WYNDHAM LEWIS was a painter, novelist, critic, and the founder of Vorticism, the avant-garde art movement based in London before the First World War. Lewis was born in 1882 in Nova Scotia and moved with his mother to London in 1893. Following a brief formal education at the Slade School of Art, Lewis moved to Paris, where he painted, travelled widely on the continent, and gathered material for his fiction, returning to England in 1909. In 1914 and 1915 Lewis published the only two issues of the Vorticist review, *Blast*, with the participation of Ezra Pound and the sculptor Henri Gaudier-Brzeska.

During the War, Lewis enlisted in the English army, serving as a gunner and bombardier. His first novel, *Tarr*, was published in 1918 in America and England with the wartime assistance of Ezra Pound. After the War, Lewis produced a wide range of art works, volumes of aesthetic and political criticism, such as *The Art of Being Ruled* (1926) and *Time and Western Man* (1927), the collection of short stories *The Wild Body* (1927), and the novels *The Childermass* (1928), *The Apes of God* (1930), *The Revenge for Love* (1937), and *Self-Condemned* (1954). During the Second World War, Lewis moved with his wife to the United States and Canada. He returned to England in 1945, where he continued to paint and write, until a pituitary tumour robbed him of his sight. He died in 1957 in London.

SCOTT W. KLEIN is Associate Professor of English at Wake Forest University in North Carolina. He is the author of *The Fictions of James Joyce and Wyndham Lewis: Monsters of Nature and Design* (Cambridge University Press, 1994).

OXFORD WORLD'S CLASSICS

*For over 100 years Oxford World's Classics have brought
readers closer to the world's great literature. Now with over 700
titles—from the 4,000-year-old myths of Mesopotamia to the
twentieth century's greatest novels—the series makes available
lesser-known as well as celebrated writing.*

*The pocket-sized hardbacks of the early years contained
introductions by Virginia Woolf, T. S. Eliot, Graham Greene,
and other literary figures which enriched the experience of reading.
Today the series is recognized for its fine scholarship and
reliability in texts that span world literature, drama and poetry,
religion, philosophy, and politics. Each edition includes perceptive
commentary and essential background information to meet the
changing needs of readers.*

OXFORD WORLD'S CLASSICS

WYNDHAM LEWIS

Tarr

Edited with an Introduction and Notes by
SCOTT W. KLEIN

OXFORD
UNIVERSITY PRESS

OXFORD
UNIVERSITY PRESS

Great Clarendon Street, Oxford ox2 6DP

Oxford University Press is a department of the University of Oxford.
It furthers the University's objective of excellence in research, scholarship,
and education by publishing worldwide in

Oxford New York

Auckland Cape Town Dar es Salaam Hong Kong Karachi
Kuala Lumpur Madrid Melbourne Mexico City Nairobi
New Delhi Shanghai Taipei Toronto

With offices in

Argentina Austria Brazil Chile Czech Republic France Greece
Guatemala Hungary Italy Japan Poland Portugal Singapore
South Korea Switzerland Thailand Turkey Ukraine Vietnam

Oxford is a registered trade mark of Oxford University Press
in the UK and in certain other countries

Published in the United States
by Oxford University Press Inc., New York

First published as an Oxford World's Classics paperback 2010

British Library Cataloguing in Publication Data

Data available

Library of Congress Cataloging in Publication Data

Data available

Typeset by Cepha Imaging Private Ltd., Bangalore, India
Printed in Great Britain
on acid-free paper by
Clays Ltd., Elcograf S.p.A.

ISBN 978-0-19-956720-1

12

ACKNOWLEDGEMENTS

AN editor necessarily receives many kinds of help along the way, particularly when dealing with a novel such as *Tarr*, which expects many kinds of knowledge of its readers. I particularly thank Thomas Pfau, who assisted with translations from the German and with navigating some unfamiliar byways of German philosophy; Stephanie Pellet, who helped clarify subtleties of French usage; Paul Edwards, for his helpful comments on the annotations; and my wife Karen Potvin Klein, both for her substantial editorial assistance, and for many other varieties of patient support. My gratitude also to Wanda Balzano, Ian Duncan, Claudia Kairoff, Maria Makela, Carrie Preston, Jessica Richard, Dick Schneider, and David Weinstein, who provided advice in their respective fields of expertise.

The staffs at the Cornell University Library Division of Rare and Manuscript Collections and the Poetry Collection at the library of the University at Buffalo (State University of New York) provided invaluable help when using their archives of Wyndham Lewis's letters and working materials. Finally, I am grateful to the Provost's Office and the Archie Fund for the Arts and Humanities at Wake Forest University, whose support enabled me to work at these collections.

CONTENTS

CONTENTS

INTRODUCTION

Tarr, the first published novel by the writer, painter, and intellectual gadfly Wyndham Lewis, is the least known, most intractable, and arguably the funniest, of major early twentieth-century English novels. Where other once-shocking novels of the Modernist period have become domesticated by the universities and comfortably assimilated by contemporary taste, *Tarr* still snarls, as though through the bars of a cage, challenging approach by adventurous readers only. Recognition of its mixture of originality and vitality was part of the praise accorded to *Tarr* on first publication in 1918. Lewis's friend and colleague Ezra Pound called *Tarr* 'the most vigorous and volcanic English novel of our time', comparing it to the early work of James Joyce and claiming, 'The English prose fiction of my decade is the work of this pair of authors'.[1] T. S. Eliot wrote in the literary journal *The Egoist*, 'In the work of Wyndham Lewis we recognize the thought of the modern and the energy of the cave-man', an encomium that Lewis would later often quote. But Eliot had also earlier declared that both *Tarr* and *Ulysses*, sections of which were appearing in the *Little Review*, 'are terrifying. That is the test of a new work of art . . . *Tarr* is a commentary upon a part of modern civilization: now it is like our civilization criticized, our acrobatics animadverted upon adversely, by an orang-outang of genius, Tarzan of the Apes.'[2]

Lewis's explosive sensibility became one of the novel's early selling points. Recognizing the value of controversy, *The Egoist*—which serialized *Tarr* and then became its English publisher as a novel—ran a full-page advertisement containing press extracts of the novel's reviews. According to this advertisement, the *Weekly Dispatch* echoed Pound's and Eliot's series of brilliant and destructive comparisons, calling *Tarr* 'a thunderbolt', while the *Manchester Guardian* warned 'one must bring a fine persistence and an insatiable appetite for both aesthetic theory and squalor'. *Everyman* perhaps summed up the general paradoxical literary attitude towards *Tarr*, declaring, 'In spite

---

[1] Ezra Pound, 'Wyndham Lewis' (1920), in *Literary Essays of Ezra Pound* (New York: New Directions, 1968), 424.

[2] T. S. Eliot, 'Tarr', *The Egoist*, 5/8 (Sept. 1918), 106, and 'Contemporanea', *The Egoist*, 5/6 (June–July 1918), 84.

of its perverseness, nastiness, and bad temper, *Tarr* bears the marks of
a strong, though unbalanced, intellect.'[3]

Energy, scandal, and alleged intellectual imbalance are scarcely
attributes of a novel or author destined for the pantheon, let alone
of a work to be admitted into the libraries of the drawing rooms of
the period, which were more likely to contain the best-sellers of
H. G. Wells and Arnold Bennett—or even Edgar Rice Burroughs's
Tarzan—than the novels of Joseph Conrad or Ford Madox Ford.
Nor, with some notable exceptions, has the contemporary academy
known quite how to place Lewis among his contemporaries. Some
scholars find his work too idiosyncratic or disagreeable to enter the
literary canon, while others simply wonder why Lewis has not yet
been accorded the attention he so obviously deserves.[4] None of this
would have surprised Lewis, who predicated his career as a writer and
painter on his recognition of the status of the artist as avant-gardist
outsider and as a critic of both the ethos of Edwardian England and
of the dominant forms of Modernism that were supposed to present
an alternative to British stolidity.

Lewis was born in Canada in 1882, but relocated to England with
his mother when he was young. After two years of formal art training
at the Slade School he moved to Paris to live among artists and hone
his skills as draughtsman and painter. It was against this aesthetic
background that *Tarr* took shape. Between 1907 and 1909 Lewis had
begun working on a story that featured a German protagonist and
a duel, which he wrote to a friend would be called 'Otto Kreisler'.
By 1910–11 Lewis had expanded the manuscript, and referred to
it as 'The Bourgeois-Bohemians', a title used in the finished work
to refer both to the novel's milieu and one of its seven sections.
By 1911 the work in progress was of full novel length—between
400 and 500 pages—and the shape had changed: the story of the
German Kreisler would now be framed by the observations and love
life of the English artist Frederick Tarr. At this stage of the manuscript's development—it was still several years from publication—
Lewis debated calling the novel either 'Otto Kreisler's Death' or
'Between Two Interviews'. In a letter to his friend Sturge Moore, he
called Tarr's two long philosophic conversations at the beginning and

---

[3] *The Egoist*, 5/9 (Oct. 1918), 124.
[4] See e.g. Fredric Jameson, *Fables of Aggression: Wyndham Lewis, the Modernist
as Fascist* (Berkeley and Los Angeles: University of California Press, 1979), and other
critical works listed in the Select Bibliography.

end of the book the 'psychological pillars' between which the rest of the story would hang 'like a grotesque tapestry'.[5]

These rejected titles, and Lewis's comments on them, underscore some of the aspects of *Tarr* that run counter to most readers' expectations of an English novel of its period. Along with its descriptive experimentation and arguably jaundiced view of human nature, *Tarr* demonstrates an open declaration of narrative fatality (the rejected title 'Otto Kreisler's Death' is subsumed in the published novel by the introduction of Kreisler as 'DOOMED, EVIDENTLY', [p. 64]). It juxtaposes traditional novelistic exposition with philosophic reflection, and it presents its long central section—from which the titular character virtually disappears—as not only a visual artefact (a 'tapestry') but a 'grotesque' one at that. How do these varied intentions coalesce?

In synopsis, the plot of *Tarr* is straightforward enough. It concerns the Parisian adventures of Frederick Sorbert Tarr, a young English painter, and Otto Kreisler, a failed German artist in his mid-thirties who is engaged on a path of self-destruction. Tarr considers himself to be a true artist in a world of 'bourgeois bohemians', the pseudo-artists of Paris who lack talent but can afford to rent studios for themselves, and who declare their independence from bourgeois society even as they create their own hypocritical community with its own equally predictable societal mores. Tarr acts as the spokesman for the novel's aesthetic ideas, and he proclaims, as the model post-Nietzschean his first name 'Frederick' suggests, that he stands beyond conventional morality. The plot follows his romantic and sexual involvement with two women. The long-suffering Bertha Lunken, a German, is soft-hearted, simplistic, and filled with conventional ideas about romance, while the stylish cosmopolitan Anastasya Vasek exemplifies the new woman of the early twentieth century, intellectually self-sufficient and sexually independent perhaps to the point of alarm. The novel describes a sort of roundelay between these four characters, who change partners in a quasi-symmetrical dance of coupling and uncoupling.

Its shape suggests that *Tarr* should be a specific kind of European comedy. The pre-War European setting, the romantic foursome in which both men become involved with both women, and in which

[5] See Paul O'Keeffe, *Some Sort of Genius: A Life of Wyndham Lewis* (London: Jonathan Cape, 2000), 93, 106, and 108.

the men are respectively a military man and an artist and the women respectively versions of the 'peasant girl' and the 'aristocrat'—such are the makings of a Viennese operetta, or the cinematic farces of Ernst Lubitsch that created contemporary analogues to those works beginning in the late 1920s. But Lewis has a considerably darker humour in mind. Like the disruptive Kreisler at the Bonnington Club dance, who 'mistook the waltz for a more primitive music' (p. 129), Lewis provides us with an alarming dance of art and sexuality closer to the *fin de siècle* of Arthur Schnitzler or Egon Schiele than to the confections of Strauss.

Part of the pleasure of *Tarr* is the juxtaposition of its formal patterns against its corrosive vision of human nature. Lewis deploys his debunking humour at a number of targets. *Tarr* skewers Kreisler, but it also satirizes the pretensions of his fellow Parisian pseudo-artists. It holds up to scorn the absurdity of the Germanic Romanticism that underlies both Kreisler and Bertha, the former a product of Prussian militarism, the latter steeped in received middle-class worship of the culture of Goethe and Beethoven. It scathingly reveals the inability of many of its characters to keep separate those human energies antithetically appropriate to the making of art versus the making of love.

Tarr's relationship with Bertha, with which the novel begins, is a model of emotional and sexual co-dependency. It combines mutual erotic attraction with Tarr's distaste both for Bertha's national and womanly commonplaces. Tarr patronizes Bertha for her lapses of taste and sophistication, while Bertha, in her suffering, nonetheless gets to play the role of the world-weary victim of a man, in her indulgent view, too young and intellectually abstracted to know what he really wants out of life. At the novel's opening Bertha's comic status as Tarr's 'official fiancée' marks only the novel's first disruptive treatment of sexual and other social relationships. In *Tarr* the desires of the body and the needs of the mind are at loggerheads, and conventional mores are no more capable of accounting for their complexities than are the techniques of conventional psychological fiction.

Tarr's later attraction to Anastasya, with her overt 'swagger sex', counterbalances Tarr's relationship with Bertha both in theme and structure. In the novel's opening chapters Tarr declares to his various male acquaintances that the man of genius needs to preserve his authentic vitality for his art, and that women must remain mere physical pendants to masculine creative energies. Anastasya's appearance throws Tarr's certainties into question, for Lewis presents her as being in every way Tarr's match—as an intellect, as a sexual being, as a game-player in relationships, and as a manipulator of images. Anastasya tellingly explains how she arranged to be booted out by her family: 'I inundated my home with troublesome images—it was like vermin; my multitude of little figures swarmed everywhere! They simply *had* to get rid of me' (p. 89). Lewis creates Anastasya to be Bertha's opposite in every way. If she seems therefore less well rounded in fictional terms, she nonetheless corresponds to an actual historic type, the women associated with the avant-garde of the pre- and inter-War periods as creators or consorts, such as French dancer and author of feminist Futurist manifestos Valentine de Saint-Point, the poet Mina Loy (whom Lewis knew before the War), and photographer Man Ray's model and companion Alice Prin, better known to the world as Kiki de Montparnasse.

Anastasya is the embodiment of the newly emergent twentieth-century woman, a flamboyant mixture of two journalistic constructions of the times, the intellectual 'New Woman' and the sexually open 'Modern Girl', and as such she hurtles down upon Tarr's and Bertha's late-nineteenth-century conceptions of women like a roller coaster. The sections of the novel dealing with Tarr—particularly the 'two interviews' with his male friends and with Anastasya at the restaurant towards the novel's end—interrogate the relationship between male and female, art and sexuality, and the claims of the intellect against the claims of lived experience. Tarr and Bertha, Tarr and Anastasya, create as couples a set of narrative possibilities that are also a set of thematic oppositions, setting art against 'life' and Tarr's theories against his behaviour. By its end, with Tarr married to Bertha in name only but continuing his dalliance with Anastasya, the novel poses a challenge to its reader: does Tarr emerge as everything he claims to be? Does Lewis intend readers to accept Tarr at his own valuation, including endorsing what most would consider to be his virulent misogyny?

The body of the novel places Tarr's intellectual consistency into stark relief, as it details a series of absurd disruptions and upheavals caused by the frustrated and self-loathing Kreisler. In a near mirror-reversal of Tarr—for Kreisler is in some ways Tarr's doppelgänger—Kreisler pursues first Anastasya and then Bertha, and in one of the novel's most memorable set-pieces, he disrupts a society dance with his increasingly erratic and bitter behaviour. Other disasters accrue, as do the novel's memorable descriptions of Kreisler's growing violence and emotional imbalance. In these scenes comedy veers closer and closer to its all-too-serious opposite. An unexpected act of sexual violence serves as the novel's most sober example of the ridiculous pushed to the edge of tragedy, as does Kreisler's participation in a duel so stunningly mismanaged that its absurd motivation is matched only by the nihilistic comedy of its decline into chaos, and the dissolution of Kreisler himself.

In his conversations with Anastasya, Tarr acts as an explicit analyst of Kreisler's behaviour, and by the novel's end readers are invited to judge Tarr's self-proclaimed superior objectivity and aesthetic sensibility. The novel balances Tarr's nominal ability to look at life objectively, 'from the outside', and to separate his relationship to art from his relationship to sex, against Kreisler's increasingly clear inability to separate art from life and sexuality from violence. At the same time, the novel presents Kreisler's dilemma as the inheritance of his Romantic Prussia, which stands in more generally for the entropic and destructive behaviour of the militarism that threatened European culture in the first decades of the twentieth century.

Satire and Society

Tarr indeed questions throughout whether one can separate life and thought, sex and art, so readily. Although Tarr does at times engage directly with Kreisler, he is largely an observer of Kreisler from afar, an effect that is reproduced for the reader, for we observe and judge Tarr much as Tarr observes and judges Kreisler. And the novel's nearly anthropological treatment of Kreisler as both a psychologically complex individual and a representative of a particular kind of culture asks us to contemplate more generally the nature of character in Lewis's world—how men and women define themselves in couples, in groups, as individuals. Kreisler, for instance, and his climactic duel, embody one of the novel's pervasive truisms: that all human relationships are tinged, when they are not wholly defined, by aggression and violence. All of the relations between characters in *Tarr* are duels of one kind or another—sexual, social, or emotional.

Etymologically, the word 'duel' derives from the Latin words *duo* and *bellum*—a war for two. Tarr's initial tirade against Hobson sets the model for relationships *à deux*, which are built on the desire for control in a relationship which protects the self while attacking the other. The long scene early on between Tarr and Bertha, in which he proudly displays his 'feeling of indifference' while she parries with a world-weary stoicism, is a kind of emotional and social battle that Lewis describes as 'a combat between two wrestlers of approximately equal strength: neither could really win' (p. 48). Tarr's dinner conversation with Anastasya is a kind of intellectual game-cum-challenge with high stakes for both egos. Her apparent initial rejection of him is a form of military strategy, and her seductive nudity in his studio thereafter becomes a challenge to which Tarr must verbally accede, crying 'I accept, I accept!' (p. 272). Bertha and Anastasya's rivalry is portrayed in terms of a joust: Anastasya's alternative story about Bertha's relationship with Kreisler, Lewis writes, 'charged hers full tilt' (p. 157). When Kreisler approaches Bertha's apartment building Lewis writes that she stands, with good reason as it turns out, 'with the emotions of an ambushed sharp-shooter' (pp. 158–9). Other examples abound: Tarr's dilemma at the novel's opening is literally to 'dis-engage' himself from Bertha, his 'official fiancée'; both terms, 'engagement' and 'disengagement', suggest military as much as sexual manoeuvres. Kreisler's duel with Soltyk depends upon a different kind of dis- and re-engagement. Kreisler displaces rage over a fantasized relationship with Anastasya upon both Bertha and the hapless Soltyk, taking sexual revenge upon the former and murderous revenge upon the latter. Lewis describes another Romantic approach only half-jokingly as a 'siege' (p. 117), and Tarr proclaims that he would like to be able to generalize the disengagement of divorce to any social bond: he complains to Hobson, 'Oh for multitudes of divorces in our *mœurs*, more than the old vexed sex ones!' (p. 8).

Tarr's distaste for wider connections stems in part from the novel's wide satire of the social world, which is presented as often comically inane and as an agglomeration of potentially inauthentic identities. In *Tarr* character is frequently a kind of mask. In Fraulein Liepmann's salon, we are told, social facts 'appeal to the mind with the strangeness of masks' (p. 114), and characters in *Tarr* frequently appear as mere personae. Throughout the Bonnington Club dance scene, for instance, Lewis casts Kreisler in the role of a 'graceless Hamlet' (p. 133), and he 'act[s] satanically' (p. 169); in conjunction with other theatrical images, Kreisler becomes a kind of bargain-basement version of Goethe's Mephistopheles. (It is possible, indeed, to see his violation of Bertha as a grotesque echo of Gretchen's betrayal in *Faust*.) In *Tarr* the generalized masking of the world threatens to become endless theatre, where character becomes role. Lewis makes explicit Kreisler's entrapment in a kind of theatre: 'Womenkind were Kreisler's Theatre,' he writes; 'they were for him art and expression: the tragedies played there purged you periodically of the too violent accumulations of desperate life' (p. 86).

Yet where most novels laud the integrity of the authentic character and treat harshly those who wear multiple societal masks, *Tarr* does the reverse. According to Tarr, Bertha and Kreisler are paradoxically limited because they are too much themselves. They lack the capacity to adapt, to play roles knowingly instead of being taken over by prefabricated identities. Late in the novel Tarr philosophizes to Anastasya about an 'authentic' art whose greatest advantage would be its deadness and its externality, and he thinks of his own self as a kind of set of nested Matryoshka dolls that have only a painting at the core. Tarr considers this multiplicity to be an advantage, a way to manoeuvre in a society whose clichés and hypocrisy endanger the artist. He boasts of his insouciant multiplicity: 'I'm an indifferent landlord, I haven't the knack of handling the various personalities gathered beneath my roof' (p. 19).

This scepticism about whether there is such a thing as an essential self, or whether the self is merely a matter of successful stage-management, explains in part why selfhood in *Tarr* is often conflated with nationality, the degree to which being 'German' or 'English' may be said to define one's character. For Tarr, at least, individuals without a robust sense of self become merely predictable products of their national upbringing, an assemblage of the tics and prejudices of their national ethos. For this reason, one of the novel's most contrarian jokes is that its Paris contains not a single significant French character. Everyone is a foreigner, and Tarr and Anastasya, the characters who are the most 'international', are also most able to adapt in a world that Lewis describes in pervasive imagery of fluidity, flooding, and survival. Kreisler and Bertha, who are in Tarr's view the characters most mired in nationality, are also the least changeable. Even their names suggest their limitations. Bertha's surname 'Lunken' carries the opprobrious echo of that English term of stupidity, 'lunkhead'. 'Kreisler'—a name borrowed from German fantasist E. T. A. Hoffmann—derives from '*kreis*', the German for 'circle', an apt appellation for a character stuck in a repetitive rut of his own making. ('Kreisler' may also suggest the German *kreisel*, 'spinning top', a mechanism that is set to furious movement from without, yet paradoxically gets nowhere, and finally collapses.)

Yet despite these 'limitations'—or perhaps because of them— Bertha and particularly Kreisler often strike contemporary readers as the most engaging, the most 'realistic' of *Tarr*'s characters, the most psychologically plausible among Lewis's otherwise constructed and externalized Parisians. Early reviewers in particular singled out Lewis's characterization of Kreisler—self-loathing and self-destructive, prone to humiliation and black comic disaster—as the novel's most noteworthy success. Kreisler's clearest fictional ancestors are the tormented protagonists of Dostoyevsky, a heritage clearly on Lewis's mind as he worked on *Tarr*.[6] But Kreisler's character also explains the novel's sheer strangeness for readers coming to *Tarr* expecting anything like the world view of the conventional English novel, which has seldom taken neurosis as its subject matter, let alone self-destructive pathology. For much like Tarr himself, *Tarr* refuses to be defined as being only 'one thing', or limited by a narrowly nationalist heritage. It takes the psychically charged worlds of Dostoyevsky and Goethe as its models, rather than basing itself upon the provincial worlds of class and social niceties typical of the English novel. Or, more precisely, it transposes the intellectual concerns of Continental novelists upon the microcosm of class and social niceties of its idiosyncratic bourgeois-bohemia. Ezra Pound wrote in his review of *Tarr*, 'Lewis is the rarest of phenomena, an Englishman who has achieved the triumph of being also a European.'[7] 'Being also

---

[6] See O'Keeffe on Lewis's early infatuation with Dostoyevsky and Goethe (*Some Sort of Genius*, 70) and how Lewis urged the 'disreputable Slav literature' of Dostoyevsky on Kate Lechmere around 1912 (ibid. 122). Rebecca West notably compared Kreisler to Dostoyevsky's character Stravrogin from *The Possessed* in an early review ('*Tarr*', *The Nation* (10 Aug. 1918); repr. in *Agenda*, 7/3 and 8/1 (Autumn–Winter, 1969–70), 67) and Pound wrote 'He is the only English writer who can be compared with Dostoyevsky' ('Wyndham Lewis', 424).

[7] Pound, 'Wyndham Lewis', 424.

a European' is also one of *Tarr*'s greatest achievements. John Rodker
once called Ford Madox Ford's novel *The Good Soldier*, because of
its sophisticated treatment of sexual mores, the finest 'French' novel
in the English language.[8] *Tarr*, with its international cast, its import-
ation of a continental sensibility into English, and its tweaking of the
English tradition of character and social analysis, may be thought
of as perhaps the finest 'Russian' or 'German' novel in the English
tradition.

Style and the Visual Arts

Where *Tarr* turns to Russia or Germany for its novelistic models, its
practices of style are a writer's response to the early twentieth-century
visual avant-gardes of France and Italy. During Lewis's apprentice-
ship as a painter Paris was an international laboratory for aesthetic
experimentation. The most advanced artists were displaying in the
salons and galleries; the Fauvists were emerging, and Picasso's and
Braque's Cubism was in full flourish. When Lewis returned from
Paris to London in 1908 he was eager to see equally innovative artists in London. But Lewis was disappointed that most English artists and critics were unwilling to move beyond Impressionism; at
their most radical, they approved of the decorative effects of Matisse.
Lewis displayed his paintings briefly under the aegis of Bloomsbury
art critic and tastemaker Roger Fry, and for a time Lewis worked at
Fry's Omega Workshop, where artisans translated French aesthetics
into home decoration. Lewis became restive with such 'middlebrow'
activity, however, and broke acrimoniously away from Fry, founding the Rebel Art Centre in 1914. There, with the collaboration of
Ezra Pound and the sculptor Henri Gaudier-Brzeska, Lewis launched
a new journal of the arts, the oversized and shockingly pink avant-
garde *Blast*, pre-War London's only significant attempt to establish
a home-grown avant-garde movement in visual and literary art:
Vorticism.

Vorticism elevated visual geometry and rhetorical paradox to the
status of theory, even as the paintings of Lewis's Vorticist period found
a new style in its synthesis of elements of analytic Cubism with the

[8] Ford Madox Ford, 'Dedicatory Letter to Stella Ford', in *The Good Soldier*, ed.
Thomas C. Moser (Oxford: Oxford University Press, 1990), 4.

colouristic effects of both the Fauvists and the German Expressionists (in *Tarr* the German artist Vokt says of his own show in Berlin 'It has not gone badly. Our compatriots improve—', p. 101). *Blast*'s manifestos, however, derive their energy largely from a highly articulate opposition to Futurism, the first of the fully articulated twentieth-century European avant-gardes. In his founding manifesto of Futurism, published on the front page of the French newspaper *Le Figaro* on 20 February 1909, the Italian poet and journalist Filippo Tommaso Marinetti declared the principles of his new art, which would embrace technology and speed, reject tradition, praise both youth and war, and trumpet intuition over intellect. The ideas of Futurism emerged thereafter in torrents of hyperbolic individual and group manifestos, which promised to transform both painting, which should extol speed, and literature, which should become a pure field of word objects. Marinetti became a *succès de scandale* in London with his lectures and presentations, but Lewis and Pound objected to the Futurist rejection of aesthetic traditions, its praising of intuition above intellect, and its quasi-Romantic fetishizing of speed, which had the effect, in Futurist canvases by painters such as Giacomo Balla, Gino Severini, and Umberto Boccioni, of disrupting Lewis's preferred stable geometrics with blurred and multiple images. In response, the manifestos of *Blast* declared that the Vorticist would extol intellect over emotion, form over (or in conjunction with) nature, space over time, balance over movement, and contemplation over action. Rather than declaring a straightforwardly singular aesthetic, Vorticism would erect in the place of Futurism a rhetoric of opposition and paradox, turning Marinetti's call to total war into an aesthetic alarum aimed at both the academicism of British art and Marinetti's then-pervasive influence. Vorticism would be both coruscating and object-ive, destructive and intellectually creative. It would, in the words of one of Lewis's manifestos, 'fight first on one side, then on the other, but always for the SAME cause, which is neither side or both sides and ours'.[9]

Many of *Tarr*'s ideas are identifiably the same as those of the *Blast* manifestos: his programmatic and egoistic opposition to the conflation of 'art' and 'life', his vaunting of paradox above consistency,

---

[9] Wyndham Lewis (ed.), *Blast* 1 (1914; repr. Santa Barbara: Black Sparrow Press, 1981), 30.

and his preference for art that emphasized exteriors and stable objects rather than interiors and the behaviour of objects in time. (Arguably, differences of tone between the Kreisler and the Tarr sections of *Tarr* may be explained as artefacts of the novel's prolonged composition, the 'Vorticism' of Tarr a later accretion upon the earlier psychological 'realism' of Kreisler.) But just as importantly, Lewis's implicit dialogue with the painterly avant-gardes produces some of *Tarr*'s most striking descriptive and narrative effects. When Lewis describes Tarr as having only 'the cumbrous [machinery] of the intellect . . . full of sinister piston-rods, organ-like shapes, heavy drills' (p. 9), his sentence transforms a particularly avant-garde fetishizing of mechanism into a new kind of English prose style, one that attempts to translate painterly abstraction into words, to represent intangible qualities by the accretion of absurdist visual shapes. That accretion becomes a source for virtuoso experimental set-pieces. When Lewis introduces Anastasya with her 'egotistic code of advanced order, full of insolent strategies' (p. 84) his subsequent description is as densely and visually constructed as a painting. Anastasya becomes a kind of Vorticist canvas—'When she laughed, this commotion was transmitted to her body as though sharp sonorous blows had been struck upon her mouth', 'her head was an elegant bone-white egg'—the details of which overwhelm Kreisler by their multiplicity, a 'cascade, a hot cascade' (p. 84). These passages are also keys to characterization. Lewis's Vorticist-inflected descriptions tend to cluster around Tarr, Anastasya, and Paris itself, reaffirming the continuity of those characters and that location with Lewis's approved ideas about art and selfhood. Conversely, Lewis's descriptions of Bertha and Kreisler tend to visualize their outmoded Romanticisms as a reflection and partial parody of Futurism. For instance, when Lewis describes Bertha's leg as appearing 'like the sanguine of an Italian master in which the leg is drawn in several positions, one on top of the other' (p. 39), he invokes not only a Renaissance sketch, but also the 'multiple exposures' of Futurist canvases, in which action through time is represented by the superimposition of shapes in space.[10]

[10] For an exemplary instance of this effect, see Giacomo Balla's painting *Dynamism of a Dog on a Leash* (1912), which represents the frenetic movements of a dachshund's legs and tail as a blur of overlapping images.

This description helps to suggest that Bertha's identity is 'out of focus', and descriptions of Kreisler throughout are overtly anti-Futurist in their comic exposure of the limitations of Marinetti's fetishizing of instinct, masculine power, militarism, and the Futurists' programmatic 'contempt for women'. Kreisler's mayhem at the Bonnington Club, in which he becomes a pure mechanism of movement as violence, is as Futurist as a speeding automobile, and as ultimately doomed to crash and burn. Kreisler's perversely mixed feelings of hate and love for Soltyk at the duel owe as much to Marinetti as to Dostoyevsky.[11] And Kreisler's rape of Bertha, which is both the most painful and the most technically virtuosic sequence of *Tarr*, can be understood as both an apotheosis of Futurist ideology and the logical endpoint of the sexual politics of *Mitteleuropa* that produced the very idea of the duel. Kreisler's cultural inheritance elevates 'woman' (*das Weib*) into an abstraction of purity that is worthy of masculine protection, even as it simultaneously reduces her to an object subject to masculine control. As such the idea of rape becomes a mere extension of the ideology of the duel, and both dovetail all too neatly with Marinetti's praise of intuitive action, destruction, and hatred of the conventionally feminine. As John Cournos wrote in *The Egoist* in a wartime essay 'The Death of Futurism', 'Some day a book may be written to show how closely war is allied with sex. For the Futuristic juxtaposition of the glorification of war and "contempt for women" is no mere accident. This contempt does not simply imply indifference, but the worst form men's obsession with sex can take, that is rape!'[12]

Cournos could not have known that the book he was seeking was being serially published in the same issue in which he wrote. Yet Lewis's ideological analyses are most powerfully delivered not by harangue but by means of visuality. *Tarr*'s single most memorable and disturbing image is perhaps the description of Bertha, after the rape, perceiving Kreisler as four disconnected figures impossible to reconcile with one another in space or time (p. 167). As a reflection of psychology the image tells us much about Kreisler's increasingly fractured and

[11] See e.g. Marinetti's statement in 'The Founding and Manifesto of Futurism' that younger Futurists will in the future 'attempt to kill us, driven by a hatred all the more implacable because their hearts will be intoxicated with love and admiration for us' (*Futurism: An Anthology*, ed. Lawrence Rainey, Christine Poggi, and Laura Whitman (New Haven and London: Yale University Press, 2009), 53).
[12] 'The Death of Futurism', *The Egoist*, 4/1 (Jan. 1917), 7.

discontinuous selfhood, as well as Bertha's attempt to cope with the
trauma of her physical and psychic violation. But as pure imagery it
also presents readers with an experiment in representation comparable to the fracturing of time and space by the human body in Marcel
Duchamp's painting *Nude Descending a Staircase* (1912), or to the
sequences of stop-motion photography made by Eadweard Muybridge
in the 1870s that inspired both Duchamp's painting and the creation
of cinema.

   As this comparison suggests, the prose of *Tarr* responds not
only to modern painting, but also to that other increasingly important visual innovation, the movies. When Kreisler appears in Bertha's
hallway 'like a great terrifying poster, cut out on the melodramatic stairway' (p. 170), he becomes a nightmarish advertisement
out of German Expressionist cinema, a kind of Nosferatu before
the great 1922 vampire film of that name by F. W. Murnau; before
his death as a 'tramp' jerked around by waiters and in need of
Time (p. 244) Kreisler becomes a kind of ghastly parody of screen
comedian Charlie Chaplin, whose international popularity Lewis
criticized in the prologue to the 1918 version of *Tarr* (see Appendix).
Lewis tells us at one point that Kreisler grasps his situation with
Anastasya 'cinematographically' (p. 88) and in so doing Lewis
implicitly alerts his readers to the dangers of living life 'filmically'—
melodramatically, prey to the vagaries of time—no less so than
when criticizing the Futurists. Bertha and Kreisler are doomed to
be the victims of such aesthetic flux and its associated psychological
and emotional upheaval. Only the aesthetically advanced Tarr and
Anastasya, who embrace highbrow art, casual ('swagger') sex, and the
life of the mind, have the tools to survive as observers of life rather
than its hapless subjects, the theatrical or cinematic audience rather
than its performers.

Tarr *and Contemporary Fiction*

But do Tarr and Anastasya indeed become life's masters, by the novel's end? One way to gauge their ultimate 'success' in Lewis's world
is to disengage *Tarr* temporarily from the traditions of the European
novels and avant-garde visual experimentation, and consider it
among its contemporaneous novels of English and Irish Modernism.

Thematic and formal linkages are surprisingly plentiful between *Tarr* and Ford's *The Good Soldier* (1915), Lawrence's *Women in Love* (1920), and Joyce's *A Portrait of the Artist as a Young Man* (1916). Ford's and Lawrence's novels tell stories, as does *Tarr*, of two sets of intertwined couples, whose social and sexual experiences become the subject of philosophical observation by one of the male members of its foursome. Lewis's novel shares with Lawrence's, whose fiction he loathed, a sometimes surprisingly sexual candour. (John Lane, who had published *Blast*, refused to publish *Tarr* in part because he worried it was 'too strong a book' in the wake of criminal proceedings brought against Methuen for publishing Lawrence's novel *The Rainbow*.[13]) Lawrence's novel shares with *Tarr* a concern for the place of sexuality and marriage in modern culture (albeit in a very different tonal register), as well as its inclusion of one male character who is largely defined by his theories about life, Rupert Birkin, and another, Gerald Crich, whose path to self-destruction is predicated in part, as is Kreisler's, as a criticism of Futurism.[14] Ford's novel shares with *Tarr* a structure in which one male character observes the self-destruction of a second male character whose motivations he tries to understand, while Joyce's novel presents a male protagonist who struggles to grow into his nominally mature status as an artist. And like Joyce, Lewis presents his readers with a portrait of an artist as a young man, for he introduces Tarr as being in his early twenties, roughly the same age as Joyce's Stephen Dedalus when he goes off to Paris at the end of *A Portrait*. It is tempting, indeed, to read the beginning of *Tarr* as a near-parodic continuation of Joyce, with Stephen transformed into Lewis's very different young artist in Paris, no longer delivering aesthetic lectures on the streets of Dublin but rather theorizing about aesthetics in a series of cafés and studios.

But what *Tarr* mainly shares with all of these novels is a pervasive ironizing that ultimately undermines the readers' uncomplicated endorsement of their protagonists' visions of the world. Early in *The Good Soldier* the reader comes to suspect that Ford's Dowell, the

[13] See O'Keeffe, *Some Sort of Genius*, 173.

[14] Lawrence's best-known statement on Marinetti and Futurism is found in his letter of 5 June 1914 to Edward Garrett. See *The Letters of D. H. Lawrence*, vol. ii. *1913–1916*, ed. George J. Zytaruk and James T. Boulton (Cambridge: Cambridge University Press, 2002), 180.

first-person narrator, is an arrantly untrustworthy guide to himself or to others, and Lawrence's and Joyce's novels present their protagonists Birkin and Stephen as quasi-autobiographical versions of their authors as both inspired and self-absorbedly egoistic. One can identify both Birkin's and Stephen's ideas, often presented at didactic length, with ideas held by their novelists' younger selves. But the novels also demonstrate their protagonists' arrogance and failures of insight. Lawrence's Ursula acts as a kind of surrogate for the reader in criticizing Birkin's self-importance throughout *Women in Love*, and the final chapter of Joyce's *Portrait* demonstrates that Stephen may be aesthetically brilliant, but that he is also self-important, quixotic, superior to his peers in intellect but inferior to them in empathy.

And so it is with Tarr. In a preface to the first edition, which he chose to omit in the 1928 revision published here (see Appendix), Lewis endorses Tarr's ideas about art but firmly distances himself from Tarr's management of his personal life. As the novel progresses, the attentive reader will note more and more flaws in Tarr's dogged dependence on humour, anti-feminism, and egoism. After Tarr visits Kreisler in his rooms, for instance, Tarr feels 'There was something mean and improper in everything he had done, which he could not define' (p. 208). Later in the passage Lewis becomes yet more straightforward about Tarr's misanthropy: 'His contempt for everybody else in the end must degrade him: for if nothing in other men was worth honouring, finally his self-neglect must result, like the Cynic's dishonourable condition' (p. 209). These moments of temporary self-realization come in the wake of Tarr's contemplations of Kreisler and Bertha, as he, and Lewis, begin to understand that jokes can be hurtful, that they may turn 'too deep for laughter' (p. 164) and are 'able to make you sweat, even break your ribs and black your eyes' (p. 211). As Tarr's ability to juggle his 'various selves' threatens to desert him, he becomes at times defined by a Kreislerian theatricality: he is not only an actor, but an awkward one. Lewis describes Tarr at one juncture as 'an untalented Pro on a provincial first-night' (p. 187), and further declares that within the temporary triangle formed with Bertha and Kreisler 'Tarr had the best rôle, and did not deserve it' (p. 189).

Lewis has suggested this inconsistency earlier in the novel. When Tarr threatens to return to England from the Vitelotte Quarter, the furthest he can bring himself to flee from Bertha is Montmartre, an easy bus ride away on the other side of Paris. His reaction to the scandal of Bertha being seen kissing Kreisler in the street is positively Victorian. When he writes in a letter, 'for God's sake get married quickly. It's all up with you otherwise' (p. 143), he sounds less like an advanced artist than an outraged maiden aunt. And when Tarr ultimately marries Bertha 'For form's sake' (p. 281) one wonders if he is truly turning social expectation to his own advantage. On the one hand, Tarr outrages convention to underwrite his continued dalliance with Anastasya, 'his illicit and more splendid bride' (p. 284), but on the other, he may have simply fallen into the trap of bourgeois expectations he has earlier criticized, exchanging artistic for social 'form'.

Tarr's limitations are not lost on the novel's other characters. Lewis initially mutes those criticisms, however, by putting them in the mouths of characters whom Tarr considers inferior. Hobson may appear passive in the face of Tarr's prolonged tirade in the opening chapter, but he may also be all too used to hearing Tarr's repeated invective to take it seriously. Indeed, Hobson rejects Tarr's theorizing outright, saying 'Your creative man sounds rather alarming. I don't believe in him' (p. 16). Bertha dismisses some of Tarr's overt emotional cruelty, chalking it up to his immaturity ('tu es *si jeune*,' she tells him, p. 184), and one must recall throughout *Tarr* that Kreisler is in his mid-thirties, while Tarr is only in his early twenties. Hobson and Bertha, of course, are scarcely presented as authoritative witnesses within the world of the novel. But when even Anastasya hears of Tarr's marriage, she looks blankly into his eyes and sees only a blasted landscape, in Lewis's memorable phrase, 'as though he contained cheerless stretches where no living thing could grow' (p. 282).

Tarr may be a genius, but that does not mean that he is not also something of a fool. His name tells us so. 'Tarr' suggests several possible origins. It may be the nickname for a British sailor who can stay masterfully afloat in the metaphorical sea of Paris ('All the nice girls love a tar!' Lewis later writes in another context[15]); it may suggest the sticky tenacity, and perhaps the blackness, of his intellectualism; it may allude to a story by Edgar Allan Poe, 'The System of Doctor Tarr

[15] *Blasting & Bombardiering* (2nd rev. ed., Berkeley and Los Angeles: University of California Press, 1967), 30.

and Professor Fether', in which madmen take over an asylum. But it also suggests the German '*Tor*' ('blockhead'), a near-homophone that appears in Kreisler's consciousness in the text (p. 99). And although '*Tor*' can mean 'fool' in the sense of a spiritual innocent (as in the libretto for Wagner's *Parsifal*), Tarr is no holy *naif*, no Dostoyevskian Myshkin to counterbalance Kreisler's Stavrogin. He is at bottom just another version of the self-important artist, one of the 'unscrupulous heroes' that haunt the Vitelotte Quarter, who, as Lewis warns in the novel's first paragraph, are 'largely ignorant of all but their restless personal lives' (p. 7). Tarr's Apollonian pronouncements ultimately prove no more capable of securing for him a 'healthy' division between sex and art than do the Dionysiac excesses of Kreisler. The novel's final words introduce the names of Tarr's future sexual partners, and they suggest that the supposedly superior artist will become trapped in an irresolvable vacillation between women like Bertha—who are maternal, Romantic, and intellectually unthreatening—and women like Anastasya, who are intellectual extroverts and thus dangerous to the male ego.

In a final twist of the knife, Anastasya also falls victim to Lewis's satire. Her conventionally feminine reaction to the news of Tarr's marriage suggests the limitations of even her code of 'swagger sex'; indeed, Lewis signals this somewhat earlier by noting that 'Her romanticism, in fact, was of the same order as Bertha's but much better class' (p. 252). So by the novel's end, both Tarr and Anastasya have been debunked, the biters have been bitten, and Lewis reveals the novel's most pervasive, if subtlest, insight. No one, including the critic of inauthenticity in society and in art, can step outside the analytic gaze: the avant-gardist looks directly into the mirror when he condemns the world around him.

'a sincerely ironic masterpiece'

The interest of *Tarr* goes well beyond its formal balances and intellectual patterning of theory evaluated against practice. Its treatment of fatality, its philosophizing, and its grotesque visuality serve to underline its representation, as Lewis writes of the opening meeting between Tarr and Hobson, of a kind of 'camouflage of intricate accommodations' (p. 8) with received novelistic form. In its paradoxical box-within-box admiration and satire of its represented critics and their critiques, *Tarr* looks to the reader to be many different things at the same time, for it feints and parries like a skilled fencer against the reader's expectations. It is undeniably bleak and at times still unsettling. But if readers can bring themselves to view its world from Lewis's detached perspective, it is also smart, provocative, and blackly entertaining. Its intertwining of violence and humour may seem quizzical, but for Lewis the two are inseparable, as are both qualities from the world itself. 'Mine is a repulsive task,' he later writes, 'I discourse matter-of-factly upon the most repulsive matters. But however ugly (and I have agreed that they are that), those things are quite *real*.'[16] This is one respect in which Lewis may be said to concur with Marinetti, who proclaimed in his 1912 'Technical Manifesto of Futurist Literature': 'Let us boldly make "the ugly" in literature, and let us everywhere murder solemnity.'[17]

That *Tarr* murders solemnity is beyond doubt. No novel before the work of Samuel Beckett so thoroughly introduces to the English tradition the idea of the Absurd ('we represent *absolutely nothing* thank God!', Anastasya drunkenly proclaims in the restaurant with Tarr, as though she has reached an apotheosis, p. 270). No other English novel sets its action in play with so little concern for morality: in his later *Rude Assignment*, Lewis writes that the story of Kreisler is expected 'to awaken neither sympathy nor repulsion from the reader . . . His death is a tragic game.'[18] No other novel would have the temerity to begin a scene of rape with a man telling a woman 'Your arms are like bananas!' (p. 166), or to introduce an entirely new character in its last two words. Yet Lewis was sensitive to English charges that *Tarr*'s satire was an affront to all that was good in the novelistic tradition. He insisted that *Tarr* was 'not (if you cared to cross the Channel) the first book in European literature to display a certain indifference to bourgeois conventions, and an unblushing disbelief in the innate goodness of human nature.'[19]

[16] Wyndham Lewis, *Doom of Youth* (Chatto and Windus, 1932; repr. Haskell House Publishers, 1973), 10.

[17] *Futurism: An Anthology*, 119.

[18] Wyndham Lewis, *Rude Assignment: An Intellectual Autobiography*, ed. Toby Foshay (Santa Barbara: Black Sparrow Press, 1984), 165.

[19] *Blasting & Bombardiering*, 88.

For *Tarr* crosses many kinds of channels—between comedy and tragedy, between philosophy and satire, and ultimately between antihumanism and humanism. Lewis was initially concerned that Harriet Shaw Weaver, the first publisher of *Tarr*, might find the tone of the book 'too heartless, bitter and material'. But he also wrote 'if the book has a moral, it is that it describes a man's revolt or reaction against his reason'.[20] If we accept his description of *Tarr* as a kind of treatise on reason and detachment gone wrong, we may also understand the novel as part of a line of twentieth-century art whose themes Lewis anticipated, even if he did not directly influence them. Its haranguing philosophizing and its mordant criticism of a society that demands ferocious attack from within can be seen in such later Austrian novels as Robert Musil's *The Man Without Qualities* (1930–42) and the works of Thomas Bernhard. Postmodern English art recapitulates many of Lewis's central aesthetic concerns. Like *Tarr*, a film such as Peter Greenaway's *The Cook, the Thief, His Wife, and Her Lover* (1989) blends rebarbative intellectuality with social satire, sexuality, and anti-humanism, all treated with the most formal visual and aesthetic rigour. And a work of art such as Damien Hirst's installation *Away from the Flock* (1994), which notoriously displays a sheep in a glass box filled with formaldehyde, addresses the same concerns as Lewis's Vorticism: how art, in framing organic form by rigorous aesthetic geometries, can make the viewer reconsider the status not only of art, but of life itself.

And if these comparisons seem to be trying to rescue a form of humanism from Lewis's often fiercely held anti-humanism (as Lewis himself would begin to do in such later novels as *The Revenge for Love*), it is worth remembering Horace Walpole's claim that the world is a tragedy for those who feel, but a comedy for those who think. For *Tarr*, in containing opposites, can ultimately be read either as a comic endorsement of its rather heartless world, or by challenging the reader to bring to bear an understanding resistant to its satiric surfaces, as a denunciation of those who, like Tarr, would suppress the world of feeling beneath an all-powerful intellect. We may read Lewis's signature novel both as saying what it means and as ironizing

---

[20] Letter of Mar. 1916, *The Letters of Wyndham Lewis*, ed. W. K. Rose (Norfolk, Conn.: New Directions, 1963), 76.

its own first principles. And in this respect, as in many others, *Tarr* should be better known. With the passage of time its status becomes clearer, like the multi-purpose Bonnington Club it describes within its pages, as the 'sincerely ironic masterpiece' (p. 127) it was acclaimed on its first publication.

NOTE ON THE TEXT

THE text reproduced in this edition is the revised second version of *Tarr* published in 1928 by Chatto and Windus. *Tarr* has an unusually complex publication history. As John Xiros Cooper has noted: 'Just ask any one of the two-dozen Lewis scholars in the world which of the versions of *Tarr* is the best or most complete text. Be prepared for a lively response.'[1] The first version of *Tarr* appeared in three different forms: as a serial in somewhat abridged form in *The Egoist*, published from April 1916 to November 1917; in an American edition published by Alfred A. Knopf on 27 June 1918; and in an English edition published by the Egoist Press on 18 July 1918, published under the name 'P. Wyndham Lewis'. These three earlier editions contain significant variants. Lewis had worked on *Tarr* roughly from 1908 to 1915, but he put the novel in final form rather quickly during a period of illness before he enlisted to fight for Britain in the First World War. Lewis wanted to leave a literary legacy that would consist of more than *Blast* and a few published short stories if he were to be killed in action, and he placed responsibility for the publication of *Tarr* largely in the hands of his friend and collaborator Ezra Pound.

Pound found the manuscript difficult to place, in part because of the novel's frankness about sexual matters. However, he was able to convince Harriet Shaw Weaver, with Lewis's only reluctant approval, to publish *Tarr* in her journal *The Egoist*. Weaver further promised that she would publish *Tarr* thereafter in book form if Pound were unable to secure another English publisher. At the same time, Pound convinced John Quinn, the American lawyer and patron of Modernist authors, to interest Alfred A. Knopf in publishing an American edition. All of these early versions were problematic. Place-holding phrases that Lewis had intended to change made their way into the incomplete serial *Egoist* version. The Knopf edition was set from a mixture of the printed *Egoist* serial materials and pieces of manuscript that Pound was able to gather while Lewis was at the front, and Lewis was never presented with proofs to correct for this edition. Moreover, John Quinn became ill during the

[1] *Modernism and the Culture of Market Society* (Cambridge: Cambridge University Press, 2004), 215.

production of the Knopf *Tarr*, and the proofreading on this edition was thus done so sloppily that Lewis later referred to this edition as 'the bad American *Tarr*'.[2] Finally, while Lewis was able to correct the proofs for the *Egoist* book publication, this edition appeared in small enough numbers that by the mid-1920s it was difficult to find. For example, a sales flyer from W. Jackson (Books) Ltd. London, dated for the week ending 18 May 1928, describes a copy of the *Egoist Tarr* as 'considered by many people as one of the finest novels in our language . . . out of print and practically impossible to obtain second hand.'[3]

Lewis was thus pleased to create a new version of *Tarr* in 1928 for Chatto and Windus's 'Phoenix Series', a line of inexpensive editions of modern novels. However, rather than present the publisher with a corrected or aggregate recension of the earlier versions of *Tarr*, and because Lewis had come to consider the 1918 *Tarr* to be 'a hasty piece of workmanship',[4] he produced an entirely rewritten and expanded version of the text. He did this by unusual means—adding new material in black pen directly to the margins of a copy of the 1918 American edition. This working copy is preserved in the Wyndham Lewis Collection at the Poetry Room of the University at Buffalo, State University of New York, and it demonstrates graphically that after the first chapter of the 1918 version—which is crossed through entirely, and for which no revised manuscript exists—Lewis did not leave a single page of the earlier *Tarr* unrevised. Some of these changes are minor, such as alterations of character and place names. But in most cases the changes are substantial. Although Lewis cancels some earlier passages, his revisions are overwhelmingly additive. Many pages contain multiple accretions, the margins filled with balloons of new text and arrows that criss-cross so densely as to render some pages nearly impenetrable.

In places where Lewis added even larger passages of text, he pasted new manuscript material over passages to be cancelled, and attached extra sheets to the bottoms of the pages of the working text that needed to be unfolded by the printers (Chapter 9 of Part IV, 'A Jest Too Deep for Laughter', is particularly densely revised in this way).

[2] See Paul O'Keeffe, *Some Sort of Genius: A Life of Wyndham Lewis* (London: Jonathan Cape, 2000), 206.

[3] Wyndham Lewis Collection, Cornell University, Box 164.

[4] *Blasting & Bombardiering*, 2nd rev. edn. (Berkeley and Los Angeles: University of California Press, 1967), 90.

For two sequences that he expanded yet more substantially— the preparation for Kreisler's duel (Chapter 4 of Part VI, 'Holocausts') and Tarr's later conversations with Anastasya (Chapter 1 of Part VII, 'Swagger Sex')—Lewis directs the printers to separate manuscripts and typescripts to be incorporated into the already densely revised text. Although no doubt a challenge for Chatto and Windus's typesetters, the 1928 version of *Tarr* proved to be a success. Unpublished letters at Cornell show that Lewis's editor C. H. C. Prentice reported to him in 1929 that the publisher had sold almost two thousand copies of the new *Tarr*; while a much later communication from the publisher notes that *Tarr* was one of three of Lewis's books, along with *The Art of Being Ruled* and *Time and Western Man*, that had repaid their advances.[5]

Lewis intended *Tarr* to be known solely in its revised version. The 1928 text served as the basis for all subsequent editions of *Tarr* in Lewis's lifetime, including an edition published by Methuen in 1951 to which Lewis contributed a few further minor alterations. Nonetheless, some contemporary readers prefer the original 1918 *Tarr* on the grounds that its greater stylistic roughness is closer in spirit to the avant-gardism of *Blast* and Vorticism than is the relative polish of the revision. Such readers regret in particular the loss of Lewis's use of an idiosyncratic form of punctuation in some sections of the 1918 Knopf *Tarr*, doubled dashes that look like equals signs ('=') and that Lewis used to divide sentences from one another. The 1928 *Tarr*, in compensation, is fuller and more complexly novelistic, containing more expansive descriptive and character detail without compromising the integrity of its aesthetics or its world view. With the availability of Paul O'Keeffe's edition of the 1918 *Tarr*, readers can make such judgements for themselves.[6]

Finally, it is worth noting two idiosyncrasies of usage and orthography in the 1928 *Tarr*. Lewis often prints foreign words and phrases in roman type, reserving italics for specific emphasis. He also prints adjectives referring to national, cultural, and religious groups without initial capitals. At times Lewis uses this orthography

[5] Wyndham Lewis Collection, Box 96, folders 37 and 135.
[6] For more complete discussions of the differences between the various editions and their editorial histories, see *Tarr: The 1918 Version*, ed. Paul O'Keeffe (Santa Rosa: Black Sparrow Press, 1990), and Stephen Sturgeon, 'Wyndham Lewis's *Tarr*: A Critical Edition', unpublished PhD diss., Boston University Graduate School of Arts and Sciences, 2007.

playfully (as when he writes 'But being a Pole, Soltyk participated in a hereditary polish of manner', p. 119). But this orthography also represented Lewis's considered belief that standard English usage overemphasized the importance of national differences compared to other bases for comparison or self-definition. As he explained in his journal *The Enemy*:

[My] use of capitals and lower case departs from current english usage. This has been objected to by some critics, and I agree with them that there is a good deal against it. Only between the german habit of over-capitalisation and the soberness of the French in their use of the capital letter ('un français', for instance, is what we write 'a Frenchman') the english usage seems rather illogically to hesitate . . . if you write 'a gymnosophist' or 'an aristocrat' with a small letter, I do not see why the name that describes another and no more important attribute of a person should receive a different treatment.[7]

This edition thus reproduces exactly Lewis's orthography as it appears in the 1928 Chatto and Windus edition, for as Lewis's opening epigraph from Montaigne commands, one should 'correct the faults of inadvertence, not those of habit'. And with that injunction in mind, this edition silently corrects also a small number of obvious typesetting errors, and a single misattribution by Lewis—where else?—to the source of his second epigraph from Montaigne.

[7] *The Enemy* 2 (1929), p. ix.

SELECT BIBLIOGRAPHY

Life, Letters, and Writings on Art

Lewis, Wyndham, *Blasting & Bombardiering* (London: Eyre & Spottiswoode, 1937; 2nd rev. edn, Berkeley and Los Angeles: University of California Press, 1967).

—— *The Letters of Wyndham Lewis*, ed. W. K. Rose (Norfolk, Conn.: New Directions, 1963).

—— *Rude Assignment: A Narrative of My Career up-to-Date* (London and New York: Hutchinson & Co., Publishers, Ltd., 1950); repr. as *Rude Assignment: An Intellectual Autobiography*, ed. Toby Foshay (Santa Barbara: Black Sparrow Press, 1984).

—— *Wyndham Lewis on Art: Collected Writings 1913–1956*, ed. Walter Michel and C. J. Fox (London: Thames and Hudson, 1969).

Meyers, Jeffrey, *The Enemy: A Biography of Wyndham Lewis* (London: Routledge & Kegan Paul, 1980).

Michel, Walter, *Wyndham Lewis: Paintings and Drawings* (Berkeley and Los Angeles: University of California Press, 1971).

O'Keeffe, Paul, *Some Sort of Genius: A Life of Wyndham Lewis* (London: Jonathan Cape, 2000).

Pound, Ezra, and Lewis, Wyndham, *Pound/Lewis: The Letters of Ezra Pound and Wyndham Lewis*, ed. Timothy Materer (New York: New Directions, 1985).

Tarr: Specific Criticism and Contemporary Reviews

Ardis, Ann L., '*The Lost Girl*, *Tarr*, and the "Moment" of Modernism', in *Modernism and Cultural Conflict, 1880–1922* (Cambridge: Cambridge University Press, 2002), 78–113.

Cooper, John Xiros, '*La bohème*: Lewis, Stein, Barnes', in *Modernism and the Culture of Market Society* (Cambridge: Cambridge University Press, 2004), 215–42.

Currie, Robert, 'Wyndham Lewis, E. T. A. Hoffmann, and *Tarr*', *Review of English Studies*, NS, 30/118 (May 1979), 169–81.

Davies, Alistair, '*Tarr*: A Nietzschean Novel', in Jeffrey Meyers (ed.), *Wyndham Lewis, a Revaluation: New Essays* (London: Athlone Press, 1980), 107–19.

Edwards, Paul, 'Symbolic Exchange in *Tarr*', in *Wyndham Lewis: Painter and Writer* (New Haven: Yale University Press, 2000), 35–51.

Eliot, T. S., '*Tarr*', *The Egoist*, 5/8 (Sept. 1918), 105–6.

Levenson, Michael H., 'Form's Body: Lewis' *Tarr*', in *Modernism and the Fate of Individuality: Character and Novelistic Form from Conrad to Woolf* (Cambridge: Cambridge University Press, 1991), 121–44.

Lewis, Wyndham, *Tarr: The 1918 Version*, ed. Paul O'Keeffe (Santa Rosa: Black Sparrow Press, 1990).

Peppis, Paul, 'Anti-Individualism and Fictions of National Character in Lewis's *Tarr*', in *Literature, Politics, and the English Avant-Garde: Nation and Empire, 1901–1918* (Cambridge: Cambridge University Press, 2000), 133–61.

Pound, Ezra, ' "*Tarr*" by Wyndham Lewis', *Little Review*, 4/11 (Mar. 1918), 35.

Sheppard, Richard W., 'Wyndham Lewis's *Tarr*: An (Anti-)Vorticist Novel?', *Journal of English and Germanic Philology*, 88/4 (Oct. 1989), 510–30.

Starr, Alan, '*Tarr* and Wyndham Lewis', *ELH*, 49/1 (Spring 1982), 179–89.

Sturgeon, Stephen, 'Wyndham Lewis's *Tarr*: A Critical Edition', unpublished PhD diss., Boston University Graduate School of Arts and Sciences, 2007.

West, Rebecca, '*Tarr*', *The Nation*, 10 Aug. 1918; repr. in *Agenda*, 7/3 and 8/1 (Autumn–Winter, 1969–70), 67.

Wutz, Michael, 'The Energetics of *Tarr*: The Vortex-Machine Kreisler', *Modern Fiction Studies*, 38/4 (Winter 1992), 845–69.

Lewis and Vorticism: General Criticism

Ayers, David, *Wyndham Lewis and Western Man* (New York: St Martin's Press, 1992).

Cork, Richard, *Vorticism and Abstract Art in the First Machine Age* (Berkeley and Los Angeles: University of California Press, 1976).

Dasenbrock, Reed Way, *The Literary Vorticism of Ezra Pound and Wyndham Lewis: Towards the Condition of Painting* (Baltimore: Johns Hopkins University Press, 1985).

Edwards, Paul, *Wyndham Lewis: Painter and Writer* (New Haven: Yale University Press, 2000).

Foshay, Toby, *Wyndham Lewis and the Avant-Garde: The Politics of the Intellect* (Montreal: McGill-Queen's University Press, 1992).

Foster, Hal, *Prosthetic Gods* (Cambridge, Mass.; London: MIT Press, 2004).

Gasiorek, Andrzej, *Wyndham Lewis and Modernism* (Tavistock: Northcote House, 2003).

Hickman, Miranda B., *The Geometry of Modernism: The Vorticist Idiom in Lewis, Pound, H.D., and Yeats* (Austin: University of Texas Press, 2005).

Jameson, Fredric, *Fables of Aggression: Wyndham Lewis, the Modernist as Fascist* (Berkeley and Los Angeles: University of California Press, 1979; new edn, London and New York: Verso, 2008).

Kenner, Hugh, *Wyndham Lewis* (London: Methuen, 1954).

Klein, Scott W., *The Fictions of James Joyce and Wyndham Lewis: Monsters of Nature and Design* (Cambridge: Cambridge University Press, 1994).

Mao, Douglas, *Solid Objects: Modernism and the Test of Production* (Princeton: Princeton University Press, 1998).

Mao, Douglas, and Walkowitz, Rebecca L. (eds), *Bad Modernisms* (Durham, NC: Duke University Press, 2006).

Materer, Timothy, *Vortex: Pound, Eliot, and Lewis* (Ithaca, NY: Cornell University Press, 1979).

—— *Wyndham Lewis, the Novelist* (Detroit: Wayne State University Press, 1976).

Meyers, Jeffrey, *Wyndham Lewis, a Revaluation: New Essays* (London: Athlone Press, 1980).

Miller, Tyrus, *Late Modernism: Politics, Fiction, and the Arts between the World Wars* (Berkeley and Los Angeles: University of California Press, 1999).

Normand, Tom, *Wyndham Lewis the Artist: Holding the Mirror up to Politics* (Cambridge and New York: Cambridge University Press, 1992).

Peppis, Paul, *Literature, Politics, and the English Avant-Garde: Nation and Empire, 1901–1918* (Cambridge: Cambridge University Press, 2000).

Peters Corbett, David (ed.), *Wyndham Lewis and the Art of Modern War* (New York: Cambridge University Press, 1998).

Puchner, Martin, *Poetry of the Revolution: Marx, Manifestos, and the Avant-Gardes* (Princeton: Princeton University Press, 2006).

Sherry, Vincent B., *Ezra Pound, Wyndham Lewis, and Radical Modernism* (New York: Oxford University Press, 1992).

Wagner, Geoffrey, *Wyndham Lewis: A Portrait of the Artist as the Enemy* (New Haven: Yale University Press, 1957).

Wees, William C., *Vorticism and the English Avant-Garde* (Toronto: University of Toronto Press, 1972).

Further Reading in Oxford World's Classics

Ford, Ford Madox, *The Good Soldier*, ed. Thomas Moser.

Joyce, James, *A Portrait of the Artist as a Young Man*, ed. Jeri Johnson.

Lawrence, D. H., *Women in Love*, ed. David Bradshaw.

A CHRONOLOGY OF WYNDHAM LEWIS

1882   (18 Nov.) Percy Wyndham Lewis born to Charles Edward and
              Anne Stuart Lewis in Amherst, Nova Scotia, Canada, by
              Lewis's account on his father's yacht.

1888–93   Family lives on Isle of Wight.

1893   Parents separate. Lives with mother in England.

1897–8   Educated at Rugby School.

1898–1901   Attends Slade School of Art in London; expelled.

1904–8   Moves to Paris. Travels within France, Germany, Holland,
              and Spain, which provided the subject matter for his earliest
              fiction.

c.1908   Begins to draft first version of *Tarr*, a narrative about
              a German and a duel, to be called 'Otto Kreisler'.

1908   (Dec.) Returns to London.

1909   Meets Ezra Pound and Ford Madox Ford (then known as Ford
              Madox Hueffer). Earliest stories published in *English Review*.

1910   Art critic Roger Fry mounts revolutionary art exhibition
              'Manet and the Post-Impressionists' in London. Early sto-
              ries appear in *The Tramp: an Open Air Magazine*.

1911   Joins the Camden Town Group of artists.

1912   Displays large canvas *Kermesse* (now lost) at the
              Allied Artists' Association exhibition at the Royal
              Albert Hall. Other artwork included in Fry's 'Second Post-
              Impressionist Exhibition'.

1913   Briefly joins Roger Fry's Omega Workshop, then breaks
              with Fry over accusation of stolen commission for the Ideal
              Home Show. Portfolio of drawings for Shakespeare's *Timon
              of Athens* published.

1914   Founds Rebel Art Centre with Kate Lechmere.
              (20 June) first issue of Vorticist journal *Blast* appears
              under Lewis's editorship, including play *Enemy of the
              Stars* and contributions by Pound, Ford Madox Ford, and
              T. E. Hulme. (4 Aug.) England declares war on Germany,
              entering the First World War.

1915   Meets T. S. Eliot. (July) Second and last issue of
           Blast, 'WAR NUMBER' appears, including contribution
           by Eliot and announcement of death of Vorticist sculptor
           Gaudier-Brezska in the war. Completes original version of
           Tarr.

1916   Enlists in the Royal Garrison Artillery, as Gunner
           and then Bombardier. Fights in third battle of Ypres.
           Tarr begins to appear in serial form in *The Egoist*
           (Apr. 1916–Nov. 1917). While Lewis is at the front, Pound
           helps arrange sale of *Tarr* to Knopf in New York.

1917   Gains commission as an official war artist for Canadian
           Corps headquarters. Short story 'Cantleman's Spring Mate'
           published in *Little Review*: its sexual frankness leads to sup-
           pression of the issue by the US Post Office. *The Ideal Giant*
           (play). T. E. Hulme killed near Lewis's battery.

1918   *Tarr* appears in America and England. Returns to London.
           Meets future wife Gladys Anne Hoskins ('Froanna').

1919   First one-man show, exhibition of war art, 'Guns' at Goupil
           gallery. *The Caliph's Design: Architects! Where is your Vortex?*
           published by Egoist Press.

1920   (9 Feb.) Mother dies. Lewis forms 'Group X', which dis-
           bands after single exhibition in March. Meets James Joyce
           with T. S. Eliot during trip to Paris.

1921   (Apr.) Edits first issue of arts journal *The Tyro*. Exhibition,
           'Tyros and Portraits'. Begins period of 'going underground'
           to work on massive book project *The Man of the World*.

1922   (Mar.) Second and last issue of *The Tyro*.

1924   (Feb.–Apr.) Two excerpts from *The Apes of God* published in
           T. S. Eliot's journal *The Criterion*.

1926   *The Art of Being Ruled* (political and cultural analysis).

1927   *Time and Western Man* (philosophical, cultural, and literary
           analysis). *The Wild Body* (short stories). *The Lion and the
           Fox* (study of Shakespeare). Edits first issue of *The Enemy:
           A Review of Art and Literature* (three issues to 1929).

1928   *The Childermass* (novel). (Dec.) Revised version of *Tarr*
           published by Chatto and Windus.

1929   *Paleface: The Philosophy of the 'Melting Pot'*. Meets W. B.
           Yeats.

1930   *The Apes of God* (novel). *Satire and Fiction.* (9 Oct.) Marries Froanna.

1931   *Hitler. The Diabolical Principle.*

1932   *The Doom of Youth. Filibusters in Barbary. Snooty Baronet* (novel).

1933   *The Old Gang and the New Gang. One Way Song* (poetry).

1934   *Men Without Art* (literary and cultural criticism).

1936   *Left Wings over Europe, or How to Make a War about Nothing. The Roaring Queen* (novel; suppressed).

1937   *Blasting and Bombardiering* (autobiography). *Count Your Dead: They are Alive! The Revenge for Love* (novel). Exhibition of paintings and drawing at Leicester Galleries. Begins to lose his sight from pituitary tumour. *Twentieth Century Verse* special Lewis issue.

1938   *The Mysterious Mr Bull.* Portrait of T. S. Eliot rejected by Royal Academy.

1939   *The Jews, Are They Human?* (polemic against anti-Semitism). *The Hitler Cult: and How it will End.* Tate Gallery acquires *Portrait of Ezra Pound.* (3 Sept.) England declares war on Germany. Lewis and wife move to Canada and United States for six years.

1940   *America, I Presume.*

1941   *Anglosaxony: A League that Works. The Vulgar Streak* (novel).

1945   (Aug.) Returns to London.

1946–51 Art critic for *The Listener.*

1948   *America and Cosmic Man.*

1949   (May) Retrospective Exhibition, Redfern Gallery.

1950   *Rude Assignment* (autobiography). Tumour diagnosed.

1951   Loses sight. 'The Sea-Mists of the Winter' (essay on blindness). *Rotting Hill* (short stories).

1952   *The Writer and the Absolute.*

1953   Special Lewis issue of *Shenandoah.*

1954   *Self Condemned* (novel). *The Demon of Progress in the Arts.*

1955   *Monstre Gai* and *Malign Fiesta* (novels, *The Human Age, Books 2 and 3*; sequels to *The Childermass*).

1956   *The Red Priest* (novel). (18 July) Dramatization of *Tarr* broadcast on the BBC Third Programme. (July–Aug.) Tate Gallery exhibition *Wyndham Lewis and Vorticism*.

1957   (7 Mar.) Death, Westminster Hospital, London.

1973   *The Roaring Queen* (novel), published posthumously.

1977   *Mrs Dukes' Million* (novel, *c.*1908–9), published posthumously.

1979   (Apr.) Death of Froanna.

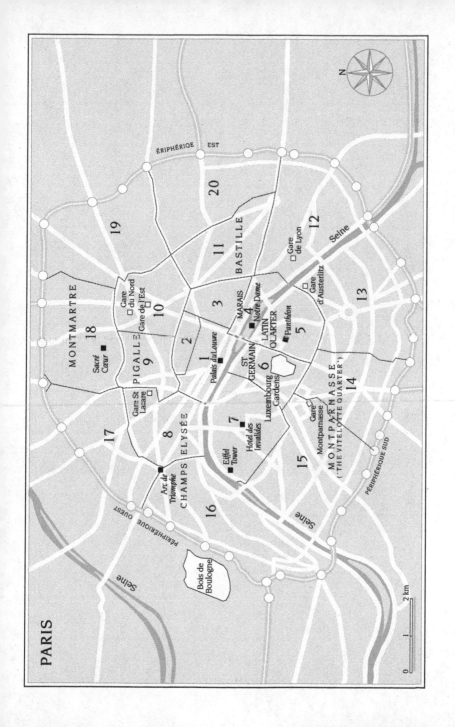

TARR

PREFACE

PUBLISHED ten years ago, *Tarr*, my first book, in a sense the first book of an epoch in England, is often referred to and a new edition has, for several years, been in demand. But in turning back to it I have always felt that as regards form simply it should not appear again as it stood, for it was written with extreme haste, during the first year of the War, during a period of illness and restless convalescence.* Accordingly for the present edition I have throughout finished what was rough and given the narrative everywhere a greater precision. A few scenes have been expanded and some material added.

WYNDHAM LEWIS.

November 1928

CONTENTS

L'ouvrage eust été moins mien: et sa fin principale et perfection, c'est d'estre exactement mien. Je corrigerois bien une erreur accidentale, dequoy je suis plain, ainsi que je cours inadvertemment: mais les imperfections qui sont en moy ordinaires et constantes, ce seroit trahison de les oster. Quand on m'a dit ou que moy-mesme me suis dict: 'Tu es trop espais en figures: Voilà un mot du cru de Gascoingne: Voilà une frase dangereuse (je n'en refuis aucune de celles qui s'usent emmy les rues françoises; ceux qui veulent combattre l'usage par la grammaire se mocquent): Voilà un discours ignorant: Voilà un discours paradoxe: En voilà un trop fol. [Tu te joues souvent, on estimera que tu dies à droit ce que tu dis à feinte.]—Ouy, fais-je, mais je corrige les fautes d'inadvertence non celles de coustume. Est-ce pas ainsi que je parle par tout? Me represente-je pas vivement? suffit.'

Montaigne, Liv. III, ch. v.

Le plus simplement se commettre à nature, c'est s'y commettre le plus sagement. O que c'est un doux et mol chevet, et sain, que l'ignorance et l'incuriosité, à reposer une teste bien faicte!'

Montaigne, Liv. III, ch. xiii, 'De l'expérience.'*

PART I

BERTHA

CHAPTER 1

PARIS hints of sacrifice. But here we deal with that large dusty facet known to indulgent and congruous kind: it is in its capacity of delicious inn and majestic Baedeker,* where western Venuses* twang its responsive streets and hush to soft growl before its statues, that it is seen. It is not across its Thébaïde* that the unscrupulous heroes chase each other's shadows: they are largely ignorant of all but their restless personal lives.

Inconceivably generous and naïve faces haunt the Vitelotte Quarter.*—We are not, however, in a Hollywood camp of pseudo-cowpunchers (though 'guns' tap rhythmically the buttocks).* Art is being studied.—But 'art' is not anything serious or exclusive: it is the smell of oil paint, Henri Murger's *Vie de Bohème*,* corduroy trousers, the operatic Italian model: but the poetry, above all, of linseed oil* and turpentine.

The Vitelotte Quarter is given up to Art: Letters and other things are round the corner. Its rent is half paid by America. Germany occupies a sensible apartment on the second floor. A hundred square yards at its centre is a convenient space, where the Boulevard du Paradis and the Boulevard Kreutzberg* cross with their electric trams: in the middle is a pavement island, like vestige of submerged masonry. Italian models festoon it in symmetrical human groups; it is also their club.

The Café Berne, at one side, is the club of the 'grands messieurs du Berne.' So you have the clap-trap Campagnia* tribe outside, in the Café twenty sluggish commonsense Germans, a Middle West group or two, drinking and playing billiards. These are the most permanent tableaux of this place, disheartening and admonitory as a Tussaud's of the Flood.*

———

Hobson and Tarr met in the Boulevard du Paradis.—They met in a gingerly, shuffling fashion: they had so many good reasons for not slowing down when they met, numbers of antecedent meetings when it would have been better if they had kept on, all pointing to *why* they *should* crush their hats over their eyes and hurry forward, so that it was a defeat and insanitary to have their bodies shuffling and gesticulating there. ('Why cannot most people, having talked and annoyed each other once or twice, rebecome strangers simply? Oh for multitudes of divorces in our *mœurs*, more than the old vexed sex ones! Ah yes, ah yes—!' had not Tarr once put forward, and Hobson agreed?)

'Have you been back long?' Tarr asked with despondent slowness.

'No. I got back yesterday' said Hobson, with pleasantly twisted scowl.

('Heavens! one day here only, and lo I meet him.')

'How is London looking, then?'

'Very much as usual.—I wasn't there the whole time; I was in Cambridge* last week.'

('I wish you'd go to hell from time to time instead of Cambridge, as it always is, you grim grim dog!' Tarr wished behind the veil.)

They went to the Berne to have their drink.

They sat for some minutes with a stately discomfort of self-consciousness, staring in front of them. It was really only a dreary boiling anger with themselves and against the contradictions of civilized life; the hatred that personal diversities engender was fermenting under the camouflage of intricate accommodations and in each other's company they were conscious of this stir. 'Phew, phew!'—a tenuous howl, like a subterranean wind, rose from the borderland of their consciousness. There they were on the point of opening, with tired ashamed fingers, well-worn pages of their souls, soon to be muttering between their teeth the hackneyed pages to each other: in different degrees and disproportionate ways they were resentful.

So they sat with this absurd travesty of a Quaker's Meeting,* shyness appearing to emanate masterfully from Tarr. And in another case, with almost any one but Hobson, it might have been shyness: for Tarr had a gauche puritanical ritual of self, the result of solitary habits. Certain observances were demanded of those approaching him, and were quite gratuitously observed in return. The fetish* within—soul-dweller that is strikingly like a wood-dweller, and who was not often enough disturbed to have had the sylvan shyness mitigated—would still cling to these forms. Sometimes Tarr's crafty daimon,* aghast at its nakedness, would manage to borrow or purloin some shape of covering from elegantly draped visitor.

But for Hobson's outfit Tarr had the most elaborate contempt. This was Alan Hobson's outfit: a Cambridge cut disfigured his originally manly and melodramatic form. His father was said to be a wealthy merchant somewhere in Egypt. Very athletic, his dark and cavernous features had been constructed by nature as a lurking-place for villainies and passions: but Hobson had double-crossed his rascally sinuous body. He slouched and ambled along, neglecting his muscles: and his full-blooded blackguard's countenance attempted to portray delicacies of common sense and gossamer-like backslidings into the inane that would have puzzled any analyst unacquainted with his peculiar training. Occasionally he would exploit his criminal appearance and blacksmith's muscles for a short time, however: and his strong piercing laugh threw A B C waitresses* into confusion. The art-touch, the Bloomsbury* technique, was very noticeable. Hobson's Harris tweeds were shabby, from beneath his dejected jacket emerged a pendant seat, his massive shoes were hooded by the superfluous inches of his trousers: a hat suggesting that his ancestors had been Plainsmen or some rough sunny folk shaded unnecessarily his countenance, already far from open.

The material for conversation afforded by a short sea voyage, an absence, a panama hat on his companion's head, had been exhausted. Tarr possessed no deft hand or economy of force: his muscles rose unnecessarily on his arm to lift a wine-glass to his lips: he had no social machinery at all at his disposal and was compelled to get along as well as he could with the cumbrous one of the intellect. With this he danced about it is true: but it was full of sinister piston-rods, organ-like shapes, heavy drills. When he tried to be amiable he usually only succeeded in being portentous.

It was an effort to talk to Hobson: for this effort a great reserve of nervous force was brought into play: it got to work and wove its large anomalous patterns. Taking crudely the subject that was foremost in his existence he imposed it upon their talk.

Tarr turned to Hobson and seized him, conversationally, by the hair.

'Well Walt Whitman, when are you going to get your hair cut?'

Hobson lifted up startled astonished eyes and sniggered.

'*Why* do you call me Walt Whitman?'

'Would you prefer Buffalo Bill, or is it Thomas Carlyle?'*

'It is not Thomas Carlyle.'

' "Roi je ne suis: prince je ne daigne."* That's Hobson's choice.* But why so much hair? I don't wear my hair long: if you had as many reasons for wearing it long as I have we should see it flowing round your ankles!'

'I might ask you under those circumstances why you wear it short. But I expect you have excellent reasons of your own. I can't see why you should resent my innocent device: however long I wore it you would not suffer, we do not compete.'

Tarr rattled the cement match-stand upon the suety marble and the *garçon* sang prettily 'Tout de suite, tout de suite!'

'Hobson, you were telling me about a studio to let before you left.—I forget the details—.'

'Was it one behind the Panthéon?'*

'That's it. Was there electric light?'

'No I don't think there was electric light. But I can find out for you.'

'How did you come to hear of it?'

'Through a German I know—Salle, Salla, or something.'

'What was the street?'

'The Rue Lhomond.* I forget the number.'

'I'll go and have a look at it after lunch.—What on earth possesses you to know so many Germans?' Tarr asked, sighing, as a burdensome afterthought.

'Don't you like Germans?—You've just been too intimate with one, that's what it is.'

'Perhaps I have.'

'A female of the species, too.'

'The sex weakens the "German," surely.'

'In Fräulein Lunken's case does it have that effect?'

'Oh you know her, do you?—Of course you would know her, as she's a German.'

Alan Hobson cackled morosely.

Tarr's unwieldy playfulness might, in the chequered north-ern shade, in conjunction with nut-brown ale, gazed at by some Rowlandson (he on the ultimate borders of the epoch)* have pleased by its à propos. But when the last Rowlandson dies, the life, too, that he saw should vanish. Anything that survives the artist's death is not life but belated drama. This homely, thick-waisted affectation!— Hobson yawned and yawned as though he wished to swallow Tarr and have done with him. Tarr yawned more noisily, rattled his chair, sat up, haggard and stiff, as though he wished to frighten this crow away: 'Carrion-Crow'* was his name for him.

Why was he talking to this individual at all? However, he shortly began to lay bare the secrets of his soul. Hobson opened:

'It seems to me, Tarr, that you know far more Germans than I do: but *you're ashamed of it.* Hence your attack. I met a Fräulein Unger the other day, a German, who claimed to know you—I'm *always* meeting Germans who know you! She also referred to you as the "official fiancé" of Fräulein Lunken.—Are you an "official fiancé"—and if so what is that may I ask?'

Tarr was taken aback, he looked round with surprise. Hobson laughed stridently: the real man emerging, he came over quickly on another wave.

'You not only get to know Germans, masses of them, on the sly, you make them your bosom friends, engage yourself to them in marriage and make heaven knows how many more solemn pacts and undertakings to cement yourself still more closely to them.'

Tarr was recovering gracefully from his relapse into discomfort: if ever taken off his guard he made a clever use immediately afterwards of his naïveté: he beamed upon his slip: he would swallow it tranquilly, assimilating it with ostentation to himself. A personal weakness slipped out, he picked it up unabashed, looked at it smilingly, and put it back in his pocket.

'As you know' he soon replied ' "engagement" is a euphemism. But as it happens my betrothed publicly announced the dissolution of our fiançailles yesterday.'

He looked no more responsible than a young child, head thrown up as though proclaiming something of which he had reason to be particularly proud.—Hobson laughed convulsively, cracking his yellow fingers.

'Yes, it is funny, if you look at it in that way: I let her announce our engagement or the reverse just as she thinks fit—that has been our arrangement from the start. I never know at any given time whether I'm engaged or not, I leave all that sort of thing entirely in her hands.

After a severe quarrel I know it's fairly safe to say that I am temporarily unattached. Somewhere or other the link will have been publicly severed.'

'Possibly that is what is meant by officially—.'

'Very likely.'

He had been hustled—through his vanity, thought the Cairo cantab*—somewhere where the time could be passed: Tarr's curiosities could now be lifted out and handled. On his side the secrets and repressions that it is the pride of the modern to disclose with a conventional obscene heroism Tarr flourished about with Hobson's assistance. He pulled a wry face once or twice at the other's *sans gêne*: but he was too good a modern not to court the ordeal.

There was a considerable pause in which Tarr obtruded complacently this strange new-fangled weakness for the unlikeliest of things, his philogermanic* patent.

'Will you go so far in this clandestine life of yours as to *marry* anybody?' Hobson then enquired.

'No.'

Staring with bright meditative sweetness down the boulevard Hobson remarked

'There must be a great difference between your way of approaching Germans and mine.'

'Ay: it is different things that take us respectively amongst them.'

'All the same you like the national flavour.'

'I like the national flavour!' (Hobson was familiar with this habit of Tarr's, namely of beginning a reply with a parrot-like echo of the words of the other party to the dialogue: also he would repeat *sotto voce* one of his own sentences, a mechanical rattle following on without stop): 'Sex is nationalized, more than any other essential of life, Hobson, it's just the opposite of art there: in german sex there is all the german cuisine, the beer-cellar, and all the plum-pudding mysticism of german thought. But then if it is the *sex* you are after that does not say you want to identify your being with your appetite: quite the opposite. The condition of continued enjoyment is to resist assimilation. A man is the opposite of his appetite.'

'Surely, a man *is* his appetite.'

'No, a man is always his *last* appetite, or his appetite before last. And that is no longer an appetite.'

'A man is nothing.' Hobson picked his teeth, laughing.

'Of course. Nobody *is* anything or life would be intolerable. You are me, I am you.—The Present is the furthest projection of our steady appetite; imagination, the commander-in-chief, keeps in the rear. Imagination is the man.'

'*What* is the Present?' asked Hobson politely, with much aspirating, sitting up a little and slightly offering his ear.

But Tarr only repeated things arbitrarily. He extinguished Hobson with a glance, then he proceeded with considerable pomp:

'Sex is a monstrosity. Sex is a monstrosity. It's the last and ugliest piece of nonsense of a long line. I can see you raising your eyebrows. No? You should do so: I'm a pessimist—.'

'A german pessimist!'

'A pessimist. I'm a new sort of pessimist. I think I'm the sort that will go down.'

'Why not? But you must—.'

'No! I am the panurgic*-pessimist, drunken with the laughing-gas of the Abyss: I gaze upon squalor and idiocy, and the more I see them the more I like them. Flaubert built up his *Bouvard et Pécuchet** with maniacal and tireless hands, it took him ten years: that was a long draught of stodgy laughter from the gases that rise from the dung-heap.'

'Flaubert—.'

'No' (Tarr raised his flat hand, threatening Hobson's mouth) 'he had an appetite like an elephant for this form of mirth, but he grumbled and sighed over his food. I take the stuff up in my arms and bury my face in it!'

As Tarr's temperament spread its wings, whirling him with menace and mockery above Hobson's head, the cantab philosopher did not consider it necessary to reply. He was not winged himself. Tarr looped the loop and he looked on. A droll bird! He wondered, as he watched him, if he was a *sound* bird. People believed in him: his exhibition flights attracted attention. What sort of prizes could he expect to win by these a little too professional talents? Would this notable *ambitieux* be satisfied?

The childish sport proceeded, with serious interludes.

'I bury my face in it!'—(He buried his face in it!)—'I laugh hoarsely through its thickness choking and spitting, choking and spitting. (He choked and spat.) That is my daily ooze: as far as sex is concerned I took to it like a duck to water. Sex, Hobson, is a german study: a german study.' He shook his head in a dejected drunken manner, protruding his lips. He seemed to find analogies for his *repeating* habits in pictures provided by the human digestion.

'All the same you must take my word for a good deal at this point. The choice of a wife is not practical in the way that, oh, buying a bicycle—think rather of the dishes of the table. Rembrandt paints decrepit old Jews.* Shakespeare deals in tubs of grease—Falstaff,* Christ in sinners. As to sex—Socrates married a shrew,* most wise men marry fools, picture post cards,* cows, or strumpets.'

'That's all right, but it's not true.' Hobson resurrected himself dutifully. 'The more sensible people I can think of off-hand have more sensible and on the whole prettier wives than other people.'

'Prettier wives?—You are describing a meaningless average like yourself and their wives. The most suspicious fact about any man with pretensions to intelligence is the possession of an intelligent wife. No, you might just as well say in answer to my art-statement that Tadema* did not paint decayed meat, Rembrandt's octogenarian burghers.'

Hobson surged up a little in his chair and collapsed.—He had to appeal to his body to sustain the argument.

'Neither did Raphael*—I don't see why you should drag Rembrandt in. Rembrandt—.'

'You're going to sniff at Rembrandt! You accuse me of truckling to the fashion in my support of cubism.* You're much more fashionable than I am, if we can be compared without absurdity. Would you mind my "dragging in" cheese, high game—?'

Hobson allowed cheeses with a rather drawn expression: but he did not see what that had to do with it, either.

'It is not purely a question of appetite' he said.

'Sex, sir, is *purely* a question of appetite!' Tarr exclaimed.

Hobson inclined himself mincingly, with a sweet chuckle.

'If it is *pure* sex, that is' Tarr added.

'Oh, if it is *pure* sex—that naturally—.' Hobson convulsed himself and crowed thrice.

'Listen Hobson!—you must not make that noise. It's very clever of you to be able to: but you will not succeed in rattling me by making me feel I am addressing a rooster.'

Hobson let himself go in whoops and caws, as though Tarr had been pressing him to perform.

When he had finished Tarr enquired coldly:

'Are you willing to *consider sex seriously or not?*'

'Yes I don't mind.'—Hobson settled down, his face flushed from his late display.—'But I shall begin to believe before very long that your intentions are honourable as regards the fair Fräulein.—What exactly is your discourse intended to prove?'

'*Not* the desirability of the marriage tie, if that's what you mean, any more than a propaganda for representation and anecdote in art: but *if* a man marries or a great painter represents (and the claims and seductions of life are very urgent) he will not be governed in his choice by the same laws that regulate the life of an efficient citizen or the standards of a eugenist.'*

'I should have said that the considerations that precede a proposition of marriage had many analogies with the eugenist's outlook, the good citizen's—.'

'Was Napoleon successful in life or did he ruin himself and end his days in miserable captivity?*—*Passion* precludes the idea of success: worldly failure is its condition.—Art and sex—the real thing—we're talking at cross-purposes—make tragedies and *not* advertisements for health-experts or happy endings for the Public, or social panaceas.'

'Alas that is true.'

'Well then, well then, Alan Hobson—you scarecrow of an advanced fool-farm—.'

'What is that?'

'You voice-culture practitioner—.'*

'I? My voice—? But that's absurd! If my speech—.'

Hobson was up in arms about his voice: although it was not his.

Tarr needed a grimacing tumultuous mask for the face he had to cover. He had compared his clowning with Hobson's pierrotesque* variety: but Hobson, he considered, was a crowd. You could not say he was an individual, he was in fact a set. He sat there, a cultivated audience, with the aplomb and absence of self-consciousness of numbers, of the herd—of those who know they are not alone.—Tarr was shy and the reverse by turns; he was alone.

A distinguished absence of personality was Hobson's most personal characteristic. Upon this impersonality, of crowd origin, Tarr gazed with the scorn of the autocrat.

'As I said we're talking at cross-purposes, Hobson: you believe I am contending that affection for a dolt, like my fiancée, is in some way a merit; I don't mean that at all. Also I do not mean that sex is my tragedy, but only art.'

'I thought we were talking about sex?'

'No. Let me explain. Why am I associated sexually with that irritating nullity? First of all, I am an artist. With most people, who are not artists, all the finer part of their vitality goes into sex if it goes anywhere: during their courtship they become third-rate poets, all their instincts of drama come out freshly with their wives. The artist is he in whom this emotionality normally absorbed by sex is so strong that it claims a newer and more exclusive field of deployment. Its first creation is *the Artist* himself. That is a new sort of person; the creative man.'

'All artists are not creative.'

'All right, call yourself an artist if you like. For me the artist is creative. Now for a bang-up first-rate poet nothing short of a queen or a chimera* is adequate, the praising-power he's been born with exacts perfection. So on all through his gifts: one by one his powers are turned away from the usual object of a man's personal poetry or passion and so removed from the immediate world. One solitary thing is left facing any woman with whom he has commerce, that is his sex, a lonely phallus.'

'Your creative man sounds rather alarming. I don't believe in him.'

'Some artists are less complete than others: more or less remains to the man.'

'I'm glad some have more than the bare phallus of them.'

'But the character of the artist's creation comes in. What tendency has my work as an artist, for I am one of your beastly *creative* persons you will readily allow. You may have noticed that an invariable severity distinguishes it. Apart from its being good or bad, its character is ascetic rather than sensuous, and it is divorced from immediate life. There is no slop of sex in *that*. But there is no severity left over for the work of the cruder senses either. Very often with an artist whose work is very sensuous or human, his sex instinct, if it is active, will be more discriminating than with a man more fastidious and discriminating than he in his work. To sum up this part of my disclosure: no one could have a coarser, more foolish, slovenly taste than I have in women. It is not even sluttish and abject, of the Turner type (the landscape-artist) with his washerwoman at Gravesend.* It is bourgeois, and it is pretty, a cross between the Musical Comedy stage and the dream of the Eighteenth-Century gallant.'*

At Eighteenth-Century Hobson moved resentfully.

'What's the Eighteenth-Century got to do with it?'

'All the delicate psychology another man naturally seeks in a woman, the curiosity of form, windows on other lives, love and passion, I seek in my work and not elsewhere.—Form would perhaps be thickened by child-bearing; it would perhaps be damaged by harlotry. Why should sex still be active? That is an organic matter that has nothing to do with the general energies of the mind.'

Hobson yawned with sullen relish.

'I see I am boring you—the matter is too remote. But you have trespassed here, and you must listen. I cannot let you off before you have heard, and shown that you understand. If you do not sit and listen, I will write it all to you in a letter. YOU WILL BE MADE TO HEAR IT!—And *after* I have told you this, I will tell you why I am talking to an idiot like you!'

'You ask me to be polite—.'

'I don't mind how impolite you are provided you listen.'

'Well I am listening—I have even betrayed interest.'

Tarr as he saw it was tearing at the blankets swaddling this spirit in its inner snobberies. At all events here was a bitter feast piping hot and going begging, it seemed, and a mouth must be found for it: this jaded palate had to serve under the circumstances and it had, its malicious appetite satisfied, to be taught to do justice to the fare.—He had something to *say*; it must be said while it was living: once it was said, it could look after itself.—As to Hobson, he had shocked something that was ready to burst out: he must help it out: Hobson must pay as well for the intimacy. *He must pay Bertha Lunken afterwards.* Tarr at this point felt like insisting that he should come round and apologize to her.

'A man only goes and importunes the world with a confession when his self will not listen to him or recognize his shortcomings. The function of a friend is to be a substitute for this defective self, to be the World and the Real without the disastrous consequences of reality.— Yet punishment is one of his chief offices. The friend enlarges also substantially the boundaries of our solitude.'

*

This statement was to be found in Tarr's diary. The self he had rebuked in this way for not listening was now again suffering rebuke by his act of confession with the first-met, a man he did not regard as a friend even. Had a friend been there he could have interceded for his ego.*

'You have followed so far?'

Tarr looked with slow disdainful suspicion at Hobson's face staring at the ground.

'You have understood the nature of my secret? Half of myself I have to hide. I am bitterly ashamed of a slovenly common portion of my life that has been isolated and repudiated by the energies of which I am so proud. I am *ashamed* of the number of Germans I know, as you put it. In that rôle I have to cower and slink away even from an old fruit-tin* like you. It is idle to protect that section of my life, it's no good sticking up for it, it's not worth it. It is not even up to *your* standards. I have, therefore, to deliver it up to your eyes and the eyes of the likes of you, in the end—if you will deign to use them! I even have to beg you to use your eyes; to hold you by the sleeve and crave a glance for an object belonging to me!'

'You've succeeded in making me sorry I ever mentioned your precious fiancée!'

'In this compartment of my life *I have not a vestige of passion*. That is the root reason for its meanness and absurdity. The closest friend of my Dr. Jekyll would not recognize my Mr. Hyde,* and vice versa: the rudimentary self I am giving you a glimpse of is more starved and stupid than any other man's: or to put it more pathetically, I am of that company who are reduced to looking to Socrates for a consoling lead.—But consider all the *collages** marriages and affairs that you know, in which some frowsy or foolish or some doll-like or log-like bitch accompanies everywhere the form of an otherwise sensible man: a dumbfounding disgusting and septic ghost! Oh Sex! oh Montreal!* How foul and wrong this haunting of women is!—they are everywhere—confusing, blurring, libelling, with their half-baked gushing tawdry presences! It is like a slop and spawn of children and the bawling machinery of the inside of life, always and all over our palaces. The floodgates of their reservoirs of illusion, that is cheap and vast, burst, and sex hurtles in between friendships or stagnates complacently around a softened mind.—I might almost take some

credit to myself for at least having the grace to keep this bear-garden*
in the background.'

Hobson had brightened up while this was proceeding. He now
cried out:

'You might almost. Why don't you? I am astonished at what you tell
me: but you appear to take your german foibles too much to heart.'

'Just at present I am in the midst of a gala of the heart: you may
have noticed. I'm an indifferent landlord, I haven't the knack of handling the various personalities gathered beneath my roof. In the present instance I am really blessed: but you ought to see the sluts that get
in sometimes! They all become steadily my fiancée too. Fiancée!—
observe how we ape the forms of conventional life in our emancipated
Bohemia:* it does not mean anything so one lets it stop. It's the same
with the Café fools I have for friends—there's a greek fool, a german
fool, a russian fool—an english fool! There are no "friends" in this
life any more than there are authentic "fiancées": so it's of no importance what we choose to call each other: one drifts along side by side
with this live stock—friends, fiancées, "colleagues" and what not in
our unreal gimcrack artist-society.'

Hobson sat staring with a bemused seriousness at the ground.

'Why should I not speak plainly and cruelly of my poor ridiculous
fiancée to you or to anyone? After all it is chiefly myself I am castigat-
ing. But you, as well, must be of the party! Yes: the right to *see* implies
the right to be *seen*. As an offset for your prying scurvy way of poking
your nose into my affairs you must offer your own guts, such as they
are—!'

'How have I pried into your affairs?' Hobson asked with a circum-
spect surprise.

'Anyone who *stands outside*, who hides himself in a deliquescent
aloofness, is a sneak and a spy.'

'That seems to me to be a case of pot calling the kettle black:
I should not have said that you were conspicuous—.'

'No. You know you have joined yourself to those who hush their
voices to hear what other people are saying! Everyone who does not
contend openly and take his share of the common burden of ignominy of life is a sneak, unless it is for a solid motive. The exemption
you claim is not to work in, there is no personal rationale for your
privileges, you make no claim to deserve your state, only to be lucky.
But against what have you exchanged your temper, your freedom, and

your fine baritone voice? You have exchanged them for an old hat that
does not belong to you and a shabbiness you have not merited by
suffering neediness. Your untidiness is a sentimental indulgence: we
should insist upon every man dressing up to his income, it should
be understood that he make willy-nilly a smart *fresh* appearance.
Patching the seat of your trousers, instead of—!'

'Wait a minute' Hobson said, with a cracked laugh. 'I don't admit
I am shabby, of course, but when you say I am sentimental because
I am not fashionably dressed, I wonder if you mean that you are
peculiarly free of sentimentality—?'

'As to that I don't care a fig, perbacco, put that away, I'm talking
about *you*: let me proceed. With your training you are decked in the
plumes of very fine birds indeed: but what does it amount to, your
plumes are not meant to fly with but merely to slouch and skip along
the surface of the earth. You wear the livery of a ridiculous set, you are
a cunning and sleek domestic: no thought can come out of your head
before it has slipped on its uniform: all your instincts are drugged
with a malicious languor—an arm, a respectability, invented by a
group of giggling invert-spinsters* who supply you with a fraudulent
patent of superiority.'

Hobson opened his mouth, had a movement of the body to speak;
but he relapsed.

'You reply "What are the grounds of all this censure? I know
I am not morally defensible, I am lazy and second-rate, that's not my
fault, I have done the best for myself. I was not suited for any heroic
station, like yours: I live sensibly and quietly, cultivating my vegetable ideas,* and also my roses and Victorian lilies:* I do no harm to
anybody."'

Hobson had a vague gesture of assent and puzzled enquiry.

'That is not quite the case. That is a little inexact. Your proceedings
possess a herdesque astuteness; in the scale against the individual
weighing less than the Yellow Press* yet being a closer and meaner
attack. Also you are essentially *spies*, in a lousy safe and well-paid service, as I told you before: you are disguised to look like the thing it
is your function to betray—What is your position? you have bought
have you not for eight hundred pounds at an aristocratic educational
establishment a complete mental outfit, a programme of manners: for
four years you trained with other recruits: you are now a perfectly dis-
ciplined social unit, with a profound *esprit de corps*. The Cambridge

set that you represent is, as observed in an average specimen, a hybrid of the Quaker, the homosexual and the Chelsea artist.* Your Oxford brothers, dating from the Wilde* decade, are a more muscular body: the Chelsea artists have at least no pretensions to be anything but philistine: the Quakers are powerful ruffians. You represent, my good Hobson, the *dregs* of anglo-saxon civilization: there is absolutely nothing softer upon the earth. Your flabby potion is a mixture of the lees of Liberalism,* the poor froth blown off the decadent Nineties, the wardrobe-leavings of a vulgar bohemianism with its headquarters in the suburb of Carlyle and Whistler.* You are concentrated, highly-organized barley-water:* there is nothing in the universe to be said for you: any efficient state would confiscate your property, burn your wardrobe—that old hat and the rest—as infectious and prohibit you from propagating.'

Tarr's white collar shone dazzlingly in the sun. His bowler hat bobbed, striking out clean lines in space as he spoke.

'A breed of mild pervasive cabbages has set up a wide and creeping rot in the West: it is the lost generations described in Chekov* over again, that any resolute power will be able to wipe up over-night, with its eyes shut. Your kind meantime make it indirectly a peril and tribulation for live things to remain in your neighbourhood. You are systematizing and vulgarizing the individual: you are the advance-copy of communism, a false millennial middle-class communism.* You are not an individual: you have, I repeat, no right to that hair and to that hat: you are trying to have the apple and eat it too. You should be in uniform and at work, *not* uniformly *out of uniform* and libelling the Artist by your idleness. Are you idle?'

Tarr had drawn up short, turned squarely upon Hobson, in an abrupt and disconnected voice screeching his question.

Hobson stirred resentfully in his chair: he yawned a little.

'Am I idle, did you say?' he asked. 'Yes, yes, I'm not particularly industrious. But how does that affect you? You know you don't mean all that farrago. But where are you coming to?'

'I have explained already where I come in. It is stupid to be idle: it is the most stupid thing. The only justification for your slovenly appearance it is true is that it is perfectly emblematic.'

'My dear Tarr, you're a very odd stick and if you'll allow me to say so you should take water with it.* But I can't follow you at all: why should these things occupy you? You have just told me a lot of things that may be true or may not: but at the end of them all——? Et alors?——alors?——*quoi?* one asks.'

He gesticulated, got the French guttural *r* with satisfaction, and said the *quoi* rather briskly.

'You deafen me with your upside-downness. In any case my hat is my business!' he concluded quickly, after a moment, getting up with a curling luscious laugh.

The waiter hastened towards them and they paid him.

'No I am responsible for you.——I am one of the only people who *see*: that is a responsibility.' Tarr walked down the boulevard with him, speaking in his ear almost and treading on his toes.

'You know Baudelaire's fable* of the obsequious vagabond, cringing for alms? For all reply the poet seizes a heavy stick and lays about the beggar with it. When he is almost battered to pieces the man suddenly straightens out under the blows, expands, stretches; his eyes dart fire! He rises up and falls upon the poet tooth and nail: in a few seconds he has laid him out flat and is just going to finish him off, when a cop arrives. The poet is enchanted: he has accomplished something! Would it be possible I wonder to accomplish something of that sort with you? No. You are meaner-spirited than the most currish hobo. I would seize you by the throat at once if I thought you would black my eye. But I feel it my duty at least to do this for your hat: your misnamed wideawake,* at least, will have had its little drama to-day.'

Tarr knocked his hat off into the road, and stepping after it propelled it some yards farther with a running kick. Without troubling to wait for the possible upshot of this action he hurried away down the Boulevard Kreutzberg.

CHAPTER 2

A GREAT many of Frederick Tarr's resolutions came from his conversation. It was a tribunal to which he brought his hesitations. An active up-and-coming spirit presided over this department of his life.

Civilized men have for conversation something of the superstitious feeling that ignorant men have for the written or the printed word.

Hobson had attracted a great deal of steam to himself. Tarr was unsatisfied. He rushed away from the Café Berne still strong and with much more to say. He rushed towards Bertha to say it.

A third of the way he encountered a friend who should have been met before Hobson. Then Bertha and he could have been spared.

As he rushed along then a gaunt car met him, rushing in the opposite direction. Butcher's large red nose stood under a check cap phenomenally peaked. A sweater and stiff-shouldered jacket, of gangster cut,* exaggerated his breadth. He was sunk in horizontal massiveness in the car—almost in the road. A quizzing, heavy smile broke his face open in an indifferent business-like way. It was a sour smile, as though half his face were frozen with cocaine.*

Butcher was the sweetest old kitten, the sham *tough guy* in excelsis.* He might have been described as a romantic educating his english schoolboyish sense of adventure up to the pitch of drama. He had been induced by Tarr to develop an interest in commerce: had started a motor business in Paris, and through circularizing the Americans resident there and using his english connections, he was succeeding on the lines suggested.

Tarr had argued that an interest of this sort would prevent him from becoming arty and silly: he would have driven his entire circle of acquaintances into commerce if he could. At first he had cherished the ambition of getting Hobson into a bank in South Africa.

Guy Butcher pulled up with the air of an Iron-Age mechanic, born among beds of embryonic machinery.

'Ah, I thought I might see you.' He rolled over the edge and stood grinning archly and stretching in front of his friend.

'Where are you off to?' Tarr asked.

'Oh, there's a rumour that some roumanian gypsies are encamped over by Charenton—.'* He smiled and waited, his entire face breaking up expectantly into arch-cunning pits and traps. Mention of 'gypsies' generally succeeded in drawing Tarr—Guy's Romanys* were a survival of Butcher's pre-motor days.

'Neglecting business?' was all Tarr said, however. 'Have you time for a drink?'

'Yes!' Butcher turned with an airy jerk to his car.

'Shall we go to the Panthéon?'

'How about the Univers? Would that take long?'

'The Univers? Four or five minutes. Jump in!'

When they had got to the Univers and ordered their drink, Tarr said:

'I've just been talking to Alan Hobson. I've been telling him off.'

'That's right. How had he deserved it?'

'Oh, he happened to drop on me when I was thinking about my girl. He began congratulating me on my engagement. So I gave him my views on marriage and then wound up with a little improvisation about himself.'

Butcher maintained a decorous silence, drinking his Pernot.*

'You're not engaged to be married, are you?' he asked.

'Engaged to be married? Well, that's a difficult question.' Tarr laughed with circumspection and softness. 'I don't know whether I am or whether I'm not.'

'Would it be the german girl, if you were?'

Tarr chewed and spat out a skein of pale tobacco, eyeing Butcher.

'Yes, she'd be the one.'

There was a careful absence of comment in Butcher's face.

'Ought I to marry the Lunken?'*

'No' Butcher said with measured abruptness, flat but soft.

'In that case I ought to tell her at once.'

'That is so.'

Tarr had wings to his hips. He wore a dark morning-coat whose tails flowed behind him as he walked strongly and quickly along, and curled on either side of his lap as he sat. It was buttoned halfway down the body. He was taller than Butcher, wore glasses, had a dark skin and a steady, unamiable, impatient expression. He was clean-shaven with a shallow square jaw and straight thick mouth. His hands were square and usually hot—all these characteristics he inherited from his mother, except his height. That he seemed to have caused himself.

He impressed the stranger as having inherited himself last week, and as under a great press of business to grasp the details and resources of the concern. Not very much satisfaction at his inheritance was manifest and no arrogance. Great capacity was written all over him. As yet he did not appear to have been modified by any sedentary, sentimental or other discipline or habit: he was at his first push in an ardent and exotic world, with a good fund of passion from a somewhat frigid climate of his own. His mistakes he talked over without embarrassment—he felt them deeply. He was experimental and modest.

A rude and hard infancy, if Balzac is to be believed, is quite the best thing for development of character.* Thereby a child learns duplicity and hardens in defence.

An enervating childhood of mollycoddling, on the other hand, such as Tarr's, has its advantages.—He was an only child of a selfish vigorous little mother. The long foundation of delicate trustfulness and irresponsibility makes for a store of illusion to prolong youth and health beyond the usual term. Tarr, with the Balzac upbringing, would have had a little too much character, like a rather too muscular man. As it was he was a shade too nervous. But his confidence in the backing of character was unparalleled: you would have thought he had an Age of Iron behind him, instead of an Age of Bibs and Binders.

When he solicited advice, as now he was doing of Butcher, it was transparently a matter of form. No serious reply was expected from anyone except himself: but he appeared to need his own advice to come from himself in public.

Did he feel that a man was of more importance in public? Probably not: but his relation to the world was definite and complementary. He preferred his own word to come out of the air; when, that is, issuing from his mouth, it entered either ear as an independent vibration. He was the kind of person who, if he ever should wish to influence the world, would do it so that he might touch himself more plastically through others. If he wanted a picture, he would paint it for himself. He was capable of respect for his self-projection, it had the authority of a stranger for him.

Butcher knew that his advice was not in fact solicited. This he found rather annoying, as he wanted to meddle, loving Tarr and desiring to have a finger in all Tarr's pies, especially where tenderness was in question. But his opportunity would come.

Tarr's affairs with Bertha Lunken were very exasperating: of all the drab, dull and disproportionately long liaisons, that one was unique! What on earth was this young master doing in this instance? Butcher could not fathom it. But it seemed that Tarr had acquiesced as an incomprehensible and silly joke.

'She's a very good sort; you know, she is phenomenally kind. It's not quite so absurd as you think, my question as to whether I should marry her. Her love is quite beyond question.'

Butcher listened with a slight rolling of the eyes, which was a soft equivalent for grinding his teeth. These women! These men!

Tarr proceeded:

'She has a nice healthy bent for self-immolation, not unfortunately, I must confess, directed by any considerable tact or discretion. She is apt to lie down on the altar at the wrong moment—even to mistake all sorts of unrelated things for altars. She once lay down on the pavement of the Boulevard Sebastopol* and continued to lie there heroically till, with the help of a cop, I bundled her into a cab. She is decidedly genial and fond of a gross pleasantry, very near to "the people"—"le peuple," as she says, purringly and pityingly in her clumsy german french. All individuals who have class marked upon them strongly resemble each other don't you agree—a typical duchess is much more like a typical nurserymaid than she is like anybody not standardized to the same extent as the nurserymaid and herself. So is Bertha, a bourgeoise or rather bourgeois-bohemian, reminiscent of the popular maiden: she is the popular maiden, at one remove.— I am not in love with the popular maiden.'

'No!' Butcher hastened to agree to that healthy sentiment.

Tarr relighted his cigarette.

'She is full of good sense. Bertha is a high-grade aryan* bitch, in good condition, superbly made; of the succulent, obedient, clear peasant type. At least it is natural that in my healthy youth, living in these Bohemian wastes, I should catch fire. I have caught fire; not much, slightly, at the tip.'

'Stamp on it!'

'No. That is not the whole of the picture. She is unfortunately not a peasant. She has german culture, and a florid philosophy of love. She is an art student. She is absurd.'

Butcher did not dare to speak, but he shifted about approvingly, his eyes very bright indeed.

Tarr struck a match for his cigarette.

'You would ask then how it is that I am still there? The peasant—if such it were—would not hold you for ever; even less so the *spoiled* peasant.—But that's where the mischief lies. That bourgeois, spoiled, ridiculous element was the trap, I discover. I was innocently depraved enough to find it irresistible: had it not the charm of a vulgar wallpaper, a gimcrack ornament? I fell to a cosy banality set in the midst of a rough life. Youthful exoticism has done it, the something different to oneself. Bertha is the one thing on earth I am not like myself, probably.'

Butcher did not roll his eyes any more, they looked rather moist. He was thinking of love and absurdities that had checkered his own past, he was regretting a downy doll. But his friend's statement had won him over as was always the case; such conviction lay very near the surface with the moist-eyed Guy Butcher.

Tarr, noticing the effect of his words, laughed. Butcher was like a dog, with his rheumy eyes.

'My romance, you see, is exactly the opposite to yours' Tarr proceeded. 'Pure unadulterated romanticism, look you Butch, is, when found in me, in much the same rudimentary state as sex. So they had perhaps better keep together? What do you say? I only allow myself to philander with *little* things. I have succeeded in shunting our noxious illusionism away from the great spaces and ambitions, that is my main claim to fame, so far. I have billeted it with a bourgeoise in a villa.' He beamed suddenly at Butcher, who taken by surprise, coughed, staggered in his chair and mildly choked, his eyes filling with tears.

'In a villa.' Tarr pointed at the summit of a dusty little tree. 'These things are all arranged above our heads, they are no doubt self-protective. All of a man's ninety-nine per cent of submerged mechanism is daily engaged in organizing his life in accordance with his deepest necessity: each person boasts some invention of purely personal application. So there I am fixed with my bourgeoise in my skin, dans ma peau. What is the next step? The body is the main thing. But I think I have made a discovery. In sex I am romantic and backward. It would be healthier for all sex to be so: but that's another matter. Well, I cannot see myself attracted by an exceptional woman, a particularly refined and witty animal—I do not understand attraction for such beings. Their existence puzzles me though I am sure they serve some purpose: but, not being as fine as men—not being as fine as pictures or poems—not being as fine as housewives or classical Mothers of Men—accordingly they appear to me to occupy an unfortunate position on this earth. No properly demarcated person as I am, is going to have much to do with them: they are beautiful to look at, it may be, but they are unfortunately alive, and usually cats: if you married one of them, out of pity, you would have to support the eternal grin of a Gioconda* fixed complacently upon you at all hours of the day, the pretensions of a piece of canvas that had sold for thirty thousand pounds. You could not put your foot through the canvas without being hanged. You would not be able to sell it yourself for that figure and so get some little compensation. At the most, if the sentimental grin would not otherwise come off, you could break its jaw, perhaps. No!'

Butcher flung his head up, and laughed affectedly.

'Ha! Ha!' he went again.

'Very good!—Very good!—I know who you're thinking of' said he.

'Do you? Oh, the "Gioconda smile," you mean? Yes. In that instance, the man had only his sentimental idiot of a self to blame. He has paid the biggest price given in our time for a *living* master-piece. Sentimentalizing about masterpieces and the *sentimental prices* that accompany that will soon have seen their day, I expect: then new masterpieces in painting will appear again perhaps, where the live ones leagued with the old dead ones disappear.—Really, the more one considers it, the more creditable my self-organisation appears, I have a great deal to congratulate myself upon—you agree? Yes, you agree!'

Butcher blinked and pulled himself together with a grave dissatis-fied expression.

'But will you carry it into effect to the extent—will you—would marriage be the ideal termination?' Butcher had a way of tearing up and beginning all over again on a new breath.

'That is what Hobson asked. No, I don't think marriage has anything to do with it. That is another question altogether.'

'I thought your remarks about the housewife suggested—.'

'No. My relation to the idea of the housewife is platonic;* I am attracted to the housewife as I might be attracted to the milliner. But just as I should not necessarily employ the latter to make hats—I should have some other use for her—so my connection with the other need not imply an establishment. But my present difficulty centres round that question.—What am I to do with Fräulein Lunken? What, Butcher, is to be done with Miss Lunken?'

Butcher drew himself up, and hiccuped solemnly and slowly.

He did not reply.

'Once again, is marriage out of the question?' Tarr asked. 'Must marriage be barred out? Marriage. Marriage.'

'You know yourself best. I don't think you ought to marry.'

'Why, am I—?'

'No. You wouldn't stop with her. So why marry?'

Guy Butcher hiccuped again, and blinked.

Tarr gazed at his oracle with curiosity. With eyes glassily blood-shot, it discharged its wisdom on gusts of flatulent air. Butcher was always surly about women, or rather men's tenderness for them: he was a vindictive enemy of the sex. So he invariably stood, a patient constable, forbidding Tarr respectfully a certain road. He spoke with authority and shortness, and hiccuped to convey the irrevocable quality of his refusal.

'Well, in that case' said Tarr, 'I must make a move. I have treated Bertha very badly.'

Butcher smothered a hiccup. He ordered another lager, to justify the hiccups and prolong the interview.

'Yes, I owe my girl anything I can give her. It is hardly my fault: with that training you get in England, how can you be expected to realize anything? I have the greatest difficulty sometimes in doing so. Listen. The University of Humour—that is what it is—that prevails everywhere in England for the formation of youth, provides you with nothing but a first-rate means of evading reality. All english training is a system of *deadening feeling*, a stoic prescription—a humorous stoicism is the anglo-saxon philosophy. Many of the results are excellent: it saves from gush in many cases; in times of crisis or misfortune it is an excellent armour. The english soldier gets his special cachet from that. But for the sake of this wonderful panacea—english humour—the English sacrifice so much. It is the price of empire, if you like. It would be better *to face* our imagination and our nerves without this drug. And then once this armature breaks down, the man underneath is found in many cases to have become softened by it; he is subject to shock, *over*-sensitiveness, and indeed many ailments not met with in the more direct races. Their superficial sensitiveness allows of a harder core: our core is soft, because of course our skin is so tough. To set against this, it is true you have the immense reserves of delicacy, touchiness, sympathy, that this envelope of cynicism has accumulated. It has served english literary art in a marvellous way: but probably it is more useful for art than for practical affairs. Then the artist could always look after himself. Anyhow, the time seems to have arrived in my life, as I consider it has arrived in the life of the nation, to discard this husk. I'm all for throwing off humour: life must be met on other terms than those of fun and sport now. The time has come. Otherwise—disaster!'

Butcher guffawed provocatively: Tarr joined him. They both quaffed their beer.

'You're a dangerous man' said Butcher. 'If you had your way you'd leave us stark naked—we should all be standing on our little island in the state of the Ancient Britons with coracles* on our backs and curls on our shoulders. Figuratively.' He hiccuped.

'Yes, figuratively' hiccuped Tarr and spat lightly. 'But in reality the country would be armed better than it ever had been before, really to the teeth I declare: by throwing over these famous "national characteristics" to which we cling sentimentally, and which are merely the accident of a time, we should lay a foundation of unspecific force on which new and more masculine "national flavours" would very soon sprout. The humorist is not so masculine as he thinks himself.'

'I quite agree' Butcher jerked out energetically.

He ordered another lager, hiccuping toughly.

'I agree with what you say! If we don't give up dreaming we shall get spanked, I mean whipped. Look at me! I've given up my gypsies. That was very public-spirited of me?' He looked coaxingly sideways at his friend, who patted his knee and went on from there.

'If everyone would give up their gypsies their jokes and their gentlemen—. "Gentlemen" are worse than gypsies. It would do perhaps if they reduced them considerably, as you have your beastly Romanys. I'm going to swear off Humour for a year to set all Englishmen an example. Even upon you, Guy, I shall gaze inhumanly. All these mock matrimonial difficulties of mine come from humour. I am going to gaze on Bertha inhumanly, and not humorously any longer, that's flat.'

He gazed at an imaginary Bertha without a spark of humour.

'Humour' he said 'does paralyse the sense for Reality, people are rapt by their sense of humour in a phlegmatic and hysteric dreamworld, full of the delicious swirls of the switch-back, the intoxication of the merry-go-round—screaming leaps from idea to idea. My little weapon for bringing my man to earth—shot-gun or what not—gave me good sport, too, and was of the best workmanship: I carried it slung jauntily for some time at my side—you may have noticed it. But I am in the tedious situation of a crack marksman who hits the bull's-eye every time. Had I not been disproportionately occupied with Miss Lunken's absurdities, really out of all reasonable proportion, I should never have allowed that charming girl to engage herself to me. But that is all over. My first practical step now will be to take this question of "engaging" myself or not into my own hands. I shall *dis-engage* myself on the spot.'

'So long as you don't engage yourself again next minute, and so on. If I felt that the time was not quite ripe, I'd leave it in Fräulein Lunken's hands a little longer. I expect she does it better than you would.'

Butcher filled his pipe, then he began laughing. He gave high-pitched crackling laughs, throwing his head backwards and forwards, until Tarr stopped him.

'What are you laughing at?'

'You are a bum!* Ha! ha! ha!'

'How am I a *bum*, Butcher! Ever since you've worn that pullover you've employed that jargon.'

Butcher composed himself, theatrically.

'I had to laugh! You repent of your thoughtlessness: your next step is to put things right.—I was laughing at the way you go about it. Ha! ha! ha! I like the way you—! Kindly but firmly you set out to break off your engagement and discard the girl: that is very neat. Yes. Ha! ha! ha!'

'Do you think so? Well, it may be a trifle overtidy: I hadn't looked at it from that side.'

'You can't be too tidy' Butcher said dogmatically. He talked to Tarr, when a little worked up, as Tarr talked to him, but he did not notice that he did. Partly it was calinerie and flattery.

Tarr pulled out of his waistcoat pocket a very heavy and determined looking watch. Had he been compelled to use a small watch he would have suffered: for the time to be microscopic and noiseless would be unbearable—the time *must* be human, upon that he insisted. He liked it loud and large.

'It is late. I must go. Must you get back to Passy* or can you stop—?'

'Do you know, I'm afraid I must get back. I have to lunch with a feller at one who is putting me on to a good thing. But can I take you anywhere? Or are you lunching here?'

'No.—Take me as far as the Samaritaine,* will you?'

Butcher took him along two sides of the Louvre, to the river.

'Good-bye, then. Don't forget Saturday, six o'clock.' Butcher nodded in bright clever silence. He shuffled into his car again, working

his shoulders like a verminous tramp. He rushed away, piercing
blasts from his horn rapidly softening as he became smaller. Tarr was
glad he had brought the car and Butcher together; opposites they
decidedly were, but with some grave essential in common.

His usual lunch time an hour away, his so far unrevised programme
was to go to the Rue Lhomond and search for Hobson's studio. For
the length of a street it was equally the road to the studio and to
Bertha's rooms. He knew to which he was going. But a sensation of
peculiar freedom and leisure possessed him. There was no hurry. Was
there any hurry to go where he was going?

With a smile in his mind, his face irresponsible and solemn, he
turned sharply into a narrow street, rendered dangerous by motor
buses, and asked at the porter's lodge of a large residence if Monsieur
Lowndes were in.

'Monsieur Lounes? Je pense que oui. Je ne l'ai pas vu sortir.'*

He ascended to the fourth floor and rang a bell.

Lowndes was in: he heard him approaching the door on tiptoe,
and felt him gazing at him through the customary crack. He placed
himself in a favourable position.

CHAPTER 3

TARR's idea of leisure recognized no departure from the tragic theme
of existence: pleasure could take no form that did not include death
and corruption—at present Bertha and Humour. Only he wished to
play a little longer: it was the last chance he might have. *Work* was in
front of him with Bertha, he recognized.

He was giving up *play*, that was quite understood; but the giving
up of play, even, had to take the form of play. He had viewed everything in terms of sport for so long that he had no other machinery
to work with: and sport might perhaps, for the fun of the thing, be
induced to cast out sport.

As Lowndes crept towards the door, Tarr said to himself, with
ironic self-restraint, '*bloody* fool—*bloody* fool! bloody—*fool.*'

Lowndes was a colleague, who was not very active, but had just
enough money to be a cubist, that was to say quite a lot. He was
extremely proud of being interrupted in his work, for Lowndes'
'work' was a serious matter, a very serious matter indeed. He 'found

great difficulty in working'; always he implied that *you* did not. He suffered from a form of persecution mania as regards his 'mornings.' To start with, it was plain, from what he said, that he was very much in request: people, seemingly, were *always* attempting to get into his room: such was the fatal attraction he exercised. But although you were led to fancy the existence of a long queue of unwelcome visitors, in reality the only person you definitely knew had been guilty of interrupting his 'work' was Thornton. This man, because of his admiration for Lowndes' mordant wit, and through moth-like attraction for his cubism and respect for his income, had to suffer much humiliation. He was to be found (even in the morning, strange to say) in Lowndes' studio, rapidly sucking a pipe, blinking, flushing, stammering the rakish locutions of an inexpensive almost nameless second-rate Public School. When you entered, he looked timidly and quickly at the inexorable Lowndes, and began gathering up his hat and books.

Lowndes' manner became withering—you felt that, before your arrival, his master had been less severe, tête à tête life might have been almost bearable for Thornton. When at length he had taken himself off, Lowndes would hasten to exculpate himself: Thornton was a fool, but he could not always keep Thornton out etc.

'Oh. Come in Tarr' Lowndes said, looking at the floor of the passage. 'I didn't know who it was—.' The atmosphere became thick with importunate phantom intruders. The wretched Thornton seemed to hover timidly in the background.

'Am I interrupting you—?' Tarr asked politely.

'No-o-o!' a long, reassuring, musical negative.

His face was very dark and slick, bald on top, pettily bearded, pointlessly handsome. Tarr always detected a tinge of indecency in these particular good looks. His celtic head was allied with a stocky commercial figure: behind his spectacles his black eyes had a way of scouring and scurrying over the floor: they were often dreamy and burning and it was then that the indecency most plainly declared itself: he waddled slightly—or rather confided himself first to one muscular little calf, then to the other.

Tarr had come to talk to him about Bertha.

'I'm afraid I must have interrupted your work—?' Tarr said, and looked stolidly at the floor.

'No it's quite all right: I was just going to have a rest. I'm rather off colour.'

Tarr misunderstood him.

'Off colour? What is the matter with colour now—?'

'No, I mean I'm seedy.'

'Oh ah. I see.'

His eyes searching the floor, Lowndes pottered about like an aim-less preoccupied dog: he felt more independent as he examined the floor boards and had something to do—it was a form of 'work' in fact to count the nail heads.

As with most leisured nobodies who do things, and like to foresee the analysis that waits upon fame, Lowndes had an autobiographic streak—he did not aspire to a Boswell.* His character sketch would run somewhat as follows: 'A fussy and exacting man, even avuncular, strangely, despite the fineness and breadth of his character, minute precious and tidy.' In this way he made a virtue of his fuss. Or to show how the general illusion would work in a particular case:—'He had been disturbed in his "work" by Tarr, who by his visit had just caused him to emerge from that state of wonderful concentration called "work": he had not been able at once to accommodate himself: his nerves drove him from object to object. But he would soon be quiet now.'

Tarr looked on with an ugly patience.

'Lowndes, I have come to ask you for a little piece of advice.'

Lowndes was flattered and relished the mystery.

'Yes-es' he said, smiling, in a slow 'sober,' professional sing-song.

'Or rather, for an opinion. What is your opinion of german women?'

Lowndes had spent two years in Berlin and Munich. Many of his friends were austrian.

'German women? But I must know first why you ask me that question. You see, it's a wide subject.'

'A wide subject—wide. Yes, very good! Ha! ha! Well, it is like this. I think that they are superior to our women, you know, the English. That is a very dangerous opinion to hold, because there are so many german women knocking about just now. I want to get rid of it: can you help me? Yes or no?'

Lowndes mused upon the ground. Then he looked up brightly.

'No I can't. For I share it!'

'Lowndes, I'm surprised at you.'

'How do you mean?'

'I did not expect you to be flippant. Still, perhaps you can help me: our ideas about girls may not be the same.'

Tarr always embarrassed him: Lowndes huddled himself tensely together, worked at his pipe, and met his visitor's jokes painfully. He hesitated.

'What are your ideas on the subject of girls?' he asked in a moment.

'Oh I think they ought to be convex if you are concave—stupid if you are intelligent, hot if you are cold, refrigerators if you are a volcano. Always *white* all over—clothes, underclothes, skin and all. My ideas do not extend much beyond that for the present on the subject of girls—white girls, I mean.'

Lowndes organized Tarr's statement, with a view to an adequate and easy reply. He gnawed at his pipe.

'Well, german women are usually convex. There are also concave ones. There are cold ones and hot ones.' He looked up. 'It all seems to depend what *you* are like!'

'I Lowndes am cold; inclined to be fat; strong i' the head; and uncommonly swarthy, as you see.'

'In that case, if you took plenty of exercise' Lowndes undulated himself as though for the passage of the large bubbles of the chain of an ever-growing chuckle, 'I should think that german women would suit you very well!'

Tarr rose.

'I wish I hadn't come to see you, Lowndes. Your answer is disappointing.'

Lowndes got up, disturbed at Tarr's sign of departure.

'I'm sorry. But I'm not an authority.' He leant against the fireplace to arrest Tarr's withdrawal for a minute or two. 'Are you doing much work?'

'I? No.'

'Are you ever in in the afternoons?'

'Not much. I'm just moving into a new studio.'

Lowndes looked suddenly at his watch, with calculated, apelike impulsiveness.

'Where are you having lunch? I thought of going down to Vallet's to see if I could come across a beggar of the name of Kreisler: he could tell you much more about german women than I can. He's a German. Come along won't you? Are you doing anything?'

'No, I know quite enough Germans. Besides, I must go some-where—I can't have lunch just yet. Good-bye. Thank you for your opinion.'

'Don't mention it' Lowndes replied softly, his head turned obliquely to his shoulder, as though he had a stiff neck, rocking upon his pneumatic calves.

He was rather hurt at the brevity of Tarr's visit. His 'morning' had not received enough respect: it had been treated, in fact, cavalierly by this imperious visitor. As to his 'work' that had never been so much as mentioned, directly.

When Tarr got outside he stood on the narrow pavement, looking into a shop window. It was a florist's and contained a great variety of flowers. The Spring for him was nameless: he could not give a single flower its name. He hung on in front of this shop before pushing off, as a swimmer clings to a rock, waving his legs. Then he got back into the street from which his visit to Lowndes had deflected him. Down it he drifted, paddling his sombrero* at his side. He still had some way to go before he need decide between the Rue Martine (where Bertha lived) and the Rue Lhomond.

Resolution had not come to him out of his talks: that already existed, the fruit of various other conversations on his matrimonial position—held with the victim, Fräulein Lunken, herself.

Not to go near Bertha was the negative programme for that particular day. To keep away was seldom easy. But ever since his conversation at the Berne he had been conscious of the absurd easiness of doing so, if he wished. He had not the least inclination to go to the Rue Martine! This sensation was so grateful and exhilarating that its object shared in its effect. He determined to go and see her. This present magisterial feeling of full-blooded indifference was born to be enjoyed: where best to enjoy it was beyond question where Bertha was.

As to the studio, he hesitated. A new situation had been created by this new feeling of indifference. Its duration could not be gauged.

Tarr wished to stay in Paris just then to finish two large paintings begun some months before. With him, for the impressionist's necessity to remain in front of the object to be represented* was substituted a sensation of the desirability of finishing a canvas in the place where it had been begun. From this point of view he had an impressionist's horror of change.

So he had evolved a plan. At first sight it was wicked, though not blacker than most of his ingenuities of the same order. Bertha, as he had suggested to Butcher, he had in some lymphatic manner within his skin. It appeared a matter of physical discomfort to leave her altogether. It must be effected gradually. In consequence he had resolved that, instead of going away to England, where the separation might cause him restlessness, he had perhaps better settle down in her neighbourhood. Through a series of specially tended ennuis, he would soon find himself in a position to depart. Thus the extreme nearness of the studio to Bertha's flat was only another inducement for him to take it. 'If it were next door, so much the better!' thought he.

Now for this famous feeling of indifference. Was there anything in it? That was the question. The studio for the moment should be put aside: he would go to see Bertha. Let this visit solve this question.

CHAPTER 4

THE new summer heat drew heavy pleasant ghosts out of the ground, like plants disappeared in winter; spectres of energy, bulking the hot air with vigorous dreams. Or they had entered into the trees, in imitation of pagan gods, and nodded their delicate distant intoxication to him. Visions were released in the sap, with scented explosion, the Spring one bustling and tremendous reminiscence.

Tarr felt the street was a pleasant current, setting from some immense and tropic gulf, neighboured by Floridas of remote invasions:* he ambled down it puissantly, shoulders shaped like these waves, a heavy-sided drunken fish. The houses, with winks of the shocked clock-work, were grazed, holding along their surface a thick nap of soft warmth. The heat poured weakly into his veins—a big dog wandering on its easily transposable business, inviting some delightful accident to deflect it from maudlin and massive promenade: in his mind, too, as in the dog's, his business was doubtful—a small black spot ahead in his brain, half puzzling but peremptory.

The mat ponderous light-grey of putty-coloured houses—like a thickening merely of hot summer atmosphere without sun—gave a spirituality to this deluge of animal well-being, in weighty pale sense-solidarity. Through the opaquer atmosphere sounds came lazily or tinglingly. People had become a balzacian species, boldly tragic and comic.*

Tarr stopped at a dairy. He bought saladed potatoes, a Petit Suisse.* The coolness, as he entered the small tiled box, gave an eerie shock to his sharply switched senses. The dairy-man, in blue-striped smock and black cap, peaked and cylindrical, came out of an inner room. Through its glasses several women were visible, busy at a meal. The isolation of this person from the heat and mood of the world outside impressed his customer as he came forward with truculent 'Monsieur!' Tarr, while his things were done up, watched the women. The discreet voices, severe reserve of keen business preoccupations, showed the usual Paris commerçante; the white, black and slate-grey of the dresses, the extreme neatness, silent felt over-slippers, make their commercial devotions rather conventual. With this purchase—followed by one of strawberries at a fruiterer's opposite—his destination was no longer doubtful.

He was going to Bertha's to eat his lunch. Hence the double quantity of saladed potatoes. He skirted the railings of the Luxembourg Gardens* for fifteen yards. Crossing the road, he entered the Rue Martine, a bald expanse of uniformly coloured rose-grey pavement plaster and shutter. A large iron gate led into a short avenue of trees: at its extremity Bertha lived in a three-storey house.

The leaden brilliant green of spring foliage hung above him, ticketing innumerably the trees. In the distance, volume behind volume, the vegetation was massed, poising sultry smoke blocks from factories in Fairyland. Its novelty, fresh yet dead, had the effectiveness of an unnecessary mirage. The charm of habit and monotony he had come to affront seemed to have coloured, chemically, these approaches to its home.

He found Bertha's eye fixed upon him with a sort of humorous indifferent query from the window. He smiled, thinking what would be the veritable answer! On finding himself in the presence of the object of his erudite discussion, he felt he had got the focus wrong after all: this familiar life, with its ironical eye, mocked at him, too. It was aware of the subject of his late conversation. Some kind of twin of the shrewd feeling embodied in the observation 'one can never escape from oneself' appeared.

But that ironical unsurprised eye at the window, so vaguely à propos, offended him. It had the air of scoffing (with its quizzing downward cock, and puzzled frowning eyebrow on one side only) or of ironically welcoming the swaggering indifference he was bringing to bask in the presence of its object. He retaliated with a certain truculence he had not at all intended to display.

'Have you had lunch yet my dear?' he asked, as she opened the door to him—'I've brought you some strawberries.'

'I didn't expect *you*, Sorbet. No, I have not had lunch. I was just going to get it.' (Sorbet, or in english, Sherbet, was his love-name, a perversion of his strange second name, Sorbert.)

Bertha's was the intellectually-fostered hellenic type of german handsomeness. It would make you think that german mothers must have replicas and photographs of the Venus of Milo* in their rooms during the first three months of their pregnancy. Of course they in fact have. Also this arid, empty intellectualist beauty is met with in german art periodicals.

Bertha had been a heavy blond westphalian* baby: her body now, a self-indulgent athlete's, was strung to heavy motherhood. Another baby could not be long delayed. To look at a man should be almost enough to effect it.

A great believer in tepid 'air-baths,'* she would remain, for hours together, in a state of nudity about her rooms. At present she was wearing a pale green striped affair, tight at the waist. It looked as though meant for a smaller woman. It may have belonged to her sister. As a result, her ample form had left the fulness of a score of attitudes all over it, in flat creasings and pencillings—like the sanguine of an Italian master* in which the leg is drawn in several positions, one on top of the other.

'What have you come for, Sorbert?'

'To see you. What did you suppose?'

'Oh, you *have* come to see me?'

'I brought these things. I thought you might be hungry.'

'Yes, I am rather.' She stopped in the passage, Dryad-like on one foot,* and stared into the kitchen. Tarr did not kiss her. He put his hand on her hip—a way out of it—which rolled elastically beneath his fingers: with a little superficial massage he propelled her into the room. His hand remarked that she was underneath in her favourite state of nakedness. He frowned as he reflected that this might subsequently cause a hitch.

Bertha went into the kitchen with the provisions. She lived in two rooms on one side of the front door. Her friend, Fräulein Lederer, to

whom she sub-let, lived on the other side of it, the kitchen promiscu-
ously existing between, and immediately facing the entrance.

Tarr was in the studio or salon. It was a complete bourgeois-
bohemian* interior. Green silk cloth and cushions of various vegetable
and mineral shades covered everything, in mildewy blight. The cold
repulsive shades of Islands of the Dead,* gigantic cypresses, grot-
toes of teutonic nymphs, had installed themselves massively in this
french flat. Purple metal and leather steadily dispensed with expensive objects. There was the plaster-cast of Beethoven (some people
who have frequented artistic circles get to dislike this face extremely),
brass jars from Normandy,* a photograph of Mona Lisa (Tarr could
not look upon the Mona Lisa without a sinking feeling).*

A table beside the window, laid with a white cloth, square embroi-
dered holes at its edges, was where Tarr at once took up his position. Truculence was denoted by his thus going straight to his eating
place—this would be understood by Bertha.

Installed in the midst of this admittedly ridiculous life, he gave a
hasty glance at his 'indifference' to see whether it were O.K. Seen by
its light, upon opening the door, Bertha had appeared *unusual*. This
impressed him disagreeably. Had his rich and calm feeling of bounty
towards her survived the encounter, his 'indifference' might also have
remained intact.

He engrossed himself in his sense of physical well-being. From his
pocket he produced a tin box containing tobacco, papers and a little
steel machine for rolling cigarettes given him by Bertha. A long slim
hinged shell, it nipped-in a little cartridge of tobacco, which it then
slipped with inside a paper tube, and, slipping out again empty, the
cigarette was made.

Tarr began manufacturing cigarettes. Reflections from the shining metal in his hand scurried about amongst the bilious bric-à-brac.
Like a layer of water lying upon one of oil, the light heated stretch
by the windows appeared distinct from the shadowed portion of the
room.

This place was cheap and dead, but rich with the same lifelessness
as the trees without. These looked extremely near and familiar at the
opened windows, breathing the same air continually as Bertha and
her bilious barracks. But they were dusty rough and real.

Bertha came in from the kitchen. She took up where she had dropped
upon his arrival a trivial rearrangement of her writing-table: or whether

this had been her occupation or not as he appeared at the gate beneath, drawing her ironical and musing eye downwards to himself, it was at this window before which the writing-table stood that her face had appeared. A new photograph of Tarr was being placed in the centre of this writing-table now. Ten days previously it had been taken in that room. It had ousted a Klinger* and generally created a restlessness, to her eye, in the other objects. She now allowed it to fall on its back, with an impatient exclamation, then began propping it up with a comic absorption, her eye still ironic.

'Ah, you've got the photographs have you? Is that me?'

She handed it to him.

'Yes, they came yesterday!'

'Yesterday' he had not been there! Whatever he asked at the present moment would draw a softly-thudding answer, heavy german reproach concealed in it with tireless ingenuity. These photographs would under other circumstances have been produced on his arrival with considerable exclamatory abandon.

Tarr had looked rather askance at this portrait and Bertha's occupation. There was his photograph, calmly, with an air of permanence, taking up its position on her writing-table, just as he was preparing to vanish for good.

'Let's see yours' he said, still holding the photograph.

What strange effects all this complicated activity inside had on the surface, his face. A set sulky stagnation, every violence dropping an imperceptible shade on to it, the features overgrown with this strange stuff—that twist of the head that was him, and that could only be got rid of by breaking his neck.

'They're no good' said she overpoweringly offhand closing the drawer, handing her photographs, sandwiched with tissue paper, to Sorbert. 'That one'—a sitting pose, face yearning from photograph, lighted, not with a smile, but sort of sentimental illumination, the drapery arranged like a poster—'I don't think that's so bad.' She was very slangy and nimble, he knew what to expect.

'What an idiot!' he thought as he gazed at the photograph, 'what a face!'

A consciously pathetic ghost of a smile, a clumsy sweetness, the energetic sentimental claim of a rather rough but frank self. There was a photograph of her in riding-habit. This was the best of them: he softened.

Then came a photograph of them together.

How strangely that twist of his, or set angle of the head, fitted in with the corresponding peculiarities of the woman's head and bust. What abysms of all that was most automatic and degrading in human life: rubbishy hours and months formed the atmosphere around these two futile dolls!

He put the photographs down and looked up. She was sitting on the edge of the table: the dressing-gown was open and one large thigh, with ugly whiteness, slid half out of it. It looked dead, and connected with her like a ventriloquist's dummy with its master. While looking at those decorous photographs it was not possible to refrain from some enquiry as to where his good sense had gone when he had had them taken. But here was this significant object, popping out pat enough to satisfy anybody: the exhibition appeared to be her explanation of the matter. The face was not very original, perhaps: but *a thigh* cannot be stupid!

He gazed surlily. Her expression of moistly magnetized reverie at this moment was supremely absurd, as he saw it side by side with one of the two main pillars of their love: he smiled and turned his face to the window. She pretended to become conscious suddenly of something amiss; she drew the dressing-gown over the pièce de résistance with a suggestion of disgust.

'Have you paid the man yet? What did he charge? I expect—.'

Tarr took up the packet again.

'Oh, these are six francs. I forget what the big ones are. I haven't paid him yet. He's coming to photograph Miss Lederer to-morrow.'

They sat without saying anything.

Tarr examined the room as you do a doctor's waiting-room.

It was really quite necessary for him to learn to turn his back upon this convenience, things had gone too far, he had ceased even, he realized, to see it objectively. To turn the back, that appeared at first sight a very easy matter: that is why so far he had not succeeded in doing so. Never put on his mettle, his standing army of will was not sufficient to cope with it. But would this little room ever appear worth turning his back on? It was really more serious than it looked: he must not underestimate it. It was the purest distillation of the commonplace: he had become bewitched by its strangeness. It was the farthest flight of the humdrum unreal: Bertha was like a fairy visited by him, and to whom he 'became engaged' in another world, not the real one.

So much was it the real ordinary world that for him with his out-of-the-way experience it was a phantasmagoria. Then what he had described as his disease of sport was perpetually fed: sex even, with him, according to his analysis, being a sort of ghost, was at home in this gross and bouffonic* illusion. Something had filled up a blank and become saturated with the blankness.

But Bertha, though unreal, was undeniably a good kind fairy and her feelings must be taken into consideration. How much would Bertha mind a separation? Tarr saw in her one of those clear, humorous, superficial natures (like a Venetian or a Viennese only much stupider) the easy product of a genial and abundant life. But he miscalculated the depths of obedient attachment he had awakened.

They sat impatiently waiting: a certain formality had to be observed. Then the business of the day could be proceeded with. Both were bored in different degrees, with the part imposed by the punctilious and ridiculous god of love. Bertha, into the bargain, wanted to get on with her cooking: she would have cut considerably the reconciliation scene. All her side of the programme had been conscientiously observed.

'Berthe, tu es une brave fille!'

'Tu trouves?'

'Oui.'*

More inaction followed on Tarr's part. She sometimes thought he enjoyed these ceremonies.

Through girlhood her strong german senses had churned away at her, and claimed an image from her gentle and dreamy mind. In its turn the mind had accumulated its impressions of men, fancies from books and conversations, and it had made its hive. So her senses were presented with the image that was to satisfy and rule them. They flung themselves upon it as she had flung herself upon Tarr.

This image left considerable latitude. Tarr had been the first to fit—rather paradoxically, but all the faster for that.

This 'high standard aryan bitch,' as Tarr had described her, had arrived, with him, at the full and headlong condition we agree to name 'love.' Thereupon the image, or type, was thrown away: the individual, the good Tarr, took its place.

Bertha had had several *Schatzes** before Tarr. They had all left the type-image intact. At most it had been a little blurred by them. It had almost been smashed for one man, physically much of a muchness

with Sorbert: but that gentleman had never got quite near enough
in to give the coup de foudre* to the type picture or eikon.* Tarr had
characteristically supposed this image to have little sharpness of out-
line left: it would not be a very difficult matter for anyone to extort its
recognition, he would have said if asked.

'Vous êtes mon goût, Sorbet. Du bist mein Geschmack'* she would
say.

Tarr was not demonstrative when she said this. Reciprocate he
could not exactly; and he could not help reflecting whether to be her
Geschmack was very flattering.—There *must* be something the matter with him: perhaps there *was* something the matter after all, of
which he was not aware! But why no, to be a Geschmack of that sort
meant nothing at all: it was all right: he could put his mind at ease.

All Bertha's hope centred in his laziness: she watched his weak-
nesses with a loving eye. He had much to say about his under-nature:
she loved hearing him talk about that: she listened attentively.

'It is the most dangerous quality of all to possess' and he would
sententiously add—'only the best people possess it, in common with
the obscure and humble.' At this she would smile indulgently and
then brightly nod her head. 'It is like a great caravanserai* in which
scores of people congregate: a disguise in which such an one, otherwise Pasha, circulates among unembarrassed men incog.* diverting
himself and learning the secrets of men. You can't learn the secrets
of men if they smell greatness in you.' The danger that resided in
these facilities was however plain enough to this particular Pasha.
The Pasha had been given a magic mask of humbleness: but the inner
nature seemed flowing equally to the mask and the unmasked magnifi-
cence. As yet he was unformed, but he wished to form wholly Pasha.

Meantime this under-nature's chief use was as a precious *villégiature** for his energy. Bertha was the country wench encountered
by the more exalted incarnation on its holidays, or, wandering idle
Khalife,* in some concourse of his surreptitious life.

Tarr's three days' unannounced and unexplained 'leave' had made
Bertha very nervous indeed. She suffered from the incomplete,
unsymmetrical appearance her life now presented. Everything spread
out palpably before her, where she could arrange it like a roomful
of furniture, that was how she liked it: even in her present shake-
down of a life, Tarr had noticed the way he was treated as material

for 'arrangement.' But she had never been able to indulge this idiosyncrasy much in the past; this was not the first time that she had found herself in a similar position. Hence her certain air of being at home in these casual quarters, which belied her.

The detested temporary makeshift dwelling had during the last few days been given a new coat of sombre thought. Found in accidental quarters, had she not been over-delicate in not suggesting an immediate move into something more home-like and permanent? People would leave her camped there for the rest of her natural life unless she were a little brutal and got *herself* out somehow. But no shadow of unkindness ever tainted her abject genuineness. Where cunning efforts to retain this slippery customer abounded, she never blamed or turned upon him. Long ago she had given herself without ceremony and almost at sight, indeed: she awaited his thanks or no thanks patiently.

But the itch of action was on her. Tarr's absences were like light: his presence was a shadow. They were both stormy. The last three days' leave taken without comment had caused her to overhaul the precarious structure in which she had dwelt for so long: something had to be done, she saw that. There had to be a reconstruction. She had trusted too much in Fate and obedient waiting Hymen.*

So a similar ferment to Tarr's was in full operation in Bertha.

Anger with herself, dreary appetite for action, would help her over farewells: she was familiar enough with them, too, in thought. She would not on her side stir a hand to change things: he must do that. She would only facilitate such action as he cared to take, easing up in all directions for him.

The new energy delivered attack after attack upon her hope: she saw nothing beyond Tarr except measures of utility. The 'heart' had always been the most cherished ornament of her existence: Tarr would take that with him (as she would keep his ring and the books he had given her). She could not now get it back for the asking. Let it go! What use had she for it henceforth? She must indulge her mania for tasteful arrangement in future without this. Or rather what heart she had left would be rather like one of those salmon-coloured, corrugated gas office stoves, compared to a hearth with a fire of pine.

With reluctance Tarr got up, and went over to her. He had not brought his indifference there to make it play tricks, perform little feats; nor did he wish to press it into inhuman actions. It was a humane 'indifference,' essentially.

'You haven't kissed me yet' he said, in imitation of her.

'Why kiss you, Sorbert?' she managed to say before her lips were covered with his. He drew her ungraciously and roughly into his arms, and started kissing her mouth with a machine action.

Docilely she covered him with her inertia. He was supposed to be performing a miracle of bringing the dead to life. Gone about too crudely, the willing mountebank, Death, had been offended: it is not thus that great spirits are prevailed upon to flee. Her 'indifference'— the great, simulated and traditional—would not be ousted by an upstart and younger relative. By Tarr himself, grown repentant, yes. But not by another 'indifference.'

Then his brutality stung her offended spirit, that had been pursing itself up for so many hours. Tears began rolling tranquilly out of her eyes in large dignified drops. They had not been very far back in the wings. He received them frigidly. She was sure, thought he, to detect something unusual during this scene.

Then with the woman's bustling, desperate, possessive fury, she suddenly woke up. She disengaged her arms wildly and threw them round his neck, tears becoming torrential. Underneath the poor comedian that played such antics with such phlegmatic and exasperating persistence, this distressed being thrust up its trembling mask, like a drowning rat. Its finer head pierced her blunter wedge.

'Oh dis Sorbert! Dis! Est-ce que tu m'aimes? M'aimes-tu? Dis!'*

'Yes—yes—yes. But don't cry.'

A wail, like the buzzing on a comb covered with paper, followed.

'Oh dis—m'aimes-tu? Dis que tu m'aimes!'*

A blurting, hurrying personality rushed right up into his face. He was very familiar with it. It was like the sightless clammy charging of a bat. Humbug had tempestuously departed: their hot-house was suffering a blast of outside air. He stared at her face groping up as though it scented mammals in his face: it pushed to right, then to left, and rocked itself.

A complicated image developed in his mind as he stood with her. He was remembering Schopenhauer:* it was of a chinese puzzle of boxes within boxes, or of insects' discarded envelopes. A woman had at the centre a kernel, a sort of very substantial astral baby:* this brat was apt to swell—she then became *all* baby. The husk he held now was a painted mummy-case, say. He was a mummy-case, too. Only he contained nothing but innumerable other painted cases inside, smaller and smaller ones. The smallest was not a substantial astral baby, however, or live core, but a painting like the rest.—His kernel was a painting, in fact: that was as it should be! He was pleased that it was nothing more violent than that.

He was half sitting upon the table: he found himself patting her back. He stopped doing this. His face looked heavy and fatigued. A dull, intense infection of her animal despair had filled it.

He held her head gently against his neck: or he held her skull against his neck. She shook and sniffed softly.

'Bertha, stop crying, do please stop crying. I'm a brute. It's fortunate for you that I am a brute. I am only a brute. There's nothing to cry for.'

He overestimated deafness in weepers: and when women flooded their country he always sat down and waited. Often as this had happened to him, he had never attempted to circumvent it. He behaved like a person taking a small dog for a necessary walk at the end of a lead.

Turned towards the window, he looked at the green stain of the foliage outside. Something was cleared up at this point; nature was not friendly to him; its metallic tints jarred. Or at least nature was the same for all men: the sunlight seen like an adventurous stranger in the streets was intimate with Bertha. The scrap of crude forest had made him want to abstract himself from his present surroundings, but strictly unaccompanied. Now he realized that this nature was tainted with her. If he went away he would only be *playing* at liberty: he had been quite right in not availing himself of the invitations of the Spring. The settlement of this present important question stood between him and pleasure. A momentary well-being had been accepted: but the larger spiritual invitation he had rejected. That he would only take up when he was free. In its annual expansion nature sent its large unstinting invitations. But nature loved the genius and liberty in him.—Tarr felt the invitation would not have been so cordial had he proposed taking a wife and family! This was his unpleasant discovery.

Bestirring himself, he led Bertha passively protesting to the settee. Like a sick person she was half indignant at being moved: he should have remained, a perpendicular bed for her, till the fever had decently passed. But revolted at the hypocrisy required, he left her standing at the edge of the settee.

Bertha stood crouching a little, her face buried in her hands, in ruffled absurdity. The only moderately correct procedure under the circumstances would be to walk out of the door at once and never come back: but with his background of months of different behaviour this could not be compassed he was quite aware, so he sat frowning at her.

She sank down upon the couch, head buried in the bilious cushions. He composed himself for what must follow. On one side of him Bertha, a lump of half-humanity, lay quite motionless and silent, and upon the other the little avenue was equally still. He, of course, between them, was quite still as well. The false stillness within, however, now gave back to the scene without its habitual character. It still seemed strange to him: but all its strangeness now lay in its humdrum and natural appearance. The quiet inside, in the room, was what did not seem strange to him: with that he had become imbued. Bertha's numb silence and abandon was a stupid tableau vivant of his own mood. His responsibility for all this was quite beyond question: this indeed was *him*. How could he escape that conclusion? There he sat, the cause of all this. It all fitted exactly as far as it went.

In this impasse of arrested life he stood sick and useless: they progressed from stage to stage of their weary farce. The confusion grew every moment. It resembled a combat between two wrestlers of approximately equal strength: neither could really win. One or other of them was usually wallowing warily or lifelessly upon his stomach while the other tugged at him, examining and prodding his carcase. His liking, contempt, realization of her authentic devotion to him, his confused but exigent conscience, dogged preparation to say farewell, all dove-tailed with precision. There she lay a sheer-hulk, he could take his hat and go. But once gone in this manner he could not stay away, he would have to come back.

He turned round, and sitting on the window-sill, began again staring at Bertha.

Women's psychic discharges affected him invariably like the sight of a person being sea-sick. It was the result of a weak spirit, as the other was the result of a weak stomach, they could only live on the retching seas of their troubles on the condition of being quite empty. The lack of art or illusion in actual life enables the sensitive man to exist, Tarr reflected: likewise, but contrariwise, the phenomenal lack of nature in the average man's existence is lucky and necessary for him.

From a prolonged contemplation of Bertha Tarr now gathered strength, it seemed: his dislocated feelings were brought into a new synthesis.

Launching himself off the window-sill, he remained as though suspended in thought: then he sat down provisionally at the writing-table, within a few feet of the couch. He took up a book of Goethe's poems, an early present to him from Bertha. In cumbrous field-day dress of gothic characters, squad after squad, these pieces paraded their message. As he turned the pages he stopped at *Ganymed** to consider the Spring from another angle.

> Du rings mich anglühst
> Frühling, Geliebter!
> Mit tausendfacher Liebeswonne
> Sich an mein Herz drängt
> Deiner ewigen Wärme
> Heilig Gefühl,
> Unendliche Schöne!

The book, left there upon a former visit, he now thrust into his breast pocket. As soldiers used to go into battle sometimes with the Bible upon their persons, he prepared himself for a final combat, with Goethe laid upon his heart. Men's lives have been known to have been saved through a lesser devoutness.

Now he was joining battle again with the most chivalrous sentiments: the reserves had been called up, his nature was mobilized. As his will gathered force and volume (in its determination to 'throw' her once and for all) he unhypocritically keyed up its attitude. While he had been holding her just now he had been at a considerable disadvantage because of his listless emotion. But with emotion equal to hers, he could accomplish anything. Leaving her would be child's play, absolutely child's play. He projected the manufacture of a more adequate sentiment.

Any indirectness was out of the question: a 'letting down softly,' kissing and leaving in an hour or two, as though things had not changed—that must not be dreamt of, now. The genuine section of her (of which he had a troubled glimpse): that mattered, nothing else—he must appeal obstinately to that. Their coming together had been prosecuted on his side with a stupid levity: that he would retrieve in their parting. Everything that was most opposite to his previous lazy conduct must now be undertaken by him. Especially he frowned upon Humour, that inveterate enemy of anglo-saxon mankind.

The first skirmish of his comic Armageddon* had opened with the advance of his mysterious and vaunted 'indifference.' That had dwindled away at the first onset. A new and more potent principle had taken its place. This was in Bertha's eyes, a *difference* in Tarr.

'Something has happened; he is *different*' she said to herself. 'He has met somebody else' had then been her rapid provisional conclusion.

Suddenly she got up without speaking, rather spectrally; she went over to the writing-table for her handkerchief. Not an inch or a muscle would she move until quite herself again—dropping steadily down all the scale of feeling to normal—that had been the idea. With notable matter-of-factness she got up, easily and quietly, making Sorbert a little dizzy. Her face had all the drama wrung out of it: it was hard, clear and garishly white, like her body.

If he were to have a chance of talking he must clear the air of electricity completely: else at his first few words the storm might return. Once lunch had swept through the room, things would be better. So he would send the strawberries ahead to prepare his way. It was like fattening a lamb for the slaughter. This idea pleased him: now that he had recognized the existence of a possible higher plane of feeling as between Bertha and himself, he was anxious to avoid display. According to his present dispositions it was true that he ran the risk of outdoing his former callousness. Saturated with morbid english shyness, that cannot tolerate passion and its nakedness, it was a choice of brutalities, merely, in fact. This shyness, he contended, in its need to show its heart, will discover subtleties and refinements of expression, unknown to less gauche and hence less delicate nations. But if he happened to be hustled out of his shell the anger that coexisted with his modesty was the most spontaneous thing he possessed.

He got up, obsequiously reproducing in his own movements and expression her matter-of-factness.

'Well how about lunch? I'll come and help you with it.'

'There's nothing to do. I'll get it.'

Bertha had wiped her eyes with the attentiveness a man bestows on his chin after a shave, in little brusque hard strokes. She did not look at Tarr. Arranging her hair in the mirror, she went out to the kitchen.

The intensity of her recent orgasm carried her on for about five minutes into ordinary life: for so long her seriousness was tactful. Then her nature began to give way: again it broke up into fits and starts of self-consciousness. The mind was called in, did its work clumsily as usual: she became her ordinary self.

Sitting upon the stool by the window, in the act of eating, Tarr there in front of her, it was more than ever impossible to be natural. She resented the immediate introduction of lunch in this way, and that increased her artificiality. For to counterbalance the acceptance of food, she had to throw more pathos into her face. With haggard resignation she was going on again; doing what was asked of her, partaking of this lunch. She did so with unnecessary conscientiousness. Her strange wave of dignity had let her in for this?—almost she must make up for that dignity! Life was confusing her again; it was useless to struggle.

'Aren't these strawberries good? Very sweet. These little hard ones are better than the bigger strawberries. Have some more cream?'

'Thank you.' She should have said no. But being greedy in this matter she accepted it, with a heavy air of some subtle advantage gained.

'How did the riding lesson go off?' She went to a riding school in the mornings.

'Oh quite well, thank you. How did *your* lesson go off?' (This referred to his exchange of languages with a russian girl.)

'Admirably, thank you.'

The russian girl was a useful weapon for her.

'What is the time?' The time? What cheek! He was almost startled. He took his heavy watch out and presented its big bold dial to her ironically.

'Are you in a hurry?' he asked.

'No, I just wondered what the time was. I live so vaguely.'

'You are sure you are not in a hurry?'

'Oh no!'

'I have a confession to make, my dear Bertha.' He had not put his watch back in his pocket. She had asked for the watch; he would use it. 'I came here just now to test a funny mood—a quite *new* mood as a matter of fact. My visit is a sort of trial trip of this new mood. The mood was connected with you. I wanted to find out what it meant, and how it would be affected by your presence. That was the test.'

Bertha looked up with mocking sulky face, a shade of hopeful curiosity.

'Shall I tell what the mood was?'

'That's as you like.'

'*It was a feeling of complete indifference as regards yourself!*'

He said this solemnly, with the pomp with which a weighty piece of news might be invested by a solicitor in conversation with his client.

'Oh, is *that* all? That is disappointing.' The little barbaric effort was met by Bertha scornfully.

'No that is not all.'

Catching at the professional figure his manner had conjured up, he ran his further remarks into that mould. The presence of his watch in his hand had brought with it some image of the family physician or gouty attorney. It all centred round the watch, as it were, and her interest in the time of day.

'I have found that this was only another fraud on my too credulous sensibility.' He smiled with professional courtesy. 'At sight of you, my mood evaporated. But what I want to talk about is what is left. I am of opinion that our accounts should be brought up to date. I'm afraid the reckoning is enormously against me: you have been a criminally indulgent partner—.'

He had now got the image down to the more precise form of two partners, perhaps comfortable wine-merchants, going through their books or something of that sort.

'My *dear* Sorbert I am aware of that. You needn't trouble to go any further. But why are you entering into these calculations, and sums of profit and loss?'

'Because my sentimental finances, if I may employ that term, are in a bad state.'

'Then they only match your worldly ones.'

'In my worldly ones I have no partner' he reminded her.

She cast her eyes about in wide-eyed swoops, full of self-possessed wildness.

'I exonerate you Sorbert' she said, 'you needn't go into details. What is *yours* and what is *mine*—my God! what does it matter? Not much!'

'I know you to be generous—.'

'Leave that then, leave these calculations! All that means *so little* to me! I feel at the end of my strength—à bout de force!' she always heaved this french phrase out with much energy. 'If you've made up your mind to go—do so Sorbert—I release you! You owe me nothing—it was all my fault. But spare me a reckoning! I can't stand any more—.'

'No, I insist on my responsibility. It would break my heart to leave things upside down like that—all our books in a ghastly muddle, our desks open, and just walk away for ever—perhaps to set up shop somewhere else, who knows? What a prospect! I can't bear it!'

'I do not feel in any mood to "set up shop somewhere else" I can assure you!'

The unbusinesslike element in the situation had been allowed by her to develop for obvious reasons. She now resisted her Sorbert's dishonest attempt to set this right, and to benefit, first (as he had done) by disorder, and lastly to benefit by order.

'We can't in any case improve matters by talking. I—I, you needn't fear for me Sorbert, I can look after myself. Only don't let us wrangle' with appealing gesture and saintishly smiling face. 'Let us part friends. Let us be worthy of each other!'

Bertha always opposed to Tarr's treacherous images her teutonic lyricism, usually repeating the same phrases several times.

This was degenerating into their routine of wrangle. Always confronted by this imperturbable, deaf and blind, 'generosity,' the day would end in the usual senseless draw. His compelling statement still remained unuttered.

'Bertha, listen. Let us, just for fun, throw all this overboard, I mean the cargo of inflated stuff that makes us go statelily, no doubt, but—. Haven't we quarrelled enough, and said these things to each other till we're both sick of them? Our quarrels have been our undoing. Look. A long chain of little quarrels has fastened us down: we should neither of us be here if it hadn't been for them.'

Bertha gazed at Tarr half wonderingly. Something out of the ordinary was on foot, it was plain.

Tarr proceeded.

'I have accepted from you a queer sentimental dialect of life— please don't interrupt me, I have something I want particularly to say—I should have insisted on your expressing yourself in a more metropolitan speech.* Let us drop it. There is no need to converse in the drivelling idiom we for the most part use. I don't think we should lead a very pleasant married life—naturally. In the second place, you are not a girl who wants an intrigue, but to marry. I have been playing at fiancé with a certain unprincipled pleasure in the novelty, but I experience a genuine horror as the fatal consequences begin to take shape. I have been playing with you!'

He said this eagerly, as though it were a point in his argument—as it was. He paused, for effect apparently.

'You for your part Bertha don't do yourself justice when you are acting. I am in the same position. This I feel acutely, no I do in fact. My ill-humour occasionally takes your direction—yours, for its part, heading in mine when I criticize *your* acting. We don't act well together and that's a fact; though I'm sure we should be smooth enough allies off the boards of love. Your heart, Bertha, is in the right place; ah, ça! what a heart!'

'You are too kind!'

'But—but; I will go a great deal farther than that: at the risk of appearing paradoxical I will affirm that the heart in question is so much part of your intelligence too—!'

'Thanks! Thanks!'

'—despite your fatuity in the matter of personal expression. But I must not allow myself to be enticed into these by-paths. I wish to make a clean breast of my motives. I had always till I met you regarded marriage as a thing beyond all argument *not* for me, I was unusually isolated from that idea; anyway, I had never even reflected what marriage was at all. It was you who introduced me to marriage! In consequence it is you who are responsible for all our troubles. The approach of this disgusting thing, so unexpectedly friendly at nearer sight, caused revulsion of feeling beyond my control, resulting in sudden fiançailles. Like a woman luxuriously fingering some merchant's goods, too dear for her, or not wanted enough for the big price, I philandered with the idea of marriage. Then I was caught. But I find I really don't want the stuff at all. I'm sorry.'

This simplification put things in a new callous light that was all. Tarr felt that she too must, naturally, be enjoying his points: he forgot to direct his exposition in such a way as to hurt her least. This trivial and tortured landscape had a beauty for him he was able and eager to explain, where for her there was nothing but a harrowing reality.

But the lunch had had the same effect upon him that it was intended to have upon his victim—not enough to overthrow his resolution, but enough to relax its form.

As to Bertha, this behaviour seemed, in the main, 'Sorbert all over.' There was nothing new. There was the 'difference': but she recognized that 'differences' had often been noticed by her, and it was really the familiar process; he was attempting to convince himself, heartlessly, at her expense. Whether he would ever manage to do so was problematic: there was no sign of his being likely to do so more to-day than any other day. So she listened; sententiously released him from time to time.

Just as she had seemed strange to him in some way when he came in (seen through his 'indifference') so he had appeared a little odd to her: this for a moment had wiped off the dullness of habit. This husband she so obstinately wanted had been recognized: she had seized him round the shoulders and clung athletically to him, as though he had been her child that some senseless force were about to snatch.

As to his superstition about marriage the subject of his recent remarks—was it not merely the restlessness of youth, propaganda of Liberty, that a year or so would see in Limbo? For was he not a 'marrying man'? She was sure of it! She had tried not to frighten him, and to keep 'marriage' in the background: but she was quite certain that he was intended to marry: he needed a wife.

Thus Tarr's disquisition had no effect except for one thing; when he spoke of a pleasure he derived from the idea of marriage upon closer acquaintance, she wearily pricked up her ears. The conviction that Tarr was a domesticated animal was confirmed from his own lips: the only result of his sortie was to stimulate her always vigilant hope and irony, both, just a little. (He had intended to prepare the couch for her despair!)

His last words, affirming marriage to be a game not worth the candle, brought a faint and 'weary' smile to her face: once more she was obviously 'à bout de force.'

'Sorbert; I understand you. Do realise that. There is no necessity for all this rigmarole with me, if you think you shouldn't marry— why it's quite simple! Don't think that I would force you to marry! *Oh* no!' (the training guttural unctuous accent she had in speaking english filled her discourse with a dreary mechanical emphasis). 'I always said that you were too young. You are far too young.

You need a wife—you've just said yourself about your feeling for marriage—but you are *so* young!' She gazed at him with compassionate half-smiling moistened look, as though there were something deformed about being *so* young. It was her invariable habit to treat anything that obviously pointed to her as the object of pity, as though it manifestly indicated, on the contrary, *him*. 'Yes, Sorbert, you are right' she finished briskly. 'I think it would be *madness* for us to marry!'

The suggestion that their leisurely journey towards marriage was perhaps a mistake, was at once seriously and with conviction far surpassing that he had ventured on taken up by her. Let them immediately call a halt, pitch tents preliminary to turning back: a pause was essential before beginning the return journey. Next day they would be jogging on again in the same disputed direction.

Tarr now saw at once what had happened: his good words had been completely thrown away, all except his confession to a weakness for the matronly blandishments of Matrimony. He had an access of stupid brief and blatant laughter.

As the earliest Science wondered what was at the core of the world, basing its speculations on what deepest things occasionally emerge, with violence, at its holes,* so Bertha often would conjecture what might be at the heart of Tarr. Laughter was the most apparently central substance which, to her knowledge, had uncontrollably appeared: often she had heard grumblings, quite literally, and seen unpleasant lights, belonging, she knew, to other categories of matter: but they never broke cover.

At present his explosive gaiety was interpreted as proof that she had been right. There was nothing in what he had said: it had been only one of his bad fits of rebellion.

But Tarr was ashamed of this backsliding into humour, that fatal condition: laughter must be given up. In some way, for both their sakes, the foundations of an ending must be laid at once.

For a few minutes he played with the idea of affecting Bertha's weapons. Perhaps it was not only impossible to overcome, but even to approach, or to be said to be on the same field with, this peculiar amazon,* without such uniformity of engines of attack or defence. Should not he get himself a mask like hers at once and follow suit with some emphatic sentence? He stared uncertainly at her. Then he sprang to his feet. He intended, as far as he could see beyond this passionate movement (for he must give himself up to the mood, of course) to pace the room.

But his violence jerked out of him a resounding shout of the most retrograde laughter. He went stamping about the floor roaring with reluctant mirth: it would not come out properly, too, except the first outburst.

'Ay—that's right! Get on with it, get on with it!' Bertha's patient irony seemed to gibe.

This laughter left him vexed with himself, like a fit of tears.

'Humour and pathos are such near twins that Humour may be exactly described as the most feminine attribute of man—and it is the only one of which women show hardly any trace! Jokes are like snuff, a slatternly habit' said Tarr to Butcher once 'whereas Tragedy (and tears) is like tobacco, much drier and cleaner. Comedy being always the embryo of Tragedy, the directer nature weeps. Women are of course directer than men.—But they have not the same resources.'

Butcher blinked. He thought of his resources. Then he recalled his inclination to tears.

———

Tarr's disgust at this electric rush of clattering sound was commensurate with the ground he had lost by it, and Bertha came in for her share of this vexation. He was now put at a fresh disadvantage. How could he ever succeed in making Bertha believe that a person who laughed immoderately was serious? Under the shadow of this laugh all his ensuing acts or words must toil, discredited in advance.

Desperately ignoring accidents, Tarr went back beyond his first explosion, and attacked its cause—indicting Bertha, more or less, as responsible for the disturbance.

He sat down squarely in front of her, hardly breathed from his paroxysm, getting himself launched without transition: by rapid plunging from one state to another he hoped to take the wind out of the laugh's sails: his irresponsible shout should be left towering, spectral but becalmed, behind.

'I don't know from which side to approach you Bertha: frequently you complain of my being thoughtless and spoilt: but your uncorked solemnity is far more frivolous than anything I can manage. Excuse me, naturally, for speaking in this way. Won't you come down from your pedestal just for a few minutes?' And he 'sketched' a gesture, as though offering the lady, about to step off her precipitous pedestal, his hand.

'My dear child I feel far from being on any pedestal, there's too little of the pedestal if anything about me. Really Sorbert' (she leant towards him with an abortive movement as though to take his hand) 'I *am* your friend—*believe me!*' (Last words very quick, with nod of head and blink of eyes.) 'You worry yourself far too much, please don't do so. You are in no way bound to me, if you think we should part—*let us part!* Yes, let us part. By all means let us part!'

The 'let us part!' was precipitate, strenuous-prussian, almost truculent.

Tarr thought:—'Is it cunning, stupidity, is she a screw loose, or what?'

She took up the tale again, unexpectedly, and she had rapidly shunted on to another track of generosity:—

'But I agree, let us be franker, Sorbert. We waste too much time talking, talking. You are different to-day Sorbert—what is it? If you have met somebody else—.'

Sorbert looked at her in dumb expostulation. Then he said:

'If I had I'd tell you. There is besides *nobody else* to meet, you are unique! Really. Unique.'

'Someone's been saying something to you—.'

'No. I've been saying something to somebody else. But it's the same thing. It's no use. I might as well keep my mouth shut.'

With half-incredulous, musing, glimmering stare she drew in her horns.

Tarr meditated. 'This I should have foreseen. I am asking her for something that she sees no reason to give up. Next her beastly Geschmack* for me it is the most valuable thing the poor girl possesses. It is indissolubly mixed up with the Geschmack. The poor heightened self she laces herself into is the only consolation for *me* and all the troubles brought down on her by a person of my order. But I ask her brutally to "come down from her pedestal." (I owe even a good deal to that pedestal, I expect, as regards her Geschmack in the first place): this blessed protection given her by nature I, a minute or two before leaving her, make a last inept attempt to capture or destroy. What more natural than that her good sense should be contemptuous and indignant? It is only in defence of this ridiculous sentimentality that she has ever shown her teeth. This invaluable illusion has enabled her to bear things, so long: now it stands ready with redskin impassibility* to manœuvre her over the falls or rapids of Parting. The scientific thing to do, I suppose, with my liberal intentions, would be to flatter and enhance in every way this idea of herself. She should be given some final and extraordinary opportunity of being "noble."'

He looked up at her a moment, in search of inspiration.

'I must not be too vain—I exaggerate the gravity of the hit. As to my attempted rape of her fairy drapery, there are two sides to that: consider how I square up when she shows signs of annexing *my* illusion! We are really the whole time playing a game of grabs and dashes* at each other's magic vestment of imagination. Only hers makes her very fond of me, whereas mine makes me see anyone but her. That's the difference. Perhaps this is why I have not been more energetic in my prosecution of the game, and have allowed her to remain in her savage semi-naked state of pristine balderdash. Why has she never tried to modify herself in direction of my "taste"? Is it on account of her not daring to leave this protective fanciful self, while I still kept all *my* weapons? Then her initiative. She does nothing it is the man's place to do: she remains "woman" as she would say. Only she is so intensely alive in her passivity, so maelstrom-like in her surrender, so exclusive in her sacrifice, that very little remains to be done. Really with Bertha the man's position is a mere sinecure.'

As a cover for reflection he set himself to finish lunch. The strawberries were devoured mechanically, with un-hungry itch to clear the plate: he was a conscientious automaton, restless if any of the little red balls still remained in front of it.

Bertha's eyes sought to waft her out of this Present, but they had broken down, depositing her somewhere halfway down the avenue so to speak.

Tarr got up, a released puppet, and walked to the cloth-covered box where he had left his hat and stick. Then he returned in some way dutifully and obediently to the same seat, sat there for a minute, hat on knee. He had gone over and taken it up without thinking: he only realized, once back, what the action signified. Nothing was settled, he had so far done more harm than good. The presence of the hat and stick on his knees, however, was like the holding open of the front door already. Anything said with them there could only be like words said as an afterthought, upon the threshold. It was as though, hat on head, he were standing with his hand on the door knob, about to add some trifle to a thing already settled.

He got up, walked back to where he had picked up the hat and stick, placed them as they were before, then returned to the window. What should be done now? He seemed to have played all his cards. All the steps that had suggested themselves to him had now been taken. But should there be some still in reserve, that passive pose of Bertha's was not encouraging. It had lately withstood stoically a good deal, and was quite ready to absorb still more. There was something almost pugnacious in so much resignation.

But when she looked up at him there was no sign of combat. She appeared adjusted to something simple again, for this critical departure, by some fluke of a word. For the second time that day she had jumped out of her skin.

Her heart beat in a delicate exhausted way, her eyelids became moistened underneath, as she turned to her unusual fiancé. They had wandered, she felt, into a drift of silence that hid a novel and unpleasant prospect at the end of it. Suddenly it seemed charged with some alarming fancy that she could not grasp. There was something more unusual than her fiancé.—But the circular storm, in her case, was returning.

'Well Sorbert?'

'Well. What is it?'

'Why don't you go? I thought you'd gone. It seems so funny to see you standing there—what are you staring at me for?'

'Oh a cat may look at a king* I suppose, still.'

She looked down with a wild demureness, her head on one side.

Her mouth felt at some distance from her brain: her voice stood on tip-toe like a dwarf to speak. She became very much impressed by her voice, and was rather afraid to say anything more. Had she fainted? Sorbert appeared to her as a stranger, hat in hand, the black stubble on his chin and his brown neck repelled her like the symptoms of a disease. She noticed something criminal and quick in his eyes: she became nervous, as though she had admitted somebody too trustingly to her flat. This fancy played upon her hysteria: she really wished very much that he would go.

'Why don't you go?' she repeated, in a matter-of-fact way, looking down.

Tarr remained silent, seemingly determined not to answer. Meantime, he looked at her with a doubtful dislike.

What is *love?* he began reasoning. It is either *possession* or a possessive madness. In the case of men and women, it is the obsession of a personality. He had been endowed with the power of awaking love in her, it was fair to assume. He had something to accuse himself of. He had been *afraid of giving up* or repudiating this particular madness. Yet why accuse himself? How could he accuse himself of an instinct? To give up another person's love is a mild suicide. Then his tenderness for Bertha was due to her having purloined some part of himself, and covered herself superficially with it as a shield. Her skin at least was Tarr. She had captured a living piece of him and held it as a hostage. She was rapidly transforming herself, too, into a slavish dependency: she worked with all the hypocrisy of a great instinct.

People can wound by loving he said to himself (he was of course accusing her): the sympathy of this affection is interpenetrative. Love performs its natural miracle, and the people that love us become part of us; it is a dismemberment to cast them off. Our own blood flows out after them when they go.

Or love was a malady, Tarr continued: it was dangerous to live with those consumed by it. He felt an uneasiness: might not a wasting and restlessness now ensue? It would not, if he were infected, be recognizable as *love.* Perhaps he had already got it slightly: that might account for his hanging about her. He evidently was suffering from something that came from Bertha, maybe it was that.

Everybody, however, all personality was catching: we all are sicknesses for each other, he reasoned. Such contact as he had had with Bertha was *particularly* risky that was all. The photographs at which he had just been looking displayed an unpleasant solidarity. Was it necessary to allege 'love' at all however—in his case the word was superfluous. The fact was before him.

He felt suddenly despondent and afraid of the future: he had fallen beneath a more immediate infection.

He looked attentively round the room. Already his memory ached. She had loved him with all this: he had been loved with the plaster cast of Beethoven, this gentle girl had attacked him with the Klingers, had ambushed him from the Breton* jars, in a funny superficial absorbing way. Her madness had muddled everything with his ideal existence. This was not he told himself like leaving an ordinary room in which you had spent pleasant hours and would regret, you would owe nothing to that, and it could not pursue you with images of wrong. This room he was wronging, and he left it in a different way. She seemed, too, so humble in it, or through it—the appeal of the *little* again: if he could only escape from scale! The price of preoccupation with the large was this perpetual danger from the *little*. Oh dear, Tarr wished he could look coldly upon mere littleness, and not fall so easily victim to it. Oh how necessary brutality was to him, he was so unprotected against all that was little! As to love, it was so much too new to him. He was not inoculated enough with love.

Callously he had been signing his name to a series of brutalities, then, as though he were sure that when the time came he would have a quite sufficient stock of toughness to meet these debts. Yet from the first he had suspected that he had not: eventually he would have to evade them or succumb. The flourishes of the hand and mind had caused Bertha's mute and mournful attitude. She thought she knew him, but was amazed at his ignorance or pretence.

He had stirred up and brought out into the light during the last hour every imaginable difficulty, and created a number of new ones. They were there in a confused mass before him. The thought of 'settling everything before he went' now appeared fantastic. He had at all events started these local monsters and demons, fishing them out stark where they could be seen. Each had a different vocal explosiveness or murmur, inveighing unintelligibly against the other. The only thing to be done was to herd them all together and march them away for inspection at leisure. Sudden herdsman, with the care of a delicate and antediluvian* flock; well!—but what was Bertha to be told? Nothing. He would file out silently with his flock, without any horn-blasts or windings such as he customarily affected.

'I am going now' he said at last, getting up.

She looked at him with startled interest.

'You are leaving me Sorbert?'

'No. At least, now I am going.' He stooped down for his hat and cane. 'I will come and see you to-morrow or the day after.'

Closing the door quietly, with a petty carefulness, he crossed the passage, belittled and guilty. He did not wish to escape this feeling: it would be far better to enhance it while he was about it. For a moment it occurred to him to go back and offer marriage. It was about all he had to offer. He was ashamed of his only gift!—But he did not stop, he opened the front door and went downstairs. Something raw and uncertain he seemed to have built up in the room he had left: how long would it hold together? Again he was acting in secret, his errand and intentions kept to himself. Something followed him like a restless dog.

PART II

DOOMED, EVIDENTLY—THE 'FRAC'*

CHAPTER 1

FROM a window in the neighbouring Boulevard, the eye of Otto Kreisler* was fixed blankly upon a spot thirty feet above the scene of the Hobson-Tarr dialogue. Kreisler was shaving himself, one eye fixed upon Paris. It beat upon this wall of Paris drearily. Had it been endowed with properties of illumination and had it been directed there earlier in the day, it would have provided a desolate halo for Tarr's ratiocination.* Kreisler's watch had been in the Mont-de-Piété* since the beginning of the week, until some clock struck he was in total ignorance of the time of day.

The late spring sunshine flooded, like a bursted tepid star, the pink boulevard: beneath, the black-suited burgesses of Paris crawled like wounded insects hither and thither. A low corner-house terminating the Boulevard Kreutzberg blotted out the lower part of the Café Berne.

Kreisler's room resembled a funeral chamber. Shallow ill-lighted and extensive, it was placarded with nude archaic images. These were painted on strips of canvas fastened to the wall with drawing-pins. Imagining yourself in some primitive necropolis,* the portraits of the deceased covering the holes in which they had respectively been thrust, you would, pursuing your fancy, have seen in Kreisler a devout recluse who had taken up his quarters in this rock-hewn death-house.

Otto Kreisler was in one sense a recluse (although almost certainly the most fanciful mind would have gasped and fallen at his contact). But Cafés were the luminous caverns where he could be said, most generally, to dwell; with, nevertheless, very little opening of the lips and much apparent meditation; therefore not unworthy of some rank among the inferior and less fervent solitudes.

A bed like an overturned cupboard, dark, and with a red billow of foot-deep down covering its surface; a tessellated floor of red tile; a little rug, made with paint carpet cardboard and horse-hair, to represent a leopard—these, with chair, wash-stand, easel, and several weeks of slowly drifting and shifting garbage, completed its contents.

Kreisler gaily flicked the lather on to a crumpled newspaper. But his face emerging from greenish soap, garish where the razor had scraped it, did not satisfy him: life did not each day deposit an untidiness that could be whisked off by a Gillette blade,* as nature did its stubble.

His face, wearing, it is true, like a uniform the frowning fixity of the Prussian warrior, had a neglected look. The true bismarckian Prussian* would seek every day, by little acts of boorishness, to keep fresh this trenchant attitude; like the german student with his weekly routine of duels* which regimen is to keep courage simmering in times of peace, that it may instantly boil up to war pitch at the merest sign from the german War-Master.

He brushed his clothes vigorously; cleaned his glasses with the absorption and tenderness of the near-sighted. Next moment, straddling on his flat slav nose, he was gazing through them at his face again—brushing up whimsical moustaches over pink and pouting mouth. This was done with two tiny ivory brushes taken out of a small leather case—present from a fiancée who had been alarmed that these moustaches showed an unpatriotic tendency to droop.*

This old sweetheart just then disagreeably occupied his mind. But he busied himself about further small details of his toilet with increased precision. Had a person he had wished to snub been sitting there and talking to him he could not have been more elaborately engrossed in a hundred insignificant things, such as adjusting the defective spring-button that secured the moustache-brush case. That morning any reverie or troubling reflections would be treated very cavalierly. To a knock he answered with careful 'Come in.' He did not take his eyes from the glass, spotted blue tie being pinched into position by finicky finger-tips, at the end of lanky drooping hands, with extended high-held formal elbows and one knee slightly flexed. Above and around his tie the entrance of a young woman was considered with a high impassibility.

'Good morning. So you're up already' she said in French.

He treated her as coolly as he had his thoughts: appearing at that moment she gave his manner towards the latter something human to play upon with relief. Imparting swanlike undulations to a short stout person, an eye fixed quizzingly upon Kreisler's in the glass, she advanced. Her manner was one seldom sure of welcome, there was deprecation in her aggressive intrusion. She was not pretty: it was a good-natured face, brows always raised, with protruding eyes. With these she gesticulated, filling her silences with explosive significance. A skin which would become easily blue in cold weather was matched with a taste in dress inveterately blue: the Pas de Calais* had somehow produced her: Paris, shortly afterwards, had put the mark of its necessitous millions on a mean, lively child.

'Are you going to work to-day?' came in a minute or two.

'No' her taciturn host replied, putting his jacket on. 'Do you want me to?'

'It would be of certain use. But don't put yourself out!' with grin tightening all the skin of her face, making it pink and bald and her eyes drunken.

'I'm afraid I can't.' Watched with a sort of appreciative raillery, he got down on his knees and dragged a portmanteau from beneath the bed.

'Susanna, what can I get on that?' he asked simply, as of an expert.

'Ah, that's where we are? You want to pop* this? I don't know I'm sure. Perhaps they'd give you fifteen francs. It's good leather.'

'Perhaps twenty?' he asked. 'I must have them!' he clamoured suddenly, with an energy that startled her.

She grimaced, looked very serious, said, 'Je ne sais pas vous savez!'* with several vigorous yet rhythmical and rich forward movements of the head. She became the broker: Kreisler was pressing for a sum in excess of regulations. Not for the world, any more than had she been the broker in fact, would she have valued it at a penny over what it seemed likely to fetch.

'Je ne sais pas vous savez!' she repeated. She looked even worried. She would have liked to please Kreisler by saying more, but her business conscience prevented her.

'Well, we'll go together.'

This conversation was carried on strictly in dialect. Suzanne understood him, for she was largely responsible for the patois in which Kreisler carried on conversation with the French. This young woman had no fixed occupation. She disappeared for irregular periods to live with men. She sat as a model.

'Your father hasn't sent yet?' He shook his head.

'Le cochon!' she stuttered.

'But it will come to-morrow, or the day after anyway.' The idiosyncrasies of these monthly letters were quite familiar to her. The dress
clothes had been pawned by her on a former occasion.

'What do you need twenty francs for?'

'I must have not twenty but twenty-five.'

Her silence was as eloquent as face-muscles and eye-fluid could
make it.

'To get the dress clothes out' he explained, fixing her stolidly with
his principal eye.

She first smiled slowly, then allowed her ready mirth to grow,
by mechanical stages, into laughter. The presence of this small indifferent and mercenary acquaintance irritated him. But he remained
cool and stiffly detached. Just then a church clock began striking
the hour. He foreboded it was already ten, but not later. It struck
ten, and then eleven. He leapt the hour—the clock seemed rushing
with him, in a second, to the more advanced position—without any
flurry, quite calmly. Then it struck twelve. He at once absorbed that
further hour as he had the former. He lived an hour as easily and care-
lessly as he would have lived a second. Could it have gone on striking he would have swallowed, without turning a hair, twenty, thirty
strokes.

Going out of the door with Suzanne, portmanteau in hand, as he
opened it he experienced a twinge of anger. A half-hour before, on
waking, he had sat up in bed and gazed at the crevice at its foot where
a letter, thrust underneath by the concierge, usually lay. He had stared
menacingly as he found nothing there. That little square of rich bright
white paper was what he had counted on night to give him—that he
had expected to find on waking, as though it were a secretion of those
long hours. It made him feel that there had been no night—long,
fecund, rich in surprises—but merely a barren moment of sleep.
A stale and garish continuation of yesterday, no fresh day at all, had
dawned: the chill and phlegmatic appearance of his room annoyed
him. Its inhospitable character had repelled the envelope pregnant
with revolutionary joy and serried* german marks. Such a dead hole
of a place must have some effect; to shut out innovation, scare away
anything pleasant. Impossible to break this spell of monotony upon
his life. And it was this room, yes, this room that cut him off from the
world: he gazed around as a man may eye a wife whom he suspects of
intercepting his correspondence. There was no reason why the letter

with his monthly remittance should have come on that particular
morning however—already eight days overdue.

'If I had a father like yours!' said Suzanne in menacing humorous
sing-song, eyes bulging and head nodding. At this vista of perpetual
blackmail she fell into a reverie.

'Never get your father off on your fiancée,* Suzanne!' Kreisler
advised in reply.

'Comment?' Suzanne did not understand, and pulled a sour face.
When would this cursed Prussian learn French? *To get your father off
on your fiancée!* What was that then? Zut!

This is what Kreisler, in a moment of aberration, had done though,
exactly: for four years now his father, a widower for nine years, had
been married to the lady who had given Otto the brushes for the
moustache. His son had only been home once in that period.

Some months before Herr Kreisler Senior had asked Otto to give
up art, offering him the choice of two posts in german firms. On a
short refusal, the matter had been dropped: but he had infuriated his
son, calculating on such effect, by sending his allowance only when
written for, and even then neglecting the appeal for several days.
On two occasions forty marks and thirty marks had been deducted
respectively, merely as an irritative measure, no reason was given in
the letter. Otto, on his side, made no remark. The father was jealous contemptuous and sulky, Otto the same, if perhaps you substitute
'sourly roguish' for 'jealous.'

How near was the end? This might be the end. So much the
better! Kreisler's student days—a life-time in itself—embracing
a great variety of useless studies of which painting, the last, was far
the most useless—had unfitted him, at the age of thirty-six, for
practically anything. So far he had only lost one picture. This senseless solitary purchase depressed him whenever he thought of it: how
dreary that cheque for four pounds ten was! Who could have bought
it? It sold joylessly and fatally one day in an exhibition. What an
event!

He turned the key carefully in the door: the concierge or landlord were quite capable of slipping in and firing his things out in his
absence.

The portmanteau whisked up from the floor, flopped along
with him like a child's slack balloon. He frowned at Suzanne, and,
prepared for surprises, went warily down the marble stairway.

CHAPTER 2

NINE months previously Kreisler had arrived in Paris at the Gare de Lyon,* from Italy. He had left Rome because the italian creditor is such a bad-tempered fellow, and he could never get any sleep after 8—or latterly 7.30—even, in the morning.

'DEAR COLLEAGUE,

'Expect me Thursday. I am at last quitting this wretched city, driven out by the Goths and other refuse that have infested it since the second century.* I hope that the room you mentioned is still free. Will come at once to your address. With many hearty greetings,

'Yours

'OTTO KREISLER.'

He had despatched this note, before leaving, to a Herr Ernst Vokt. For some time he stood on the Paris platform, ulster thrown back, smoking a lean cigar with a straw stuck in it. He was glad to be in Paris. How busy the women, intent on travel, were! Groups of town-folk, not travellers, stood like people at a show. Each traveller was met by a phalanx of uninterested faces beyond the gangway.

His standing on the platform was a little ceremonious and military. He was taking his bearings. Body and belongings, with him, were always moved about with certain strategy. At last with racial menace he had his things swept together, saying heavily:

'Un Viagre!'*

Vokt was not in, but had left word he would be there after dinner. It was in a Pension: he rented a studio as well in the garden behind. The house was rather like a provincial Public Baths, two storied, of an unclean purple colour. Kreisler looked up at it. Looking big and idle in their rooms, catching the eye of the stranger on the pavement, he remarked several pensionnaires and was remarked by them. He was led to the studio in rear of the house, and asked to wait.

Several long canvases stood face against the wall. He turned them round and to his astonishment discovered dashing ladies in large hats before him.

'Ha! Ha! Well I'm damned! Bravo Ernst!' he exploded in his dull solitude, extremely amused.

Vokt had not done this in Rome. Even there he had given indications of latent virtuosity but had been curbed by classic presences. Since arriving in Paris he had blossomed shamelessly; he dealt out a blatant vitality by the peck to each sitter, and they forgave him for making them comparatively 'ugly.' He flung a man or woman on to nine feet of canvas and pummelled them on it for a couple of hours, until they promised to remain there or were incapable of moving, so to speak. He had never been able to treat people like this in any other walk of life and was grateful to painting for the experience. He always appeared to feel he would be expected to apologize for his brutal behaviour as an artist and was determined not to do so.

A half-hour later, upon his return, he was informed by the servant that somebody was waiting in the studio. With face exhibiting the collected look of a man of business arriving at his office, he walked out quickly across the garden.

When he saw Kreisler the bustling business look disappeared. Nothing of his private self remained for the moment: he was engulfed in his friend's personality.

'But Ernst! What beautiful pictures! What pleasant company you left me to wait amongst! How are you? I am glad to see you again!'

'Had a good journey? Your letter amused me! So Rome became too hot?'

'A little! My dear chap, it *was* a business! In this last scuffle I lost literally half the clothes off my back. But chiefly Italian clothes, fortunately.'

'Why didn't you write?'

'Oh, it wasn't serious enough to call for help' he dismissed this at once. 'This is a nice place you've got.' Kreisler looked round as though measuring it. He noticed Vokt's discomfort: he terminated his examination. Vokt coughed a stilted 'ahem!' like a stereotyped remark,

'Have you dined? I waited until eight. Have you . . . ?'

'I should like something to eat. Can we get anything here?'

'I'm afraid not. It's rather late for this neighbourhood. Let's take these things to your room—on the way—and go to the Big Boulevards.'*

They stayed till the small hours of the morning, in the midst of the 'Paris by Night'* of the german bourgeois imagination, drinking champagne and toasting the creditors left behind in Rome.

Kreisler, measured by chairs or doors, was of immoderate physical humanity: he was of that select and strapping minority that bend their heads to enter our dwellings. His long almost perfectly round thighs stuck out like poles: this giant body lounged and poised beside Vokt in massive control and over-reaching of civilized matter. It was in Rome or in Paris—it moved about a great deal: everywhere it sat down or stood up with an air of certain proprietorship. Vokt was stranger in Paris than his companion, who had only just arrived: even he felt a little raw and uncomfortable, almost a tourist. He was being shown 'Paris by Night'—almost literally, for his inclinations had not taken him much to that side of the town.*

Objects—*kokotten,** newsvendors, waiters—flowed through Kreisler's brain without trouble or surprise. His heavy eyes were big gates of a self-centred city—this was just a procession. (There was no trade in the town.)

His body had been given the freedom of the city by every other body within sight at once, heroically installed and almost unnaturally solid. So intensely real, so at home, his big guest ended by appearing to Ernst Vokt, as he sat there beside him, almost an apparition, by sheer dint of contradicting what by all rights he should have been—a little strange and not yet part of the scene.

Vokt began looking for himself: he picked up the pieces quietly. This large rusty machine of a man smashed him up like an egg-shell at every meeting; the shell grew quickly again, but never got hard enough.

But it pleased him to see him again (he told himself, expanding his chest), he was downright glad to have him there! Good old Otto, *brave* old Otto! They were great old friends. This was *good.* The drink had been much and good—the old days!—but in spite of himself Ernst Vokt was fidgety at the lateness of the hour. The next day Fräulein von Bonsels, who was sitting for him, was due at 9.30. At 9.30—it was now 4. But the first night of seeing his friend again—. He drank to banish this sense of time and became silent, thinking of his westphalian home and his sister who was not very well: she had had a bicycle accident and had received a considerable shock. He might spend the summer with her and his mother at Berck-sur-Mer.* He would have gone home for a week or so now, only an aunt he did not like was staying there.

'Well let's get back!' said Kreisler, rather thoughtful, too, at all the life he had seen.

CHAPTER 3

IN Paris Ernst Vokt, as his studio and its contents betrayed, had found himself: the french capital seemed especially constructed for him—such a wonderful large polite institution. No one looked at him because he was small: for money in Paris represented delicate things, in Germany chiefly gross ones, and his money lent him more stature than anything else could, and in a much more dignified and subtle way than elsewhere. Now for the first time his talent benefited by his money. Heavy temperament, primitive talent, well yes genius, had their big place, but money had at last come into its own, and climbed up into the spiritual sphere. A very sensible and soothing spirit reigned in this seat of intelligence: a very great number of sensible well-dressed figures perambulated all over these suave acres. Large tribes of 'types' prosecuted their primitive enthusiasms in certain Cafés, unannoyed by either the populace or the differently-minded élite. The old romantic personal values he was used to in his Fatherland were all deeply modified: money, luck and non-personal power, were the genius of the new world. American clothes were adapted for the finer needs of the Western European; cosmopolitan Paris was what America ought to be.

On the evening following Kreisler's arrival Ernst had a dinner engagement. The morning after that Kreisler turned up at half-past twelve. Ernst was painting Fräulein von Bonsels, a Berlin débutante, very parisian, very expensively dressed, her lips crepitating with correct clichés. Ernst displayed a disinclination to make Kreisler and his sitter acquainted, but he was a little confused. He was going to lunch with his sitter: they arranged to meet at dinner time.

Kreisler the night before had lavished a good deal of money in the teutonic paradise beyond the river. Vokt understood by a particular insistent blankness about Kreisler's eye that money was needed. He was familiar with this look—Kreisler owed him three thousand marks. At first Kreisler had made an effort to pay his friend back money borrowed, when his allowance arrived: but in Rome, and earlier for a short time in Munich, Vokt's money was not of so much value as it was at present: repayment was waived in an eager sentimental way, and the debt grew. The financial void caused by Vokt's going off to Paris had been felt keenly by Kreisler. The real motive of his following Vokt to Paris had scarcely been formulated by him, he had taken the step almost by instinct. He was now in a position analogous to that of a man who had been separated for some months from his wife: he was in a luxurious hurry once more to see the colour of Vokt's gold.

Kreisler was very touchy about money, like all of a certain class of borrowers. He sponged with discrimination: but for some time he had not required to sponge at all, as Vokt amply met his needs. He had got rather out of practice in consequence. He found this reopening of his account with little friend Ernst a most delicate business: it was worse than tackling a stranger. He recognized that a change might have come over Vokt's open-handedness in new surroundings; he therefore determined to ask for a sum in advance of actual needs, and by boldness at once re-establish continuity.

After dinner he said:

'You remember Ricci?—where I got my paints to start with. I had some trouble with that devil before I left. He came round and made a great scandal on the staircase. He shouted "Bandit!" Ha! ha!—Sagralctto!*—how do you say it?—Sporco Tedesco. Then he called the neighbours to witness. He kept repeating he was "not afraid of me." I took him by the ear and kicked him out!' he ended with florid truculence.

Vokt laughed obsequiously, but with discomfort. Kreisler solicited his sympathetic mirth with a too masterful eye: he laughed, himself, unnecessarily heartily. A scene of violence in which a small man was hustled (which Vokt would have to applaud) was a clever prelude. Ernst felt instinctively it was a prelude, too: he grew very fidgety. Then the violence was toned down.

'I'm sorry for the little devil. I shall have the money soon: I shall send it him. The first! He shall not suffer.—Antonio, too. I don't owe much. I had to settle most before I left. Himmel! My landlord!' He choked mirthfully over his coffee a little, almost upsetting it, then mincingly adjusted the cup to his lips.

If he had to *settle up* before he left, he could not have much now, evidently! There was a disagreeable pause.

Vokt stirred his coffee. Then he showed his hand; he looked up and with transparent innocence enquired:

'By the way Otto, you remember Fabritz at Munich—?'

'You mean the little Jew from whom everybody used to borrow money?' Kreisler fixed him severely and significantly with his eye and spoke with a very heavy deliberation indeed.

'Did people borrow money from him?—I had forgotten. Yes that's the man; he has turned up here; who do you think with? With Irma, the bohemian girl; they are living together—round the corner there.'

'Hum! Are they? She was a pretty nice girl. Do you remember the night von Thöny was found stripped and tied to his door handle? He assured me Irma had done it and pawned his clothes.'

Was Vokt thinking that the famous and admitted function of Fabritz should be resorted to as an alternative by Kreisler—he Vokt failing?

'Vokt, I can speak to you plainly; isn't that so? You are my friend. What's more, already we have—' he laughed strongly and easily. 'My journey has cost the devil of a lot. I shall be getting my allowance in a week or so. Could you lend me a small sum of money? When my money comes—.'

'Of course. But I am hard up. How much—.' These were three very jerky efforts.

'Oh, two hundred marks or if you can spare it—.'

Vokt's jaw dropped.

'I am afraid, my dear Kreisler, I can't—just now—manage that. My journey, too, cost me a lot. I'm most awfully sorry. Let me see. I have my rent next week—I don't see how I can manage—.'

Vokt had a clean-shaven depressed and earnest face: he made use of all its most uninviting attributes for this occasion.

Kreisler looked sulkily at the table-cloth, and knocked the ash sharply off his cigarette into his cup.

He said nothing. Vokt became nervous.

'Will a hundred marks be of any use?'

'Yes' Kreisler drew his hand over his chin as though stroking a beard down and then pulled his moustaches up, fixing the waitress with an indifferent eye. 'Can you spare that?'

'Yes—I can't really. But if you are in such a position that—.'

These were the circumstances under which he had lost Vokt. He felt that hundred marks, given him as a favour, was the last serious bite he would get. It was only gradually that he realized of how much more value Vokt's money now was, and what before was an unorganized mass of specie, in which the professional borrower could wallow, was now a sound and suitably conducted business. That night he was presented to the new manager.

After dinner Ernst took him round to the Berne. He did not realize what awaited him. There he at once found himself in the headquarters of many personalities of his own nation. Politeness reigned. Kreisler was pleased to find this club where german was the principal language; his roots mixed sluggishly with Ernst's in this living lump of the soil of the Fatherland deposited at the head of the Boulevard Kreutzberg.

The Germans he met here spoke a language and expressed opinions he could not agree with, but with which Vokt evidently did. They argued genially over glasses of beer and champagne. He found his level at once: he was the 'vieille barbe' of the party.

'Yes, I've seen Gauguins. But why go so far as the South Sea Islands* unless you are going to make people more beautiful? Why go out of Europe, why not save the money for the voyage?' he would bluster.

'More beautiful? What do you understand by the word "beautiful," my dear sir?' would answer a voice in the service of new movements.

'What do I call beautiful? How would you like your face to be as flat as a pancake, your nostrils like a squashed strawberry, one of your eyes cocked up by the side of your ear? Would not you be very unhappy to look like that? Then how can you expect anyone but a technique-maniac to care a straw for a picture of that sort; call it Cubist or Fauve* or whatever you like? It's all spoof. It puts money in somebody's pocket, no doubt.'

'It's not a question unhappily of how we should like our faces to be: *it is how they are.* But I do not consider the actual position of my eyes to be any more "beautiful" than any other position they might have assumed. The almond eye was long held in contempt by the hatchet eye—.'

Kreisler peered up at him, and laughed. 'You're a modest fellow. You're not as ugly as you think! Na! I like to find—.'

'But you haven't told us, Otto, what you call *beautiful.*'

'I call this young lady here'—and he turned gallantly to a blushing cocotte* at his side—'*beautiful,* very beautiful.' He kissed her amid gesticulation and applause.

'That's just what I supposed' his opponent said with appreciation.

With Soltyk he could not get on at all. Louis Soltyk was a young Russian Pole, who occasionally sat amongst the Germans at the Berne; and of him Vokt saw more than of anybody: in fact it was he who had superseded Kreisler in the position of influence as regards Vokt's purse. But Soltyk did not borrow a hundred marks: his system was far more up to date. Ernst had experienced an unpleasant shock in coming into contact with Kreisler's clumsy and slovenly money habits again.

Physically Soltyk even bore, distantly and with polish, a resemblance to Kreisler. It was as though he had been compelled to imitate Kreisler all his life, but the material at his disposal being of an unsuitable texture, something rather different had resulted. His handsome face and elegance belied the suggestion. Still Kreisler and he disliked each other for obscure physiological reasons perhaps: in some ways Soltyk was his efficient and more accomplished counterpart.

'Also wo steckt er eigentlich, unser wahrhaftlicher echter Germane? Ist wohl nicht hier gewesen?'* Soltyk would ask.

'He's in good company somewhere!'—Vokt revealed Kreisler as a lady's man. This satisfied the hilarious purposes of Soltyk: the Russian Pole now made it his business to keep an eye on Vokt's pocket while Kreisler was about; he had not been long in noting the signs of the professional borrower, the most contemptible and slatternly member of the crook family.

Louis Soltyk dealt in paintings and art-objects. In the first days of Kreisler's arrival Ernst asked his new friend if he could not dispose of a painting by Kreisler.

'What. Does he *paint*?'

'Why yes.'

'What's it like? I should like to see that! I should like to see the sort of paintings your friend Kreisler does!'

'Well, come round some day—.'

But Soltyk took Vokt by the lapel of the coat.

'Non! Sois pas bête! Here' he pulled out a handful of money and chose a dollar piece. 'Here—give him this. You buy a *picture*—if it's a picture you want to buy—you buy a picture by Picasso, or—or—. Kreisler has nothing but *Kreisler* to offer. C'est peu!'

Ernst introduced Kreisler next to another sort of Paris compatriot: this time it was a large female contingent. He took him round to Fräulein Liepmann's on her evening at home, when these ladies played the piano and met.

Kreisler felt that he was a victim of strategy: he puffed and swore outside, he complained of their music, the coffee, their way of dressing.

The Liepmann circle could have stood as a model for Tarr's bourgeois-bohemians, stood for a group. For chief characteristic this particular bourgeois-bohemian circle had in the first plan the inseparability of its members. Should a man, joining them, wish to flirt with one particularly, he must flirt with all—flatter all, take all to the theatre, carry the umbrellas and the paint boxes, of all. Eventually, should he come to that, it is doubtful if a proposition of marriage could be made otherwise than before the assembled band. And marriage alone could wrench the woman chosen away from the clinging bunch, if it did succeed in doing that.

Kreisler, despite his snorting, went again with Vokt: the feminine spell had taken effect. This gregarious female personality had shown such frank invitation to Vokt upon his arrival in Paris that, had any separate woman exhibited half as hospitable a front, he would have been very alarmed. As it was, it had at first just fulfilled certain bourgeois requirements of his lonely german soul.

Kreisler went a few weeks running to the Liepmann soirée: never finding Vokt there, he left off going as well. He felt he had been tricked and slighted. The ladies divined what had happened: Fräulein Liepmann, the leader, put a spiteful little mark down to each of their names.

CHAPTER 4

KREISLER pocketed Ernst's hundred-mark note and made no further attempts upon the formerly hospitable income of his friend, for he was a proud sponger: but debts began accumulating. Thereupon he made a disquieting discovery: he found he had suddenly grown timid with his creditors. The concierge literally frightened him: he conciliated the garçon at the Café, to whom he owed money: he even paid several debts that it was quite unnecessary to pay, in a moment of panic and discouragement. On one occasion this novel open-handedness caused him to spend a very disagreeable week until the next allowance arrived. This rapid deterioration of his will extended to his relations with his Café acquaintances: at the Berne he had lost his nerve in some way; on some evenings he would clown obsequiously, and depressed and slack the next, perhaps, resenting his companions' encores, would grow boorish.

The next thing was that he gradually developed the habit of sitting alone: more often than not he would enter the Café and proceed to a table at the opposite side of the room to that at which his german acquaintances were sitting.

Ridicule is focussed at about ten yards: the spectator is then without the sphere of average animal magnetism. For once it does not matter: but if persisted in it results without fail in a malicious growth of criticism at the expense of the solitary. This process is perfectly automatic: those who keep to themselves awaken mirth as a cartwheel running along the road by itself would. With regard to the 'lonely' man people have the sensation that he is going about with some eccentric companion, namely himself. Why did he choose this deaf and dumb companion? What do they find to say to each other? He is ludicrous as two men would be, who, perpetually in each other's company, were never seen to exchange a word—who dined together, went to theatre or Café in each other's company, without ever looking at each other or speaking.

So Kreisler became a lonely figure. It was a strange feeling: he must be quiet and not attract attention: in some way he was marked as though he had committed a theft. Perhaps it was merely the worry of perpetual 'tick'* beginning to tell. For the moment he would just put himself aside, and see what happened, he seemed to have decided. He was afraid of himself too: always up till then immersed in that self, now for the first time he stood partly outside it. This slight divorce made him less sure in his touch in everything. A little less careful of his appearance, he went sluggishly about, smoking, reading the paper a great deal, working at the art school fairly often, playing billiards with an austrian cook whom he had picked up in a Café and who disappeared owing him seven francs.

The inertia and phlegm, outward sign of depressing everyday Kreisler, had found someone, when he had found Vokt, for whom they were a charm and something to be envied. Kreisler's imagination woke shortly after Vokt's. It was as though the peasant, always regarding his life as the dullest affair, should be suddenly transformed by participating in some townsman's romantic notions of the romance of rural man. Kreisler's moody wastefulness and futility had found a raison d'être and meaning, almost.

Vokt had been a compendious phenomenon in his life, although his cheery gold had attracted him to the more complete discovery.

Vokt had ousted women, too, from Kreisler's daily needs: he had become a superstition for his tall friend.

On the other hand it was Kreisler's deadness, his absolute lack of any reason to be confident and yet perfect aplomb, that mastered his companion.

Ernst Vokt had remained for three desultory and dreamy years becalmed on this empty sea. Kreisler basked around him, never having to lift his waves and clash them together as formerly he had been forced sometimes to do. There had been no appeals to life, all that was asked of him was to be his own static essence, the deader the better: Vokt had been the guarantor of his peace. And now the defection of Vokt was the omen of the sinking ship, the disappearance of the rat.

The terms of this desertion, however, resembled in their indistinctness and taciturnity the terms of their companionship. Otto and Ernst had never arrived at terms of friendship. It had been only an epic acquaintanceship, and Kreisler had taken him about as a parasite that he pretended not to notice. There was no question, therefore, of a reproach at desertion. Ernst merely hopped off on to somebody else. At this Kreisler was more exasperated than at the defection of a friend, who could be fixed down and from whom at last an explanation must come. An unfair advantage had been taken of his hospitable nature: no man had a right to accompany you in that distant and paradoxical fashion, get all he could, make himself ideally useful, unless it were for life.

Soltyk's success he observed with an affectation of distant mockery. Vokt's loves were all husks, of illogical completeness. Off with the old and on with the new it was with him. Soltyk's turn would come.

A man appeared one day in the Berne who had known Kreisler in Munich. The story of Kreisler's marrying his fiancée to his father thereupon became known: other complications were alleged in which Otto's paternity played a part. The dot* of the bride was another obscure matter.

These backgrounds were revealed at a time when he had already become an aloof figure at the Café. He looked the sort of man, the party agreed, who would splice his sweetheart with his papa, or reinforce his papa's affairs with a dot he did not wish to pay for at last with his own person. The Berne was also informed that Kreisler had to keep seventeen children in Munich alone; that he only had to look at a woman for her to become pregnant. It was when the head of the column, the eldest

of the seventeen, emerged into boyhood requiring instruction that
Kreisler left for Rome. Since then a small society had been founded in
Bavaria to care for Kreisler's offspring throughout Germany.

The picture of Otto as universal papa was the last straw, this mis-
directed and disordered animal capacity made him into a vast Magog
of Carnival,* an antediluvian puppet of fecundity for his compatriots.
When he appeared that night everybody turned towards his historic
figure with cries of welcome. But he took a seat in the passage-way
leading to the Bureau de Tabac. As their laughter struck him through
his paper, he was unstrung enough to respond with visible annoyance.
He frowned and puckered up his spectacled eyes, and two flushed
lines descended from his brows to his jaw. On their way out one or
two of his compatriots greeted him.

'Sacré Otto vas!* Why so unsociable? You cut us. You are unkind!'

'Hush! He has much to think about. You don't understand what
the cares of a—.'

'Come, old Otto, a drink! No? Why not? No! All right.'

He shook them off with a mixture of affected anger and authentic
spitting oaths of vexed disgust. He avoided their eyes, and spat blas-
pheming at his beer. For some days he gave the Berne a wide berth.

————

Kreisler then recovered.

At first nothing much happened. He had just gone back again into
the midst of his machinery like a bone slipped into its place, with a
soft click. He became rather more firm with his creditors: he changed
his rooms (moving to the Boulevard Kreutzberg), passed an occasional evening with the Germans at the Berne and started a portrait
of Suzanne, who had been sitting at the Academy.*

'How is Herr Vokt? Is he out of Paris?' Fräulein Liepmann asked
him when they met. 'Come round and see us.'

People's actual or possible proceedings formed in very hard and
fast mould in Kreisler's mind, seen not with the flexible breadth of
the realistic intelligence but through conventions of his suspicious
irony. This solicitude as to Vokt he contrasted with their probable
indifference as regards his impoverished shabby and impolite self.

But he went round, his reception being insipid. He had shown no
signs of animation or interest in them: both he and the ladies were

rather doubtful as to why he came at all: no pleasure resulted on either side from these visits, yet they doggedly continued. A distinct and steady fall in the temperature could be observed: he sneered, as though the aimlessness of his visits were an insult that had at last been taken up. They would have been for ever discontinued except for a sudden necessity to reopen that channel of bourgeois intercourse.

CHAPTER 5

On the first morning of his letter being overdue, a convenient manner of counting, Otto rose late from a maze of shallow and sluggishly protracted dreams, and was soon dressed, wanting to get out of his room. As the clock struck one he slammed his door and descended the stairs alertly. The concierge, upon the threshold of her 'loge,' peered up at him.

'Good morning Madame Leclerc, it's a fine day' said Kreisler, in his heavy french, his direct and chilly gaze incongruously brightened with a vivid smile.

'Monsieur has got up late this morning' replied the concierge, with very faint amiability.

'Yes, I have lost all sense of time. J'ai perdu le temps! Ha! Ha!' He grinned mysteriously. The watch had gone the way of the dress clothes some days already.

'J'ai perdu' he gulped with mirth 'mon temps!'*

She followed him slowly along the passage, become extremely grave.

'Qu'est-ce qu'il raconte? Il perd son temps? En effet!' She chucked her head up and cocked her eye. 'Quel original! quel genre!'* With a look of perplexed distrust she watched him down the street. His german good humour and sudden expansiveness was always a portentous thing to Madame Leclerc. Kreisler, still beneath the eye of the concierge, with his rhythmic martial tread approached the restaurant. A few steps from the threshold he slowed down, dragging his long german boots, which acted as brakes.

The Restaurant Vallet, like many of its neighbours, had been originally a clean tranquil little creamery, consisting of a small shop a few feet either way. Then one after another its customers had lost their reserve: they had asked, in addition to their daily glass of milk, for côtes de pré salé* and similar massive nourishment, which the decent little business at first supplied with timid protest. But perpetual scenes of unbridled voracity, semesters of compliance with the most brutal appetites of man, gradually brought about a change in its character; it became frankly a place where the most full-blooded palate might be satisfied. As trade grew the small business had burrowed backwards into the ramshackle house: bursting through walls and partitions, flinging down doors, it discovered many dingy rooms in the interior that it hurriedly packed with serried cohorts of eaters. It had driven out terrified families, had hemmed the apoplectic concierge in her 'loge,' it had broken out on to the court at the back in shed-like structures: and in the musty bowels of the house it had established a broiling luridly lighted roaring den, inhabited by a fierce band of slatternly savages. The chef's wife sat at a desk immediately fronting the entrance door: when a diner had finished, adding up the bill himself upon a printed slip of paper, he paid at the desk on his way out.

In the first room a tunnel-like and ill-lit recess furnished with a long table formed a cul-de-sac to the left: into this Kreisler passed. At the right-hand side the passage led to the inner rooms.

Kreisler's military morning suit,* slashed with thick seams, carefully cut hair, short behind, a little florid and bunched on the top, his german high-crowned bowler hat and plain cane, were in distinguished contrast with the Charivari of the art-fashion and uniform of The Brush* in those about him, chiefly students from the neighbouring art schools.

He took up the bill-of-fare, stencilled in violet ink, and addressed himself to the task of interpreting its characters. Someone took the seat in front of him. He looked up, put down the card. A young woman was now sitting there, and she seemed waiting, as though Kreisler might be expected, after a few moments' intermission, to take up the menu again and go on reading it.

'Have you done with? May I—?'

At the sound of her voice he moved a little forward, and in handing it to her, spoke in german.

'Ich danke sehr' she said, smiling with a german nod of racial recognition.

He ordered his soup. Usually this meal passed in impassible inspection of his neighbours when he was not reading the newspaper.

Staring at and through the figure in front of him, he spent several minutes. He seemed making up his mind.

'Monsieur est distrait aujourd'hui' Jeanne said, who was waiting to take his order.

Contrary to custom, he sought for some appetizing dish to change the routine. There were certain tracts of menu he never explored: his eye always guided him at once to the familiar place where the 'plat du jour' was to be found, and the alternations of eggs in snow or chocolate custard following the plat du jour. He now plunged his eye down the long line of unfamiliar dishes.

On Jeanne he fixed his eye with indecision too, as she stood politely smiling. ('My vis-à-vis is pretty!' he thought.)

'Lobster salad, mayonnaise and a pommes à l'huile Jeanne' he called out.

The beauties of menu to which he had just awoken led him to survey his neighbour. She must be connected with lobster salad something told him, yet how did not seem obvious at first. He was surprised that such a very presentable girl should be sitting there. Unusually attractive people wander dangerously about in life just like ordinary folk it is true. It was in the nature of good luck that an exceptional specimen of his race should arrive there in front of him: good luck in the abstract, of course, for it could have no especial significance for him. But this man could never leave good luck alone: all his past proved it up to the hilt.

He had already been examined by the attractive newcomer. Throwing a heavy far-away look into her eyes she let them wander over him. Afterwards she cast them down into her soup. As a pickpocket, after brisk work in a crowd, hurries home to examine his spoil, so she then assessed collectedly what her dreamy eyes had noted. Perhaps in her cloudy soup she beheld something of the storm and shock* that inhabited her neighbour, for her face assumed a rather grave expression.

Without interior preparation Kreisler found himself addressing her, a little abashed when he suddenly heard his voice and with an eerie sensation when it was answered.

'From your hesitation in choosing your lunch, gnädiges Fräulein, I suppose you have not been long in Paris?'

'No, I only arrived a week ago and can't speak much French yet.' She settled her elbows on the table for a moment.

'Allow me to give you some idea of what the menu of this restaurant is like.' This was like a lesson: he started ponderously. 'At the head of each list you will find simple dishes; elemental dishes, I might call them; this is the rough material from which the others are evolved. Each list is like a dervish performance:* as it progresses it gets wilder and more confused: in the last dish you can be sure that the potatoes will taste like parsnips, and that the pork will have become a schnitzel of veal.'

'*So!*' laughed the young woman, with good german guttural. 'I'm glad to say I have ordered dishes that head the list.'

Kreisler let fall a further heavy hint.

'Garlic is an enemy usually ambushed in gigot: that is its only quite certain haunt!'

'Good. I will avoid gigot.' His facetiousness met with her indulgence, she drawled a little in sympathy. Between language and feeding Kreisler sought to gain the young lady's confidence, adhering conventionally to the primitive order of creation.

She wore a heavy black burnous,* very voluminous and severe; a large ornamental bag was on the chair at her side, which one expected to contain herbs and trinkets, paraphernalia of the witch, rather than powder lip-stick and mere beauty secrets. Her hat was immense and sinuous; generally her appearance implied an egotistic code of advanced order, full of insolent strategies. Beside her other women in the restaurant appeared dragged down and drained of vitality by their clothes, thought Kreisler, although she wore so much more than they did. Her large square-shouldered and powerful body swam in the fluidities of hers like a duck.

When she laughed, this commotion was transmitted to her body as though sharp sonorous blows had been struck upon her mouth. Her lips were long hard bubbles risen in the blond heavy pool of her face, ready to break, pitifully and gaily: grown forward with ape-like intensity, they refused no emotion noisy egress if it got so far. Her eyes were large stubborn and reflective, brown coming out of blondness: her head was an elegant bone-white egg in a tobacco-coloured nest. Personality was given off by her with alarming intensity; it was an ostentation similar to diamonds and frocks mailed with sequins; Kreisler felt himself caught in the midst of a cascade, a hot cascade.

Recognizing herself, it would seem, to be some sort of travelling circus, equipped with tricks and wonders, beauty shows and monstrosities, quite used to being looked at, she possessed the geniality of public characters and gossiped easily with Kreisler as though he were a strange loafer nothing more, without any consciousness of condescension.

Just when most out of his depth, it was scarcely the moment for Kreisler to encounter all this: with the mellowness of sunset it melted and boomed in this small alcove infernally.

By the fact of sex this figure seems to offer Otto a traditional substantiality: he clutches at it eagerly as at something familiar and unmetamorphosed—and somewhat unmetamorphosable—by Fate. In the first flush of familiarity he revolves with certain skill in this new 'champs de manœuvres,' executing one or two of his stock displays. He seems to make some headway.

'My name is Anastasya' his neighbour informs him irrelevantly, as if she had stupidly forgotten, before, this little detail.

Whew! his poor ragged eyelashes flutter, a cloud of astonishment passes grotesquely over his face; like the clown of the piece, he looks as though he were about to rub his head, click his tongue and give his nearest man-neighbour an enthusiastic kick. 'Anastasya!' It will be 'Tasy' soon!

Outwardly he becomes more solemn than ever, like an unworthy merchant who finds himself in the presence of a phenomenal dupe, and would in some way conceal his exhilaration. But he calls her carefully, at regular intervals, 'Anastasya.'

'I suppose you've come here to work?' he asked.

'I don't want to work any more than is absolutely necessary. I am overworked as it is, by living merely.' He could well believe it; she must do some overtime! But *Life* had been mentioned; all was in the authentic german note, he felt more and more at home. 'If it were not for my excellent constitution—.'

This was evidently the moment to touch on some of the more ponderous of life's burdens. Her expression was perfectly even and non-committal.

'Ah, yes' he sighed heavily, one side of the menu rising gustily and relapsing. 'Life gives one work enough.'

She looked at him and reflected 'What work does "cet oiseau-là" perform?'

'Have you many friends here, Anastasya?'

'None.'

She laughed with ostentatious satisfaction at his funniness.

'I came here as a matter of fact to be alone. I want to see *only* fresh people: that is being alone, isn't it? People become too real. After a time we give them our illusions, then they are too real. But I have had all the gusto and illusion I had lent all round steadily handed back to me where I come from: the result is that I am amazingly rich—I am *lousily* rich!' She opened her eyes wide; Kreisler pricked up his ears and wondered if this were to be taken in another sense: he cast down his eyes respectfully. 'Lousily rich: I have the sort of feeling that I have enough to go all round. But perhaps I haven't!'

Kreisler lingered over her first observation:—'wanted to be alone.' The indirect compliment conveyed (and he felt, when it was said, that he was somewhere near the frontier, surely, of a german confidence) was rather mitigated by what followed: the 'having enough to go all round,' that was very universal and included him too easily in its sweep. That was a pity—but it was something to go on with to be included.

'Do you want to go all round?' he asked, with heavy plagiarism of her accent, and best *de profundis** mask of suety insistence, almost clammy with its intensity.

'I don't want to be mean.'

His pulses gave a heavy hop: his eyes struggled with hers; he was easily thrown. But she had the regulation feminine foible of charity, he reassured himself, by her answer.

The one great optimism of Otto Kreisler was a belief in the efficacity of women. You did not deliberately go there—at least he usually did not—unless you were in straits, no: but there they were all the time—vast dumping-ground for sorrow and affliction—a world-dimensioned Pawn-shop, in which you could deposit not your dress suit or garments, but yourself, temporarily, in exchange for the gold of the human heart and any other gold that happened to be knocking about. Their hope consisted, no doubt, in the reasonable uncertainty as to whether you would ever be able to take yourself out again. Kreisler had got in and out again almost as many times as his 'smokkin'* in another sphere.

Womenkind were Kreisler's Theatre, they were for him art and expression: the tragedies played there purged you periodically of the too violent accumulations of desperate life. There life's burden of laughter as well might be exploded. Woman was a confirmed

Schauspielerin, a play-actress it was his conviction, and to this he often gave trenchant utterance: but coming there for illusion he was willingly moved. Much might be remarked of a common nature between this honest german man and the drunken navvy on saturday night, coming home bellicosely towards his wife, blows raining gladly at the mere sight of her. Thus practically all the excitement and exertion he violently needs may be obtained, without any of the sinister chances a more real encounter must present. The Missis is his little bit of unreality, his ration of play. He can declaim, be outrageous to the top of his bent and can be maudlin too—all conducted almost as he pleases, with none of the shocks of the real and too tragic world.

In this manner 'woman' was the aesthetic element in Kreisler's life. Love, too, always meant *unhappy* love for him, with its misunderstandings and wistful separations. From these encounters he emerged solemnly and all the better for them however exacting in detail. He approached a love affair as the Korps-student* engages in a student's duel—no vital part exposed, but where something spiritually of about the importance of a nose might be lost—at least stoically certain that blood would be drawn.

A casual observer of the progress of Otto Kreisler's life might have said that the chief events, the crises, consisted of his love-affairs—such as that unfortunate one with his present step-mother. But, in the light of a careful analysis, this would have been an inversion of the truth. When the events of his life became too unwieldy or overwhelming, he converted them into love; as he might otherwise have done, had he possessed a specialized talent, into some art or other. He was a sculptor—a german sculptor of a mock-realistic and degenerate school—in the strange sweethearting of the 'free-life.'

The two or three women he had left in this way about the world—although perhaps those symbolic statues had grown rather characterless in Time's weather and perhaps lumpish—were monuments of his perplexities. After weeks of growing estrangement, he would sever all relations suddenly one day—usually on some indigestible epigram, that worried the poor girl for the rest of her days. Being no adept in the science of his heart, there remained a good deal of mystery for him about the appearance of 'Woman' in his life. What was she doing there, what did she want with him? She was always connected he felt with its important periods; superstitiously he would tell himself that his existence was in some way implicated with 'das Weib.'* She was, in any case, for him, a stormy petrel.* He would be killed by a woman, he sometimes thought. This superstition had flourished with him before he had yet found for it much raison d'être. A rather serious duel having been decided upon in his early student days, this reflection 'I am quite safe; it is not thus that I shall die,' had given him uncanny coolness. His opponent nearly got himself killed, because he, for his part, had no hard and fast theory about the sort of death in store for him. But Kreisler now felt that he might find release in some other manner.

This account, to be brought up to date, would have in any case to be modified on account of Vokt. No woman had come conspicuously to disturb him since Vokt's arrival. But between this state enjoyed by him in association with Ernst—the least intense flowering of male friendship possible, a distant and soothing companionship— and more serious states occurring, with Kreisler, invariably with woman, there was no possible foothold for him. Friendship usually dates from unformed years: but Love still remains in full swing long after Kreisler's age at that time, a sort of spurious and intense friendship. Kreisler had however regarded both as extinct. Still the intensities of "Love" it would have surprised him least of the two to see reappearing.

An uncomfortable thing happened now: he realized all the possibilities of this chance acquaintanceship, plainly and cinematographically and was seized with panic. He must make a good impression. From that moment he ran the risk of doing the reverse, so unaccustomed was he to act with calculation. There he was like an individual who had gone nonchalantly into the presence of a prince but who—just in the middle of the audience, when he should have been getting over his first embarrassment—is overcome with a tardy confusion, the imagination in some way giving a jump. This is the phenomenon of the imagination, repressed and as it were slighted, revenging itself.

Casting desperately about for means of handling the situation, he remembered she had spoken of getting a dog *to guide her.* What had she meant? However, he grasped at the dog: he could regain possession of himself in romantic stimulus of this figure. He would be her dog! Lie at her feet! He would fill with a merely animal warmth and vivacity the void that *must* exist in her spirit. His imagination, flattered, came in as ally: this, too, exempted him from the necessity of being victorious. All he asked was to be her dog! Only wished to impress her as a dog! Even if she did not feel much sympathy for him now, no matter: humbly he would follow her up, put himself at her disposition, not ask too much. It was a rôle difficult to refuse him.

The sense of security ensured him by the abjectness of this resolution caused him to regain his self-possession. Only it imposed the condition, naturally, of remaining a dog. Every time he felt his retiring humbleness giving place to another sensation, he experienced qualms afresh.

'Do you intend studying here Fräulein?' he asked, with a new deference in his tone—hardly a canine whine, but the deep servient bass of the faithful St. Bernard. She seemed to have noticed this something that was novel already, and Kreisler on all fours evidently astonished her.

'A year or two ago I escaped from a bourgeois household in an original manner. Shall I tell you about that Otto?'

Confidence for confidence, he had told Anastasya that he was Otto.

'Please!' he said, with reverent eagerness.

'Well, the bourgeois household was that of my father and mother, I got out of it in this way. I made myself such a nuisance to my family that they had to get rid of me.' Otto flung himself back in his chair with dramatic incredulity. 'It was quite simple. I began scribbling and scratching all over the place—on blotting-pads, the margins of newspapers, upon my father's correspondence, the wallpaper. I inundated my home with troublesome images—it was like vermin; my multitude of little figures swarmed everywhere! They simply *had* to get rid of me. I said nothing—I pretended that I was possessed! That's the way to treat them—when you have to deal with the bourgeois.'

Kreisler looked at her dully, smiling solemnly and rolling his head up and down, with something in fact of the misplaced and unaccountable pathos and protest of dogs (although still with a slavish wagging of the tail) at some pleasantry of the master. Her expansiveness, as it happened, did embarrass him very much at this point: he was divided between his inclination to respond to it and mature their acquaintance out of hand, where everything appeared so promising, and his determination to be merely a dog. Her familiarity, if adopted in turn by him, might not be the right thing; yet, as it was, he must appear to be holding back, he must seem 'reserved' in his mere humility. He was a very perplexed dog for some time.

Smiling up at her with appealing pathos at intervals, he remained dumb: she wondered if he had indigestion or what. He undertook several desperate dog-like sorties: but she saw he was clearly in difficulties. As her lunch was finished, she called the waitress. Her bill was made out, Kreisler scowling at her all the while. Her attitude, suggesting 'Yes, you *are* funny, you know you are, I'd better go, then you'll be better' was responded to by him with the same offended dignity as the drunken man displays when his unsteadiness is remarked. Sulkily he repudiated the suggestion that there was anything amiss: then he grew angry with her. His nervousness was all her doing. All was lost: he was very near some violence. But when she stood up he was so impressed that he sat gaping after her. He remained cramped in his place until she had left the restaurant.

He moved in his chair stiffly; his limbs ached as though he had been sitting for his portrait. The analogy struck him: sitting for his portrait—that was what had been happening very likely. These people dining near him as though they had suddenly appeared out of the ground—it was embarrassing to find himself alone with them: he had not noticed that they were there all round him, overhearing and looking on. Anastasya—Otto!—it was as though he had been talking to himself and had just become aware of the fact: a tide of magnetism had flowed away, leaving him bare and stranded.

Recovering his self-possession, Kreisler at once put a stop to this empty mental racket. Only a few minutes had passed since Anastasya's departure: seizing hat and stick he hurried to the desk. Once outside he gave his glasses a new angle, started up and down the boulevard in all directions. The tall figure he was pursuing was not there: he started off, partly at a run, in the likeliest direction. At the Berne corner, where several new vistas opened, there she was some distance down the Boulevard Vitelotte: she stood beneath the trees festooning the side-walk, attending the passage of an oncoming tram to cross. Having seen so much, should he not go back? There was nothing else to be done: to catch her up and force himself on her could have only one result, he thought. He might, perhaps, follow a little way: that already he was doing at a sluggish march-step.

For some hundred yards they advanced, she a good distance ahead on the opposite pavement. Walking for a moment with his eyes on the ground, when he looked up he caught her head pivoting slowly round. She had seen him no doubt. He realized what was happening then. 'Here I am following Anastasya as though we were strangers: so I am putting the final touch to what I began in the restaurant: by following her in the street as though we had never spoken I am making a stranger of a person who has just been talking to me in a most friendly manner.' He pulled up and frowned. Either he must catch her up at once or vanish. He headed up a side street and circled round to his starting-point brooding for a few moments on the sleepy pavement encompassing the Berne.

CHAPTER 6

ANASTASYA towered bleakly in Kreisler's mind henceforth as an obstacle in his path, a sort of embodiment of optimism, totally unsought, but since she had been put there she must be dealt with. By all rights and according to the rules of the national temperament he should have committed suicide some weeks earlier: now so much a machine with the momentum of all this old blood and iron*that was Otto Kreisler he must go on: but lo he had been held up by an obstruction.

Probably his nature would have sought to fill up the wide shallow gap left by Ernst and earlier ties either by another Ernst or more likely a variety of matter: it would have been a temporary stopping only. Now a gold crown, regal person, had fallen upon the hollow.

His little dog simile was veritably carried out in his scourings of the neighbourhood, in hope of crossing his lost mistress. But these 'courses' gave no result: benignant apparition, his roughness had scared it away, and off the earth, for ever. He entered, even infested, all painting schools of the Quarter: rapidly he would give chase to distant equivocal figures in gardens and streets. Each rendered up its little quota of malignant hope, then presented him with a face of monotonous strangeness.

It was Saturday when Kreisler was found preparing to take his valise to the Mont-de-Piété. On the preceding evening he had paid one of his unaccountable calls on Fräulein Liepmann, the first for some time. He had a good reason for once. Her salon was the only place of comparatively public assembly in the Quarter he had not visited. Entering with his usual slight air of mystification he bent to kiss Fräulein Liepmann's hand in a vaguely significant fashion. He prolonged his ceremonious kiss to emphasize the significance of this particular call.

The blank indifference attending these calls on both sides was thus relieved: a vague curiosity was woken on one side, a little playful satisfaction on the other. Even this might have ripened into a sort of understanding. He did not follow up his advantage: after a half-hour of musing upon the margin of a stream of conversation, and then music, suddenly he recognized something, a flotsam bobbing past. It had bobbed past before several times: but gradually he became aware of it. A dance at the Bonnington Club,* which was to take place the following evening, it was that that finally attracted his attention. Why was this familiar?—Anastasya!—She had spoken of it: that was all he could remember.

Would Anastasya be present at the dance at the Bonnington Club—had she said she would be present? That he could not remember. At once, and as though he had come there to do so, he commenced fishing delicately in this same stream of tepid chatter for an invitation to the function. Fräulein Liepmann, the fish he particularly angled for, was backward: they did not seem to want him very much at the dance. Nevertheless, after the exertion of many powers seldom put forth in that salon, he secured the form, not the spirit, of an invitation.

Kreisler saw, in his alarmed fancy, Anastasya becoming fused in this female group-soul: the energy and resource of the devil in person would be required to extricate her. She must be beaten back from this slough for the moment he needed.

Was it too late to intercept her? He felt he might accomplish it. The eyes of these ladies, so far dull with indifference, would open: he would stand forth as a being with a novel mysterious function where they were concerned. Vokt's absence from the Liepmann reunions was due to that traitor's not wishing to meet him: they must have observed that. Now the enigmatical and silent doggedness of his visits would seem explained. Would he not appear like some unwieldy deliberate parasite got on to their indivisible body? The invitation extracted, he made haste to go: if he stayed much longer, it might be overlaid with all sorts of offensive and effacing matter, and be hardly fit for use.

A defiant and jeering look upon his departing face, he withdrew with an 'until to-morrow.'

It was at this point that the *smokkin* came into prominence.

CHAPTER 7

IMPOSSIBLE my poor old son! Five francs. Not a cent more! That's the outside!'

Suzanne stood at attention before him in the hall of the Mont-de-Piété: if before she had been inexorable she was now doubly so beneath the eyes of the authentic officials. The sight of these salaried usurers of the State combined with her half-official status of go-between and interpreter, urged her to an ape-like self-importance. With flushed and angry face, raised eyebrows, shocked at any further questioning of the verdict, she repeated:

'Five francs; it's the most.'

'No that's no good, give me the portmanteau' he exclaimed.

She gave it him in silence, eyebrows still raised, eyes fixed, staring with intelligent disapproval right in front of her. She did not look at her eminent compatriots behind the large counter: but her sagacious stare, lost in space, was meant to meet and fraternize with probable similar stares of theirs, lost in the same intelligent electrical void.

Her face fixed in distended, rubicund, discontentedly resigned mask, she walked on beside him, the turkey-like backward-forward motion of the fat neck marking her ruffled state. Kreisler sat down on a bench of the Boulevard Vitelotte, she beside him.

'Dis! Otto! couldn't you have borrowed the rest?' she said at last.

Kreisler was tired. He got up.

'No of course I couldn't. I hate people who lend money as I hate pawnbrokers.'

Suzanne listened, with protesting grin. Her head nodded energetically.

'Eh bien! si tout le monde pensait comme toi—!'*

He pushed his moustache up and frowned pathetically.

'Où est Monsieur Vokt?' she asked.

'Vokt? I don't know. He has no money.'

'Comment! Il n'a pas d'argent? C'est pas vrai! Tu ne le vois pus?'*

'Good-bye.' Kreisler left Suzanne seated, staring after him.

The portmanteau dragged forward at his side, he strode past a distant figure. Suzanne saw him turn round and examine the stranger's face. Then she lost sight of them round a corner of the Boulevard.

'Quel type!' she exclaimed to herself, nearly as the concierge had done.

In a little room situated behind the Rue de la Gaiété,* Suzanne pulled open one of two drawers in her washstand, which contained a little bread, coffee, potatoes, and a piece of cold cod. She spread out a sheet of the *Petit Parisien** beside the basin. Having peeled the potatoes and put them on the gas, she took off those outdoor things that just enabled her to impart a turkey-like movement to her person. Then, dumpy, in a salmon-check petticoat, her calves bowed backwards and her stomach thrust out, she stood moodily at the window. In the Midi* at present, a substantial traveller in pharmaceutical goods, who had enjoyed her earliest transports in the days when she worked at Arras,* sent her a few francs at irregular intervals.

This rueful spot, struck in image of this elementary dross of humanity, was Kreisler's occasional haunt. Cell of the unwieldy tragic brain of the city, alongside a million other similar cells, representing the overwhelming uniform force of brooding in that brain, it attracted him like a desert or ocean.

He would listen solemnly like a great judge to Suzanne's perpetual complaints, sitting upon the edge of her bed, hat on head. She was so humble, with such pretensions: her imagination was arrogant and constantly querulous. The form her recriminations took was always that of lies; needless dismal falsehoods. She could not grumble without inventing and she never ceased to grumble. This, then, was one of Kreisler's dwellings. He lived at large: some of his rooms, such as this, the Café Berne and Juan Soler's School of Art, he shared with others. On very troubled days his body, like the finger of a weather-glass, would move erratically. When found in Suzanne's room it might be taken as an indication of an unsettled state. A tendency to remain at home, on the contrary, denoted mostly a state of equilibrium.

CHAPTER 8

THE portmanteau fell under the bed; his body crushed into the red balloon of down. Kreisler never sat upon his bed except when about to get into it: for another man it would have replaced the absent arm-chair, but in those moments of depression in which he resorted to it he always immediately sank into a still deeper melancholy, except of course at night, when he seldom failed to sleep. Head between hands emerging from the blood-red billow, he now stared at the floor. Four hours! Five hours! He must raise that paltry sum. He could not attend the party if he did not raise that paltry sum. That paltry sum! He frowned in his hands. But how could, the devil take it, the necessary be come by—in the time, in the time?

'Small as it is, I shan't get it' he thought and began repeating this stupidly and stuck at the word 'shan't.' Brain and mouth in a sluggish tangle, he stuttered thickly in his mind. He sprang up a blustering dishevelled mass, but the slovenly hopeless quality of the bed clung to him. This was a frivolous demonstration. He wandered to the window in a sulky apathy, his nose flattened against the pane, conscious of his compressed putty-grey mask, he let his gaze stream out into space. Ah, the Mensch, the Mensch! What was that, the Mensch?*

The sudden quiet and idleness of his personality was an awakening after the little nightmare of Suzanne. But it was not a refreshing one at all.

That portmanteau was a disillusion: it had always received certain consideration, as being, next the dress suit, the most dependable article among those beneath his sway—to come to his aid if their common existence were threatened. With disgust he had cast it beneath the bed, and now observing its strap, he reflected that he and all his goods were rubbish for the gutters.

He sauntered from the window to the bed and back. Whenever he liked, in a sense, he could open the door and go out; but still, *until* then (and *when* would he like?) he was a poor prisoner. Outside the Mensch took some strength and importance from others: but truly, in here, he could be said to touch bottom and to realize what the Kreisler-self was, with four walls round it.

The thought of once more going over to the window and gazing down upon the street beneath made him draw back his chair: he sat midway in the room, looking steadily out at the depressing fleece of the stationary clouds, dusty city clouds a little yellow in the joints.

Comrades at the painting school, nodding acquaintances, even waiters and waitresses, were once more run through: but between

them this unworthy crowd did not muster, even from the most
optimistic angle, a solitary franc.

Perhaps Anastasya had left Paris? At regular intervals he thought
of that: this solution had only made his activity during the last few
days more pointless and mechanical, it converted it into the pursuit
of a shadow.

A quarter of an hour had passed: through a series of difficult
clockwork-like actions, he had got once more to Vallet's to have
lunch. With disgust he took what had been latterly his usual seat,
at the table in the recess; it was the one place, he was sure, in which
Anastasya would never be discovered again, wherever else she might
be encountered.

Lunch passed in a dull munching. Got to the coffee, he caught
sight of Lowndes.

'Hi! Master Lowndes!' he called out—always assuming great bluff-
ness and brutality, as he called it, with english people. 'How do you
do sir!'

The moment his eye had fallen upon Master Lowndes, the probable national opulence of this acquaintance had occurred to him as
a tantalizing fact. All the wealth of the Indies festered in the pockets of this Englishman. No gross decision could be come to in that
moment. Lowndes was called to be kept there a little bit, while he
turned things over in his mind and settled the moment and mode of
the *Angriff*. Their acquaintance, such as it was, throve on national
antithesis. There was not much in that: but you never knew. He had
never tapped an Englishman. Ah! A good start!

Lowndes had finished his own lunch, and was just going off. At
the sight of the German he grinned: he had almost forgotten his idea
in coming to the Restaurant, that of seeing just this acquaintance.
Swaying from side to side on his two superlatively elastic calves, he
sat down opposite the good Otto, who leered back, blinking.

Lowndes spoke german fairly well, so they used that, after a little
flourish of english.

'Well, what have you been doing? Working?'

'No' replied Kreisler truthfully. Then he added: 'I'm giving up
painting and becoming a business man. My father has offered me a
position!'

Lowndes smiled correctly, not suspecting that this statement had
any sentimental weight beyond what it purported to tell.

'Have you seen Douglas?' This was a friend, through whom they had known each other in Italy.

Why should this fellow lend him thirty francs? Why should he not? Kreisler's new type of touchiness began to operate. The grin he was looking at would not be there were this person conscious of Otto's designs. Why should it? But oh that offensive prosperity of the English, the smugness of their middleclassishness, the wonderbearing *Schweinerei* of their shopkeepingness! *Pfui!*

Kreisler pictured the change that would come over this face when he popped the question. Anger and humiliation at the imagined expression overcame him. The man was an enemy: had they been in a quiet place he would have knocked him on the head and taken his money.

The complacent health and humoristic phlegm with which this kind grinned and perambulated through life charged Kreisler with the contempt natural to his more stiff education. He saw behind Lowndes the long line of all the Englishmen he had ever known. 'Useless swine!' he thought. 'So cheerful over his average middlingness and mean as a peasant I bet!'

'Oh I was asked for my opinion on a certain matter this morning: someone asked what I thought of german women—!!'

'What reply did you make Mr. Lowndes?'

'I didn't know what to say. I was really stumped. I suggested that my friend should come along and get your opinion.'

'My opinion as an *expert*—do I understand you? My fees as an expert are fairly considerable. I charge thirty francs a consultation!'

'I'm sure he'd have paid that' Lowndes laughed with innocence. Kreisler surveyed him unsympathetically.

'What, then, is your opinion of our excellent females?' he asked.

'Oh I have no opinion. I admire your ladies, especially the pure Prussians—.'

Kreisler was thinking—If I borrow it there must be some time mentioned for paying back—next week say, next week. Where? More likely to lend if he knew where. He must have my address.

'Come and see me—some time.' Kreisler blinked. 'Eighty-eight Boulevard Kreutzberg, fourth floor. It's beside the Restaurant, just here. You see? Up there.'

'I will. I looked you up at your old address a month or so ago. Where was that? They said they didn't know where you'd gone.'

Kreisler stared at him very fixedly. The old address reminded him of several little debts. On that account he had not told the concierge where he was going. The concierge would complain of her old tenant. Even Lowndes might have been shown derelict tradesmen's bills. Not much encouragement for his proposed victim! Na!

Lowndes was writing on a piece of paper.

'There's my address, Rue des Quatre Années.'

Kreisler inspected it fussily and said over—'cinq, rue des Quatre Années. Lowndes—.' He hesitated and then repeated the name.

'R. W.—Robert Wooton. Here, I'll write it down for you.'

'Are you in a hurry? Come and have a drink at the Berne' suggested Kreisler. He made up his bill hurriedly.

On the way Lowndes continued a discourse.

'A novelist I knew told me he changed the names of the characters in a book several times in the course of writing it. It freshens them up, according to him; he said that the majority of people were killed by their names.'

'Killed, yes.' Kreisler nodded.

'I think a name is a man's soul.'

'Which? I don't understand you.'

Kreisler forged ahead, rhythmically and sullenly.

'If we had numbers, for instance, instead of names, who would take the number thirteen?'

'I' said Kreisler.

'Would you?'

Every minute Kreisler delayed popping the question increased the difficulty because his energy was giving out. Everything depended upon the first shot. It was hit or miss. Your voice had to be so modulated—but he yawned nervously. They were now sitting on the terrace at the Berne. An immense personal neurasthenia had grown up round this simple habit. Borrowing was no longer what it had been! Why Herrgott could he not *take*! Why petition? He knew that if Lowndes refused he would break out, there would be a scene—he nearly did so as it was.—With disgust and fatigue he lay back in his chair, paying no attention to what Master Bob Wooton was saying. His mind was made up: he would not proceed with his designs on this dirty pocket. He became rough and monosyllabic. He wished to purify himself in rudeness, and wash out the traces of his earlier civility.

Lowndes had been looking at a newspaper. He put it down and said he must go back to 'work': his 'morning' had of course been interrupted by Tarr.

Kreisler as he looked doggedly up still saw the expression on the Englishman's face that he had prefigured as he had prepared to pop the question. *Pfui!* he with difficulty curbed the desire to spit in it. The nearness they had been to this demand must have affected, he thought, even his thickhided *Tor* of a companion. He *had* asked and been refused to all intents and purposes. He got up, left Lowndes standing there, and went into the lavatory of the Café. There he spat and spat and spat. Afterwards he had a hand-wash, and brushed his prickly scalp with vigour. That was good, that was good.

————

He returned to the Café table: there was no sign of the Englishman. He had gone off bad luck to him! As well for him! Now he could finish his drink in peace, deciding what the next move should be.

Various pursuits suggested themselves. Might he not go and offer himself as model at some big private studios near the Observatoire?* A week's money might be advanced him. He would dress as a woman and waylay somebody or other on the lonely Boulevards in the early hours: it was often done. He would crouch down and have a big hat. He might steal some money anyway. Vokt was the last: he came just after murder. He would go to Ernst Vokt—Ernst with his little obstinate resolve in the obscurity of his mind no longer to be Kreisler's acquaintance. The perfectly exasperating thing that this obstinacy was in that weak character, something that was out of place to the nth degree! In people of weak character—what an offence! They have no right to resoluteness, does not tenacity make them look more weak and mean than the strong can bear? The submissive Vokt had broken away, somewhere he was posing as a stranger. This proceeding was indecent——*pfui!* And again *pfui!*

The massive wrinkled brow of this 'thinking' Mensch exhibited the big-dog pathos of his heavily-thinking german kind, as he sat and experienced this classic disgust, of a spirit against another with whom he has mingled, but which other suddenly covers and decks itself, wishing to regain its strangeness. It was as a protest against this strangeness that he uttered his customary *pfui!* A strange being suddenly baring itself provokes our *pfuis!* and the opposite operation has the same effect. Then the imagination wakes and the eye sees best: it is the classical situation when friendship cools and the friend becomes a stranger. His irritated eye fixed upon this transformation, Kreisler watched, through fancy's telescope, the distant and ill-omened haste of the departing rat: when suddenly he no longer, so it seemed, had need of his far-glass, for the naked eye struck, from where he sat beneath the Café awning, the familiar back of the object of his thoughts. There was the Vokt-back—surely it must be his!—disappearing round a corner, as though trying to avoid a meeting.

The blood rushed into his head with force, his body started, to spring forward in pursuit of this unsociable shape. Rushing words of insult were spawned on his struggling silent lips, he fidgeted in a sort of static fit, gazing blankly at the spot where he had seen the figure. That it was no longer there galled him beyond measure: it was as though he had considered Ernst as in duty bound to remain at the corner, immobile, his back towards him, a visible target and food for his anger. He made a sign to the waiter, to indicate that his drink would go into his 'tick' account,* the waiter nodding shortly without moving: he then at full steam headed for Vokt's house—the direction also that the back had taken—resolved to force something out of him.

Kreisler, letting instinct guide his steps, took the wrong turning, following in fact his customary morning track. Suddenly he found himself some distance beyond Vokt's street, near Juan Soler's Academy. He gazed down it towards the Atelier,* then took off his glasses and began carefully wiping them. While doing this he heard words of greeting and found Vokt at his elbow.

'Hallo! You look rather hot. You nearly knocked me over a minute ago in your haste' Ernst was saying.

Kreisler jumped—as the bravest might, if, having stoutly confronted an apparition, it suddenly became a man of flesh and blood. Had his glasses been firmly planted on his nose things might have gone differently. He frowned vacantly at his disaffected chum and went on rubbing them.

Vokt saw something was wrong. To 'have it out' and have done with it would perhaps be best, but he was sluggish.

'It's dreadfully hot!' he said uneasily, looking round as though examining the heat. He stepped up on to the pavement out of the way of a horse-meat chariot.* The large panelled conveyance, full of outlandish red carcasses of large draught horses, went rushing down the street, bearing with it an area of twenty yards of deafness. This explosion of sound had a pacifying effect upon Kreisler; it made him smile for some reason or other: and Vokt went on:

'I don't know whether I told you about my show.'

'What show?' asked Kreisler rudely.

'In Berlin you know. It has not gone badly. Our compatriots improve—. I believe we're an artistic nation—what do you think? No? I've got a commission to paint the Baroness Wort-Schrenck. What have you been doing lately?' There was a refractory pause. 'I've intended coming round to see you: but I've been sticking at home working. Have you been round at the Berne—?'

He spoke rapidly and confidentially, as though they had been two breathless stockbrokers meeting in the street at the busiest period of the day compressing into a few minutes, between two handshakes, a lot of domestic news. He sought to combine conviction that he was very anxious to tell Kreisler all about himself, and (by his hurried air) paralysis of the other's desire to have an explanation.

'I am glad you are going to paint the Baroness Wort-Schrenck. I congratulate you Mr. Vokt! I am in a hurry. Good day.'

Kreisler turned and walked towards the Juan Soler Academy. For no reason, except that it was impossible, he could not get money from Vokt: it was as though that money would not be real money at all. Supposing he got some money from him; the first place he tried to pass it, the man would say: 'This is not money.'—As for taking him to task, his red correct face made it quite out of the question; it had suddenly become a lesson and exercise that it would be ridiculous to repeat. He was not a schoolboy.

Vokt walked away ruffled: he was mortified now because, through apprehension of a scene, he had been so friendly. The old Otto had scored: he, Vokt, had humiliated himself needlessly, for it was evident Kreisler's manner had been misinterpreted by him, there had after all been no danger, since he had gone off so quickly of his own accord.

Kreisler had not intended going to Soler's that day; yet there he was, presumably got there now to avoid Ernst Vokt. *Pfui*—noch einmal! with astonishment he saw himself starting up from the Berne a quarter of an hour before, steaming away in pursuit of that skulking truant—impetus of angry thought carrying him far beyond his destination; when lo and behold (oh irony of the *Schicksal!*) Vokt comes along pat and runs him into the painting school! He compared himself

to one of those little nursery locomotives that go straight ahead without stopping; that anyone can take up and send puffing away in the
opposite direction. Humouring this fancy he entered the studio with
the gaze a man might wear who had fallen through a ceiling and
found himself in a strange apartment in the midst of a family circle.
The irresponsible, the resigned and listless air signified whimsical
expectancy. He was a thing, scarcely any longer a Mensch,—though
if given a good push he could show what he was made of! Some other
figure would now rise up no doubt and turn him streetwards again?
He waited.

He was confronted by a fellow statue. A member of the race
which has learnt to sleep standing up 'posed' upon the throne.
He had suddenly come amongst brothers: he was as torpid as the
Model was, as indifferent as these mechanical students. The clock
struck. With a glance at the Massier,* the Model slowly and rhythmically abandoned her rigid attitude, coming to life as living statues
do in ballets;* she reached stiffly for her chemise. The dozen other
figures, who had been slowly pulsing—advancing or retreating, suspended around her mustard red body—now with laboured movements dispersed, relapsing aimlessly here and there, chiefly against
walls.

He had been considering a fat hill of flesh, and especially a parting carried half way down the back of the skull. Why should not its
owner, and gardener, he had reflected, continue it the entire distance
down, dividing his head in half with a line of white scalp? This person
now turned upon him sudden, unsurprised, placid eyes. Had he *eyes*
as well as a parting, at the back of his head? He was on the point of
enquiring whether that parting should or should not be gone on with
till it reached the neck.

Three had struck. He left and returned to the Berne neighbourhood, by the same and most roundabout route, as though to efface in
some way his previous foolish journey.

Every three or four hours vague hope recurred of the delayed letter, like hunger recurring at the hour of meals. He went up to the loge
of his house and knocked.

'Il n'y a rien pour vous!'

Four hours remained: the german party was to meet at Fräulein
Liepmann's after dinner.

CHAPTER 9

OTTO'S compatriots at the Café were sober and thoughtful, with some discipline in their idleness: their monthly monies flowed and ebbed, it was to be supposed, small regular tides frothing monotonously in the form of beer and glasses of cheap sekt. This rather desolate place of chatter newspapers and airy speculative art-business had the charm of absence of gusto, of water-lilies, of the effete lotus.

Kreisler was purer german, of the true antiquated grain. He had experienced suddenly home-sickness, not for Germany, exactly, but for the romantic stiff ideals of the german student of his generation. It was a home-sickness for his early self: like the knack of riding a bicycle or anything learnt in youth, this character was easily resumed. Gradually he was discovering the foundations of his personality: many previous moods and phases of his nature were mounting to the surface, now into a conscious light.

Arrived in front of the Berne, he stood for fifteen minutes looking up and down the street, at the pavement, his watch, the passers-by. Then he chose the billiard-room door to avoid the principal one, whereby he usually entered. All the familiar ugliness of this essential establishment he hated with methodic deliberate hatred; taking things one by one as it were, persons and objects, he hated powerfully. The garçon's spasmodic running about was like a gnat's energy above stagnation. The garçon was his enemy.

Passing from the billiard-room to a gangway with several tables, his dull grey eye fell upon something it did not understand. How could it be expected to understand? It was an eye, and it stuck—it blinked—it trembled. It signalled: the gland shot a tear into it. It clouded. It was simple though: it was amazed and did not understand.

ANASTASYA.

Stolid surprise and some sort of bovine calculation was all that could be detected upon his face.

Set in the heart of this ennui, it arrested the mind like a brick wall some carter drowsed upon his waggon: stopping dead, Kreisler stupidly stared.

Anastasya was sitting there: she was seated beside Soltyk. Undoubtedly! Soltyk!

Kreisler seemed about to speak to them—they were at least under that impression: quite naturally he was about to do this, like a child surprised. As though in intense abstraction, he fixed his eyes on them: then he took a step towards them, possibly with the idea of sitting down at their side. But consciousness set in, with a tropic tide of rage, and carried him at a brisk pace towards the door, corresponding to the billiard-room door, on the other side of the establishment. Yet in the midst of this he instinctively raised his hat a little, his eyes fixed now upon his feet.

He was in a great hurry to get past this couple: and this could not be done without discovering two inches of the scalp for a moment: so as an impatient man in a crush, wishing to pass, pushes another aside, raising his hat at the same time to have the right to be rude, he passed saluting.

Same table on terrace as an hour before. But Kreisler seemed squatting on air, or upon one of those gyrating platforms in the Fêtes.*

The garçon, with a femininely pink, virile face, which, in a spirit of fun he kept constantly wooden and dour—except when, having taken the order, he winked or smiled—came up hastily.

'Was wünschen Sie?' he asked, wiping the table with a serviette. He had learned a few words of german. Supposing Kreisler rather a touchy man he always attempted to put him at his ease, as the running of bills was profitable. He had confidence in this client, and hoped the bill would assume considerable proportions.

Kreisler's thoughts dashed and stunned themselves against this wooden waiter. His mind stood stock-still for several minutes: the pink wooden face paralysed everything. As its owner thought the young gentleman was having a joke with him, it became still more humorously wooden. The more expressionless it became, the more paralysed grew Kreisler's intelligence. He stared at him more and more oddly, till the garçon was forced to give up.

As he had appeared to walk deliberately with hot intention to his seat, so he seemed gazing deliberately at the waiter and choosing his drink: then the dam gave way. He hated this familiar face; his thought smashed and buffeted it: such commercial modicum of astute good nature was too much! It was kindness that only equilibrium could ignore. The expression of his own face became distorted: the garçon fixed him with his eye and took a step back, with dog-like doubt, behind the next table—what was up with this strange Bosche* now? Oh là là!

Anastasya had smiled in a very encouraging way as Otto passed. But this had offended him extremely. Anastasya-Soltyk: Soltyk-Anastasya: that was a bad coupling! His sense of persecution seized him in a frenzy of suspicion. This had done it! Soltyk, who had got hold of Vokt, and was the something that had interfered between that borrowable quantity and himself, occupied in his life now a position not dissimilar to his stepmother. Vokt and his father, who had kept him suspended in idleness, and who now both were withdrawing or had withdrawn like diminishing jets of water, did not attract the full force of his indolent tragic anger. Behind Ernst and his parent stood Soltyk and his stepmother.

That lonely ego, in Otto's case so overworked, might at this point have said, if afforded that relief: 'Hell take that little beast Ernst! I come to Paris, I am ashamed to say, partly for him: but the little swine-dog* has given me the go-by, may his bones rot! I don't like that swine-dog Soltyk! He's a sneaking russian rascal!' It would not have said more frankly 'I've lost the access to Ernst's pocket. The pig-dog Soltyk is sitting there!'

Anastasya now provided him with an acceptable platform from which his vexation might spring at Soltyk. 'Das Weib' was there. All was in order for unbounded inflammation.

He wanted to bury his fear in her hot hair, that devilish siren—their hair was always hot, so were their lips: her lips must be kissed as he had never kissed any Weib's: he must tread her woman-body in a masterful rutting debauch, and of course subsequently spurn it having used it. But what would Soltyk be doing about it? He had met her alone, that was all right and not impossible within a world made by their solitary meeting: he had lived with her instinctively in this solitary world since then. It was quite changed at present. Soltyk had got into it. Soltyk, by implication, brought a host of other people, even if it did not mean that he was a definite rival there himself. What would he be saying to her now? Sneers and grins filled space, directed at himself—more than ten thousand men could have discharged. His ears grew hot at the massed offence. His stepmother-fiancée! he knew that story was current. But anything that would conceivably prejudice the beautiful stranger against him, he accepted as already retailed. There he sat, like a coward: he was enraged at their distant insulting equanimity.

A breath of violent excitement struck him, coming from within: he stirred dully beneath it. She was there, he had only put a thin partition between them. His heart beat slowly and ponderously. 'On hearing what the swine Soltyk has to say, she will remember my conduct in the restaurant and my appearance, she will make it all fit in. But it does fit in! What tricks I have played! Anything I did now would only be filling out the figure my ass-tricks have cut for her!'

He was as conscious of the interior, which he could not see from his place upon the street, as though, passing through, he had just found the walls, tables, chairs, painted bright scarlet. He felt he had left a wake of seething agitation in his passage of the Café. Passing the two people inside there had been the affair of a moment: it was not yet grasped; this experience apparently of the past was still going on: the senses' picture even was not yet complete. New facts, important details, were added every moment. He was still passing Anastasya and Soltyk. He sat on, trembling, at the door. There were other exits. She might be gone.—But he forgot about them, his turmoil suddenly drifting away from the exciting source.

He thought of the *frac*: a colossal relief announced itself and swept him into bliss. How he had pestered himself about the pawned suit! Fate had directed him there to the Café to save him the trouble of further racking of brains and expense of shoe-leather. Should he leave Paris? At that idea he grew mutinous. Its occurrence filled him with suspicions.

The fit was over; he was eyeing himself obliquely in the looking-glass behind his head.

He almost jumped away at two voices beside him, and the thrilling sound of the proverbial petticoat: it was as though someone had spoken with his own voice, it did not appear related to anything visible. He felt they were coming to speak to him—just as they had supposed that he was about to speak to them. The nerves on that side of his head twitched as though shrinking from a touch.

They were crossing the terrace to the street. His heart beat a slow march now. The image in the wear and tear of his recent conflicts had become somewhat used and inanimate. The Reality, in its lightning correction of this, dug into his mind. There once more the real figure had its separate and foreign life. He was disagreeably struck by a certain air of depression and cheerlessness in the two persons before him. This one thing that should have been pleasant, displeased him: he was angry as though she had been shamming melancholy.

They were not talking—the best proof of familiarity. A strange figure occurred to him; he felt he was a man with every organ—bone—tissue complete, but made of cheap perishable stuff, who could only live for a day and then die of use.

Now a reality under his nose, Anastasya had, in coming to life, drawn out all his energy, like a distinct being nourished by him: whereas the image, intact in his mind, had returned him more or less the vigour spent. Her listlessness seemed a complement of the weakness he now felt: energy was ebbing away from both.

He sent a bloodshot stare after them: then he got up and began walking after her. Soltyk, on hearing steps, turned round: but he made no remark, he took Anastasya's arm, they crossed the street and got into a passing tram. Kreisler went back to the Café.

It was like returning to some hall where there had been a banquet, to find empty chairs, empty bottles, dirt and disorder. The vacant seats around seemed to have been lately vacated. Then there was the sensation of being left high and dry—of the withdrawal of a fluid medium. The Café Berne was a solitary place. Everything began to thrust itself upon him—the people, insignificant incidents, as though this indifferent life of facts, in the vanishing of the life of the imagination, had now become important, being the only thing left. Common Life seemed rushing in and claiming him, to emphasize his defeat, and the new condition this inaugurated.

He went to Vallet's for dinner. During the whole day he had been in feverish hurry, constantly seeing time narrowing in upon him: now he had a sensation of intolerable leisure. The first glee at the absence of pressure had entirely passed.

The useless ennui of his life presented itself to him for the thousandth time, but now with a chilly clearness. It was a very obvious fact indeed, it had waited with great calm: now it said: 'As soon as you can give me your attention—well, what are you going to do with me?' Sooner or later he must marry and settle down with this stony fact and multiply its image: things had gone too far: the fact pointed that out and he did not demur.

And how about his father, what was that letter going to contain? Mr. Kreisler senior had got a certain amount of pleasure out of him: the little Otto had satisfied in him in turn the desire of possession (that objects such as your watch, your house, which could equally well belong to anybody, do not satisfy), of authority (that servants do not satisfy), of self-complacency (that self does not)—he had been to him, later, a kind of living cinematograph and *Reisebuch** combined; and, finally, he had inadvertently lured with his youth a handsome young woman into the paternal net. There was no further satisfaction that he now could ever be expected to procure to this satiated parent. Henceforth he must be a source only of irritation and expense.

Dinner completed and mind made up, he walked along the Boulevard. The dark made him adventurous: he peered into never visited Cafés as he passed. He noticed it was already eight. Supposing he should meet some of the women on the way to Fräulein Liepmann's? He made a movement as though to slink down a side street: next moment he was walking on obstinately in the direction of the Liepmann's house however. His weakness drew him on, back into the vortex:* anything at all was better than going back into that terrible colourless mood. His room, the Café, waited for him like executioners. For a time he had escaped from that world: wild horses would not drag him back, not yet. The night was young. Dressed as he was, extremely untidy, he would go to Fräulein Liepmann's flat.

Only humiliation, he knew, awaited him in that direction. If Anastasya were there (he would have it that she would be found wherever he least would care to see her) then anything might happen. But so much the better: he wanted her to be there! He asked nothing better: to suffer still more by her was his peculiar wish, up to the hilt, *physically*, as it were, under her eyes. That would be a relief from present torment. He must look in her eyes; he must excite in her the maximum of contempt and of dislike. He desired to be in her presence again, with the fullest consciousness that his mechanical idyll was vetoed by Fate. Not stoic enough to leave things as they were, he could not go away with this incomplete and, physically, uncertain picture behind him. It was as though a man had lost a prize, and then required of his judges a written stamped and sealed statement to that effect. He wished to shame her: if he did not directly insult her he would at least insult her by thrusting himself upon her. Then, at the height of her disgust, he would pretend again to make advances. He believed he would insult her. His programme, as he sketched it out, grew, at the last, obscene.

As to the rest of the party, a sour glee possessed him at thought of *their* sensations by the time he had done with them; already he saw their faces in fancy, when he should ring the flat bell and present

himself—old morning suit, collar none too clean, dusty boots, dishevelled head. His self-humiliation was wedded with the notion of retali-
ation. In his schooldays Kreisler had been the witness of a drama
affording a parallel to what he was now preparing. His memory hovered about the image of a bloodstained hand, furiously martyred. But
he could not recall to what the hand belonged. The scene he could
not reconstruct had taken place in his fourteenth year, and it had proceeded beneath the desk of his neighbour during an algebra lesson.
The boy next to him had jabbed his neighbour in the hand with a
penknife: the latter, pale with rage, had held his hand out in sinister invitation, hissing 'Do it again! Do it again!'—The boy next to
Kreisler had looked at the hand for a moment and complied. 'Do it
again!' came still fiercer. This boy had seemed to wish to see his hand
a mass of wounds and to delect himself with the awful feeling of his
own black passion.

Kreisler did not know how he should wipe out his score, but he
wanted it bigger, more crushing. The bitter fascination of suffering
drew him on, to substitute real wounds for imaginary. But Society at
the same time must be taught to suffer, he had paid for that.

Near Fräulein Liepmann's house he rubbed his shoulder against a
piece of whitewashed wall with a broad grin. He went rapidly up the
wide stairs leading to the entresol, considering a scheme for the com-
mencement of the evening. This seemed so happy that he felt further
resourcefulness in misconduct would not be wanting.

PART III

BOURGEOIS-BOHEMIANS

CHAPTER 1

KREISLER pressed the bell. A hoarse low Z-like blast, braying softly into the crowded room, announced him. Kreisler still stood safely outside the door.

There was a rush in the passage within; the hissing and spitting sounds inseparable from the speaking of the german tongue: someone was percussioning louder than the rest with a muscular german tongue, and squealing dully as well. They were square-shouldered flat-heeled Maenads,* disputing among themselves the indignity of door-opener. The most anxious to please gained the day: the door was pulled ajar: an arch voice said:

'Wer ist da?'

'Der Herr Kreisler, gnädiges Fräulein!'*

The roguish vivacious voice died away, however: the opening of the door showed in the dark vestibule Bertha Lunken with her rather precious movements imposed upon german robustness.

The social effect had been instantaneous. The disordered hair, dusty boots, the white patch on the jacket had been registered by the super-bourgeois eye that they had had the good luck at the outset to encounter.

'Who is it?' a voice cried from within.

'It's Herr Kreisler' Bertha answered with dramatic quietness. 'Come in Herr Kreisler; there are still one or two to come.' Bertha spoke in business-like accent, she bustled to close the door, to efface politely her sceptical reception of him by her handsome wondering eyes.

'Ah Herr Kreisler! I wonder where Fräulein Vasek is?' he heard someone saying.

He looked for a place to hang his hat. Fräulein Lunken preceded him into the room. Her expression was that of an embarrassed domestic foreseeing horror in his master's eye. Otto in his turn appeared. The chatter seemed to him to swerve a little bit upon his right hand: bowing to two or three people he knew near the door, sharply from the hips, he went over to Fräulein Liepmann and bending respectfully down, kissed her hand. Then with a naïve air, but conciliatory, began:

'A thousand pardons, Fräulein Liepmann, for presenting myself like this: Herr Vokt and I have been at Fontenay des Roses* all the afternoon: we made a stupid mistake about the time of the trains and I have only just got back—I hadn't time to change. I suppose it doesn't matter? It will be quite "intime," and bohemian, won't it? Herr Vokt had something to do: he's coming on later if he can manage it.'

With genuine infantile glee he delivered himself of his fairy-tale—he had hit upon it while waiting at the door. Seeing the weakness these ladies always displayed for his late friend and that he was almost sure not to turn up, he would use him to cover the self-inflicted patch from the whitewashed wall: but he would get other patches he promised himself (and find other lies to cover them up) till he could hardly move about for this plastering of small falsehoods.

His hostess had been looking at him with indecision.

'I am glad to hear Herr Vokt's coming: I haven't seen him for ages. You've plenty of time to change, you know, if you like: Herr Eckhart and several others haven't turned up yet. You live quite near don't you, Herr Kreisler?'

'Yes, third to the right and second to the left, and keep straight on!'

'So!'

'Yes. But I don't think I'll trouble about it. I shall be all right like this. I think I'll do don't you, Fräulein Liepmann?' He took a couple of steps and looked at himself complacently in a glass.

'You are the best judge of that.'

'Yes that is so of course isn't it, Fräulein? I have often thought that: how curious the same notion should occur to you! I thought I was alone in that belief. Society pretends—but it is all one!' Again Kreisler smiled and affecting to consider the question as settled, turned to a man standing near him, with whom he had worked at Juan Soler's. In doubt as to whether he intended to go and change or not (he was, perhaps, just talking to his friend a moment before going?) his slightly frowning hostess moved away.

The company was not socially brilliant but 'interesting.' On this occasion it was rather on its mettle, both men and women in their several ways, dressed and anointed, as scrupulously toiletted as if this were a provincial Court. An Englishwoman who was a great friend of Fräulein Liepmann's was one of the organizers of the Bonnington Club: through her they had been invited to go there, it was upon a correct institution that they awaited, evening-suited, the word of command to march.

Five minutes later Kreisler found Fräulein Liepmann in his neighbourhood again. She stood beside him at first without speaking. She had a pale fawn-coloured face, looking like the protagonist of a *crime passionel*. At every turn she multiplied her social responsibilities, yet her manner implied that the quite ordinary burdens of life were beyond her strength. The two rooms with folding doors, which formed her salon and where her guests were now gathered, had not been furnished casually or without design. The 'Concert' of Giorgione* did not hang there for nothing: the books lying about had been flung down by a careful hand. Fräulein Liepmann required a certain variety of admiration: but being very energetic she had a great contempt for other people, so she drew up, as it were, a list of her attributes, carefully and distinctly underlining each: with each new friend she went over again the elementary points, as a teacher would go over with each new pupil the first steps of accidence or geography—first showing him his locker, where the rulers were put and where, when he got them dirty, he could wash his hands. She took up her characteristic attitudes, one after the other, as a model might; that is, those simplest and easiest to grasp.

Her room dress and manner were a kind of chart to the way to admire Fräulein Liepmann. The different points in her *Geist* one was to gush about, the various scattered hints one was to let fall about her naturally rather tragic life-story, the particular way one was to regard her playing of the piano. The observant newcomer would feel that there was not a candlestick or antimacassar* in the room but had its lesson for him. To have two or three dozen people, her 'friends,' repeating things after her in this way did not give her very much satisfaction, she had not the sensation of its being very great; but she had many of the characteristics of the schoolmarm and she continued untiringly with her duties—namely teaching 'Liepmann' with the solemnity, resignation and half-weariness (with occasional explosions of anger) that a woman would teach 'twice two are four, twice three are six.' Her best friends were her best pupils of course. Even the rooms were furnished with somewhat the severity of the schoolroom: a large black piano—for demonstrations—corresponded more or less to the blackboard. It was in the piano that anybody would have had to look really for her *Geist*.

'Herr Spicker just tells me that dress is *de rigueur*. Miss Bennett says it doesn't matter. But it would be awkward if you couldn't get in.' She was continuing their late conversation. 'You see it's not so much an artists' club as a place where the english *Société* permanent in Paris, meet: it's a bore: you know how correct they are.'

'Yes I see; of course that makes a difference! But I asked, I happened to ask, an english friend of mine to-day—a founder of the club as it happens, a Master Lowndes' (this was a libel on Lowndes) 'he told me it didn't matter in the least, these were his very words. You take my word for it Fräulein Liepmann—it won't matter a bit—not a bit!' he reiterated a little boisterously, nodding his head sharply, his eyelids clapping to like metal shutters, rather than winking. Then, in a maundering tone, yawning a little and rubbing his glasses as though they had now idled off into gossip and confidences:

'I'd go and dress only I left my keys at Soler's: I shall have to sleep out to-night, I shan't be able to get my keys till the morning.' Suddenly in a new tone, the equivalent of a vulgar wink:

'Ah this life, Fräulein—this life, this life! Its accidents often separate one from one's Smokkin for days, sometimes months of Sundays—you know what I mean? One has no control over—well! Now my Smokkin bless its little silk lapels—it's a good one, I have always been accustomed to the very best—leads a very independent life: sometimes it's with me, sometimes not. It was a very expensive fashionable article. That has been its downfall.'

'Do you mean you haven't got a "frac"?'

'Oh how brutal—no certainly, not that heaven forbid! You misunderstand me.' He reflected a moment.

'I beg your pardon.'

'Not at all! Ah before I forget, Fräulein Liepmann! if you still want to know about that little matter—I wrote to my mother the other day as I said I would, and in her reply she tells me that Professor Heymann is still at Karlsruhe; he will probably take a class in the country this summer as usual, she had heard he would—to the Jura* I think. It is so lovely!—The remainder of the party!' he added beaming as the bell again rang.

He could not be prevented from accompanying these people to their informal dance. But with his remark about Vokt anyway he felt as safe as if he had a ticket or passe-partout in his pocket: he strutted up and down like a peacock for a few moments eyeing the assembly with disdain.

Kreisler was standing alone nearly in the middle of the room, his arms folded and staring at the door. He would use this ficti-tious authority and licence to its utmost limit. Something unusual in his presence besides his dress and the disorder even of that suggested itself to his fellow-guests, they supposed he had been drinking.

Rustlings and laughter in the hall persisted for some minutes. Social facts, abstracted in this manner, appeal to the mind with the strange-ness of masks, each sense, isolated, being like a mask upon another, and Otto speculated and dreamt, with military erectness. There was an explosion of excitement: Anastasya appeared. She came out of that social flutter astonishingly inapposite, like a mask come to life. The little fanfare of welcome continued. She was much more outrageous than Kreisler could ever hope to be, bespangled and accoutred like a bastard princess or aristocratic concubine of the household of Peter the Great,* jangling and rumbling like a savage raree show* through abashed capitals.

Her amusement often had been to disinter in herself the dust and decorations of some ancestress: she would float down the wind-ings of her Great Russian and Little Russian* blood, living in some imagined figure for a time as you might in towns met with upon a majestic river.

'We are new lives for our ancestors, not theirs a playground for us. We are the people who have the Reality.' Tarr lectured her later. To which she replied:

'But they had such prodigious lives! I don't like being anything out and out, life is so varied. I like wearing a dress with which I can enter into any milieu or circumstances: that is the only real self worth the name.'

Anastasya regarded her woman's beauty as a bright dress of a har-lot; she was only beautiful for that, so why humbug? Her splendid and bedizened state was assumed with shades of humility: even her tenderness and peculiar heart appeared beneath the common infec-tion and almost disgrace of that state.

Kreisler's sympathy, however, was not of an order to enter into these considerations. He had come there with the express object of doing her some indignity: all he saw accordingly was the fact of her being 'dressed up' and the warmth with which she returned the Liepmann's greeting. At this he frowned over at her with something like the severity of a stern pastor from his pulpit whose eye falls upon some face among his flock especially reprobate. His last meeting with her had caused the instant suicide of his dreams, from despair: now his original *béguin* was on all hands slowly giving place to hard puerile dislike: for there must be *activity* and its stimulus between him and her.

Going up to her, at her smile he took her hand and kissed it with as much devotion as any Quattrocento* lips could have displayed. 'So here we meet again' he said.

On finding himself speaking to her like this, and she apparently none the worse for anything that might have passed (he interpreted a certain hesitation—'my attire, my attire! Most natural! She'll get over that'—and smiled blandly), he felt for a moment that another nightmare was over: the *It's all right after all* feeling returned. The matter-of-fact reality favoured him: here he was talking to her, there was no obstacle really in the way at all of their becoming very friendly. He had been dreaming. But the Liepmann seemed hanging doubtfully upon their rear. There *was* something wrong. Obstacles accumulated ominously once he began reflecting.

His plan of outrage forgotten, he attempted to make the best of the situation.

'I quite forgot about the dance—I happened to be passing Fräulein Liepmann's a moment ago, I thought I would look in; I am wondering if I can go like this?' With a naïf haste he began repairing the breach.

'I feel quite out of it in this high-distinguished gathering! I expect, I hope, that our friends' preparations are pessimistic, I mean that the affair will not be so terribly correct as those suggest.'

'You mean their dressing up? For heaven's sake never wear dress clothes' she said with concern. 'It wouldn't suit you at all. I shouldn't like you so well in them.—You want me to like you I believe?'

Kreisler, at these sudden revolutions, the 'situation' all at once denying its hopelessness and protesting that it was quite an ordinary peaceful kind little 'situation' if one at all, had become anxious and nervous. For the moment he was certainly unmanned by this balmy atmosphere. And at once the 'too good to be true' sensation and despondency set in, in accustomed manner.

'Now I must just mark time—one two!' said he to himself: 'her attitude to me must be held in suspense until a better moment. I must leave her where she is just so: perhaps I'd better not keep her any longer.' He was making room for an imaginary Fräulein Liepmann or some other intruder, stepping aside, bringing his discourse to an end and looking round. There, sure enough, Fräulein Liepmann stood.

'I didn't know you knew Herr Kreisler' she said to Anastasya Vasek.

'Oh yes, very well.'

'Yes, yes' Kreisler cooed slowly.

'Did you say Herr Vokt was coming on to the Club?' Fräulein Liepmann asked him.

'Yes, a very little later.'

'Herr Spicker said he saw him about four.'

'Herr Spicker again!' Kreisler expostulated angrily; 'again this Spicker! He could not have seen Vokt at four because I had him safely at Fontenay des Roses at four!' He caught Anastasya Vasek's eye. She had seen Kreisler at about four o'clock too, but alone and a long way from Fontenay des Roses. He grinned at her stupidly.

'Herr Spicker' Fräulein Liepmann began again.

'Fräulein!' uttered Kreisler solemnly 'speak no more of Spicker! I cannot bear to hear you quote that person, It suggests a credulity that—. There he sits, a dubious oracle, in the corner': he indicated a bloated and rigid individual who was not Spicker at all: 'there he sits, encyclopaedic but misguided, uncanny—misinformed. It is as I tell you; our mutual friend Ernst Vokt is coming on very shortly! That is what I tell you: that then must be true!' Fräulein Liepmann gave up the riddle. A dissipated Swede was leering at Anastasya with greedy invitation, standing with his chest thrown out as though he were going to wrestle with her and she was now taken off to be introduced to him.

'Ah that's done it' thought Kreisler. 'That Spicker! Which is Spicker?' and he turned and surveyed the company truculently once more.

The new confidence in the turn things were taking had only been skin deep: Otto was soon back in the old rôle again. His hostess's discovery of his little deception had contributed to this. He imagined she had seen through it, and was in fact thoroughly informed. A clatter of conversation surrounded him. Table d'hôte at a boarding-house it sounds like, as though their voices were pitched one note above the clatter of forks and plates, he thought, and took a free cigarette from a box on the piano.

A viennese painter named Eckhart was one of the next arrivals. He was very uniform, all his features machine made for each other to a fraction of an inch—to go with a dull fat stock-size trunk. Eckhart had passed a year or so in Spain; from Malaga, just before returning, he had written to Fräulein Liepmann, with whom he had constantly corresponded from the most romantic spots in the Peninsula, asking if it were any use his taking Paris on his way back to Vienna—meaning should he 'take' Fräulein Liepmann of course—matrimonially absorb her on the way. Or should he, on the other hand, return by way of the Mediterranean? Fräulein Liepmann had been inclined to write back and suggest a third route by way of England, the Baltic and Berlin: but asked to fix his itinerary in this way she was really rather perplexed. Should she allow him to have a try at her on his way back? She had never heard of a General writing to a fortress in a country he was invading and asking it if he should storm it on his way, or, on the other hand, not include it in his campaign: should such a thing occur, what would the fortress answer? No doubt that it would be very honoured to be stormed by His Excellency, but, not being quite prepared, would prefer he should have a go at its neighbour instead, that was of course supposing it to be in the same condition as herself. She had replied at length: *she should be very glad to see him, but only as a friend.* This answer brought him back by way of Paris, in a state of uncomfortable suspense. On arriving there, he sat down in front of her and opened the siege.

Fräulein Liepmann knew that the most unexciting man may show up very well as a lover: but she found him the dullest of Generals, and it was the dullest siege she had ever sat through. So she made a sortie, and drove him away. She had allowed him to come back to Paris to have another look at him: she knew she would not accept him, but she would not have been quite easy in her mind, if she had not had another look at him. There he was—robust, bearded, cheap efficient blue eyes, thirty-eight, always in a hurry (except in love-making), obstinate and always reading the newspaper or his private correspondence (in a great hurry), when he was not doing dull engravings. No!

The result of the sortie however had been to arouse him to considerable activity: instead of going to Vienna he had actually settled in Paris, and Fräulein Liepmann was getting more of a siege than she had bargained for. But still worse, another admirer was about to arrive from Russia (coming in a bee-line, he, with whom there was no question of alternative routes!) and what would happen when the rival armies met before the fortress? The Russian was a parti she had quite given up as lost and her pleasure at learning of his tardy decision was impaired by the presence of Eckhart.

The bourgeois-bohemian life is a stirring one.

In this assembly almost all exuded a classic absurdity. There was a couple near the door: these were 'der Mathematiker' and Isolde. Isolde was a person bordering on the albino, very large, very golden-amber and even pink, spectacled, the upper eyelids covered with horizontal clean-cut blinkers of fat; she tramped about, her steady blue eyes, a schoolmistress's mouth and soft large jaw, made her extremely grim. But a vulgar, harsh, jocular spirit inhabited her: according to her friends the two rooms she occupied were never cleaned. It was there that much strange life was lived in company with der Mathematiker, steaks cooked and Bach played in gargantuan intermixture; much music, much meat, including her own. She was a gigantic blonde slut.

Der Mathematiker, as he was generally called in this circle, was a little man about thirty-five, rather like Paul Verlaine in old age;* a very brilliant mathematician, it was said, who would soon get a chair at a University. Therefore Isolde rather contemptuously allowed him to remain near her, in shrewd elephantine condescension. He was about a third her size, but he ate enormously, and, although he did not grow, felt perhaps that this in some way equalized matters. In the restaurant four beefsteaks one after the other would have to be brought him, and Isolde assured you that in their solitary orgies in her den she had known him eat as many as six—after six hours, say, of violin playing. When near her, he would hop and dance about as though to exaggerate the contrast.

Der Mathematiker always made faces at Fräulein Liepmann. No one knew what this signified. With teutonic intuition for such things they supposed it meant that he secretly loved her. This was not at all certain—it might be he hated her: and this mysterious circumstance helped der Mathematiker's prestige, along with his violin playing.

When, from his place in a dark corner, he was observed to be putting his tongue out at Fräulein Liepmann, everyone pretended not to notice, and they all experienced an agreeable thrill.

Isolde had apparently chopped away from some dress portions that had formerly concealed certain parts of her body, which the seductive glamour of night-light tempted out; two immense breasts coyly buried their nipples in its flamboyant cotton.

Other members were less sympathetic than these two: there were a couple of sisters named von Arnim, from the Baltic provinces whose love for each other was a byword. They were very 'grand dame': they missed no function such as this dance. There was a german Countess who was very poor and came principally to get models for nothing. One of the initiatory ceremonies in this society was to sit for the Countess: if anyone shied at this, it was a very bad mark. Then two girls from Dresden who professed a sort of adoration for Fräulein Liepmann were present: but in this group of women one and all must be in love with each other (even Isolde fell into this convention) and where their leader was concerned worship was added to love.

At the head of a formidable group of her own was a corpulent young Dutchwoman, named van Bencke. She was rather comely, with the professional pianist's pout and frown, and in a shabby 'Reformkleide,'* with a terribly rich dark-featured dutch stockbroker always on one side of her, and an equally well-off little dutch Countess on the other. This proximity of great gold-fields to this personality appeared as inevitable as the geologic dispositions of nature: evidently there was something about her that attracted large quantities of money: so these cumbrous masses of gold hung on her steps. She had only to lift a finger for gold to pour out of either of these quiescent figures.

The dutch Countess was an anaemic and silent young woman, and it was always a source of wonderment that these robust lavas of wealth could belong in that insignificant soil. But with such auxiliaries van Bencke was able to satisfy a social ambition equal to Fräulein Liepmann's.

Eckhart had hardly entered and doggedly invested Fräulein Liepmann, when the party became complete on the advent of Soltyk. He navigated about the salon with an ease that showed he had been born on smiling and treacherous seas and that he condescended in this puddle. But being a Pole, Soltyk participated in an hereditary polish of manner. He went up to Fräulein Vasek at once. After talking for a few minutes he left her, evidently in quest of somebody. It was a man in the farther room, soon found, and with whom he was still deep in conversation when they all left the house.

Fräulein Vasek had not shown any further sign of remembering Kreisler's existence, although he had followed her constantly with his eyes: this, thought he, was as it should be. To 'mark time' was his cue, until the opportunity arrived *to strike*. But marking time was a depressing occupation; he definitely accepted what his consequent despondency suggested. The little appearance things had of being better after all was only so much more playing with the mouse—he the mouse and the *Schicksal* of course the cat. Fluctuations of luck had been apparent, not real. He determined to be hard in future towards the coquetries of life, followed by nothing substantial.

Yet the actual course of events was so much more complicated than Kreisler's forecast. All was passing differently. Soltyk showed interest in nothing in the world but his discussion with an unknown man in a corner. He was the instrument designed to carry off some of Kreisler's wrath; he seemed deliberately disappointing him. All this company, the confederates of Fate, acted in an unexpected and maliciously natural way.

But if they were cool and matter-of-fact, he could be so too: for the rest of the evening he was more and more obstinately matter-of-fact in his actions, to meet this unfair advantage and wilful sobriety of nature.

Lost in thought, he was constantly forgetting his dusty worn clothes, and the ticklish nature of his position. The further rôle he had assigned himself for that evening would be equally forgotten: then he would be recalled to it all with sudden nausea, wishing for a moment to take his leave and disappear. Finding himself unconventionally dressed, he felt in fact a sort of outcast. He entered thoroughly into the part his situation and appearance suggested. He did not become deprecatory, but haughty and insurgent. Kreisler was the true revolutionary, since he was the perfect snob, with revenge for a motive.

The Bonnington Club was not far away. They had decided to walk, as the night was fine. It was about half-past nine when they started. Seven or eight led the way in a suddenly made self-centred group; once outside in the spaciousness of the night-streets, the party seemed to break up into sections, held together in the small lighted rooms.

Soltyk and his friend, whom Otto did not recognize, still deep in conversation, and then a quieter group, followed. Fräulein Lunken had stayed behind with another girl to put out the lights. Instead of running on with her companion to join the leading band, she stopped with Kreisler, whom she had found bringing up the rear alone.

'Not feeling gregarious to-night?' she asked.

Kreisler walked slowly, increasing, at every step, the distance between them and the next group, as though hoping that, should he draw her far enough back in the rear, like an elastic band she would in panic shoot forward.

'Do you know many english people?'

He couldn't say that he did, with some gruffness: and then she must enter upon a long eulogy of the english. Was that necessary? To hell with this Club, in fact with all english clubs. He muttered sceptically. She seemed then to be saying something about Soler's: eventually she was recommending him a new spanish professor. Why spanish?

'Do you happen to know of an english professor?'

'No, I don't think there are any.'

'I suppose not.'

Kreisler cursed this chatterbox and her complaisance in accompanying him.

'I must get some cigarettes' he said briskly, as a bureau de tabac was there. 'But don't you wait, Fräulein: catch the others up. You see?'

Having purposely loitered over his purchase, when he came out upon the Boulevard again there she was as before. 'Aber! aber! what's the matter with her?' Kreisler glared at her in impatient astonishment.

The answer to that irritated question was complex, though Bertha had not stopped behind to consort with this fish-out-of-water for nothing; though her motives, as he divined, had little to do with him. She did not live in a state of constant harmony with the Liepmann circle: her comeliness without distinction made her suspect, she was thought to be too interested in the ordinary world; and her finances were inadequate. So, as a dreadfully respectable adventuress, she should have been more humble. As it was, as a pretty girl, she was too insubordinate, and Tarr—he was a chronic source of difficulty. He was her fiancé she had announced: but he was uncompromisingly

absent from all their gatherings, and bowed to them, when met in
the street, as it seemed to them derisively, even. He had been excom-
municated long ago by Fräulein van Bencke most loudly and most
picturesquely.

'Homme sensuel!' she had called him. She averred she had caught
his eye resting too intently on her well-filled-out bosom.

'Homme égoïste!'* (this referred to his treatment of Bertha,
supposed and otherwise).

Tarr considered that these ladies were partly induced to continue
their friendship for Bertha through the hope of rescuing her from her
fiancé, or doing as much harm to both as possible. Bertha alternately
went to them a little for sympathy, and defied them with a display of
Tarr's opinions.

By analogy Kreisler had, in her mind, been pushed into the same
boat with Tarr. She always felt herself a little *without* the circle, since
Tarr was so much outside: here was another outsider, that was all.
So this was a little conspiracy.

So, Bertha still in this unusual way clinging to him (although
she had ceased plying him with conversation), they proceeded along
the solitary backwater of Boulevard in which they were. Pipes lay
all along the edge of excavations to their left, where a network of
old drains was being brought up to date. They tramped on under
the small uniform trees Paris is planted with, in imitation of the
scorching Midi.

Kreisler ignored his surroundings: he was escorting himself,
self-guarded siberian exile,* from one cheerless place to another.
To Bertha nature still had the usual florid note of bald romance: the
immediate impression caused by the moonlight was implicated with a
thousand former impressions; she did not discriminate. It was in fact
the lunar-illumination of several love-affairs.

Kreisler, more restless, renovated his susceptibility every three
years or so: the moonlight for him was hardly nine months old, and
belonged to Paris, where there was no romance, no romance whatever. For Bertha the darkened trees rustled with the delicious and
tragic suggestions of the passing of time and lapse of life. The black
unlighted windows of the tall houses held within, for her, breathless
and passionate forms, engulfed in intense eternities of darkness and
whispers. Or a lighted one (in its contrast to the bland light of the
moon) so near, suggested something infinitely distant. There was

something fatal in the rapid never-stopping succession of their footsteps—loud, deliberate, continual noise of their trotting.

Her strange companion's dreamy roughness, this romantic enigma of the evening, suddenly captured her fancy. The machine, the sentimental, the indiscriminate side of her, awoke.

She took his hand. Rapid soft and humble she struck the deep german chord, vibrating rudimentarily in the midst of his cynicism the germanic bass that underlies all the weighty, all-too-weighty music in the world.

'You are suffering! I know you are suffering. I wish I could do something for you.—Can not I?'

Kreisler began tickling the palm of her hand slightly. When he saw it interrupted her words, he left off, holding her hand solemnly as though it had been a fish slipped there for some obscure reason. Her hand—her often trenchant hand with its favourite gesture of sentimental over-emphasis—being captive, made her discourse almost quiet.

'I know you have been wronged or wounded: treat me as a sister, suppose that I am your own sister and let me help you if I can. You think my behaviour odd: do you think I'm a funny girl? Ach! all the same we walk about and torment each other enough! I knew you were not drunk when you came in, I saw you were half-cracked about something—. Why not go back? Perhaps it would be better not to come on to this place—? Why not go back?'

He quickened his steps, and still gazing stolidly ahead, drew her by the hand.

'I only should like you to feel I am your friend' she continued.

'Right!' with promptness came through his bristling moustaches.

'You're afraid I—' she looked at the ground, he ahead.

'No' he said. 'But you shall know my secret! Why should not I avail myself of your sympathy? You must know that my "Frac"—useful to waiters, that is why I get so much for the poor suit—this "Frac" is at present *not* in my lodgings. No: not in my apartment—my Frac! That seems puzzling to you?—Have you happened to notice an imposing edifice in the Rue de Rennes, with a foot-soldier constantly on guard? Yes, in the Rue de Rennes. Well, he mounts guard, night and day, over my suit!' Kreisler pulled his moustache with his free hand.—'Why keep you in suspense?—my "Frac" is not on my back because—it is *in pawn!* It was popped last month to meet a small debt. Now, Fräulein,

that you are acquainted with the cause of my slight, rather wistful—
meditative appearance, you will be able to sympathize adequately with
me! My suffering, as you put it, is now no longer mysterious—I have
given you the clue—the pawn-ticket, so to speak.'

She was crying a little, engrossed directly, now, in herself.
He thought he should console her and remarked:

'Those are the first tears ever shed over my "Frac." But do not
distress yourself Fräulein Lunken, the waiters have not yet got it!'

Kreisler did not distinguish Bertha from the others. At the beginning he was distrustful: if not 'put up' to doing this, she at least
hailed from an objectionable quarter. Now he accepted her bona-
fides,* but ill-temperedly substituted complete boredom for mistrust.
At the same time he would use this little episode to embellish his
programme.

He had not been able to shake her off: here she still was: he was
not even sure yet that he had had the best of it. His animosity for
her friends vented itself upon her: he would anyhow give her what
she deserved for her persistence. He took her hand again. Then suddenly he stopped, put his arm round her waist, and drew her forcibly
against him.

Bertha succumbed to the instinct to 'give up,' even sententiously
'destroy.' She remembered her resolve—a double one of sacrifice—
and pressed her lips, shaking and wettened, to his. This was not the
way she had wished: but, God! what did it matter? *It mattered so little*,
ANYTHING, and above all *she!* This was what she had wanted to do:
and now she had done it!

The 'resolve' was a simple one. In her uncertain emotional manner
she had been making up her mind to it ever since Tarr had left that
afternoon. Tarr wished to be released; he did not want her, was embarrassed, not so much by their formal engagement as by his liking for
her (this secured him to her, she thought she discerned). A stone hung
round his neck, he fretted the whole time: it would always be so. Good.
This she understood. The situation was plain. Then *she* would release
him. But since it was not merely a question of *words* (of saying 'we are
no longer engaged'—she had already been very free with them) but
of facts, she must bring these substantialities about. By putting herself in the most definite sense out of his reach—far more than if she
should leave Paris—their continued relations must be made impossible. Somebody else—and a somebody else who was at the same time

nobody, and who would evaporate and leave no trace the moment he had served her purpose—must be found. She must be able to stare pityingly and resignedly (but silently) if he were mentioned. Kreisler exactly filled this ticket. And he arose not too unnaturally.

This idea had been germinating while Tarr was still with her that morning. So, a profusion of self-sacrifice being offered her in the person of Kreisler, she behaved as she had done, with gusto. It was a clear and satisfactory action.

Should Tarr wish it undone, it could easily be conjured: the smudge on Kreisler's back was a guarantee, and did the trick in more ways than he had counted on. But in any case his whole personality was a perfect alibi for the heart, to her thinking. While at the back of her mind there always appeared that possibility, that, with the salt of jealousy, and a really big row, Tarr could perhaps be landed and secured even now?

Next moment (the point thus gained) she pushed Kreisler more or less gently away. It was like a stage-kiss: the needs of their respective rôles had been satisfied. He kept his hands on her biceps: she was accomplishing a soft withdrawal.

They had stopped at a spot where the Boulevard approached a more populous and lighted avenue. As they now stood a distinct, yet strangely pausing, female voice struck their ears:

'Fräulein Lunken!'

Some twenty yards away stood several of her companions, who, with fussy german sociableness, had returned to carry her forward with them, as they were approaching the Bonnington Club. Finding her not with them, and remembering she had lagged behind, they had walked back to the head of the Boulevard speculating as to what could have detained her. They now saw quite plainly what was before them, but were in that state in which a person will not believe his eyes, and lets them bulge until they nearly drop out, to correct their scandalous vision. Kreisler and Bertha were some distance from the nearest lamp and in the shade of the trees. But each of the spectators would have sworn to the identity and attitude of their two persons.

Bertha nearly jumped out of her skin, broke away from Kreisler, and staggered several steps. He, with great presence of mind, caught her again, and induced her to lean against a tree, saying curtly:

'You're not quite well, Fräulein. Lean—so. Your friends will be here in a moment.'

Bertha accepted this way out. She turned, indeed, rather white and sick, and even succeeded so far as half to believe her pretence, while the women came up. Kreisler called out to the petrified and quite silent group at the end of the avenue; soon they were surrounded by big-eyed faces. Hypocritical concern soon superseded the masks of scandal.

'She was taken suddenly ill.' Kreisler coughed conventionally as he said this, and flicked his trousers as though he had been scuffling on the ground. Then he coughed again.

Indignant glances were cast at him. Whatever attitude they might decide to adopt as regards their friend, there was no doubt as to their feeling towards *him*: he was to blame from whichever way you looked at it. Eventually, with one or two curious german glances into her eyes, slow, dubious, incredulous questions (with a drawing back of the head and dying away of voice) they determined temporarily to accept the explanation and to say that she had been indisposed. To one of them, very much in the know with regard to her relations with Tarr, vistas of possible ruptures opened: but here was a funny affair all were agreed. With Kreisler, of all people! Tarr was bad enough!

Bertha would at once have returned home, and confirmed the story of a sudden megrim.* But she felt the best thing was to go through with it. To absent herself at once would be a mistake. The affair would be less conspicuous with her not away: her friends must at once ratify their normal view of this little occurrence. The only thing she thought of for the moment was to hush up and wipe out what had just happened: her heroics disappeared in the need for action. So they all walked on together, a scandalized silence subsisting in honour chiefly of Kreisler.

Again he was safe, he thought with a chuckle. His position was precarious, only he held Fräulein Lunken as hostage! Exception could not *openly* be taken to him, without reflecting on their friend! He walked along with perfect composure, mischievously detached and innocent.

Fräulein Liepmann and the rest had already gone inside the club building, which was brightly illuminated. Several people were arriving in taxis and on foot. Kreisler got in without difficulty. He was it turned out the only man present not in evening dress.

CHAPTER 2

ONE certain thing (amongst many uncertainties) about the english club, the Bonnington Club, was that it could not be said as yet to have found itself quite. Its central room (and that was almost all there was of it) reminded you of a Public Swimming Bath when it was used as a Ball-room, and when used as a studio, you thought of a Concert Hall. But it had cost a good deal to build. It made a cheerful show, with pink, red and pale blue paper chains and Chinese Lanterns, one week, for some festivity, and the next, sparely robed in dark red curtains, would settle its walls gravely to receive some houseless quartet. In this manner it paid its way. Some phlegmatic divinity seemed to have brought it into existence—'Found a club, found a club!' it had reiterated in the depths of certain minds probably with sleepy tenacity.— Someone sighed, got up and went round to another individual of the same sort, and said perhaps a club had better be founded. The second assented and subscribed something, to get rid of the other. In the course of time, a young french architect had been entrusted with the job. A club. Yes. What sort of a club? The architect could not find out. Something to be used for drawing-classes, social functions, a reading-room, he knew the sort of thing! He saw he was on the wrong tack. He went away and made his arrangements accordingly. He had produced a design of an impressive and to all appearance finished house: it was a sincerely ironic masterpiece, but with a perfect gravity, and even stateliness of appearance. It was the most non-committing façade, the most absolutely unfinal interior, the most tentative set of doors, ever seen: a monster of reservations.

Not only had the building been put to every conceivable use itself, but it dragged the Club with it. The members of the Bonnington Club changed and metamorphosed themselves with *its* changes. They became athletic or sedentary according to the shifts and exigencies of this building's existence. They turned out in dress clothes or gymnasium get-ups as its destiny prompted, to back it up: one month they would have to prove that it *was* a gymnasium, the next that it *was* a drawing-school, so they stippled and vaulted, played table-tennis and listened to debates.

The inviting of the german contingent was a business move: they might be enticed into membership and would in any event spread the fame of the Club, getting and subsequently giving some conception of the resources of the club-house building. The hall had been very prettily arranged: the adjoining rooms were hung with the drawings and paintings of the club members.

Kreisler, ever since the occurrence on the Boulevard, had felt a reckless irresponsibility, which he did not care to conceal. His assurance even came to smack of braggadocio.

With his abashed english hostess he carried on a strange conversation full of indirect references to that 'stately edifice in the Rue de Rennes'* of which he had spoken to Bertha. 'That stately edifice in the Rue de Rennes—but of course you don't know it—!'

With smiling german ceremoniousness, with heavy circumlocutions, he bent down to her nervously smiling face, and poured into her startled ear symbols and images of pawn-shops, usury, three gold balls, 'pious mountains,'* 'Smokkin' or 'Frac' complets,* which he seemed a little to confuse, overwhelmed her with a serious terminology, all in a dialect calculated to bewilder the most acute philologist.

'Yes it *is* interesting' she said with strained conviction.

'Isn't it?' Kreisler replied. A comparative estimate of the facilities for the disposing of a watch in Germany and France had been the subject of his last remarks.

'I'm going to introduce you, Herr Kreisler, to a friend of mine—Mrs. Bevelage.'

She wanted to give the german guests a particularly cordial reception. Kreisler did not seem, superficially, a great acquisition to any club, but he was with the others. As a means of concluding this very painful interview—he was getting nearer every minute to the word that he yet solemnly forbade himself the use of—she led him up to a self-possessed exemplar of mid-victorian lovely womanhood, whose attitude suggested that she might even yet stoop to Folly* if the occasion arose. Mrs. Bevelage could listen to all this, and would be able to cope with a certain disquieting element she recognized in this young German.

He saw the motive of her move: and, looking with ostentatious regret at a long-legged flapper* seated next to them, cast a reproachful glance at his hostess.

Left alone with the widow, he surveyed her prosperous, velvet and cuirassed form.

'Get thee to a nunnery!'* he said dejectedly.

'I beg your pardon?'

'Yes. You have omitted "My Lord"!'

Mrs. Bevelage looked pleased and puzzled. Possibly he was a count or baron, being german.

'Do you know that stingy but magnificent edifice—.'

'Yes—?'

'That sumptuous home of precarious "Fracs," situated Rue de Rennes—?'

'I'm afraid I don't quite understand—.' The widow had not got used to his composite tongue. She liked Kreisler, however.

The music burst forth, and the club members leapt to their feet to affirm with fire their festive intentions.

'Shall we dance?' he said, getting up quickly.

He clasped her firmly in the small of the back and they got ponderously in motion, he stamping a little bit, as though he mistook the waltz for a more primitive music.

He took her twice, with ever-increasing velocity, round the large hall, and at the third round, at breakneck speed, spun with her in the direction of the front door. The impetus was so great that she, although seeing her peril, could not act sufficiently as a brake on her impetuous companion to avert the disaster. Another moment and they would have been in the street, amongst the traffic, a disturbing meteor, whizzing out of sight, had not they met the alarmed resistance of a considerable british family entering the front door as Kreisler bore down upon it. It was one of those large featureless human groups built up by a frigid and melancholy pair, uncannily fecund, during an interminable intercourse. They received this violent couple in their midst. The rush took Kreisler and his partner half-way through, and there they stood embedded and unconscious for many seconds. The british family then, with great dignity, disgorged them, and moved on.

The widow had come somewhat under the sudden fascination of Kreisler's mood: she was really his woman, the goods, had he known it: she felt deliciously rapt in the midst of a simoom*—she had not two connected thoughts. All her worldly Victorian grace and good management of her fat had vanished: her face had become coarsened in those few breathless minutes. But she buzzed back again into the dance, and began a second mad, but this time merely circular, career.

Kreisler took care to provide his actions with some plausible air of purpose: thus: he was abominably short-sighted; he had mistaken

the front door for one leading into the third room, merely! His burden, not in the best condition, was becoming more and more puffed
and heavier-footed at every step. When satisfied with this part of his
work, he led Mrs. Bevelage into a sort of improvised conservatory*
and talked about pawn-shops for ten minutes or so—in a mixture
of french english and german. He then reconducted her, more dead
than alive, to her seat, where he left her with great sweeps of his tall
figure.

He had during this incident regained his former impassivity. He
stalked away now to the conservatory once more, which he regarded
as a suitable headquarters.

Bertha had soon been called on to dance vigorously, without much
intermission. In the convolutions of the dance, however, she matured
a bold and new plan. She whirled and trotted with a preoccupied air.

Would Tarr hear of all this? Now it was done she was alarmed. Also
the Liepmann, the van Bencke's attitude towards the Kreisler kissing
was a prospect that cowed her as she got used to it. Undoubtedly she
must secure herself. The plan she hit on offered a 'noble' rôle that she
would, in any circumstances, have found irresistible.

Her scheme was plain and clever: she would simply 'tell the truth.'
This is how the account would go.

'She had recognized something distracting in Kreisler's life, in
short the presence of crisis. *On an impulse*, she had offered him her
sympathy. He had taken up her offer immediately but in the brutal manner already seen. (One against him: two for her!) Such lurid
sympathy he claimed. She was sorry for him still, but he was very
brutal.'

So she jogged out her strategies with theatrically abstracted face
and rolling eyes.

At this point of her story she would hint, by an ambiguous hesitation, that she, in truth, had been ready even for this sacrifice: had
made it, if her hearers wished! She would imply rather that from
modesty—not wanting to appear *too* 'noble'—she refrained from telling them the whole truth.

For such a confession it is true she had many precedents. Only a
week ago Fräulein van Bencke herself, inflating her stout handsome
person, had told them that while in Berlin she had allowed a young
painter to 'kiss' her: she believed 'that the caresses of a pure woman
would be helpful to him at that juncture of his life.' But this had not

been, it was to be supposed, in the middle of the street: no one had ever seen, or ever would see, the young painter in question, or the kiss.

Busy with these plans, Bertha had not much time to notice Kreisler's further deportment. She came across him occasionally, and keyed her solid face into an intimate flush and such mask as results from any sickly physical straining. '*Poor* Mensch! Poor luckless Mensch!' was the idea.

Soltyk surprised one anglo-saxon partner after another with his wonderful english—unnecessarily like the real thing. He exhibited no signs of pleasure (except as much as was testified to by his action, merely) at this sort of astonishment.

Only twice did Kreisler observe him with Anastasya. On those occasions he could not, on the strength of what he saw, pin him down as a rival. Yet he was thirsting for conventional figures. His melancholy could only be satisfied by *active* things, unlike itself. Soltyk's self-possession, his ready social accomplishment, depressed Kreisler: for it was not in his nature to respect those qualities, yet he felt they were what he had always lacked. The Russian was, more distantly, an attribute of Vokt. How it would satisfy him to dig his fingers into that flesh, and tear it like thick cloth! He Otto Kreisler was 'for it':* he was down and out (revolutionary motif): he was being assisted off the stage by this and by that. Why did he not *shout*? He longed to act: the rusty machine had a thirst for action.

Soltyk liked his soul to be marked with little delicate wounds and wistfulnesses: he enjoyed an understanding, a little melancholy, with a woman: they would just divine in each other possibilities of passion, that was yet too 'lasse' and sad to rise to the winding of Love's horns* that were heard, nevertheless, in a décor Versaillesque and polonais.* They were people who looked forward as others look back: they would say farewell to the future as most men gaze upon the past. At the most they played the slight dawning and disappearing of passion, cutting, fastidiously, all the rest of the piece. So he was often found with women. But for Anastasya, Soltyk was one of her many impresarios, who helped her on to and off the scene of Life. He bored her completely, they had something equivalent to pleasant business relations: she had recognized at once his merits as an impresario. There could not therefore have been less material for passion: even Kreisler was nonplussed. He was surrounded by unresponsive shapes.

Conventional figures of drama lacked: Kreisler had in fact got into the wrong company. But he conformed for the sake of the Invisible Audience haunting life: he emulated the matter-of-factness and aplomb that impressed him in the others: so far indeed was he successful in this that the Audience took some time to notice him—the vein of scandal running through an otherwise dull performance.

———

In the conservatory he dug himself in by a cleverly arranged breast-work of chairs. From thence he issued forth on various errands. All his errands showed the gusto of the logic of his personality: he might indeed have been enjoying himself. He invented outrage that was natural to him, and enjoyed slightly the licence and scope of his indifference.

At the first sortie he observed a rather congested, flushed and spectacled young woman, her features set in a spasm of duty. It was a hungry sex in charge of a flustered automaton. Having picked her for a partner, he gained her confidence by his scrupulous german politeness. But he soon got to work. While marking time in a crush, he disengaged his hand and appeared to wish to alter the lie of her bosom, very apologetically and holding her tight with the other hand.

'Excuse me! it's awkward—. More to the left—so! Clumsy things and some women are so proud of them! (No: I'm sure you're not!) No. Allow me. Let it hang to the left!' The young lady, very red, and snorting almost in his face, escaped brusquely from his clutch and fled towards her nearest friends.

Several young women, and notably a flapper, radiant with heavy inexperience and loaded with bristling bronze curls, he lured into the conservatory. They all came out with scarlet faces: but that did not prevent others from following him in.

For the first hour he paid no attention to Anastasya: he prosecuted his antics as though he had forgotten all about her. He knew she was there and left her alone, even in thought; he hid coquettishly behind his solemn laughter-in-action, the pleasant veil of his hysteria, Anastasya was no longer of the least importance: he had realized that she had been all along a mere survival of days when such individuals mattered. Now he was *en pleine abstraction**—a very stormy and concrete nothingness.

At length he became generally noticed in the room, although there were a great many people present. The last flapper had screamed and had escaped at the gallop. He had even been observed for a moment, an uncouth faun,* in pursuit, in the flowery mouth of the conservatory. Fräulein Liepmann hesitated now. She thought at length that he was insane. In speaking to him and getting him removed if necessary, a scandalous scene was almost certain to occur.

Again the tall, and in spite of the studied dishevelment, still preternaturally 'correct,' satyric* form appeared upon the threshold of the conservatory.—An expectant tremor invaded several backs. But on this occasion he just stalked round on a tour of inspection, as though to see that all was going along as it should. Heavily and significantly he stared at those young ladies who had been his partners, when he came across them: one he abruptly stopped in front of and gazed at severely. She did not denounce him but blushed and even tittered. He left this exhibition of cynicism in disgust, and returned to his conservatory.

In his deck chair, his head stretched back, glasses horizontal and facing the ceiling, he considered the graceless Hamlet that he was.

'Go to a nunnery, Widow!'

He should have been saying that to his Ophelia. He hiccuped. Why did he not *go to her?*—contact was the essential thing: his thoughts returned to Anastasya. He must bare her soul. If he could insult her enough she would be bare-souled. There would be the naked *weibliche Seele.** Then he would spit on it. Soltyk however offered a conventional target for violence: Soltyk was evading him with his indifference. Soltyk! What should be done with Soltyk? Why (a prolonged and stormily rising 'why'), there was no difficulty about *that.* He got up from his chair, and walked deliberately and quickly into the central room gazing fiercely to right and left. But Soltyk was nowhere to be seen.

The dancers were circling rapidly past with athletic elation, talking in the way people do when they are working. Their intelligences floated and flew above the waves of these graceful exercises, but with frequent drenchings, as it were. Each new pair of dancers seemed coming straight for him: their voices were loud, a hole was cut out of the general noise, as it were opening a passage into it. The two or three instruments behind the screen of palms produced the necessary measures to keep this throng of people careering, like the spoon stirring in a saucepan: it stirred and stirred and they jerked and huddled insipidly round and round, in sluggish currents with small eddies here and there.

Kreisler was drawn up short at the first door and had to flatten himself against the wall for a moment. He was just advancing again to work his way round to the next exit when he caught sight of Anastasya dancing with (he supposed) some Englishman. He stopped, paralysed by her appearance: the part she had played in present events gave her a great prestige in his image-life: when in the flesh she burst into his dream she still was able to disturb everything for a moment. Now he stood like somebody surprised in a questionable act. The next moment he was furious at this interference. She and her partner stood in his way: he took her partner roughly by the arm, pushing him against her, hustling him, fixing him with his eye. He passed beyond them then, through the passage he had made. The young man handled in this manner, shy and unprompt, stared after Kreisler with a 'What the devil!'—People are seldom rude in England. Kreisler, without apology, but as if waiting for more vigorous expostulation, was also looking back, while he stepped slowly along the wall towards the door beyond—the one leading to the refreshment room.

Anastasya freed herself at once from her partner, and pale and frowning (but as though waiting) was looking after Kreisler curiously. She would have liked him to stop. He had done something strange and was as suddenly going away. That was unsatisfactory. They looked at each other without getting any farther, he showed no sign of stopping: she continued to stare. She burst out laughing. They had clashed (like people in the dance). The *contact* had been brought about. He was still as surprised at his action as she was. Anastasya felt too, in what way this had been *contact*: she felt his hand on her arm as though it had been she he had seized. Something difficult to understand and which should have been alarming, the sensation of the first tugs of the maelstrom he was producing and conducting all by himself which required her for its heart she had experienced: and then laughed, necessarily; once one was in that atmosphere, like laughing gas with its gusty tickling, it could not be helped.

Now this rough figure of comic mystery disappeared in the doorway, incapable of explaining anything. She shivered nervously as she grasped her partner's arm again, at this merely physical contact. 'What's the matter with that chap?'—her partner asked, conscious of the lameness of this question. Elsewhere Kreisler was now a subject of conversation. 'Herr Kreisler is behaving very strangely. Do you think he's been drinking?' Fräulein Liepmann asked Eckhart.

Eckhart was a little drunk himself: he took a very decided view of Kreisler's case.

'Comme toute la Pologne!* as drunk as the whole of Poland!' he affirmed. He only gave it as an opinion, with no sign of particular indignation: he was beaming with greedy generosity at his Great Amoureuse.

'Ah! here he comes again!' said Fräulein Liepmann at the door.

So Kreisler disappeared in the doorway after the 'contact'; he passed through the refreshment room. In a small chamber beyond he sat down by an open window.

When Anastasya had laughed Kreisler's inner life had for a moment been violently disturbed. He could not respond, or retaliate, the door being in front of him he vanished, as Mephistopheles* might sink with suddenness into the floor at the receipt of some affront, to some sulphurous regions beneath, in a second—come to a stop alone, upright—stick his fingers in his mouth nearly biting them in two, his eyes staring: so stand stock-still, breathless and haggard for some minutes: then shoot up again, head foremost, in some other direction, like some darting and skulking fish, to the face of the earth. Kreisler sat on staring in front of him, quite forgetful where he was and how long he had sat there, in the midst of a hot riot of thoughts.

Suddenly he sat up and looked about him like a man who has been asleep for whom work is waiting; with certain hesitation he rose and again made for the door. Glancing reflectively and solemnly about he perceived the widow talking to a little reddish Englishman. He bore down upon them with courtly chicken-like undulations.

'May I take the widow away for a little?' he asked her companion.

(He always addressed her as 'Widow': all he said to her began with a solemn 'Widow!' occasionally alternating with '*Derelict!*' All uttered in a jumbled tongue, it lost most of its significance.)

On being addressed the small Briton gave the britannic equivalent of a jump—a sudden moving of his body and shuffling of his feet, still looking at the floor, where he had cast his eyes as Kreisler approached.

'What? I—.'

'Widow! permit me—' Kreisler said and encircled her with a heavy arm.

Manipulating her with a leisurely gusto, he circled into the dance.

The band was playing the 'Merry Widow' waltz.*

'*Merry* Widow!' he said smilingly to his partner. 'Yes!' shaking his head at her roguishly: '*merry* Widow!'

The music fumbled in a confused mass of memory, all it managed to bring to light was a small cheap photograph, taken at a Bauern Ball,* with a flat german student's cap. He saw this solemn lad with pity, this early Otto. Their hostess also was dancing: Kreisler remarked her with a wink of recognition. Dancing very slowly, mournfully even, he and his partner bumped into her each time as they passed: each time it was a deliberate collision. Thud went the massive buffers of the two ladies. The widow felt the impact, but it was only at the third round that she perceived the method presiding at these bumps. She then realized that they were without fail about to collide with the other lady once more: the collision could not be avoided, but she shrank away, made herself as small as possible, bumped gently and apologized over her shoulder, with a smile and screwing up of the eyes, full of dumb worldly significance. At the fourth turn of the room, however, Kreisler having increased her speed sensibly, she was on her guard. In fact she had already suggested that she should be taken back to her seat. He pretended to be giving their hostess a wide berth this time; then suddenly and gently he swerved and bore down upon her. The widow frantically veered, took a false step, tripped over her dress of state, tearing it in several places, and fell to the ground. They caused a circular undulating commotion throughout the neighbouring dancers, like a stone falling in a pond.

Several people bent down to help Mrs. Bevelage. Kreisler's assistance was angrily dispensed with, the widow was roused at last: she scrambled to her feet and limped to the nearest chair, followed by a group of sympathizers.

'Who is he?'

'He's drunk.'

'What happened?'

'He ought to be turned out!' people exclaimed who had witnessed the accident.

With great dignity Herr Otto Kreisler regained the conservatory. As he lay stretched in his chair Fräulein Liepmann, alone, appeared before him and said in a tight, breaking voice,

'I think Herr Kreisler you would do well now, as you have done nothing all evening but render yourself objectionable, to relieve us of your company.'

He sat up frowning.

'I don't understand you!'

'I suppose you're drunk. I hope so, for—.'

'You hope I'm drunk, Fräulein?' he asked in an astonished voice. He reclined at full length again.

'A lady I was dancing with fell over' he remarked 'owing entirely to her own clumsiness and intractability.—But perhaps she was drunk, I never thought of that. Of course that explains it.'

'So you're not going?'

'Certainly Fräulein—when you go! We'll go together.'

'Schurke!' Hurling hotly this epithet at him—her breath had risen many degrees in temperature at its passage, and her breast heaved in dashing it out (as though, in fact, the word 'Schurke' had been the living thing, and she were emptying her breast of it violently)— she left the room. His last exploit had been accomplished in a half-disillusioned condition. The evening had been a failure from his point of view. Everything had conspired to cheat him of the violent relief he required; his farcing proceeded because he could think of nothing else to do. Anastasya laughing had disorganized 'imaginary life' at a promising juncture. He told himself now without conviction that he *hated* her. 'Ich hasse dich! Ich hasse dich!' he hissed over to himself, enjoying the wind of the 'hasse' in his moustaches but otherwise not very impressed. His sensuality had been somewhat stirred: he wanted to *kiss* her now: he must get his mouth on hers he told himself juicily and fiercely; he must revel in the laugh, where it grew! She was a fatal woman: she was in fact evidently *the Devil.*

He began thinking about her with a slow moistening of the lips. 'I *shall possess* her!' he said to himself, seeing himself in the rôle of the berserker warrior,* ravening and irresistible: the use of the word *shall* in that way was enough.

But this *infernal* dance! He was no longer romantically 'desperate,' but bored with his useless position there. His attention was now concentrated on a practical issue, that of the 'possession' of Anastasya though even that depended on a juicy vocabulary, hissed in the form of an incantation and he lost sight of it the moment he ceased deliberately to attend to it.

He was tired as though he had been dancing the whole evening. Getting up, he threw his cigarette away; he even dusted his coat a little with his hand. He then, not being able to get at the white patch on the shoulder, took it off and shook it. A large grey handkerchief was used to flick his boots with.

'So!' he grunted, smartly shooting on his coat.

The central room, when he got into it, appeared a different place: people were standing about and waiting for the next tune. He had become a practical man, surrounded by facts: but he was much more worried and tired than at the beginning of the evening.

To get away was his immediate thought. But he felt hungry: he made for the refreshment room. On the same side as the door, a couple of feet to the right, was a couch: the improvised trestle-bar with the refreshments ran the length of the opposite wall: the room was quiet and almost empty. Out of the tail of his eye, as he entered, he became conscious of something. He turned towards the couch: Soltyk and Anastasya were sitting there, and looking at him with the abrupt embarrassment people show when an absentee under discussion suddenly appears. He flushed and was about to turn back to the door. This humiliating full-stop beneath their eyes must be wiped out at once: he walked on steadily to the bar, with a truculent swagger.

A consciousness of his physique beset him: the outcast feeling returned in the presence of these toffs—class-inferiority-feeling beset him. He must be leisurely: he *was* leisurely. He thought when he stretched his hand out to take his cup of coffee that it would never reach it. He felt a crab dragged out of its hole, which was in this case perhaps the conservatory. *Inactive*, he was ridiculous: he had not reckoned on being watched. This was a fiasco: here he was posing nude for Anastasya and the Russian.

He munched sandwiches without the faintest sense of their taste. Suddenly conscious of an awkwardness in his legs, he changed his position: his arms were ludicrously disabled. The sensation of standing neck-deep in horrid filth beset him. The noise of the dancing began again and filled the room: this purified things somewhat.

But his anger kept rising. He stood there deliberately longer now: in fact on and on, almost in the same position. She should wait his pleasure till he liked to turn round, and—then. He allowed her laughter to accumulate on his back, like a coat of mud. In his illogical vision he felt her there behind him laughing and laughing interminably. Soltyk was sharing it of course. More and more *his* laughter became intolerable: the traditional solution again presented itself. Laugh! Laugh! He would stand there letting the debt grow, they might gorge themselves upon his back. The attendant behind the bar began observing him with severe curiosity: he had stood in almost the same position for five minutes and kept staring darkly past her, very red in the face.

Then suddenly a laugh burst out behind him—a blow, full of insult, in his ears: he nearly jumped off the ground: after his long immobility the jump was of the last drollery: fists clenched, his face emptied of every drop of colour, in the mere action he had almost knocked a man standing beside him off his feet. The laugh, for him, had risen with tropic suddenness, a simoom of intolerable offence: it had swept him from stem to stern, or whirled him completely round rather, in a second. A young english girl, already terrified at Kreisler's appearance, and a man, almost as much so, stood open-mouthed in front of him. As to Anastasya and Soltyk, they had entirely disappeared, long before in all probability.

To find that he had been struggling and perspiring in the grasp of a shadow, was a fresh offence merely. It counted against the absentees but even more it swelled the debt against a more terrible, abstract, antagonist. He had been again beating the air: this should have been a climax—of blows, hard words, definite things. But still there was *nothing.*

He smiled, rather hideously, at the two english people near him and walked away. All he wanted now was to get away from the English Club as soon as possible, this ill-fated Club.

While making towards the vestibule he was confronted again with Fräulein Liepmann.

'Herr Kreisler, I wish to speak to you' he heard her say.

'Go to the devil!' he answered in a muffled voice, without paying more attention. Her voice bawled suddenly in his ear:

'Besotted fool! if you don't go at once I'll get—.'

Turning on her like lightning, with exasperation perfectly meeting hers, his right hand threatening, quickly raised towards his left
shoulder, he shouted with a crashing distinctness:

'Lass' mich doch, gemeine alte Sau!'*

The hissing, thunderous explosion was the last thing in teutonic
virulence: the muscles all seemed gathered up at his ears like reins,
the flesh tightened and white round his mouth, everything contributed to the effect.

Fräulein Liepmann took several steps back: with equal quickness
Kreisler turned away, rapped upon the counter, while the attendant
looked for his hat; then passed out of the club. Fräulein Liepmann
was left with the heavy, unforgettable word 'sow' deposited in her
boiling spirit, that, boil as it might, would hardly reduce this word to
tenderness or digestibility. *Sow*, common-old-sow—the words went
on raging through her spirit like a herd of Gadarene Swine.*

PART IV

A JEST TOO DEEP FOR LAUGHTER*

CHAPTER 1

WITH a little scratching (as the concierge pushed it with her finger-tips) with the malignity of a little, quiet, sleek animal, the letter
from Germany crept under the door the next morning. It lay there
through the silence of the next hour or two, until Kreisler woke.
Succeeding to his first brutal farewells to his dreams, no hopes leapt
upon his body, a magnificent stallion's, uselessly refreshed: big and
limp, upon his back, he had no desire to move his limbs. Soon he
saw the letter across the room, quiet, unimportant, rather matter-
of-fact and sly.

Kreisler felt it an indignity to have to open this letter: until
his dressing was finished it remained where it was. He might have
been making some person wait. Then he took it up and, opening
it, drew out, between his forefinger and thumb, the cheque: this he
deposited with as much contempt as possible and a *pfui* of the best
upon the extreme edge of his washhand stand. He turned to the letter: he read the first few lines, pumping at a cigarette, reducing it
mathematically to ash. Cold fury entered his mind with a bound at
the first words.

'Here is your monthly cheque, but it is the last——.'

They were the final words giving notice of a positive stoppage: this
month's money was sent to enable him to settle up his affairs and
come to Germany at once.

He read the first three lines over and over, going no further,
although the news begun in these first lines was developed throughout the two pages of the letter. Then he put it down beside the cheque,
and crushing it under his fist, said monotonously to himself, without
much more feeling than the sound of the word contained: 'Schwein.
Schwein. Schwein!'

He got up and pressed his hand upon his forehead; it was wet: he
put his hands in his pockets and one of these came into contact with
a fifty-centime piece.* He took his hands out again slowly, went to his

box and underneath an old dressing-gown found writing paper and envelopes. Then, referring to his father's letter for the date, he wrote the following lines:

'*7th June* 19—

'Sɪʀ,—I shall not return as you suggest, not in person, but my body will no doubt be sent to you about the middle of next month. If—keeping to your decision—no money is sent, it being impossible to live without money, I shall on the seventh of July, this day next month, shoot myself.

'Oᴛᴛᴏ Aᴅᴏʟꜰ Kʀᴇɪsʟᴇʀ.'

Within half an hour this was in the post: then he went and had breakfast with more tranquillity and relish than he had known for many days. He sat up stiffly at his Café table. He smacked his lips as he drank. The coffee was very hot.

He had come to a respectable decision: his revolt of the night before had been the reverse of that. Death—like a monastery—was before him, with equivalents of a slight shaving of the head, a handful of vows, some desultory farewells: there would be something like the disagreeableness of a dive for one not used to deep water. His life might almost have been regarded as a long and careful preparation for voluntary death, or self-murder.

Instead of rearing pyramids against Death, if you imagine some more uncompromising race meeting its obsession by means of an unparalleled immobility in life, a race of statues, in short, throwing flesh in Death's path instead of basalt, there you would have a people among whom Kreisler would have been much at home.

CHAPTER 2

Iɴ a large fluid but nervous handwriting, the following letter lay, read, Bertha still keeping her large blue ox-eye* upon it from a distance:

'Dᴇᴀʀ Bᴇʀᴛʜᴀ,—I am writing at the Gare St. Lazare,* on my way to England. You have made things much easier for me in one way of course, but more difficult in another. (I may mention that

the whimsical happenings between you and your absurd countryman in full moonlight are known to me: they were recounted with
a wealth of detail that left nothing to the imagination. I don't know
whether that little red-headed bitch—the colour of Iscariot,* so
perhaps she is—is a friend of yours? Kreisler! I was offered an
introduction to him the other day, which I refused: it seems he has
introduced himself.) Before, I had contemplated retiring to a little
distance for the purpose of reflection: this last *coup* of yours neces-
sitates a much further withdrawal—a couple of hundred miles at
least, I have judged: and as far as I can see I shall be some months—
say ten—away. You are now a free woman (is that right?) Let your
new exploit develop naturally, right up to *fiançailles*, or elsewhere I
mean. I release you, Bertha. But for God's sake get married quickly.
It's all up with you otherwise. My address for the next few months
will be 10 Waterford Street, London, W.C.—Yours,

'SORBETT.'

Sorbert was his second name; and Sorbett or Sherbet his *nom
d'amour:* he spelt it with two T's because his fiancée had never discip-
lined herself to suppress final consonants.*

Bertha was in her little kitchen. It was near the front door: next
to it was her studio or *salon*, then bedroom: along a passage at right
angles the rooms rented by Clara Vamber, her friend.

The letter had been laid upon the table, by the side of which stood
the large gas-stove, its gas stars blasting away luridly at sky-blue
saucepans with Bertha's breakfast. While attending to the eggs and
coffee, she gazed over her arm reflectively at the letter: it was a couple
of inches too far away for her to be able to read it.

Ten minutes before the postman had hurled it in at the door. It was
now four days after the dance, and since she had last seen Tarr. On this
particular morning she had 'felt' he would turn up. 'Could he have
heard anything about the Kreisler incident?' she had speculated:—
the possibility of this was terrifying! But perhaps it would be as well
if he had. It might at any future time crop up: she would tell him
if he had not already heard: he should hear it from her! The great
boulevard-sacrifice of the other night had appeared folly long ago: but
so peculiarly free from any form of spite, she did not feel unkindly
towards Kreisler, poor devil, that would be absurd. She would take
the blame herself.

So Sorbert had been expected to breakfast, on the authority of
intuition; bread was being fried in fat. What manner of man would
appear, how far informed—or if *not* informed, still all their other
difficulties were there inevitably were they not, enough to go on
with. Could fried toast and honey play a part in such troubles?
Ach! troubles often reduced themselves to fried bread and honey:
they could sow troubles, why not help to quell troubles? She had had
a second intuition however that he *knew*: not knowing how stormy
their interview might be (and the stormier the better of course—it
might all along have been just that storm that they had needed!)
she neglected no minute precautions, any more than the sailor
would neglect to stow away even the smallest of his sails at the
sulky approach of a simoom.—The simoom, however, had left her
becalmed and taken the train for Dieppe* instead of coming in her
direction!

CHAPTER 3

BERTHA went on turning the bread over in the pan, taking the but-
ter from its paper and dropping it into its earthenware dish: rinsing
and wiping cutlery and plates, regulating the gas. Frequent truculent
exclamations spluttered out if anything went wrong: 'Verdammte
Zündhölzchen!' 'Donnerwetter!'* She employed the oaths of
Goethe* which had become rakish and respectable; one eyebrow was
raised in humorous reflective irritation. She would flatten the letter
out and bend down to examine a sentence, stopping her cooking for
a moment.

'Salaud!' she exclaimed, after having read the letter all through
again, putting it down. She turned with coquettish contemptuous-
ness to her frying-pan. Clara's door opened, and Bertha crumpled
the letter into her pocket. Clara entered sleepy-eyed and affecting
ill-humour. Her fat body was a softly distributed burden, which she
carried with aplomb: she had a gracefully bumpy forehead, a nice
whistling mouth—a nest of plump tissue, soft, good and discreet grey
eyes. The Library of the Place Saint-Sulpice was where she spent her
days.

'Na ja also, lass mich in Ruhe denn!* Attend to your cooking!'
she shouted as Bertha began her customary playful greetings.

Bertha always was conscious of her noise, of shallowness and worldli-
ness: this shrewd, slow, monosyllabic bookworm brought out all that
was worst in her: she wanted to caper round it, inviting it to cumbrous
play, like a small flippant mongrel around a mastiff. She was much
more *femme,** she said, but Clara did not regard this as an attainment,
she knew. Being *femme* had taken up so much of her energy and life
that she could not expect to be so complete in other ways as Clara
however, Clara would occasionally show impatience at Bertha's skit-
tishness: a gruff man-like impatience entering grimly into the man-
part, but claiming at the same time its prerogatives.

'Clara, Soler has told me to send a picture to the Salon
d'Automne.'*

'Oh!' Clara was not impressed by success: the large insensitive
poster-landscapes of her companion had been removed from her
walls. She was preparing her own breakfast and jostled Bertha,
usurping more than half the table. Bertha delighted, retorted with
trills of shrill indignation. She recaptured the positions lost by her
plates. Her breakfast ready she carried it into her room, pretending
to be offended with Clara.

Breakfast over she wrote to Tarr. The letter was written quite
easily and directly: the convention of her passion was so trium-
phantly fixed that there was no scratching out or hesitation. 'I feel
so far away from you'—there was nothing more to be said; as it
had been said often before, it came promptly to the pen. All the feeling that could find expression was fluent large and assured, like the
handwriting. It never questioned the adequacy of these conventional
forms.

'Let Englishmen thank their stars—the good stars of the Northmen
and early seamen—that they have such stammering tongues and such
a fierce horror of grandiloquence. They are still true in their passion
because they are afraid, like children.'

This passage, from an article in the *English Review,** Tarr had
shown to Bertha with great relish. She relished it too, as the national
antithesis, she knew, was very interesting to this schoolboy. She agreed
that Englishmen were very strong and silent.

On the receipt of Tarr's letter she had felt, to begin with, very
indignant and depressed. That he should have had the strength to go
away without coming to see her was disquieting and unexpected. So
her letter began with a complaint about that. He had at last gone off,

with the first likelihood of permanence since they had known each other. Despite her long preparation, and although she had been the immediate cause of it, she was mortified at her success.

The Kreisler episode had been for her own private edification: she would free Sorbert by an act, in a sort of impalpable way: it had not been destined for publicity. The fact of the women surprising Kreisler and herself had destroyed the perspective. Tarr was not only in the right this time, but he had witnesses to confirm the justice of his action. To end nobly, on her own initiative, had been the idea; to make a last sacrifice to Sorbert in leaving him irrevocably, as she had sacrificed her feelings all along in allowing their engagement to be indefinitely protracted: and now, instead, everything had been turned into questionable meanness: she got no credit anywhere for her noble action.

She wrote her letter quite easily, as usual, but she did not, most unusually, believe in its efficacy. She even wrote it a trifle *more* easily than usual for that reason: its fluency seemed too fluent even to her. She rose a little startled from the table, and for some minutes held it in her hand, about to tear it up. But instead she sealed up the letter, sat down and addressed it.

In the drawer where she was putting Sorbert's latest letter away were some old ones. A letter of the year before she took out and read. With its two sentences it was more cruel and had more meaning than the one she had just received:—

'Put off that little Beaver woman. Let's be alone.'

It was a note she had received on the eve of an expedition to a village near Paris. She had promised to take a girl down with them. She was to show her the place, its hotel and the sketchable woods at the back. The girl had seen the place in her slashing bold and buxom canvases and so they had come to talk about it. The Beaver girl had not been taken: Sorbert and she had spent the night at an inn on the outskirts of the forest. They had come back in the train next day without speaking, having quarrelled in the inn. Wild regret for him suddenly struck her a series of sharp blows: she started crying again, quickly and vehemently.

The whole morning her methodic dusting and arranging depressed her. What was she doing it for? At four o'clock in the afternoon, as often happened, she was still in her dressing-gown and had not yet had lunch.

The *femme de ménage* came at eight every morning, doing Clara's rooms first. Bertha was in the habit of talking about Sorbert with Madame Vannier.

'Mademoiselle est triste?' this good woman said, noticing her dejection. 'C'est encore Monsieur Sorbert qui vous a fait du chagrin?'

'Oui madame, il est un salaud!' Bertha replied, half crying.

'Oh, il ne faut pas dire ça, mademoiselle: comment, il est un salaud?'* Madame Vannier worked silently with the quiet thud of felt slippers. Work was not without dignity for her. Bertha was playing at life. She admired and liked this handsome open-handed young german child of Fortune—she was clean, and educated. Monsieur Tarr was too young for her, though: also too dirty.

At two Madame Vannier took the letter to the post. She remarked that the address was London, England. She gave her head a slight toss.

CHAPTER 4

BERTHA'S friends looked for her elsewhere, nowadays, than at her rooms: Tarr was always likely to be found there in impolite possession. She made them come as often as she could; her coquetry as regards her carefully arranged rooms demanded numerous visitors: so it now suffered in the midst of her lonely tastefulness.

Since the dance none of her women friends had come to see her. She had spent an hour or two with them at the Restaurant however. At the dance itself she had kept rather apart: dazed, after a shock, and needing self-collection, was the line indicated by her sinewy but mournful movements. Her account of things could not of course be blurted out, it had to grow out of circumstances. Indeed as long a time as possible must be allowed to elapse before she referred to it directly. It must almost seem as though she were going to say nothing; impressive silence—nothing. Their minds, accustomed to her silence, would, when it came, find the explanation all the more impressive.

At a Café after the dance her account of the thing flowered grudgingly. They were as yet at the stage of exclamations.

'He came there on purpose to create a disturbance. Whatever for, I wonder!'

'I expect it was the case of Fräulein Fuchs over again.' (Kreisler had, on a former occasion, paid his court to a lady of this name, with resounding unsuccess.)

'If I'd have known what was going on I'd have dealt with him!' said one of the men.

'Didn't you say he told a pack of lies, Renée—?'

Fräulein Liepmann had been sitting, her eyes fixed upon a tram near by, watching the people crawling in and out. The exclamations of her friends did not, it appeared, interest her. It would have been no doubt scandalous if Kreisler had not been execrated: but anything they could say was inadequate when measured with the 'gemeine alte Sau.' The terrific corroding of that epithet (known only to her) made her sulky and impatient.

Applied to in this way directly about the lies, she turned to the others slowly and said:—

'Ecoutez—listen!' leaning towards the greater number of them (seeming to say "it's really simple enough, as simple as it is disagree-able: I am going to settle the question for you: let us then discuss it no more"). Her lips were a little white with fatigue, her eyes heavy with disgust at it all: fighting these things she however came to their assistance.

'Listen: we none of us know anything about that man'; this was an unfortunate beginning for Bertha, as thoughts, if not eyes, would leap in her direction, and Fräulein Liepmann even paused as though about to qualify this: 'We none of us, I think, want to know anything about him: therefore why this idiot—the last sort of beer-drinking brute—treated us to his bestial and—and—despicable foolery—?'

Fräulein Liepmann shrugged her shoulders with contemptuous indifference.

'I assure you it is not one of the things that interest me to know *why* such brutes behave like that at certain times. I don't see any mys-tery, for my part. Where is the mystery? It seems odd to you does it that HERR KREISLER should be an offensive brute?' she eyes them a moment. 'To me NOT!'

'We do him far too much honour by discussing him, that's certain' said one of them. But Fräulein Liepmann had something further to say.

'When one is attacked, one does not spend one's time in considering *why* one is attacked, but in defending oneself. I am just fresh from the "souillures de ce brute."*—If you knew the words he had addressed to me!'

Eckhart was getting very red, his eyes were shining, and he was moving rhythmically in his chair something like a steadily rising sea.

'Where does he live, Fräulein?' he asked.

'*Nein, Eckhart*: one could not allow anybody to embroil themselves with that useless brute.' The 'nein, Eckhart' had been drawled fondly at once, as though that contingency had been weighed. It implied as well an 'of course' for his red and dutiful face. 'I myself, if I meet him anywhere, shall deal with him better than you could: this is one of the occasions for a woman—.'

Bertha's story had come uncomfortably and difficultly to flower. No one seemed to want to hear it. She wished she had not waited so long. But, the matter put in the light given it by Fräulein Liepmann, she must not delay: she was, there was no question about it, in some sense responsible for Kreisler. It was her duty *to explain* him: but now Fräulein Liepmann had put an embargo on explanations: there were to be no more explanations.

The subject was drawing perilously near the point where it would be dropped: Fräulein Liepmann was summing up, and doing the final offices of the law over the condemned and already unspeakable Kreisler. No time was to be lost. The breaking in now involved inevitable conflict of a sort with Fräulein Liepmann: for she was going to 'say a word for Kreisler' *after* Fräulein Liepmann's address: (how much better it would have been before!).

So at this point, looking up from the table, Bertha (listened to with uncomfortable unanimity) began. She was smiling with an affectedly hesitating, timid and drooping face, the neighbourhood of her eyes suffused slightly with blood, her lips purring the words a little:—

'Renée, I feel that I ought to say something—.'

Renée Liepmann turned towards her composedly.

'I had not meant to say anything—about what happened to me, that is: I, as a matter of fact, have something particularly to complain of. But I had nothing to say about it. Only, since you are all discussing it, I thought you might not quite understand if I didn't—. I don't think, Renée, that Herr Kreisler was quite in his right mind this evening. I may be wrong, but I must say, Renée, he doesn't strike me as méchant: I don't think he was really accountable for his actions. Of course, I know no more about him than you do: this evening was the first time I have ever exchanged more than a dozen words with him in my life and then should not have done so except for—.'

This was said in the sing-song of quick parenthesis, eyebrows lifted, and with little gestures of the hand.

'He caught hold of me—like this' she made a violent snatching gesture all of a sudden at Fräulein Liepmann, who did not like this attempt at intimidation and withdrew to a safe distance out of reach. 'He was kissing me when you came up' turning to one or two of the others. This was said with dramatic pointedness, the 'kissing' spat with a sententious brutality and a luscious disparting of the lips.

'We couldn't make out *whatever* was happening—' one of them began.

'When you came up I felt quite dazed: I didn't feel that it was a man kissing me. He was mad, I'm sure he was. It was like being mauled by a brute!' She shuddered, with rather rolling eyes. 'He *was* a brute to-night—it was a brute we had with us to-night: he didn't know what he was doing.'

They were all silent. Her view only differed from the official one in supposing that he was not *always* a brute. She had drawn up short: their silence became conscious and septic. They appeared as though they had not expected her to stop speaking, and were like people surprised naked, with no time to cover themselves.

'I think he's in great difficulties—it's money or something: but all I know for certain is that he was *really* in need of somebody—.'

'But what makes you think, Bertha—' one of the girls said, hesitating.

'I let him in at Renée's; he looked very peculiar to me, didn't you notice? I noticed him first when I let him in.'

Anastasya Vasek was sitting with them: she had not joined in the Kreisler-palaver. With the air of a newcomer in some community, participating for the first time at one of their debates on a local and stock subject, she followed their remarks with a polite attention: Bertha she examined as a person would some particularly eloquent chief airing his views at a clan-meeting.

'I felt he was *really* in need of some hand to help him, he seemed just like a child.' She sugared her gaze with the maternal illumination. 'The poor man was ill as well—I thought he would drop—he can't have eaten anything all day: I am sure he hasn't. He was walking slower and slower—that's how it was we were so far behind—he could hardly totter along—when he had smoked a cigarette he went quicker—but he was light-headed all the time. I should have realized, I know—! It was my fault—what happened: at least—.'

The hungry touch had been an improvisation: she had then almost said 'until he had bought a packet of cigarettes' but saw just in time that that would draw the retort 'if he had the money to buy cigarettes, why not food?'

'You make him quite a romantic figure: I'm afraid he's been working on your feelings my dear girl! I saw no signs of an empty stomach myself' said Fräulein van Bencke.

'He refreshed himself extensively at the dance in any case! You can put your mind at rest as to his present emptiness' Renée Liepmann said.

The subject languished. The Liepmann had taken her stand on boredom: she was committed to the theory of the unworthiness of this discussion. Bertha's speeches provoked no further comment: it was as if she had been putting in her little bit of abuse of the common enemy.

The certain lowering of the vitality of the party when she came on the scene with her story offended Bertha, there should have been noise and movement. It was not quite the lifelessness of scepticism: but it bore an uncomfortable resemblance to the manner of people listening to speeches they do not believe. She persevered, but her intervention had killed the topic and they merely waited until she had ended her war-dance upon its corpse.

As to Tarr and the references to Iscariot in his letter, he had fallen in with the red-headed member of the party by chance: learning that he had not seen Bertha since the night of the ball with roguish pleasantness this girl had remarked that 'he'd better look after her better, why hadn't he come to the dance with his fiancée? Oh là là! the goings-on, the goings-on!' Tarr had not understood.

Bertha had had an adventure, he then was told; *all* of them, for that matter, had had an adventure, but *especially Bertha*.—Oh,

Bertha would tell him all about it. But, upon Tarr insisting, Bertha's adventure, in substance, had been told.

Now retrospectively, her friends insisted upon passing by the two remarkably unanimous-looking forms on the Boulevard, in stony silence: she shouted to them and kissed Kreisler loudly; it was no use! They refused to take any notice. She sulked and kept to herself day after day. She would make a change in her life: she might go back to Germany; she might go to another quarter of Paris. To go on with her daily life as though nothing had happened was out of the question. A series of demonstrations were called for, of a fairly violent order.

Her burly little clock struck four. Hurrying on reform-clothes,* she went out to buy lunch. The dairy lay almost next door to Vallet's restaurant. Crossing the road in front of the restaurant she caught sight of Kreisler's steadily marching figure approaching. First she side-stepped and half turned: but the shop would be reached before they met, so she went on, with quickening step and downcast eye. But her eye, covertly observing him (calculating distances and speeds) saw him hesitate—evidently having just caught sight of *her*—and then turn down a side street nearly beside the dairy for which she was making. There was something depressing about this action of Kreisler's. Even the pariahs fled from her. How alone she was in this world, *mon Dieu*!

CHAPTER 5

BUT Herr Kreisler, on his side, had been only a few paces from his door when he caught sight of Bertha. As his changed route would necessitate a good deal of tiresome circling to bring him back practically to the spot from which he had started, he right-about-faced in a minute or two, the danger past, as he thought. The result was, that, as Bertha left the shop, there was Kreisler, approaching again, with the same fatal, martial monotony, almost in the same place as before.

She was greeted affably, as though to say 'Caught! both of us!' He was under the impression, however, that she had lain in wait for him: he was so accustomed to think of her in that character. Had she been in full flight he would have imagined that she was only decoying him: she was a woman of that sort—one of the stickers!

'How do you do? I've just been buying my lunch.'

'So late?'

'I thought you'd left Paris!' She had no information of this sort, but was inclined to rebuke him for *not* leaving Paris.

'I? Who told you that I should like to know! I shall never leave Paris; at least—.'

There was a sudden wealth of enigmatic significance in this, said lightly—the heartbreak note—the colossal innuendo did not escape her, sensible to such nuances.

'How are our fair friends?' asked he.

'Our—? Why Fräulein Liepmann I suppose you mean and—. Oh I haven't seen them since the other night.'

'Indeed! Not since the other night—?'

She made her silence swarm with unuttered thoughts, like a glassy shoal with innumerable fish: her eyes, even, stared and darted about, glassily.

It was very difficult, now she had stopped, to get away: the part she had adopted with her friends, of Otto's champion, seemed to have imposed itself on her. Her protégé could not be hurried away from exactly: the fact that he did not this time hurry away from her, even, had its weight.

His more brutal instincts had latterly remained within close call: even quite novel appetites had put in an appearance. The fact that she was a pretty girl did its work on a rather recalcitrant subject.

Surely for a quiet ordinary existence pleasant little distractions were suitable? The time had to be filled up somehow.

Without any anxiety about it, he began to talk to Bertha with the idea of a subsequent meeting. Like other women, she no doubt had a—she no doubt had all—had what all—. He had avoided her not to be reminded of disquieting events: but she turned, as he stood in front of her, into a bit of comfort. What he particularly needed was a certain quietude, enlivened by healthy appetites.

'I was cracked the other night, quite potty!* I'm not often in that state' he said. Bertha's innuendoes had to receive recognition.

'I'm glad to hear that' she answered.

To have been kissed was after all to have been kissed: Bertha threw a little fascination into her attitude—she flexed one knee, juiced her lips a little and cocked a serious eye into non-committal distances.

'I'm afraid I was rather rude to Fräulein Liepmann before leaving: did she speak about it?'

'I think you were rude to everybody!'

'Ah well—.'

'I must be going. My lunch—.'

'Oh I'm so sorry, have I kept you from your lunch? I was so glad to meet you—under more normal conditions! I had some things I wished to say to you. Ahem!' He gave the stiff little cough of his student days. 'I wonder if you would procure me the extreme pleasure of seeing you again?'

Bertha looked at him in astonishment, taking in this sensational request. See Kreisler again! How—when—why? The result as regards the Liepmann circle! This pleaded for Kreisler: it would be carrying out her story: this insistence upon it would destroy that subtle advantage, now possessed by her friends. Presented with rather the same compromising spectacle again they would be somewhat nonplussed! All the arguments in favour of seeing more of Kreisler marshalled themselves with rapidity. In deliberately exposing herself to criticism, she would be effacing, in some sense, the extreme *involuntariness* of the Boulevard incident. It was in a jump of defiance or 'carelessness,' her mind's eye on those cattish troublesome friends, that she exclaimed:—

'Yes, of course, if you wish it! Why not!'

'You like Cafés? There's such a good concert—.'

'Good! Very well!' she answered very quickly, in her trenchant tone, imparting all sorts of unnecessary meanings to her simple acceptance: she had answered as men accept a bet or the Bretons clinch a bargain in the fist. 'Certainly! Fine! Cafés! Schön. Thanks a thousand times. Good-bye! *Auf wiedersehen!*'

Kreisler was leisurely: he met her vehemence with sleepy amusement.

'I should then like to go with you to the Café de l'Observatoire to-morrow evening!' He stood smiling down at her 'faraway' frowning ox-eye. 'When can I meet you?'

'Will you come and fetch me at my house?'

Shivers went down her back as she said it. She was now thoroughly committed. She was delighted, or rather excited. Each fresh step was a thrill. But the details had not been reckoned on: of course they would have to *meet*: Kreisler was like a physician conducting a little, unpleasant, operation, in an ironical, unhurrying way.

'Well it's understood: we shall see each other tomorrow' he said. With a smile of half raillery at her rather upset expression, he left her upon his invariable stiff bow, his hat held up in the air, derisively high. So much fuss about a little thing, such obstinacy in doing it! What was it after all? Meeting him!—his smiling was only natural. She showed with too little disguise the hazardous quality, as she considered it, of this consent: she would wish him to feel the largeness of the motive that prompted her, and for him to participate too in the certain horror of meeting himself! Well well well! What a goose! A plump and pleasing goose, however! Yes! He marched away with the rather derisive smile still upon his face.

CHAPTER 6

Back in her rooms, Bertha examined, over her lunch, with stupefaction, the things she had been up to—her conversations, farewell letters, appointments, and all the rest. All in a few hours! What a strange proceeding though! Was she quite responsible for her actions?

She was prevented from brooding over Sorbert's going. Of Kreisler she thought very little: her women friends held the centre of the stage. As she imagined their response to the new situations she was creating, she saw them staring open-mouthed at her supersession: Tarr to Kreisler: from bad to worse.

The key to her programme was a cumulative obstinacy: a person has made some slip in grammar, say: he makes it again on purpose so that his first involuntary speech may appear deliberate.

She resumed her customary pottering, dawdling from one domestic task to another. Fräulein Elsa von Arnim, one of the Dresden sisters, interrupted her. At the knock she thought of Tarr and Kreisler simultaneously, welded in one, and her heart beat in double-time. Elsa had a cold reception.

'Isn't it hot? It's simply grilling out in the street. I had to go into the gardens and get under the trees. I left the studio quite early.'

Fräulein von Arnim sat down, giving her hat a toss and squinting up at it.

These dirty anaemic sisters had a sort of soiled, insignificant handsomeness. They explained themselves, roughly, by describing in a cold-blooded lazy way their life at home. A stepmother, prodigiously smart, well-to-do, neglecting them; sent first to one place, then another (now Paris) to be out of the way. Yet the stepmother supplies them superfluously from her superfluity.

They talked about themselves as twin parcels, usually on the way from one place to another, expensively posted here and there sealed and registered, the Royal Mail, but without real destination. They enjoyed nothing at all; unless it was the society of Fräulein Liepmann. Their stepmother neglected them, she was very smart and well-off, she gave them plenty of money, and despatched them hither and thither, always out of the way.

'Oh! Bertha, I didn't know your dear "Sorbert" was going to England.'—*Deiner Sorbert* was the bantering formula for Tarr. Bertha was incessantly talking about him—to them, to the charwoman, to the greengrocer opposite, to everybody she met: so Tarr was for them her possession, her Tarr.

'Didn't you? Oh yes he's gone.'

'You've not quarrelled—with your Sorbert?'

'What's that to do with you, my dear?' Bertha gave a brief, indecent laugh. 'By the way, I've just met Herr Kreisler. He's going to take me to a wine-restaurant tomorrow night, isn't it lovely!'

'Wine-restaurant with—! Well! I like your taste!'

'What's the matter with Herr Kreisler? You were all friendly enough with him a week ago.'

Elsa looked at her with a cold-blooded scrutiny, puffing cigarette smoke towards her as though in an attempt to reach her with its impalpable scented cloud.

'But he's a vicious brute, but above all a brute, simply. Besides, there are other reasons for avoiding Herr Kreisler: you know the reason of his behaviour the other night? It was, it appears, because Anastasya Vasek snubbed him. He was nearly the same when the Fuchs wouldn't take an interest in him. He can't leave women alone: he follows them about and annoys them, and then becomes—well, as you saw him the other night—when he's shaken off. He is impossible. He is a really hopeless brute who should be given as wide a berth as possible.'

'Where did you hear all that! I don't think that Fräulein Vasek's story is true for a moment, I am certain—.'

'Well, he once was like that with me. Yes think of it! Even with me. He began hanging around, and—. You know the story of his engagement?'

'What engagement?'

'He was engaged to a girl and she married his father instead of marrying him.'

Bertha struggled a moment a little baffled.

'Well what is there in that? I don't see anything in that. You are all so unfair—that's my complaint. His fiancée married! I've known several cases—.'

'Yes. That *by itself*—.'

Elsa was quite undisturbed. She was talking to a child. She offered it advice but it must take it or leave it. In a few moments Bertha returned to the charge.

'Did Fräulein Vasek give that particular explanation of Herr Kreisler's behaviour?'

'No. We put two and two together. She did say something, yes, she did as a matter of fact say that she thought she had been the cause of Kreisler's behaviour.'

'How funny! I can't stand that girl! she's so unnatural, she's such a *poseuse*! Don't you think, Elsa? But what a funny thing to say! You can depend on it that *that*, anyhow, is not the explanation.'

'No?'

'Why no! Certainly not!'

'Sorbert has a rival perhaps?'

This remark was met in staring silence. It was an unnecessary intrusion of something as inapropos as unmanageable: it deserved no reply, it would get none from her. She had no intention of conceding the light tone required.

Elsa had admitted that Fräulein Vasek was responsible for the statement '*I* was the cause of Kreisler's behaviour,' etc. That was one of those things (seeing there was no evidence to confirm or even suggest it) which at once place a woman on a peculiar pinnacle of bad taste, incomprehensibleness and horridness. Bertha's personal estimation of Kreisler received a complex fillip.*

This ridiculous version—coming after her version and superseding it with her cats of friends was, why, a sort of *rival version*. And in such exquisite taste! Such pretentiousness should discredit it in advance, it should with decent people.

Bertha took some minutes to digest Elsa's news: she flushed and frowned: the more she thought of this rival version of Fräulein Vasek's the more repulsive it appeared. It was a startlingly novel view, it gave proof of a perfect immodesty. It charged hers full tilt. For three days now this story of hers had been her great asset, she had staked her little all upon it. Now some one had coolly set up shop next door, to sell an article in which she, and she alone, had specialized. Here was an unexpected, gratuitous, *new* inventor of Versions come along: and what a version, to start with!

Bertha's version had been a vital matter: Fräulein Vasek's was a matter of vanity clearly. The contempt of the workman, sweating for a living, for the amateur, possessed her.

But there was a graver aspect to the version of this poaching Venus. In discrediting Bertha's suggested account of how things had happened, it attacked indirectly her action, proceeding, ostensibly, from those notions. Her meeting Kreisler at present depended for its reasonableness upon the 'hunger' theory; or, if that should fail, something equally touching and primitive. Were she forced to accept, as Elsa readily did, the *snub-by-Anastasya* theory, with its tale of ridiculous reprisals, further dealings with Kreisler would show up in a bare and ugly light. Her past conduct also would have its primitive slur renewed. She saw all this immediately: her defiance had been delivered with great gusto—'I am meeting Herr Kreisler to-morrow!' The shine had soon been taken off that.

The weak point in Anastasya's calm and contradictory version was the rank immodesty of the form it took.

Bertha's obstinacy awoke: in a twinkling her partisanship of Kreisler was confirmed. She had a direct interest now in their meeting: she was most curious to hear what he had to say as to his alleged attempt in Fräulein Vasek's direction.

'Well, I'm going to Renée's now to fetch her for dinner. Are you coming?' Elsa said, getting up.

'No. I'm going to dine here to-night' and Bertha accompanied her to the door, humming an especially 'gay' air, with the most off-hand of expressions to leave in no doubt the true meaning of the tune.

CHAPTER 7

PEOPLE appear with a startling suddenness sometimes out of the fog of Time and Space: so Kreisler appeared—such an apparition! Bertha did not visualize her countryman very readily: and the next day she was surprised when she saw him below her windows. He stared up at the house with eager speculation: he examined the house and studio opposite. Behind the curtains Bertha stood with the emotions of an ambushed sharp-shooter; she felt on her face the blankness of the house wall, all her body was as unresponsive as a brick: the visitor beneath appeared almost to be looking at her face, magnified and exposed instead of at the walls of the house and its windows.

Then it appeared to her that it was *he*, the enemy, getting in: she wished to stop him there, before he came any farther: he was a bandit, a house-breaker, after all a dangerous violent person.

Yet in the processes of his uncertainty he looked so innocuous and distant, for the moment. His first visit: there he was, so far, a stranger. Why should these little obstacles of strangeness—which gate to enter, which bell to ring—be taken away from this particular individual? He should remain 'stranger' for her, where he came from: *she* did not want him any nearer to her. But he had burrowed his way through, was at the bell already, and would soon be at herself: he would be at her! He would be breaking into her: she did not wish him inside, he was well enough where he was. *She* found here, in her room, was very different from *she* found outside, in restaurant or street: the clothing of this décor was a nakedness: she revolted immobile and alarmed.

For a moment she struggled up from the obstinate dream, made of artificial but tenacious sentiments, shaped by 'contretemps'* of all sorts which had been accumulating like a snow-ball ever since her last interview with Tarr. Still somewhat rapt in this interview she rolled in its nightmarish, continually metamorphosed substance, through Space: where would it land her—this electric, directionless, vital affair? The 'Indifference' and the 'Difference,' they had floated her, successfully, away in *some* direction. Again the bell rang: then the knocker, the little copper gargoyle, began to thunder. She could see him, almost, through the wall, standing phlegmatic and erect. They had not spoken yet: but they had been some minutes 'in touch.'

Perhaps this visitor was after all *mad?* Elsa, with her warnings for her, came into her mind: however much she resisted the facts, there was very little reason for this meeting. It was now unnecessary. It had been exploded actually by Anastasya. She was going through with something that no longer meant anything at all.

As the bell rang a third time she walked to the door. Kreisler was a little haggard, different from the day before. He had expected to be asked in: instead, hardly saying anything, she came out on the narrow

landing and closed the door behind her with a bang. Surprised, he felt
for the first stair with his foot: it was eight in the evening, very dark
on the staircase and he stumbled several times. Bertha felt she *could*
not say the simplest word to him. She had the impression that some
lawyer's clerk had come to fetch her for a tragic interview; and she,
having been sitting fully dressed for unnecessary hours in advance,
was now urging him silently and violently before her, following.

That afternoon she had received a second letter from Sorbert.

'MY DEAR BERTHA.—Excuse me for the quatsch* I wrote the
other day. Simply, I think we had better say, finally, that we will
try and get used to not seeing each other, and give up our idea of
marriage. Do you agree with me? As you will see, I am still here, in
Paris. I am going to England this afternoon.—Yours ever,
                                                        SORBETT.'

On the receipt of this letter—as on the former occasion a little—
she first of all behaved as she would have done had Sorbert been
there: she acted silent resignation, and 'went about her work as
usual,' for the benefit of the letter, in the absence of its author. The
reply, written an hour or so before Kreisler arrived, had been an
exaggerated falling in with the view expressed.—'Of course, Sorbert:
far better that we should part! far far better!' and so forth. But soon
this letter of his began to molest her. It even threatened her manner-
isms. She was just going to take up a book and read, when, as though
something had claimed her attention, she put it down: she got up,
her head turned back over her shoulder, then suddenly flung herself
down upon the sofa as though it had been rocks and she plunging
down on to them from a high cliff. She sobbed until she had tired
herself out.

So Kreisler and she now walked up the street as though compelled
by some very strange circumstances, only, to be in each other's company. He appeared depressed, he too had come under the spell of
some meaningless duty: his punctuality even suggested fatigued and
senseless waiting, careful timing. His temporary destination reached,
he delivered himself up indifferently into her hands. He remarked
that it was hot: she did not answer. They said nothing but walked on
away from her house: neither seemed to require any explanation for
these peculiar manners.

Before they got to the Café de l'Observatoire Kreisler attempted to make up for his lapse into strangeness: he discovered, however, that he had not been alone, and desisted.

Bertha looked in at the door, at the clock inside, as they took up their place on the quieter 'terrasse.' She asked herself how long she would stop. A half-hour, she thought.

CHAPTER 8

'Who is that, then—Anass—what?' Kreisler asked, after some moments of gradually changing silence, when Miss Vasek began to be mentioned by Bertha. He was stretched out in massive abandon and seemed interested in nothing in the world.

This meeting had been the only event of the day for him: at first he had looked forward to it a little, but as it approached he had grown fidgety, he began counting the time, it became a burden. What useless errand was he on now, he pondered, and could not make out how he had come to let himself in for this at all. It was a mystery. He would not have gone. But the appointment being made, and fixed in his mind, and he having felt it in the distance all day, he knew if he did *not* go that he would be still more uncomfortable. In the empty evening he would have been at the mercy of this thing-not-done, like an itch.

Bertha, for her part, had now recovered: Kreisler's complete abstraction and indifference were a soothing atmosphere. He seemed to know as little why he was there as she, or less. He was plainly only waiting for her to disappear again. As to there being anything compromising in this meeting, that could be dismissed on every count: and he looked very unlikely to suggest another. Elsa's description of his conduct with women came to mind, as she sat beside this aloof and lounging statue. *This* was the man who had caused her fresh misgivings! When a dog or cow has passed a trembling child without any signs of doing it mischief, the child sometimes is inclined to step after it and put forth a caressing hand. She felt almost drawn to this inoffensive person.

Kreisler had created a situation not unlike that of the Dance-night: there they sat, she pressing him a little now, he politely apathetic. It seemed for all the world as though Bertha had run after him somewhere and forced a meeting upon him, to which he had grudgingly consented. Bertha was back in what would always be for him her characteristic rôle. And so now she appeared still to be following him up, to the discomfort of both, for some unexplained reason.

'No I don't know who you mean' he said, replying to descriptions of Anastasya. 'A tall girl you say? No, I can't bring to mind a tall girl, answering to that description.'

He liked fingering over listlessly the thought of Anastasya, but as a stranger: the subject gave him a little more interest in Bertha, just as, for her, it had a similar effect in his favour. Forthwith she was quite convinced that Fräulein Vasek had been guilty of the most offensive, the most self-complacent, mistake. *Pfui!*

Bertha now had achieved a simplification or synopsis of the whole matter as follows:

Anastasya Vasek, alleged bastard of a Grand Duke, a beautiful and challengingly original Modern Girl,* arrives, bespangled and replete with childish self-confidence, upon the scene of her (Bertha's) simple little life—her plain blunt womanhood contrasted with this pretentious super-sex: this audacious interloper had discovered her kissing, and being kissed in return by an absurd individual in the middle of the street. Bertha had disengaged herself rapidly from this compromising embrace, and had explained that she had been behaving in that way solely because he had captured her pity through his miserable and half-starved appearance; that, even then, he had assaulted her, and she had been found in that delicate situation entirely independent of her own will. Anastasya's lip had curled, and she had received these explanations in silence. Then, upon their nervous repetition, she had negligently observed, with the perfect effrontery of the minx that she was—'You were no doubt being hugged by Herr Kreisler in the middle of the pavement as you admit and as we all were able to observe, the motives the ordinary ones. You might have waited till—but that's your own business. On the other hand, the reason of his devastated appearance this evening and of all the rest of his goings-on, was *this*. He had the colossal neck* to wish to make up to me: I sent him about his business, and he "manifested" in the way you know.'

Reducing all the confused material of this affair to such essential proportions, Bertha saw clearly the essence of her action. Definite withdrawal from the circle of her friends had now become essential. It was being accomplished with as much style as possible: Kreisler provided the style. She cast a glance upon this at her silent abstracted companion, and smiled. The smile was not ill-natured.

It was her first instinct now to wallow still more in this unbecoming situation. She desired even to be seen with Kreisler. The meanness, the strangeness, the *déchéance*, in consorting with this sorry bird, must be heightened into poetry and thickened with luscious fiction. *They had driven her to this—they were driving her!* Very well—she was weary, she was *lasse* (she drooped beside Otto as she pondered), she would satisfy them. She would satisfy Sorbert—it was what he wanted, was it not? She would be faithful to his wishes, his last wishes.

Kreisler was the central, irreducible element in this mental pie: he was the egg-cup that kept up the crust. She tried to interest herself in Kreisler and satisfy Tarr, her friends, the entire universe, more thoroughly.

CHAPTER 9

DESTINY has more power over the superstitious: they attract constantly bright fortunes and disasters within their circle. Destiny had laid its trap in the unconscious Kreisler. It had fixed it with powerful violent springs.—Eight days later (dating from the Observatoire meeting) it snapped down upon Bertha.

Kreisler's windows had been incandescent with steady saffron rays coming over the roofs of the Quarter: it was a record conflagration of *der Gang*. His small shell of a room had breasted them with pretence of antique adventure: the old boundless yellow lights streamed from their abstract Eldorado:* they were a Gulf Stream* for our little patch of a world, making a people as quiet as the English. Men once more were invited to be the motes in the sunbeam and to play in the sleepy surf upon the edge of remoteness.

Now, from within, his windows looked as suddenly harsh and familiar: unreasonable limitations gave its specific colour to thin glass.

The clock struck eight: like eight metallic glittering waves dashing discordantly together in a cavern, its strokes rushed up and down in Bertha's head. She was leaning upon the mantelshelf, head sunk forward, with the action of a person about to be sick.

A moment before she had struggled up from the bed—the last vigour at her disposal being spent in getting away from that at all costs.

'Oh Schwein! Schwein! Ich hass dich—ich hass dich! Schwein! *Pfui!* du hässlicher Mensch du!'*

All the repulsion of her being, in a raw indecent heat, seemed turned into this tearful sonority, pumped up in spasms and hissing on her lips as she spat out the usual epithets for the occasion. The deepening sing-song of the 'hässlicher Mensch!' was accompanied by a disgusting sound like the brutal relishing and gobbling of food. The appetite of hatred spat and gobbled while it lasted. Her attitude was reminiscent of the way people are seen to stand, bent awkwardly forward, neck craned out, slowly wiping the dirt off their clothes, or spitting out the remains of their polluted drink, cursing the person who has victimized them, after the successful execution of some practical joke. This had been, too, a practical joke of the primitive and whimsical order, in its madness and inconsequence. But it was of a solemn and lonely kind, more like the tricks that desperate people play upon themselves: at its consummation there had been no chorus of intelligible laughter.—An uncontrolled satyrlike figure had suddenly leapt away from the battling Amazon—it was all over, the day was lost, she lay convulsed upon her back, her mouth smeared with blood: in a struggle that had been outrageous and extreme, rolling in each other's arms, like confederates beneath the same ban of the world's law, only calling to each other hoarsely under their breaths, Bertha and he had fought out the simple point, mysteriously fierce, like snarling animals. A joke too deep for laughter, parodying the phrase alienating sorrow and tears, had been achieved in this encounter.

A folded blouse lay upon the corner of Kreisler's bleak trunk. Bertha's arms and shoulders were bare, her hair hanging in wisps and strips: generally, a Salon picture* was the result. For purposes of work (he had asked her to sit for him) the blouse had been discarded. A jagged tear in her chemise over her right breast also seemed the doing of a Salon artist of facile and commercial invention: a heavy Susanna-like breast* heaved uncontrollably.

Kreisler stood at the window. His eyes had an expressionless lazy stare, his lips were open. His conscious controls and the entire body were still spinning and stunned: his muscles teemed with actions not finished, sharp, when the action finished: he was still swamped with violence. His sudden immobility, as he stood there, made the posthumous riot of movement rise to his brain like wine from a feeble body. Satisfaction however had damped and softened everything except this tingling prolongation of action.

Bertha's hidden face was strained into an old woman's bitter mask, inane tears soaking into it. A watchful fate appeared to be inventing morals to show her the folly of her perpetual romancing: this was its last cynical invention: what had occurred was senseless, there was not a visible pinshead of compensation. It never occurred to her that such things could be arrived at without traversing romance. But where oh where was the romance in this occurrence? The terrible *absence of romance* crushed her.

The famous embrace upon the evening-boulevard had been followed by a vast scaffolding of fable and ingenious explanation. What was this to be followed by? By nothing. Her heart sank: with the ultimate thud of nightmare it struck bottom. This was an end of all explanations. She recognized the logic of this act—more repulsive by far than its illogic. Oh what a fool she had been, for this was a dark insult—the *Shicksal*, the Shicksal had spat in her face.

A separate framework of time had been arranged for it to happen in, this last disrespectful attack. A moment before, it was quite impossible to say how long, Otto Kreisler, the swine-man standing at that window over there, had been tranquilly scratching away at his wretched drawing. In a pose improvised by her with quick ostentatious understanding—it represented the most captivating moment of a lady's toilette, the hair down, a comb in her hand—she had sat a humorous indulgence in her eye for her not very skilful colleague: she had been partly undressed: the scene was significant.

That stage had been preceded (as she dizzily went backwards) by one in which she had been assailed by sudden anxieties: startled by his request to draw her 'shoulders'—her bare shoulders, arms and probably breasts, she could not refuse her breasts—immediately she had repressed the unworthy prejudice by which she had been assailed: she had come to sit for him and her body of course was a most beautiful thing, whereas the mere idea that there was any danger was extremely repulsive where there was any question of a beautiful thing—*Pfui!* He was an artist (a bad one, poor chap, but professional!) they were two priests of Beauty.

'Shall I strip?' she had asked jauntily, cocking her big blue eye. 'I have rather good legs.'

'I don't want your legs at the moment' Kreisler had replied.

'No? Oh. To the waist?'

'Just the arms and breasts, I think.'

'The arms and breasts? Good.'

While he was working they had not talked. Then he had put down his paper and chalk, stretched, and delivered himself of the unusual remark:

'Your arms are like bananas!'

'Oh!'

A shiver of anxiety had penetrated her at the word 'bananas': anybody who could regard her arms in that light was inartistic: she was distinctly glad that her 'good' legs had not been wanted. He was a modern artist of course and it was natural, perhaps inevitable, that he should compare her arms to bananas.

'Oh are they like that? they are rather flat. I hope you've made a good drawing. May I see?'

The rationale of the exposure must be emphasized a little now that she was not posing and that she had scented a freshness in his manner. He had got up: before she quite knew what was happening he had caught hold of both her arms above the elbow, chafing them violently up and down, remarking:

'You have pins and needles Fräulein?' Fräulein used here had a disquieting sound: she drew herself away, with understanding, but upon the defence.

'No thank you: now I will put my clothes on if you have finished. I'm a little cold. It's fresh.'

He knew it was not fresh as she was perspiring; he smiled—a 'dangerous,' a very equivocal, smile.

They had eyed each other uncertainly for a moment, he with a flushed fixed extremely stupid smile. She was afraid to move away now—she fixed him absent-mindedly with knit brow, her large eye revolving slightly. He straddled close up to her, growing more male every moment, his eyes settling down 'masterfully' into her one heavily-focussed optic, and then he coughed.

'Let me chafe your arm! I like doing it.'

'No.—Thanks!' she had replied sharply without moving.

She could see a gold-stopping and a gap on the right of his mouth as his lip curved up in the extension of his grin, become now an even lurid danger-signal. His eye fell some inches and with dismay she observed its lid drooping with a suggestive promise of a 'dangerous' passion. His gaze reposed with obvious boldness upon her bust.

'Your breasts are good!' he almost shouted, shooting up a hand to finger one—she thrust his hand away with force and shouted back:

'Yes: they are good. But I don't wish you to touch me: you understand that?'

With the fury of a person violently awakened to some insult he had flung himself upon her: her tardy panting expostulation, defensive prowess, disappeared in the whirlpool towards which they had both with a strange deliberateness and yet aimlessness, been steering.

An iron curtain rushed down upon that tragedy: he was standing there at the window now as though to pretend that nothing had passed to his knowledge; she had been dreaming things, merely. The monotony and silence of the posing had prepared her for the strangeness now: that other extreme joined hands with this. She saw side by side and unconnected, the silent figure engaged in drawing her bust and the other one full of blindness and violence. Then there were two other figures, one getting up from the chair, yawning, and the present lazy one at the window—four in all, that she could not for some reason bring together, each in a complete compartment of time of its own. It would be impossible to make the present idle figure at the window interest itself in these others. The figure talked a little to fill in an interval; it had drawn: it had suddenly flung itself upon her and done something disgusting: and now it was standing idly by the window, becalmed, and completely cut off from its raging self of the recent occurrence. It could do all these things: it appeared to be in a series of precipitate states: in this it resembled a switchback, rising slowly, in a steady innocent way, to the top of an incline, and then plunging suddenly down the other side with a catastrophic rush. The fury of her animal hostility did not survive this phase for long.

She had come there, got what she did not expect, and must now go away again, it was simple enough: to Kreisler there was nothing more to be said. There never had been anything to say to him: he was a mad beast as everyone had always been right in remarking.

Now she had to take her departure as though nothing had happened. It was nothing actually, nothing in fact had happened: what did it matter what became of her? The body was of little importance: what was the good (seeing what she knew and everything) of storming against this person?

She had done up her hair; her hat was once more on her head: she went towards the door, her face really haggard, the inevitable consciousness of drama providing the customary unnecessary emphasis. Kreisler turned round, went towards the door also, unlocked it, let her pass without saying anything, his eyes severely fixed upon the floor at his feet, and, waiting a moment, closed it indifferently again with a slight bang. She was let out as a workman would have been, who had been there to mend a shutter or rectify a bolt.

CHAPTER 10

BERTHA made her way home in a roundabout fashion. She did not court at that moment a meeting with anyone she knew. The streets were loftily ignorant of her small affairs. Thank God for bricks and mortar, for strangers, for the indifference of nature and its great extent! Ha! ha! with fat dejected back guffawed the shattered Bertha, the importance of our human actions! Is it more than the kissing of the bricks?

As she tramped on she experienced anger and astonishment at finding herself walking away in this matter-of-fact manner. That the customary street scene would absolutely not mix with the obsessional nature of her late experience perplexed her.

Nature no doubt was secret enough: but not to tell this experience of hers to *anybody* would be shutting her in with Kreisler, somehow for good: she would then never be able to escape the contamination of that abominable little attic of his. Was it not one of those things that in some form one should be able to tell? She had a growing wish to make it known at once somewhere or other.

The moral of the late event had had its chance of influencing her radically but it had not succeeded: nothing *radically* was changed: she began dreaming immediately of sacrifices, of the proper presentation of this harsh event: yet, spasmodically, disgust with Kreisler reappeared. *Kreisler by doing this had made an absolute finishing with Kreisler perhaps impossible?* That was an evil notion that she shook roughly off. No! Of Otto Kreisler—*enough!* No more of him, at least. *Pfui!* Of *that* no more!

There was nobody now on her side in any sense whatever, or upon whose side she could range herself. She was a sort of Kreisler now. Kreisler himself had taken his place beside her women friends, Tarr and so on, in a disgusting and dumbfounding way: the list of people who preyed on her mind and pushed her to all these ill-assorted actions. Kreisler she had set up as a 'cause' against her friends: in a manner peculiar to himself he had betrayed her and placed himself in the ranks of her critics. He had certainly carried out in the fullest fashion their estimate of him. So Kreisler had acted satanically on behalf of her friends.

She had seen Elsa and her sister twice that week. The others had not been near her. Now she could hardly go on talking about Kreisler. In examining likelihoods of the immediate future, she concluded that she would have to break still more with her women friends to make up for having to retire from her Kreisler positions. To counteract their satisfaction she must accentuate her independence, even to insult and contempt.

The recent outrage took up too much space: it seemed to require the other factors in the situation to come back and be referred to it. But this was not admissible: getting closed in with Kreisler—a survival, perhaps, of her vivid fear of a little time before, when he had locked the door, and she knew that resisting him would be useless—must be at all costs avoided. Everything pointed to the necessity of a confidante.

Whom could she tell? Clara? Madame Vannier?

Once home, she lay down and cried for some time. She did this in a businesslike way: she lay down, put her face into a pillow and bellowed softly.

She now began to regret a lost opportunity: should she have left Kreisler so undramatically? *Something* should have been done: there would have been the normal relief. Dramatic revenge even occurred to her: she thought of going back at once to his room: life could not get started quite clearly again until something had been done against him, or in some way where he was. She rolled over and cried on the other side.

Kreisler grew in importance: he had been a shadowy and unimportant nobody. Of this he had shown no consciousness. Rather dazed and machine-like, Bertha had treated him as she had found him: suddenly, without any direct articulateness, he had revenged himself as a machine might do, in a nightmare of violent action. At a leap he was in the rigid foreground of her life: in an immense clashing wink he had drawn attention to himself, but for such a comparatively short time, and the next moment there he had stood, abstracted and baffling as before: once more it was difficult to realize he was there, he was the machine again, a bone-headed nobody.

The real central figure all along, but purposely veiled, had been Tarr. He had been as really all-important (though to all appearance eliminated) as Kreisler had been of no importance, though propped up in the foreground. Sorbert at last could no longer be suppressed. He kept coming forward now in her mind. But his presence, too, was perplexing: she had grown so used to regarding him, though seeing him daily, as an uncertain, a departing figure, that now he had really gone that did not make much difference. So his proceedings, a carefully prepared anaesthesia for himself, had had their due effect, and drugged her too.

The bell rang. She stood up in one movement and stared towards the door. The bell rang a second and third time. How much persistence on the part of this visitor would draw her to the door? She did not know. Was it Elsa? She had lighted her lamp, and her visitor could therefore have seen that she was at home.

At length Bertha went to the door with affected alacrity, and opened it sharply. Kreisler was there. The opening of the door had been like the tearing of a characterless mask off a hideous and startling face.

There did not seem room for them where they were standing: like a great terrifying poster, cut out on the melodramatic stairway, he loomed in her distended eyes. She remained stone-still in front of him with a pinched expression, as though about to burst out crying. There was something deprecating in her paralysed gesture, like a child's.

Caricatured and enlarged to her eyes, she wanted to laugh for a moment: the surprise was complete. Her mind formed his image rather like a person compelled to photograph a ghost. Kreisler! It was as though the world were made up of various animals, each of a different kind and physique even, and this were the animal Kreisler, whose name alone conjured up certain peculiar and alarming habits: a wild world, not of uniform men and women, but of very divergent and strangely-living animals—Kreisler, Liepmann, Tarr. This was not an apparition from the remote Past, but from a Past almost a Present, a half-hour old, far more startling: the too raw and too new colours of an image hardly digested, much less faded were his. Last seen she had been still in the sphere of an intense agitation: his ominous and sudden reappearance, so hardly out of that crashing climax, had the effect of swallowing up the space and time in between. It was like the chilly return of a circling storm: she had taken it for granted that it depended on her to see him or not, that in short he was passive except when persistently approached. But here he was, this time, at last, *following*! 'The Machine' was following her!

CHAPTER 11

HE took a step forward: her room was evidently his destination.

'Schurke!' Bertha exclaimed shrilly, at the same time retreating into the passage way. 'Go!'

Arrived in the room, he did not seem to know what next to do. So far he had been evidently quite clear as to his purpose: he had in fact been experiencing the same necessity as she—he, to see his victim. To satisfy this impulse he decided that he would seek for pardon. So he had come.

A moment before she had felt that she *must* see him again, at once, before going further with her life: he, more vague but more energetic, had come, at the end of twenty minutes.

They now stood together, quite tongue-tied. He stood leaning on his cane, and staring in front of him. Bertha stood quite still, as she would sometimes do when a wasp entered the room, waiting to see if it would blunder about and then fly out again. He was dangerous, he had got in, he might in the same manner go off again in a minute or two.

He stood there without saying anything, just as though he had been sent for and it were for her to speak. She would have been inclined to send him back to his room, and *then*, perhaps, go to *him*: but she could not find anything to say to him now any more than before.

Constantly on the point of 'throwing him out,' in her energetic german idiom, it yet evidently would then be the same as before, nothing would be gained. Meantime she was intimidated by his unexplained presence. So she stood, anxious as to what he might have come there to do, gradually settling down into a 'proud and silent indignation,' behind which her curiosity became active.

Kreisler was unable to prevail upon himself to go through the stupid form of apology. He had got there, that would have to be sufficient.

In order to be able to do something, she attempted to represent to herself the *outrage*—the thing this gentleman had done to her. But she discovered she could not. She could not feel as normally she should that anything in particular had happened. It was nothing, it was a bagatelle! How could it be of any importance, she could not feel that it was anything but necessary.

She had wished to *free* Sorbert, all her actions derived from that. So what did Kreisler mean? At last his significance was as clear as daylight. He meant *always* and *everywhere* merely that *she could never see Tarr again!* Kreisler always could only mean one thing, that Tarr had gone out of her life.

She now faced him, her face illuminated with happy tragic resolve.—Supposing she had *given* herself to a man to compass this sacrifice? as it was, everything (except the hatefulness and violence of the act) had been spared her: and in informing Sorbert that there was something, now, between them, she would be nobly lying, and turning an involuntary act into a voluntary one.

Even with Kreisler now she could, too, be tragically forbearing.

'Herr Kreisler I think I have waited long enough: will you please leave my room?'

He stirred gently like a heavy flower in a light current of air: but he turned towards her and said:

'I don't know what to say to you. Is there nothing I can do to make up to you—? I shall go and shoot myself, Fräulein—I cannot support the thought of what I have done!'

This dreadful man appeared to possess a genius for making things more difficult.

'All I ask you is to go, you hear?' she exclaimed angrily. 'That will be the best thing you can do for me.'

'Fräulein, I *can't*, it's quite impossible, do listen to me for a moment, I cannot even refer to what has happened without offence, Fräulein—I am mad—mad—mad! You have shown yourself a good friend, heavens! that is the way I repay you! Were you anywhere but here and unprotected, there would be a man to answer to for this outrage!'*

He drew himself up and placed his hand upon his breast.

'I will be that man myself! I come to ask your permission!'

His appetite directed him to a more and more urgent, dramatic hypocrisy. His eye shone and he even smiled at the conclusion of his mock-eloquence.

Bertha was very dignified, she warmed to her new clemency as she proceeded:

'Let us leave all that, if you please. It was my fault. You must have been mad, as you say, but if you wish to show yourself a gentleman now, the obvious thing is to go away, as I have said, and not to molest or remind me any further of what has passed. There is nothing more to say, is there? Go now, please!'

Kreisler flung himself upon his knees, and seized her hand. She received this with puzzled protestation, retreating, while he followed her upon his knees.

'Fräulein you are an angel, you don't know how much good you do me! You are *so* good, so good! There is nothing too much you can ever ask of Kreisler, I have done something I can never undo. It is as though you had saved my life. Enough! Excuse me! Otto Kreisler you can always count on! Adieu, Fräulein. Adieu! Adieu!'

Giving her hand a last hug, he sprang to his feet, and Bertha heard him next stormily descending the stairs: then, further away, she heard him passing rapidly down the Avenue.

A brilliant light of grateful confusion on all the emotions emanating from Kreisler had been afforded by this demonstration: the notion he had evoked in parting, that they had been doing something splendid together—a life-saving, a heroism—found a hospitable ground in her spirit. Taking one thing with another, things had been miraculously transformed. Her late depression now merged in a steadily growing exaltation.

CHAPTER 12

TARR had not gone to England. Still practising his self-indulgent system of easy stages, he had settled upon a spot a bus-ride distant from the buxom attraction: now he had a rival it would be doubly easy to keep away, so there was no need to go to England, nor anywhere else for that matter. For his present studies Paris was necessary: he must not be driven out of it. Behind the Place Clichy,* in what had been a convent, he found a room big enough for a regiment, an enormous room. Its size appalled him once he was installed.

The insouciant, adventurous (Those who needed no preparation to live) the adventurous or rather the improvising hand-to-mouths, he did not admire, but felt he should imitate: with Tarr a new room had to be fitted into as painfully as a foot into some new and too elegant shoe. The things deposited on the floor, the door finally closed upon this new area to be devoted exclusively to himself, the sheerest discomfort began to undo him. To unpack and let loose upon the room his portmanteau's squashed and dishevelled contents—brushes, photographs and books like a flock of birds flying to their respective places on dressing-table, mantelpiece, shelf or bibliothèque;* boxes and parcels creeping dog-like under beds and into corners—this initial disorder taxed his character to the breaking point. The sturdy optimism shown by these inanimate objects, the way they occupied stolidly and quickly room after room, made a most disagreeable impression. Then they were *packed-up* things, with the staleness of a former room about them, and charged with the memories of a depressing time of tearing up, inspecting and rejecting. These sensations were the usual indigestion of Reality, from which this fastidious soul suffered acutely, without ever recognizing the cause.

These preliminary discomforts were less than ever spared him here: he had cut his way to this decision through a bristling host of incertitudes. This large studio-room was worse than any desert: it had been built for something else, it would never be right. A largish white-washed box was what he wanted, to pack himself into: this was the ceremonious carved chest of a former age. Even the awful size of his new easel was dwarfed: the high divan in the centre of its background appeared a toy. Once he had packed this place with consoling memories of work it would improve and might become quite perfect: he would see, time would tell. He started work at once, in fact. This was his sovereign cure for new rooms.

For the present he would not remain in this squalid cathedral a moment longer than he could help. A half-hour after entering into possession he left it tired out and swam out into the human streams of his new Quarter, so populous in contrast to the one he had left. The early lunch-breakfasts were started. In front of the Café near the Place Pigalle* that he chose there were a few clusters of men. The Spanish men dancers were coloured earth-objects, full of basking and frisking instincts: the atmosphere of the harlot's life went with them, along with spanish reasonableness and civility. The hideous ennui of large gim-crack shops and dusty public offices pervaded other groups of pink mostly dark-haired Frenchmen, drinking appetizers: they responded with their personalities on the Café terraces to the emptiness of the Boulevard.

Even before his drink had been brought, there was a familiar unwelcome face approaching. It was Berthe, a model (though bringing no reminder with her of the other 'Berthe' he knew), she was with an english painter. He knew the painter by sight. Berthe chose a table near him, with a nod. She meant to talk to him.

'Do you wish me to present you?' she said, looking towards her protector. 'This is Mr. Tarr, Dick.'

It was done.

'Why don't you come and sit here?' That too was done.

The young Englishman annoyed Tarr by pretending to be alarmed every time he was addressed. He had a wide-open, wondering eye, fixed, upon the world in timid serenity. This inoffensive eye did not appear at first to understand what you said and would roll a little with alarm. Then it seemed suddenly to be laughing. It had understood all the time! It had only been its art to surprise you, and its english unreadiness. This was a great big youngster, he wandered through life! Why is it, Tarr over and over again asked himself, that the young Latin wishes to impress you with his ability to look after himself, whereas idiocy of demeanour has always been considered stylish in England, both with old and young? The present specimen was six foot one, with a handsome Wellington beak* in front of his face. His wideawake was larger if anything than Hobson's: innumerable minor Tennysons* had planted it upon his head, or bequeathed a desire for it to this ultimate Dick of long literary line. Dick's family was allied to much Victorian talent: but, alas! thought Tarr, how much worse it is when the mind gets thin than when the blood loses its body, in merely aristocratic refinement: intellectual aristocracy in the fifth generation!—but Tarr gazed at the conclusive figure in front of him, words failing him for the moment. Words failed, too, for maintaining conversation with this dummy: how he hoped Berthe would bleed him of some of his Victorian cash and perhaps give him syphilis! He soon got up and left. He had found one place in his new home to give a wide berth to!

After dinner Tarr went to a neighbouring Music Hall, precariously amused, soothed by the din: but he eventually left with a headache. The strangeness of the streets, Cafés and places of entertainment depressed him deeply. Had it been an absolutely novel scene, he would have found stimulus in it. Tarr liked his room and some familiar streets with their traces of familiar men: where more energetic impulses suggested some truer solitude to him, he would never have sought it where a vestige of inanimate familiarity remained.

Unusually for him, Tarr felt alone, that was a nondescript, lowered and unreal state, for him.

Sleeping like a log, he woke his legs rather cramped and tired and not thoroughly rested. But as soon as he was up, work came quite easily. He got his paints out, and without beginning on his principal canvas, took up a new and smaller one, by way of diversion to avoid characteristically a frontal attack. Squaring up a drawing of three naked youths sniffing the air, with rather worried hellenic faces and heavy nether limbs, he stuck it on the wall with pins, and then drew his camp-easel up alongside it. He squared up his canvas upon the floor with a walking-stick, and fixed it upon the easel. A pencil had to be shaved continually for some time until its leaden point satisfied him.

By the end of the afternoon he had got a witty pastiche on the way suggestive of the work of the hellenizing world—it might have been the art of some malicious Syrian poking fun at the greek culture.* Two colours principally had been used, mixed in piles upon two palettes: the first was a smoky, bilious saffron, the second a pale transparent lead. The significance of the thing depended first upon the suggestions of the pulpy limbs, strained dancers' attitudes and empty faces; secondly, the two colours, and the simple yet contorted curves.*

The day's work done, his depression again grasped him, like an immensely gloomy companion who had been idling impatiently while he worked: he promenaded this personality in 'Montmartre-by-Night,' without improving his character. Nausea glared at him from every object met: sex surged up and martyrized him, but he held it down rather than satisfy himself with the first-met, probably poxed.*

The next day, même jeu. He sat for hours in the fatiguing evening among a score of relief ships or pleasure boats,* hesitating, but finally rejecting relief and pleasure, mainly because of his besetting fear of the pox. For many minutes he would sit and look at a 'fire-ship,'* calculating risks and clinical pros and cons: he peered into their mouths when they laughed and carefully noted if they touched spirits and with what freedom. But he paid for the drink and left. The next day it was the same thing.

Meantime his work made some progress: but to escape these persecutions he worked excessively. His eyes began to prick; and on the sixth day he woke up with a headache. All that day he was sick and unable to work.

The fascination of the omnibuses bound for the Rive Gauche* became almost irresistible: Tarr decided that he should have left Paris for a while. He had been granted the necessary resolution to break: he could have gone away—anywhere, even. Yet he had decided to go no farther than Montmartre, in the robust conceit of his young freedom.

He sat in his Cafés asking himself why he did not simply take the bus down the hill or hail a passing taxi: she was not of the least importance, so why make so much fuss as though she were.

His resentment against Bertha was quite active: there was plenty of room for the satisfaction of this impulse, and the equally strong one to see her again. The road back to the Quartier Berthe would probably have been taken immediately, but it needed as much of an effort, in the contrary direction, to get back, as it had to get away.

At last one evening he started. He went deliberately up to an omnibus 'Clichy—St. Germain' and took his seat under its roof. He was resolved to luxuriate in his weakness, now he had got started: he would do most thoroughly what he had been wanting to do for a week.

He would be treading the floor of Bertha's absurd flat again now and basking in her banality: the terrible german middle-classishness would again hem him in. Also he would make it his business to find out what had been happening in his absence: perhaps even, he might condescend to hang about a little outside and attempt to surprise her in some manner. Then he would behave 'en maître,' there would be no further question of his having given her up and renounced his rights: he would behave just as though he had never gone away at all: he would claim his full rights with quite superfluous appeals to her love. In brief, he would conduct himself without any dignity or honesty at all—he was on his mettle.

But once on the way in his bus, a wave of excitement overran him: what awaited him? She might really have given him up. She might not be there any more. But like Kreisler he found it difficult to think of her as fleeing, and not pursuing.

PART V
A MEGRIM OF HUMOUR

CHAPTER 1

SOME days later, in the evening, Tarr was to be found in a strange place. Decidedly, his hosts could not have explained it, how he got there: he displayed no consciousness of the anomaly. For the second time—after dining with her and her following at Restaurant Séguin, he had returned to Fräulein Liepmann's flat. As inexplicable as Kreisler's former visits, these ones that Tarr began to make were not so perfectly unwelcome: also of course there was a glimmering of meaning in them for Bertha's women friends. Two nights before he had presented himself at the door of the flat as though he had been an old and established visitor there, shaken hands and sat down. He had listened to their music, drunk their Mokka and gone away apparently satisfied. Did he regard his official standing with Bertha as a sanction, giving him a right to their hospitality? At all events it was a prerogative he had never exercised before, except on one or two occasions in her company, quite at the start.

Their explanation of this occurrence was that the young Englishman was in despair. His separation from Bertha (or her conduct with Kreisler) had hit him hard: he wished for mediation, or merely consolation.

Neither of these guesses was right: it was really something quite absurd: in reality Tarr was revisiting the glimpses of the moon, or the old, distant battlefields of love, in a tourist spirit, not without some preoccupations of a distinctly scientific or historical nature. It was rather as if he had been an official despatched by the Tarr Society to find where Tarr had slept, or taken his meals, with a view to putting up medallions or brass-plates: also for the collection of data for the Society's archives. But ten days away from his love affair with Bertha, Tarr was now coming back to the old haunts and precincts of his infatuation: he was living it all over again in memory, the central and all the accessory figures still in exactly the same place. Quite suddenly, everything to do with 'those days,' as he thought of a week or two before (or what had ended officially then) had become of absorbing interest, though curiously remote. Bertha's women friends were delightful landmarks: Tarr could not understand how it was he had not taken any interest in them before. They had so much the german savour of that life lived with Bertha about them.

But not only with them, but with Bertha herself he was likewise carrying on this mysterious retrospective life: he was so delighted, in fact, to be free of her, that he willingly poetized her personality and everything to do with it. It was, as a taste, on a par with the passion for the immediate past of the great Victorian Epoch.

On this second visit to Fräulein Liepmann's Tarr met Anastasya Vasek. She, at least, was nothing to do with his souvenirs:*yet, not realizing her as an absolute newcomer at once, he accepted her as another proof of how delightful all these people in truth were. He patronized her as a modern aesthete would patronize an antima-cassar.

So far he had been a very silent guest. What would this enigma eventually say, when it decided to speak? the Liepmann circle wondered.

'How is Bertha?' they had asked him.

'She has got a cold' he had answered. It was a fact that she had caught a summer cold several days before. How strange! they thought. So he sees her still!

'She hasn't been to Flobert's lately' Renée Liepmann: said, 'I've been so busy or I'd have gone round to see her: she's not in bed is she?'

'Oh no, she's just got a slight summer cold, she's a little hoarse that's all. She's very well otherwise' Tarr answered.

Bertha disappears: Tarr turns up tranquilly in her place. Was he a substitute? It was most mysterious, and might turn out to be aggravating. The first flutter over, their traditional hostility for him reawakened: had he not always been an arrogant, eccentric and unpleasant person—*Homme égoïste. Homme sensuel!* in van Bencke's famous words. So what was he up to?

On observing him talking with new liveliness, to which they were quite unaccustomed and which he never showed with them, with the beautiful Anastasya, their suspicions began to take form. They did not of course say: '*Perhaps getting to like Germans, and losing his first, he has come here to find another.*' And yet the conclusions to which they eventually came could without much alteration have been reduced to this simple statement. On his side, comfortable in his liberty, Tarr was still enjoying the satisfactions of slavery.

Tarr had been *Homme égoïste* so far it was certain, but *Homme sensuel* was an exaggeration. His sensual nature had remained undeveloped: his Bertha, if she had not been a joke, would not have satisfied him. Her milkmaid's physique—the *oreiller de chair fraîche où on ne peut aimer**—had not succeeded in waking his senses: there was no more reality in their sex relations than in their other relations. But he had never wished for that sort of reality: his intellect had conspired to the effect that his senses never should be awakened, in that crude way: it was some such soothing milking process that nature wished him to have in place of passion, as he dimly understood.

The whole of the meaning of his attachment to stupidity became more clear and consistent as he persevered, indeed: his artist's asceticism could not support anything more serious than such an elementary rival: when he was on heat, it turned his eyes away from the highest beauty, and deliberately it dulled the extremities of his senses, so that he had nothing but rudimentary inclinations left.

But perhaps that chapter was closing: in the interests of his animalism he was about to betray the artist in him: for he had of late been saying to himself that he must really endeavour to find a more suitable lady-companion, one he need not be too ashamed of. 'Life' would be given a chance.

Anastasya's highly artistic beauty suggested an immediate solution.

Sorbert was now dragged out of his luxury of reminiscence without knowing it, he began discriminating between the Bertha enjoyment felt through the pungent german medium of her friends, and this novel artistic sensation. Yet as an intruder this novelty met with some resistance.

Tarr asked Fräulein Vasek from what part of Germany she came.

'My parents are russian. I was born in Berlin and brought up in America. We live in Vienna' she answered. 'I am a typical Russian, therefore.'

So she accounted for her jarring on his maudlin german reveries.

'Lots of russian families have settled latterly in Germany haven't they?' he asked.

'Russians are still rather savage: the more bourgeois a place or thing is the more it attracts them. German watering places, musical centres and so on, they like about as well as anything. Often they settle there if they can afford to.'

'Do you regard yourself as a Russian or a German?'

'Oh a Russian. I'm thoroughly russian.'

'I'm glad of that' said Tarr impulsively quite forgetting where he was and the nature of his occupation.

'Don't you like Germans then?'

'Now you remind me of it I suppose I do: very much, in fact.' He shook himself with self-reproach and gazed round benignly upon his hosts. 'Else I shouldn't be here,' he added. 'They're such a nice, modest, assimilative race: I admire their sense of duty so much; they make perfect servants, they're excellent mercenary troops.* I much prefer them to people of aristocratic or artistic race, who are apt to make a nuisance of themselves.'

'I see you know them really à fond.' She laughed in the direction of the Liepmann.

He made a deprecating gesture.

'Not much. But they are an accessible and friendly people.'

'You are English?'

'Yes.'

He treated his hosts with a warm affability which sought to make up for past affronts: this was only partially successful, it appeared.

The two von Arnims came over and made an affectionate demonstration around and upon Anastasya. She got up, scattering them abruptly, and went over to the piano.

'What a big brute!' Tarr thought. 'She would be just as good as Bertha to make a fuss of, though on the large side, and you get a respectable human being into the bargain!' He was not convinced offhand that she would be as satisfactory. Let us see how it would be, he reflected, when it came to the point; this even more substantial machine, of repressed, moping senses, did attract certainly: to take it to pieces, bit by bit, and penetrate to its intimacy, might give a similar pleasure to undressing Bertha. But he fell into a reverie—it was really because she was so big that he was sceptical: women possessed of such an intense life as Anastasya always appeared on the verge of a dark spasm of unconsciousness: with their organism of fierce mechanical reactions their self-possession must be rather a bluff, and to have on your hands a blind force of those dimensions! He shuddered: for the moment he was saved.

Surrender to a woman was a sort of suicide for an artist. Nature, who never forgives an artist, would never allow *her* to forgive. So he has two enemies instead of one. With any 'superior' woman he had ever met, this feeling of being with a parvenu* never left him and Fräulein Vasek was not an exception. An artist, she would be a vulgar one.

On leaving, Tarr recognized that he no longer would come back to enjoy a diffused form of Bertha there: the prolongations of his Bertha period had passed its climax. On leaving Renée Liepmann's, nevertheless, he went to the Café Toucy, some distance away, but with an object. To make his present frequentations quite complete, it only needed Kreisler. Otto was there, very much on his present visiting list. He visited him regularly at the Café Toucy, where he was constantly to be found.

CHAPTER 2

THE following is the manner in which Tarr had become acquainted with Kreisler. Upon his first return from his exile in Montmartre he had arrived at Bertha's place about seven in the evening. He hung about for a little: in ten minutes' time he had his reward. She came out, followed by Herr Kreisler.

At first Bertha had not seen him. He followed on the other side of the street, some fifteen yards behind. He did this with sleepy gratification. All was well: this was most amusing.

Relations with her were now, it must be clear even to her, substantially at an end: a kind of good sensation of alternating jealousy and regret made him wander along with obedient gratitude. Should she turn round and see him, how uncomfortable the poor creature would be! How naturally alike in their mechanical marching gait she and the German were! He was a distinct third party—at last! Being-a-stranger, with very different appearance, thrilled him agreeably. Now by a little strategic manœuvre of short-cuts he would get in front of them. This he did.

As he debouched from his turning some way ahead Bertha at once recognized him. She stopped dead and appeared to the astonished Otto to be about to take to her heels. It was flattering in a way that his mere presence should produce this effect: Tarr went up to her his hand stretched out. Her palm a sentimental instrument of weak, aching, heavy tissues, she gave him her hand. Her face was fixed on him in a mask of regret and reproach: fascinated by the intensity of this, he had been staring at her a little too long, perhaps with some reflection of her expression. He turned towards Kreisler: there he met a, to him, conventional meaningless countenance, of teutonic make.

'Herr Kreisler' Bertha said with laconic energy, as though she were uttering some fatal name. Her 'Herr Kreisler' said hollowly 'It's done!' It tolled 'My life is finished!' It also had an inflexion of 'What shall I do?'

A sick energy saturated her face, the lips were indecently compressed, the eyes wide, dull, with watery rims.

Tarr bowed to Kreisler as Bertha said his name. Kreisler raised his hat. Then, with a curious feeling of already thrusting himself on these two people, he began to walk along beside Bertha.

She moved like an unconvinced party to a bargain, who consents to walk up and down a little, preliminary to a final consideration of the affair. 'Yes, but walking won't help matters' she might have been saying continuing to walk aimlessly on. Kreisler's indifference was absolute. There was an element of the child's privilege in Tarr's making himself of the party ('Sorbet, tu es *si jeune*'* in other words, to quote his late fiancée). There was the claim for indulgence of a spirit not entirely serious because so much at the beginning of life, so immature. The childishness of turning up as though nothing had happened, with such wilful resolve not to recognize the passionate seriousness of Bertha's drama, the significance of the awful words 'Herr Kreisler!' and so on, was not lost upon Tarr, but he did not understand the nature of the forces upon which his immunity reposed. Bertha must know the meaning of his rapid resurrection—she knew him too well not to know that that was as far as his argument got. So they walked on, without conversation. Then Tarr enquired if she were 'quite well.'

'Yes Sorbert, quite well' she replied, with soft tragic banter.

As though by design, he always found just the words or tone that would give an opening for her lachrymose irony.

But the least hint that he had come to reinstate himself must not remain: it must be clearly understood that *Kreisler* was the principal figure now: he, Tarr, was only a privileged friend—that must be emphasized!

With surely unflattering rapidity somebody else had been found: her pretension to heroic attachment was compromised. Should not he put in for the vacant rôle? He would try his hand at it. He found a formula, where Kreisler was concerned: he had the air to a marked extent now of welcoming this newcomer. 'Make yourself at home, take no notice of me' his manner said in the plainest way. As to showing him over the premises he was taking possession of—he had made the inspection himself, no doubt that was unnecessary.

'We have a mutual friend, Lowndes' Tarr said to Kreisler pleasantly. 'A week or two ago he was going to introduce me to you, but it was fated—.'

'Ah yes, Lowndes' said Kreisler. 'I know him.'

'Has he left Paris do you happen to know?'

'I think not. I thought I saw him yesterday, there, in the Boulevard Steinberg' Kreisler nodded over his shoulder, indicating precisely the spot on which he had observed Lowndes on the preceding day: his gesture implied that Lowndes might still be found thereabout.

Bertha shrank in clumsy pantomime from their affability. From the glances she pawed her german friend with, he deserved nothing, it was more than plain, but horrified avoidance. Sorbert's astute and mischievous way of saddling her with Kreisler, accepting their being together as the most natural thing in life, brought out her fighting spirit. Tarr honoured him, clearly out of politeness to her: very well: all she could do for the moment was to be noticeably distant with Kreisler. She must display towards him the disgust and reprobation that Tarr ought to feel, and which he refused to exhibit in order to vex her.

During the last few days Kreisler had persisted in seeing her: he had displayed some cleverness in his choice of means. As a result of overtures and manœuvres, Bertha had now consented to see him. Her demoralization was complete. She could not stand up any longer against the result, personified by Kreisler, of her romantic actions. At present she had transferred her hatred from herself to Kreisler.

Tarr's former relations with Bertha were known to Otto; he resented the Englishman's air of proprietorship, the sort of pleasant 'handing-over' that was going on; it probably had for object, he thought, to cheapen his little success, and he did not like it. Bertha was of course responsible.

'I don't think Herr Kreisler I'll come to dinner after all.' She stood still and rolled her eyes wildly in several directions, and stuck one of her hands stiffly out from her side.

'Very well Fräulein' he replied evenly. The dismissal annoyed him: his eyes took in Tarr compendiously in passing. Was this a resuscitation of old love at his expense? Tarr had perhaps come to claim his property: this was not the way that is usually done.

'Adieu Herr Kreisler' sounded like his dismissal. A 'never let me see you again, understand that here things end!' was written blackly in her eyes. With some irony he bid good-day to Tarr.

'I hope we shall meet again.' Tarr shook him warmly by the hand.

'It is likely' Kreisler replied at once.

Kreisler as yet was undisturbed. He had no intention of relinquishing his acquaintance with Bertha Lunken: if the Englishman's amiability were a polite way of reclaiming property left ownerless and therefore susceptible of new rights being created in it, then in time those *later* rights would be vindicated.

Kreisler's first impression of Tarr was not flattering. But no doubt they would meet again, as he had said.

CHAPTER 3

BERTHA held out her hand brutally, in a sort of spasm of will: said, in the voice of 'finality,'

'Good-bye Sorbert. Good-bye!'

He did not take it. She left it there a moment, saying again 'Good-bye!'

'Good-bye if you like' he said at length. 'But I see no reason why we should part in this florid manner: if Kreisler wouldn't mind'—he looked after him—'we might go for a little walk: or will you come and have a drink—?'

'No Sorbert, I'd rather not. Let us say good-bye at once, will you?'

'My good Bertha don't be so stupid! You are you know the world's goose!' He took her arm and dragged her towards a Café, the first one on the Boulevard they were approaching.

She hung back, prolonging the personal contact, yet pretending to be resisting it *with wonder*—her eyes rolled.

'I can't Sorbert. Je ne peux pas!' purring her lips out and rolling her eyes furiously. In the end she allowed herself to be dragged and pushed into the Café. For some time conversation hung back.

'How is Fräulein Liepmann getting on?'

'I don't know. I haven't seen her.'

'Ah!'

Tarr felt he had five pieces to play. He had played one. The other four he toyed with in a lazy way.

'Van Bencke?'

'I have not seen her.'

That left three.

'How is Isolde?'

'I don't know.'

'Seen the Kinderbachs?'

'One of them.'

'How is Clare?'

'Clare? She is quite well I think.'

The solder for the pieces of this dialogue was a dreary grey material supplied by Bertha. Their talk was an unnecessary column on the top of which she perched herself with glassy quietude.

She turned to him abruptly as though he had been hiding behind her and tickling her neck with a wisp of straw, in bucolic horseplay.

'Why did you leave me Sorbert! *Why* did you leave me?'

He filled his pipe, and then said, feeling an untalented Pro on a provincial first-night: 'I went away at that particular moment, as you are aware, because I had heard that Herr Kreisler—.'

'Don't speak to me about Kreisler—don't mention his name, I *beg* you. I hate that man. *Pfui!*'

Her violence made Tarr have a look at her. Of course she would say that: she was using too much hatred though, not to be rather flush of it for the moment.

'But I don't see—.'

'Don't, don't!' She sat up suddenly in her chair and shook her finger in his face. 'If you mention Kreisler again Sorbert I shall *hate you too!* I especially *pray* you not to mention him! It is unfair to me and—I cannot bear it!'

She collapsed, mouth drawn down at corners.

'As you like.' In insisting farther he would appear to be demanding an explanation: hints of exceptional claims upon her confidence must be avoided, there must be no explanations.

'*Why* did you leave me? You don't know, I have been mad ever since but *completely* off my head. One is as helpless as possible! I have felt just as though I had got out of a sick-bed. I have had no strength at all, I still don't know where I am nor why I am here. Sorbert!' He looked up with feigned astonishment.

'Very well!' She relapsed with a sigh at his side in a relaxed and even careless attitude.

From the Café they went to Flobert's. It was after nine o'clock and the place was empty. She bought a wing of chicken, at a dairy a salad and eggs, two rolls at the baker's, the material for two suppers. It was more than she would need for herself: Sorbert did not offer to share the expense. At the gate leading to her house he left her.

Immediately afterwards, walking towards the terminus of the Montmartre omnibus, he realized that he was well in the path that led away, as he had not done while still with her. He was glad and sorry, doing homage to her and the future together. As a moribund Bertha she possessed a novel fascination: the immobile short sunset of their friendship should be enjoyed. A rich throwing-up and congesting of souvenirs on this threshold were all the better for the weak and silly sun: ah what a delightful imperturbable clockwork orb!

On the next day at a rather earlier hour Tarr again made his way across Paris. He invited himself to tea with her. They talked to each other as though posing for their late personalities.

Deliberately he took up one or two controversial points. In a spirit of superfluous courtesy he went back to the subject of several of their old typical disputes, and proceeded to argue, with a sober eloquence, against himself. He seemed concerned to show her how very wrong he had been.

All their difficulties seemed swept away in a relaxed humid atmosphere, most painful and disagreeable to her. He agreed entirely with her, now agreeing no longer meant anything! But the key was elsewhere: enjoyment of and acquiescence in everything Berthaesque and Teutonic was where it was to be found. Just as now he went to see Bertha's very german friends, and said 'How delightful' to himself at every moment so he appeared to be resolved to come back for a week or two and to admire and patronize everything that formerly he had found most irritating in Bertha herself. Before retiring for good like a man who hears that the rind of the fruit he has just been eating is good and comes back to his plate to devour the part he has discarded, Tarr returned to have a last leisurely tankard of german beer. Or still nearer the figure, his claim in the unexceptionable part of her now lapsed, he had returned demanding to be allowed to live *just a little while longer* on the absurd and disagreeable section.

On her side Bertha suffered more than in all the rest of the time she had spent with him put together. To tell the whole Kreisler story might lead to a fight. Her beloved Sorbert might be shot by that brute. She had a vivid picture of her Young Werther breathing his last almost *im blauen Frack mit gelber Veste*, the assembly beside themselves with sorrow, 'hanging upon his lips,' as she and he in the golden summer of their early friendship had read, beside a goethean brook, the ending of those imaginary Sorrows.* Nothing would ever induce her, she thought in terror, to expose him to those dangers. It was too late now. She could not, in honour, seek to re-entangle Tarr.

Nor could she disown Kreisler. She had been found with Kreisler; she had no means of keeping him away for good. An attempt at suppressing him might produce any result—the most fearful vile things might happen. Should she have been able, or had she desired, to resume her relations with Tarr, Kreisler would not have left him uninformed of all the things that had happened, shown in the most uncongenial light, she could see Kreisler describing his actions to Tarr, watching him like a cat with a mouse. If left alone, and not driven away with ignominy, he might gradually quiet down and disappear.— Sorbert would be gone, too, by that time!

Their grand, beautiful friendship into which she had put all the romance of which her spirit was capable, in generous shovelfuls, was ending in shabby shallows. Tarr had the best rôle, and did not deserve it. No cruel implacable creditor, coming between a person and his happiness, was ever more detested than she at the last detested Kreisler.

CHAPTER 4

Tarr left Bertha punctually at seven. She looked very ill. He resolved not to go there any more.

Very low, feeling strangely upset, he made towards Vallet's; when he reached it, it was full of Americans. He gave all these merry school-children, with their nasal high-spirits, a dark look and sat down. Kreisler was not there: afterwards he went on a hunt for him and ran him to earth at the Café Toucy.

Kreisler was not cordial. He emitted sounds of gruff surprise, shuffled his feet and blinked. But Tarr sat down in front of him. Kreisler grinned unpleasantly, summoning the waiter he offered him a drink. After that he settled down to contemplate Bertha's Englishman at his leisure, and to await developments. He was always rather softer with people with whom he could converse in his own harsh tongue.

Tarr naturally sought out Kreisler on the same principle that he thrust himself upon the Liepmann group: a bath of Germans was his prescription for himself, a voluptuous immersion. To heighten the effect, he was being german himself—being Bertha as well.

But he was more german than the Germans, Kreisler did not recognize the portrait entirely. Successive lovers of a certain woman fraternizing, husbands hobnobbing with their wives' lovers or husbands of their unmarried days is a commonplace of german or scandinavian society, and Tarr brought an alien intensity into the situation.

Kreisler had not returned to Bertha's. He was too lazy: but he concluded that she had better be given scope for anything the return of Tarr might suggest. He, Otto Kreisler, might be supposed no longer to exist: his mind in short was working up for some truculent action. Tarr was no obstacle: he would just walk through this fancy-man like a ghost when he saw fit to 'advance' again.

'You met Lowndes in Rome didn't you?' Tarr asked him.

Kreisler nodded.

'Have you seen Fräulein Lunken to-day?'

'No.' As Tarr was coming to the point Kreisler condescended to speak—'I shall see her to-morrow morning.'

A space for protest or comment seemed to be left: but Tarr smiled at the tone of this piece of information. Kreisler at once grinned, mockingly, in return.

'You can get out of your head any idea that I have turned up to interfere with your proceedings' Tarr then said. 'Affairs lie entirely between Fräulein Lunken and yourself.'

Kreisler met this assurance truculently.

'You could not interfere with my proceedings. I do what I want to do in this life!'

'Capital! *Wunderbar!* How I admire you!'

'Your admiration is not asked for!'

'It leaps up involuntarily! Prosit! But I did not mean, Herr Kreisler, that my desire to interfere, had such desire existed, would have been tolerated. Oh no! I meant that no such desire existing, we had no cause for quarrel. Prosit!'

Tarr again raised his glass expectantly and coaxingly, peering steadily at the German. He said 'Prosit' as he would have said 'Peep-oh!'*

'Pros't!' Kreisler answered with alarming suddenness, and an alarming diabolical smile. 'Prosit!' with finality. He put his glass down with a crash. 'That is all right. I have no *desire*' he wiped and struck up his moustaches 'to *quarrel* with anybody. I wish to be left alone. That is all.'

'To be left alone to enjoy your friendship with Fräulein Lunken— that is your meaning? Am I not right? I see.'

'That is my business. I wish to be left *alone*.'

'Of course it's your business, my dear sir. Have another drink!' He called the waiter. Kreisler agreed to another drink.

Why was this Englishman sitting there and talking to him? It was in the german style and yet it wasn't. Was Kreisler to be shifted, was he meant to go? Had the task of doing this been put on Bertha's shoulders? Had Tarr come there to ask him, or in the hope that he would volunteer a promise, never to see Bertha again or something of that sort? On the other hand, was he being approached by Tarr in the capacity of an old friend of Bertha's, or in her interests or at her instigation?

With frowning impatience he bent forward quickly once or twice, asking Tarr to repeat some remark. Tarr's german was not so good as it might have been. But another glass of french Pilsener, and Kreisler became engagingly expansive.

'Have you ever been to England?' Tarr asked him.

'England?—No—I should not mind going there at all! I like Englishmen! I feel I should get on better with them than with these French. I hate the French! They are all actors.'

'You should go to London.'

'Ah to London. Yes, I should go to London, it must be a wonderful town! I have often meant to go there. Is it expensive?'

'The journey?'

'Well, once you're there. Life is dearer than it is here, I have been told.' For the moment Kreisler forgot his circumstances. The Englishman seemed to have hit on a means of escape for him: he had never thought of England! A hazy notion of its untold wealth made it easier for him to put aside momentarily the fact of his tottering finances.

Perhaps this Englishman had been sent him by the *Schicksal*. He had always got on well with Englishmen!

The notion then crossed his mind that Tarr perhaps wanted *to get him out of Paris*. That was it. He had come to make him some offer of hospitality in England. At once, in a bargaining spirit he began to run England down. He must at all costs not appear too anxious to go there.

'They say, though, things have changed. England's not what it was' he said, shaking his head heavily from side to side.

'No. But it has changed for the better.'

'I don't believe a word of it! It's rotten. I've heard!'

'No, it's quite true. The last time I was there it had improved so much that I thought of stopping. Merrie England is played out, there won't be a regular Pub in the whole country in fifty years. Art will flourish you see if it doesn't! There's not a *real* gypsy left in the country. It's fantastic: not one genuine one. The sham art-ones are dwindling!'

'Are the *Zigeuner* disappearing?'

'Rather! There's not a true-blue Romany Rye* from Land's End to John o' Groat's!'*

'The only Englishmen I know are very *sympathisch*.'

'Of course.'

They pottered about, on the subject of England, for some time. Kreisler was very tickled with the idea of England.

'English women—what are they like?' Kreisler then enquired with a grin. Their relations made this subject delightfully delicate and yet, Kreisler thought, very natural. This Englishman was evidently a description of pander, and no doubt he would be as inclined to be hospitable with his countrywomen in the abstract as with his late fiancée in concrete fashion.

'A friend of mine who had been there told me they were very
"pretty" '—he pronounced the english word with mincing slowness
and mischievous interrogation marks in his distorted face.

'Your friend did not exaggerate: the britannic lasses are like lan-
guid nectarines! The Tiller girls* are a pale shadow of what you see in
Britain. You would enjoy yourself there.'

'But I can't speak english—only a little. "I spik ingleesh a leetle" '
he attempted with pleasure.

'Very good! You'd get on splendidly! They're most partial to the
german brogue.'

Kreisler brushed his moustaches up, sticking his lips out in a hard
gluttonous way. Tarr watched him with sympathetic curiosity.

'But—my friend told me—they're not—I don't know how to
describe it—not very kind. Are they easy? They are great flirts—so
far—and then *bouf!*—you are sent flying! They are teasers, what, are
they not!'

'You would find nothing on the lines of *Fasching**—no official
Ausgelassenheit, you understand me. No you would not find anything
to compare with the facilities of your own country. But you would not
wish for that?'

'No?—But, tell me, then. They are cold?—They are of a calculating nature?'

'They are practical, I suppose, up to a certain point. But you must
go and see.'

Kreisler ruminated.

'What do you find particularly attractive about Bertha?' Tarr asked
in a discursive way. 'I ask you as a German. I have often wondered
what a German would think of her.'

Kreisler looked at him with resentful uncertainty for a moment.
He took a draught of beer and smacked his lips.

'You want to know what I think of the Lunken?—She's a sly prostitute, that's what she is!' he announced loudly and challengingly.

'Ah!'

When he had given Tarr time for any demonstration and decided
that nothing was forthcoming he thawed into his sociable self.
He then added:

'She's not a bad girl! But she tricked you my friend! She never
cared *that*'—he snapped his fingers inexpertly—'for you! Not that!
She told me so!'

'Really? That's interesting.—But I expect you're only telling lies. All Germans do!'

'All Germans *lie*?' Kreisler exclaimed shrilly.

'"*Deutsches Volk—the folk that deceives!*"* is your philosopher Nietzsche's account of the origin of the word Deutsch.'

Kreisler sulked a moment.

'No. We don't lie! Why should we? We're not *afraid of the truth*, so why should we?'

'Perhaps, as a tribe, you lied to begin with, but have now given it up?'

'What?'

'That may be the explanation of Nietzsche's etymology. Although he seemed very stimulated at the idea of your national certificate of untruthfulness: he felt that, as a true patriot, he should react against your blue eyes, your beer, and the childish frankness.'

'*Quatsch!* What did Nietzsche know about the Germans? He was a Jew! Nietzsche!'

'You've mixed him up with Wagner.'*

'Nietzsche was always *paradoxal*: he would say anything to amuse himself. You English are the greatest liars and hypocrites on this earth!'

'"See the Continental Press"!* I only dispute your statement because I know it is not first-hand. Hypocrisy is usually a selfish stupidity.'

'The English are *stupid* hypocrites then! We agree. Prosit!'

'The Germans are uncouth but zealous liars! Prosit!'

He offered Kreisler a cigarette. A pause occurred to afford the acuter national susceptibilities time to cool.

'You haven't yet given me your opinion of Bertha. You permitted yourself a truculent flourish that evaded the question.'

'I wish to evade the question!—I told you that she has tricked you. She is very underhand—*malin!** She is tricking me now, or she is trying to. She will not succeed with me!'

He put his finger to the side of his nose.

'"When you go to take a woman you should be careful not to forget your *whip*!" *That* Nietzsche said too!'*

'Are you going to give her a beating?' Tarr asked.

Kreisler laughed in ferocious ironical fashion.

'You consider that you are being fooled in some way by Fräulein Lunken?'

'She would if she could. She is nothing but deceit. She is a snake. *Pfui!*'

'You consider her a very cunning and double-faced woman?'

Kreisler nodded sulkily.

'With the soul of a prostitute?'

'She has an innocent face, like a Madonna. But she is a prostitute.' He paused: then he shouted 'I have proofs of it!'

'In what way has she tricked *me*?'

'In the way that women always trick men!'

With resentment partly, and with hard picturesque levity, Kreisler met Tarr's discourse.

This solitary drinker, particularly shabby, who could be 'dismissed' so easily, whom Bertha with accents of sincerity 'hated, hated!' was so different from the sort of man that Tarr expected might attract her, that he began to wonder. A certain satisfaction resulted from these observations.

For that week he saw Kreisler nearly every day: a regulation 'triangle' was then set up. Bertha (whom Tarr saw constantly too) did not actually refuse admittance to Kreisler (although he usually had first to knock a good many times), yet she prayed him repeatedly not to come any more. Standing always in a drooping and desperate condition before him, she did her best to avert a new outburst on his part. She sought to mollify him as much as was consistent with the most absolute refusal. Tarr, unaware of how things actually stood, seconded his successor.

Kreisler, on his side, was rendered obstinate by her often tearful refusal to have anything more whatever to do with him. On one occasion he attempted to repeat his initial performance. They were fighting on the floor when Tarr entered. With curses, panting and dishevelled, Kreisler desisted and retired to the kitchen. Tarr placed himself upon the settee. Bertha remained where she was, rolling over upon her face. Shortly Tarr heard Kreisler leave the house.

'I'm sorry to have barged in' he said.

As Bertha did not speak, he withdrew, quietly closing the two doors after him—he had still retained his latchkey.

Kreisler had come to regard Tarr as part of Bertha, a sort of masculine extension of her: at the Café he would look out for him, and drink deeply in his presence.

'I *will* have her. *I will have her!*' he once shouted towards the end of the evening, springing up and calling loudly for the waiter. It was all Tarr could do to prevent him from going, with assurances of inter-cession.

His suspicions of Tarr at last awoke once more. What was the mean-ing of this Englishman always there—what was he there for after all? If it had not been for him, several times he would have rushed off and had his way with this disaffected mistress, the eagle's way. But he was always there between them: and in secret, too, probably, and away from him—Kreisler—he was working on Bertha's feelings, and preventing her from seeing him. Tarr was the obstacle! Yet there he was, arguing and palavering, offering to act as an intermediary, and meantime preventing him from acting. He alone was the obstacle, and yet he talked as though he were nothing to do with it, or at the most a casually interested third party:—that is how Kreisler felt on his way home after having drunk a good deal. But so long as Tarr paid for drinks he staved him off his prey.

CHAPTER 5

TARR soon regretted this last anti-climax stage of his adventure: he would have left Kreisler alone, but he felt that by frequenting him he could save Bertha from something disagreeable. With disquiet and misgiving every night now he sat in front of his prussian friend; he watched him gradually swallowing enough spirits to work him up to his pitch of characteristic madness.

'After all let us hear really what it all means, your Kreisler stunt, and Kreisler?' he said to her four or five days after his reappearance. 'Do you know that I act as a dam, or rather a dyke, to his outrageous flood of liquorous spirits every night? Only my insignificant form is between you and destruction, or you and a very unpleasant Kreisler, at any rate. I'm afraid he may do you some mischief one of these fine days. Have you seen him when he's drunk?—What, after all, does *Kreisler* mean? Satisfy my curiosity.'

Bertha shuddered and looked at him with dramatically wide-open eyes, as though there were no answer.

'It's nothing Sorbert, nothing' she said, as though Kreisler were the bubonic plague* and she were making light of it.

'Why aren't you kinder to him? He really has something to complain of.'

He had neglected the coincidence of his own reappearance and Bertha's refusal to see Kreisler. He must avoid finding himself manœuvred into appearing the cause: a tranquil and sentimental revenant* was the rôle he had chosen. He encouraged Bertha to see his boon companion and relax her sudden exclusiveness: but he hesitated to carry out thoroughly his part of go-between and reconciler. At length he began to make enquiries. After all, to have to hold back his successor to the favours of a lady, from going and seizing those rights (temporarily denied him presumably), was an uncomfortable situation. At any moment now it seemed likely that Kreisler would turn upon him.

Better leave lovers to fight out their own quarrels! All his retrospective pleasure was being spoilt. Bertha was tempted to explain, in as dramatic a manner as possible, the situation to Tarr: but she hesitated always because she thought it would lead to a fight. She was often, as it was, anxious for Tarr.

'Sorbert, I think I'll go to Germany at once' she said to him, on the afternoon of his second visit to Renée Liepmann's.

'Why, because you're afraid of Kreisler?'

'No but I think it's better.'

'But why, all of a sudden?'

'My sister will be home from Berlin, in a day or two——.'

'And you'd leave me here to "mind" the dog.'

'No. Don't see Kreisler any more, Sorbert. Dog is the word indeed! He is mad: he is worse than mad. Promise me, Sorbert'——she took his hand——'not to go to the Café any more!'

'Do you want him at your door at twelve to-night?——I feel I may be playing the part of——gooseberry* do you call it——.'

'Don't Sorbert. If you only knew!——He was here this morning, hammering for nearly half an hour. But all I ask you is to go to the Café no more. There is no need for you to be mixed up in all this: I alone am to blame.'

'Have you known Otto long——before you knew me for instance?'

'No only a week or two——since you went away.'

'I must ask Kreisler. But he seems to have very primitive notions about himself.'

'Don't bother any more with that man Sorbert. You don't do any good. Don't go to the Café to-night!'

'Why to-night?'

'Any night.'

The chief cause of separation had become an element of insidi-ous *rapprochement*.* He left her silently apprehensive face at the front door, staring after him mournfully.

So that night, after his second visit to Fräulein Liepmann's, he did not seek out Kreisler at his usual headquarters with his first enthusiasm.

CHAPTER 6

ALREADY before a considerable pile of saucers, representing a consid-erable bill up-to-date for the accommodating Tarr, Kreisler sat quite still, his eyes very bright, smiling to himself. Tarr did not at once ask him 'what Kreisler meant' as he had intended; 'Kreisler' looked as though it meant something a little different on that particular even-ing. He acknowledged Tarr's arrival slightly, seeming to include him in his reverie. Then they sat without speaking, this meeting redolent of the unpleasant atmosphere of police-court romance.*

Tarr still kept his retrospective luxury before him, as it maintained the Kreisler side of the transaction in a desired perspective. Anastasya, whom he had just left, had come as a diversion. He got back, with her, into the sphere of 'real' things again, not fanciful retrospective ones. This would be a reply to Kreisler (an Anastasya for your Otto) and restore the balance: at present they were perched upon a sort of three-legged affair. The fourth party would make things solid and less precarious.

To maintain his rôle of intermediary and go on momentarily keeping his eye on Kreisler's threatening figure, he must himself be definitely engaged in a new direction, beyond the suspicion of hankerings after his old love. Did he, however, wish to enter into a new attachment with Anastasya? That could be decided later: he would take the first steps, retain her if possible, and out of this charming expedient pleasant things might arise. For the moment he was compelled to requisition her. She might be regarded as a casual travelling companion: thrown together on a casanovaesque stage-coach journey,* anything might happen. Delight, adventure and amusement were always achieved: his itch to see his humorous concubine is turned into a 'retrospective luxury,' visits to the Liepmann circle, mysterious relationship with

Kreisler: this, in its turn, suddenly turning rather prickly and per-plexing, he now, through the agency of a beautiful fourth party, turns it back again into fun; not serious enough for Beauty—destined, therefore, rather for her subtle, rough, satiric sister.

Once Anastasya had been relegated to her place rather of expedi-ency, he could think of her with more freedom: he looked forward to his work in her direction. There would be no harm at all in anticipat-ing a little: she might at once be brought upon the boards, as though the affair were already settled and ripe for publicity.

'Do you know a girl called Anastasya Vasek? She is to be found at your german friend's, Fräulein Liepmann's.'

'Yes I know her' said Kreisler, looking up with unwavering blank-ness. His introspective smile vanished. 'What then?' was implied in his look. What a fellow this Englishman was, to be sure! What was he after now? Anastasya was a much more delicate point with him than Bertha.

'I've just got to know her. She's an attractive girl, don't you agree?' Kreisler's reception of these innocent remarks he could not make out at all.

'Is she?' Kreisler looked at him almost with astonishment.

There is a point beyond which we must hold people responsible for accidents: innocence then loses its meaning. Beyond this point Tarr had transgressed. Whether Tarr knew anything or not, the essential reality was that Tarr was beginning to get at him with Anastasya, just having been for a week a problematic figure suddenly appearing between him and his prey of the rue Martine. The habit of civilized restraint had done something to keep Kreisler baffled and passive for a week. His new self-elected boon companion also was an open-handed person: he had been preparing lately to borrow money from him. Anastasya brought on the scene was another kettle of fish. What did this new stunt signify? 'Bertha Lunken will have nothing more to do with you. You mustn't annoy her any more. In the meantime, I am getting on very well with Anastasya Vasek!' Was that the idea?

Kreisler ruminated the question as to whether Tarr had heard the whole story of his assault upon his late fiancée: the possibility of his knowing increased his contempt for this shifty gentleman.

Kreisler was disarmed for the moment by the remembrance of Anastasya.

'Is Fräulein Vasek working in a studio?' he asked.

'She's at Serrano's, I think' Tarr answered.

'So you go to Fräulein Liepmann's?'

'Sometimes.'

Kreisler reflected a little.

'I should like to see her again.'

Tarr began to scent another mysterious muddle. Would he never be free of Herr Kreisler? Perhaps he was going to be followed there as well. In deliberate meditation Kreisler appeared to be coming round to Tarr's opinion: for his part too, Fräulein Vasek was a nice young lady. 'Yes, she is attractive, as you say!'—his manner began to suggest that Tarr had put her forward as a substitute for Bertha.

For the rest of the evening Kreisler would talk of nothing but Anastasya. How was she dressed? Had she mentioned him? and so forth. Tarr felt inclined to say 'But you don't understand! She is for *me. Bertha* is your young woman now!' Only in reflecting on this possible remark, he was confronted with the obvious reply 'But *is* Bertha my young woman? I have been denied my male rights since you put in an appearance! It's up to you to find me a substitute.'

CHAPTER 7

TARR had Anastasya in solitary promenade two days after this conversation. He had worked the first stage consummately: he swam with ease beside his big hysterical black swan, seeming to guide her with a golden halter. They were swimming at the moment with august undulations of thought across the Luxembourg Gardens on this sunny and tasteful evening, about four o'clock. The Latins and Scandinavians who strolled upon the Latin terrace were each of them a microscopic hero, but better turned out than the dubious too spacious and slapdash heroes of 1840's Vie de Bohème and revolutionary storm and stress.*

The inviolate, constantly sprinkled and shining lawns by the Lycée Henri Trois* were thickly fringed with a sort of seaside humanity, who sat facing them and their coolness as though it had been the sea. Leaving these upland expanses to the sedentary swarms of mammas and papas, Tarr and Anastasya crossed over beneath the trees past the children's carousals grinding out their antediluvian lullabies.

This place represented the richness of three wasted years, three incredibly gushing, thick years—what had happened to this delightful muck? He had just turned seventeen when he had arrived there, and had wandered in this children's outdoor nursery almost a child himself. All this profusion had accomplished for him was to dye the avenues of a Park with personal colour for the rest of his existence. *No one*, he was quite convinced, had squandered so much of the imaginative stuff of life in the neighbourhood of these terraces, ponds, and lawns. So this was more nearly *his Park** than it was anybody else's: he should never walk through it without bitter and soothing recognition from it. Well, that was what the 'man of action' accomplished. In four idle years he had been, when most inactive, experimenting with the man of action's job. He had captured a Park!—well! he had spent himself into the earth, the trees had his sap in them.

He remembered a day when he had brought a newly purchased book to the bench there, his mind tearing at it in advance, almost writing it in its energy. He had been full of such unusual abounding faith: the streets around these gardens, in which he had lodged alternately, were so many confluents and tributaries of memory, charging in upon it on all sides with defunct puissant tides. The places, he then reflected, where childhood has been spent, or where, later, dreams of energy have been flung away, year after year, are obviously the healthiest spots for a person where such places exist: but perhaps, although he possessed the Luxembourg Gardens so completely, they were completely possessed by thousands of other people! So many men had begun their childhood of ambition in this neighbourhood. His hopes, too, no doubt, had grown there more softly because of the depth and richness of the bed. A sentimental miasma made artificially in Paris a similar good atmosphere where the mind could healthily exist as was found by artists in brilliant, complete and solid times. Paris was the most human city we had.

'*Elle dit le mot, Anastase, né pour d'éternels parchemins.*'* He could not, however, get interested: was it the obstinate Eighteenth-Century animal vision? Those Eighteenth-Century hams—the rosy cheeks and cupid mouths and gigantic bottoms, those shapes once they got into your head, perhaps got in the way and obstructed? When you plunge into these beings, must they be all quivering with unconsciousness, like life with a cat or a serpent?—But her sex would throw clouds over

her eyes: she was a woman—it was no good. Again he must confess
Anastasya could only offer him something too *serious*: he could not
play and joke so well with that.

Then to his Bertha he was after a fashion true;* the protective
instinct that people with a sense of their own power have for those
not equals with whom they have been associated existed with him: he
would have given to Bertha the authority of his own spirit, to prime
her with himself that she might meet on equal terms and vanquish
any rival. A slight hostility to Anastasya made itself felt, like a part of
Bertha left in himself protesting and jealous.

'I suppose she knows all about Bertha' he thought. ('Homme sensuel! Homme égoïste!' he remembered.) She seemed rather shy with
him.

'How do you like Paris?' he asked.

'I don't know yet. Do you like it?' She had a flatness in speaking
english because of her education in the United States.

'I don't like to be quite so near the centre of the world, you feel
the machinery at work. Then it's too exciting and prevents you from
working. But here I am. It's certainly difficult to live in London after
Paris.'

'I should have thought everything was so perfected here that the
machinery did not obtrude—' she objected.

'Perhaps that is so; but I think that Paris works that the other
countries may live and create: that is the rôle France has chosen. The
french spirit seems to me rather spare and impoverished at present.'

'You regard it as a mother-drudge?'

'More of a drudge than a mother—we really get very little from
France except tidiness.'

'I expect you are ungrateful.'

'Perhaps so. But I cannot get over a dislike for latin facilities. Suarès
finds a northern rhetoric of ideas in Ibsen,* for instance, exactly similar to the word-rhetoric of the South: but in latin countries you have
a democracy of vitality, the best things of the earth are in everybody's
mouth and nerves. *The artist has to go and find them in the crowd.* You
can't have "freedom" both ways and I prefer the *artist* to be free,
and the crowd not to be "artists"—I don't know if you understand
what I mean? What does all our emotional talk about the wonderful artist-nation, etc., amount to?—we exclaim and point because we
find thirty-five million petits-maîtres,* each individually possessing

very little taste, really, living together and prettifying their towns and themselves. Imagine England an immense garden city, on Letchworth lines (that is the name of a model Fabian township near London),* or Germany (it almost has become that) a huge reform-dressed,* bestatued State. Every individual Frenchman has the trashiest taste possible: you are more astonished when you come across a severe artist in France than elsewhere: for his vitality is hypnotically beset by an ocean of cheap Salon artistry: his best instinct is to become rather aggressively harsh and simple. The reason that a great artist arouses more fury in France than in England is not because the French are *more interested in Art*—they are less interested: it is because they are all "artistic" and all artists—little ones. In their case it is professional jealousy.'

'But what difference does the attitude of the crowd make to the artist?'

'Well, we were talking about Paris, which is the creation of the crowd. The man really thinking in these gardens to-day (a rare event) the man thinking on the quays of Amsterdam three centuries ago, think much the same thoughts. The thought is one thing, the form another: the artist's work I believe is nowhere so unsafe as in the hands of an "artistic" public. As to living in Paris, Paris is very intelligent: but no friendship is a substitute for the blood-tie; and intelligence is no substitute for the response that can only come from the narrower recognition of your kind.'

'Do you think blood matters?'

'I have been talking about an average: what I said would not apply to works of very personal genius: country is left behind by that. Intelligence also.'

'Don't you think that work of very personal genius often *has* a country?'

'I don't believe it has.'

'May it not break through accidents of birth and reach perfect conditions somewhere in a different time or place?'

'I suppose you could find a country or a time for almost *anything*: but I am sure the *best* has in reality no Time and no Country—that is why it accepts without fuss any country or time for what they are worth, and is "up-to-date," usually.'

'But is the best work always up-to-date?'

'It always has that appearance, its manners are perfect.'

'I am not so sure that a personal code is not as good as the current code. The most effectual men have always been those whose notions were diametrically opposed to those of their time' she said carefully.

'I don't think that is so, except in so far as all effectual men are always the enemies of every time. Any opinion of their contemporaries that they adopt they support with the uncanny authority of a plea from a hostile camp. All activity on the part of a good mind has the stimulus of a paradox. To produce is the sacrifice of genius.'

They seemed to have an exotic grace to him as they promenaded their sinuous healthy intellects in this elegant landscape: there was no other pair of people who could talk like that on those terraces. They were both of them barbarians, head and shoulders taller than the polished stock around; they were highly strung and graceful. They were out of place.

'Your philosophy reminds me of Jean-Jacques' she said.

'Does it? How is that I wonder?'

'Well, your hostility to a tidy rabble, then what you say about an uncultivated bed to build on brings to mind the doctrine of the natural man.* You want a human landscape similar to Jean-Jacque's rocks and waterfalls.'

'I see what you mean: but I think you are mistaken about that: what I think is really the exact opposite of what Jean-Jacques thought.—He preached wild nature and unspoilt man: his was propaganda for instinct as against intellect. I don't say that at all: it is a question of expediency and the temporal and physical limitations of our human state. For a maximum human fineness much should be left crude and unformed: for instance, crudity in an individual's composition is necessary for him to be able to create. There is no more absolute value in stupidity and formlessness than there is in dung, but they are necessary. The conditions of creation and of life disgust me—the birth of a work of art is as dirty as that of a baby. But there is no alternative to creation except the second-rate. Of course if you like the second-rate, as so many people do, there's nothing more to be said.'

'So you would discourage virtue, self-sacrifice and graceful behaviour?'

'No, praise them very much: also praise deceit, lechery and panic.'

'But they cancel each other.'

'No, whatever a man does, praise him: in that way you will be acting as the artist does: if you are not an artist, you will not act in that way.

An artist should be impartial like a god. Our classifications are inartistic.'

'Rousseau again—?'

'If you really want to saddle me with him, I will help you. My passion for art has made me fond of chaos. It is the artist's fate almost always to be exiled among the slaves: he gets his sensibility blunted.'

'He becomes in fact less of an artist?'

'He's hard-boiled.'

'If that is so, wouldn't it be better to be something else?'

'No I think it's about the best thing to be.'

'With women he is also apt to be undiscriminating.'

'For that he is notorious at all times!'

'I think that is a pity: that is no doubt because I am a woman, and am conscious of not being a slave.'

He looked at her pleasantly, the first time he had turned to her since they had been talking, and replied:

'But such women as you are condemned to find themselves surrounded by slaves!'

Her revolving hips and thudding skirts carried her forward with the orchestral majesty of an ocean-going ship. He suddenly became conscious of the monotonous racket. At that moment the drums began beating to warn everybody of the closing of the gates. They had dinner in a Bouillon* near the Seine. They parted about ten o'clock.

CHAPTER 8

FOR the first time since his 'return' Tarr found no Kreisler at the Café Toucy. The waiter told him that Kreisler had not been there at all that evening. Tarr reconsidered his responsibilities. He could not return to Montmartre without first informing himself of Kreisler's whereabouts and state of mind. The 'obstacle' had been eluded: he must get back into position again.

To Bertha's he had no intention going if he could help it. A couple of hours at tea-time was what he had constituted as his day's 'amount' of her company. Kreisler's own room would be better, so he turned in that direction. There was a light—the window had been pointed out to him on several occasions by Otto. This perhaps was sufficient, Tarr felt: he might now go home, having located him. Since he was there on second thoughts he decided to go up and make sure. Striking matches as he went, he plodded up the dark staircase. Arrived at the top floor, he was uncertain at which door to knock. He chose one with a light beneath it.

In a moment someone called out 'Who is it?' Recognizing the voice, Tarr answered, and the door opened slowly. Kreisler was standing there in his shirt sleeves, glasses on and a brush in his hand.

'Ah come in' he said.

Tarr sat down and Kreisler went on brushing his hair. When he had finished he put the brush down quickly, turned round and pointing to the floor, said, in a voice suggesting that that was the first of several questions:

'Why have you come *here?*'

Tarr at once recognized that he had gone a step too far. Otto felt no doubt that his keeper had come in search of his charge, and to find out why he had absented himself from the Café.

'Why have you come here?' Kreisler asked again, in an even tone, pointing steadily with his forefinger to the centre of the floor.

'Only to see you of course. I thought perhaps you weren't well.'

'Ah, so! I want you, my dear english friend, now that you are here, to explain yourself a little. Why do you honour me with so much of your company?'

'Is my company disagreeable to you?'

'I wish to know, sir, why I have so much of it!' The Korps *student* was coming to the top: his voice had risen and the wind of his breath appeared to be making his moustaches whistle.

'I, of course, have reasons, besides the charm of your society, for seeking you out.'

Tarr was sitting stretched on one of Kreisler's two chairs looking up frowningly. He was annoyed at having let himself in for this interview. Kreisler stood in front of him without any expression in particular, his voice rather less guttural than usual, even a little shrill. Tarr felt ill at ease at this sudden breath of storm, he kept still with difficulty.

'You have reasons? You have reasons! Heavens! Outside! Quick! Out! Out!'

There was no doubt this time that it was in earnest: he was intended rapidly to depart. Kreisler was pointing to the door. His cold grin was slightly on his face again, and an appearance of his hair having receded on his forehead and his ears gone close against his head warned Tarr definitely where he was. He got up. For a moment he stood in a discouraged way, as though trying to remember something.

'Will you tell me what on earth's the matter with you to-night?' he asked.

'Yes! I don't want to be followed about by an underhand swine like you any longer! By what devil's impudence did you come here to-night? For a week I've had you in the Café: what did you want with me? If you wanted your girl back, why hadn't you the courage to say so? I saw you with another lady to-night. I'm not going to have you hovering and fawning around me. Be careful I don't come and pull your nose when I see you with that other lady! You hear me? Be careful!'

'Which?'

'Oh *that*! You're welcome to that little tart—go and stick your nose in it, I give you leave!'

'I recommend you to hold your tongue! I've heard enough, you understand, enough! Where her senses were when she picked up a bird like you—.' Tarr's german hesitated. He had stepped forward with an air as though he might strike Kreisler.

'Heraus, Schwein!' shouted Kreisler, in a sort of incredulous drawling crescendo, shooting his hand towards the door and urging his body like the cox of a boat:* like a sheep-dog he appeared to be collecting Tarr together and urging him out.

Tarr stood staring at him.

'What—.'

'Heraus! Out! Quicker! Quicker! Out!'

His last word dropped like a plummet to the deepest tone his throat was capable of: it was so absolutely final that the grace given, even after it had been uttered, for this hateful visitor to remove himself, was a source of astonishment to Tarr. Should he maintain his position it could only be for a limited time, since after all he had no right where he was: sooner or later he would have to go and make his exit unless he established himself there and made it his home, henceforth: a change of lodging he did not contemplate. In such cases the room even must seem on its owner's side, and to be vomiting forth the intruder: the instinct of ownership makes it impossible for any but the most indelicate to resist a feeling of hesitation before the idea of resistance in another man's shell!

He stood for a few seconds in a tumultuous hesitation, when he saw Kreisler run across the room, bend forward and dive his arm down behind his box. He watched with uncomfortable curiosity this new move, as one might watch a surgeon's haste at the crisis of an operation, searching for some necessary instrument, mislaid for the moment. He stepped towards the door: the wish not to 'obey' or to seem to turn tail either, had alone kept him where he was. He had just reached the door when Kreisler, with a bound, was back from his box, flourishing an old dog-whip in his hand.

'Ah you go? Look at this!' He cracked the whip once or twice. 'This is what I keep for hounds like you! Crack!' He cracked it again, in rather an inexperienced way. He frowned as though it had been some invention he were showing off, but which would not quite work at the critical moment.

'If you wish to see me again you can always find me here. You won't get off so easily next time!' He cracked the whip smartly: then he slammed-to the door.

Tarr could imagine him throwing the whip down in a corner of the room and then going on with his undressing.

When Kreisler had jumped to the doorway Tarr had stepped out with a half-defensive, half-threatening gesture and then gone forward with strained slowness, lighting a match at the head of the stairs.

The thing that had chiefly struck him in the Kreisler under this new aspect was a pettiness in his movements and behaviour, a nimbleness where perhaps he would have expected more stiffness and heroics; the clown-like gibing form his anger took, a frigid disagreeable slyness and irony, a juvenile quickness and coldness.

With the part he had played in this scene Tarr was extremely dissatisfied. First of all, he felt he had withdrawn too quickly at the appearance of the whip, although he had, in fact, commenced his withdrawal before it had appeared. Then, he argued, he should have stopped at the appearance of this instrument of disgrace. To stop and fight with Kreisler, what objection was there to that, he asked himself? It was to take Kreisler too seriously? But what less serious than fighting? He had saved himself from something ridiculous, merely to find himself outside Kreisler's door with a feeling of primitive dissatisfaction.

There was something mean and improper in everything he had done, which he could not define. Undoubtedly he had insulted this man by his attitude, his manner often had been mocking; but when the other had turned, whip in hand, he had—walked away? What really should he have done? He should, no doubt, having humorously instituted himself Kreisler's keeper, have humorously struggled with him, when the idiot became obstreperous. But at that point his humour had stopped. Then his humour had limitations?

Once and for all no one had a right to treat a man as he had Kreisler and yet claim, when turned upon, immunity from action on the score of the other's imbecility. In allowing the physical struggle any importance he allowed Kreisler an importance, too: this made his former treatment of him unjustified. In Kreisler's eyes was he not a 'blagueur'—without resistance at a pinch, who walks away when turned on? Yet this opinion was of no importance, since he had not a shadow of respect for Kreisler. Again he turned on himself:—If he was so weak-minded as to care what trash like Kreisler thought or felt—! Gripped in this ratiocination he wandered back towards the Café.

His unreadiness, his dislike for action, his fear of ridicule, he treated severely in turn: he laughed at himself: but it was no good. At last he surrendered to the urgency of his vanity: plans for retrieving this discomfort came crowding upon him. He would go to the Café as usual on the following evening, sit down smilingly at Kreisler's table as though nothing had happened: in short, he would altogether endorse the opinion that Kreisler had formed of him. And yet why this meanness, even assumed? His contempt for everybody else in the end must degrade him: for if nothing in other men was worth honouring, finally his own self-neglect must result, like the Cynic's dishonourable condition.*

Still, for a final occasion and since he was going this time to accept any consequences, he would follow his idea: he would be to Kreisler's mind, for a little, the strange 'fawner and hoverer' who had been kicked out on the previous night. He would even have to 'pile it on thick' to be accepted at all, he must exaggerate what especially provoked Kreisler's unflattering notion of him. Then he would aggravate Kreisler by degrees and with the same bonhomie. As he reached this point he laughed aloud, as a sensible old man might laugh at himself on arriving at a similar decision. The picture of Kreisler and himself setting about each other was not edifying.

The parallel morals of his Bertha affair and his Kreisler affair became increasingly plain to him. His sardonic dream of life got him, as a sort of quixotic dreamer of inverse illusions, blows from the swift arms of windmills and attacks from indignant and perplexed mankind. But he—unlike Quixote—instead of having conceived the world as more chivalrous and marvellous than it was, had conceived it as emptied of all dignity, sense and generosity. *The drovers and publicans were angry at not being mistaken for a legendary chivalry, for knights and ladies!* The very windmills resented not being taken for giants!*—The curse of humour was in him, anchoring him at one end of the seesaw whose movement and contradiction was life.

Reminded of Bertha, he did not, however, hold her responsible: but his protectorate would be wound up. Acquaintance with Anastasya on the other hand would be definitely developed despite the threatened aggression against his nose.

PART VI

HOLOCAUSTS*

CHAPTER 1

PAINTING languished in the Montmartre studio, which was no longer anything but an inconvenient address, requiring a long bus or taxi ride at the end of the day. At this time Tarr's character performed repeatedly the following manœuvre: his best energies would, once a farce was started, gradually take over the business from the play department, and continue the farce as a serious line of its own. It was as though it had not the go to initiate anything of its own accord: it appeared content to exploit the clown's discoveries. But as for painting he ceased almost to think of it: he rose late, breakfasted near at hand, and proceeded to the Rive Gauche and his daily occupations.

The bellicose visit to Kreisler now projected was launched to a slow blast of Humour, ready, when the time came, to turn into a storm. His contempt would not allow him to enter into anything seriously against him: Kreisler was a joke. Jokes, it had to be admitted (and in that they became more effective than ever) were able to make you sweat, even break your ribs and black your eyes.

That Kreisler could be anywhere but at the Café Toucy on the following evening never entered Tarr's head. As he was on an unpleasant errand, he took it for granted that Fate would on this occasion put everything punctually at his disposal: had it been an errand of pleasure, he would instinctively have supposed the reverse.

At ten, and at half-past, the other comedian* had not yet put in an appearance. At last Tarr set out to make a rapid tour of the other Cafés. But Otto might be turning over a new leaf: he might be going to bed, as on the previous evening. He must not be again sought, though, on his own territory: the moral disadvantage of this position, on a man's few feet of most intimate floor space, Tarr had too clearly realized to repeat the experiment.

The Café des Sports Aquatiques,* the most frequented of the Quarter, entered merely in a spirit of german thoroughness, turned out to be the one. More alert, and brushed up a little, Tarr thought, there sat Kreisler sure enough with another man, possessing a bearded, naïf, and rather pleasant face. No pile of saucers this time attended him. A Mokka was in front of each of them.

The stranger was a complication: perhaps the night's affair should be put off until the conditions were more favourable. But Tarr's vanity was impatient: his protracted stay in the original Café had made him nervous. On the other hand, it might come at once—an opposite complication: Kreisler might open hostilities upon the spot. This would rob Tarr of the subtle benefits to be derived from his gradual strategy. That must be risked.

He was not very calm. He crudely went up to Kreisler's table and sat down. The necessary good humour was absent from his face: he had carefully preserved this expression for some time, even walking lazily and quietly as if he were carrying a jug of milk; now it vanished in a moment. Despite himself, he sat down opposite Kreisler as solemn as a judge, pale, his eyes fixed upon the object of his care with something like a scowl.

But, his first absorption in his own sensations lifting a little, he recognized that something very unusual was in the air.

Kreisler and his friend were not speaking or attending to each other at all: they were just sitting still and watchful, two self-possessed malefactors. The arrival of Tarr to all appearance disturbed and even startled them, as if they had been completely wrapped up in some engrossing game or conspiracy.

Kreisler had his eyes trained across the room. The other man, too, was turned slightly in that direction, although his eyes followed the tapping of his shoe against the ironwork of the table, and he only looked up occasionally.

Kreisler turned round, stared at Tarr without at once taking in who it was. 'It's only Bertha's Englishman' he seemed then to say: he took up his former wilful and patient attitude, his eyes fixed straight ahead.

Tarr had grinned a little as Kreisler turned his way, rescued from his solemnity: there was just a perceptible twist in the German's neck and shade of expression that would have said 'Ah there you are? Well, be quiet, we're having some fun. Just you wait!'

But Tarr was so busy with his own feelings that he didn't quite understand this message: he wondered if he had been seen by Kreisler in the distance, and if this reception had been concerted between Otto and this other fellow. If so, why?

Sitting, as he was, with his back to the room, he stared at his neighbour. His late boon companion distinctly was waiting, with absurd
patience, for something. The poise of his head, the set of his yellow
prussian jaw, were truculent, although otherwise he was peaceful and
attentive. His collar looked *new* rather than clean, it was of a dazzling
white: his necktie was not one familiar to Tarr. Boots shone impass-
ibly beneath the table.

Screwing his chair sideways, Tarr faced the room. It was full of
people—very athletically dressed american men, all the varieties of
the provincial in american women, powdering their noses and ogling
Turks, or sitting, the younger ones, with blameless curiosity never at
peace, and fine Schoolgirl Complexions:* and there were many many
Turks, Mexicans, Russians and other 'types' for the american ladies!
In the wide passage-way into the further rooms sat the orchestra,
playing the 'Moonlight Sonata.'*

In the middle of the room, at Tarr's back, he now saw a group
of eight or ten young men whom he had seen occasionally in the
Café Berne. They looked rather german, but smoother and more vivacious: Poles or Austrians, then? Two or three of them appeared to be
amusing themselves at his expense. Had they noticed the little drama
that he was conducting at his table? Were they friends of Kreisler's,
too?

Tarr flushed and felt far more like beginning on them than on his
complicated idiot of a neighbour, who had grown cold as mutton on
his hands.

He had moved his chair a little to the right, towards the group at
his back, and more in front of Kreisler, so that he could look into his
face. On turning back now, and comparing the directions of the various pairs of eyes engaged, he at length concluded that he was without
the sphere of interest; *just* without it.

At this moment Kreisler sprang up. His head was thrust forward,
his hands were in rear, partly clenched and partly facilitating his swift
passage between the tables by hemming in his lean sweeping coat-
tails. The smooth round cloth at the top of his back, his smooth head
above that, with no back to it, struck Tarr in a sudden way like a whiff
of sweat: Germans had no backs to them, or were like polished peb-
bles behind, was the deliverance of this impression.

Tarr had mechanically moved his hand upwards from his lap to
the edge of the table on the way to ward off a blow when Kreisler first

rose to his feet: he was dazed by all the details of this meeting, and
the peculiar miscarriage of his plan. But Kreisler brushed past him
with the swift deftness of a person absorbed by some overmastering
impulse. The next moment Tarr saw the party of young men he had
been observing in a blur of violent commotion: Kreisler was in among
them, working on something in their midst. There were two blows—
smack—smack; an interval between them. He could not see who had
received them.

Tarr then heard Kreisler shout in german:

'For the *second* time to-day! Is your courage so slow that I must do
it a *third* time?'

Conversation had stopped in the Café and everybody was standing.
The companions of the man smacked, too, had risen in their seats:
they were expostulating, in three languages. Several were mixed up
with the waiters, who had rushed up to engage in their usual police
work on such occasions. Over Kreisler's shoulder, his eyes carbon-
ized to a black sweetness, his cheeks a sweet sallow-white, with a red
mark where Kreisler's hand had been, Tarr saw the man his german
friend had singled out. He had sprung towards his aggressor, but by
that time Kreisler had been seized from behind and was being hustled towards the door. The blow seemed to hurt his vanity so much
that he was standing half-conscious till the pain abated. He seemed
to wish to brush the blow off, but was too vain to raise his hands to
his cheek: it was left there like a scorching compress. It was surprising how much he seemed to mind. His friends—Kreisler wrenched
away from them—were left standing in a group, in attitudes of violent
expostulation and excitement.

Otto Kreisler receded in the midst of a band of waiters towards
the door. He was resisting and protesting, but not too much to retard
his quick exit. The Café staff had the self-conscious unconcern of
civilian braves.*

The young man attacked and his friends were explaining what
had happened, next, to the manager of the Café who had hastened
to the scene. A waiter brought in a card upon a plate.* There was
a new outburst of protest and contempt from the others. The plate
was presented to the individual chiefly concerned, who brushed
it away, as though he had been refusing a dish that a waiter was,
for some reason, pressing upon him. Then suddenly he took up the
card, tore it in half, and again waved away the persistent platter.

The waiter looked at the manager of the Café and then returned to the door.

———————

So this was what Kreisler and the little bearded man had been so busy about! Kreisler as well had laid his plans for the evening. And Tarr's scheme was destined not to be realized—unless he followed Kreisler at once and got up a second row, a more good-natured one, just outside the Café? Should he go out now and punch Kreisler's head, fight about a little bit, and then depart, his business done, and leave Kreisler to go on with his other row? For he felt that Kreisler intended making an evening of it. His companion had not taken part in the fracas, but had followed on his heels at his ejection, protesting with a vehemence that was intended to hypnotize.

Tarr felt relieved. Just at the moment when he had felt that he was going to be one of the principal parties to a violent scene, he had witnessed, not himself at all, but another man snatched up into his rôle. As he watched the man Kreisler had struck, he seemed to be watching himself. And yet he felt rather on the side of Kreisler. With a mortified chuckle he prepared to pay for his drink and be off, leaving Kreisler for ever to his very complicated, mysterious and turbulent existence.

Just then he noticed that Kreisler's friend had come back again, and was talking to the man who had been struck. He could hear that they were speaking in russian or polish. With great collectedness, Kreisler's emissary, evidently, was meeting their noisy expostulations. He could not at least, like a card, be torn in half! On the other hand, in his person he embodied the respectability of a visiting card. He was dressed with perfect 'correctness' suitable to such occasions and such missions as his appeared to be: by his gestures (one of which was the taking an imaginary card between his thumb and forefinger and tearing it in half) Tarr could follow a little the gist of his remarks.

'That, sir' he seemed to assert 'is not the way to treat a gentleman. That, too, is an insult no gentleman will support.' He pointed towards the door. 'Herr Kreisler, as you know, cannot enter the Café; he is waiting there for your reply. He has been turned out like a drunken workman.'

The Russian was as grave as he was collected, and stood in front of the other principal in this affair, who had sat down again now, with the evident determination to get a different reply. The talking went on for some time. Then he turned towards Tarr, and, seeing him watching the discussion, came towards him, raising his hat. He said in french:

'You know Herr Kreisler, I believe. Will you consent to act for him with me, in an affair that unfortunately—? If you would step over here, I will put you "au courant." '

'I'm afraid I cannot act for Herr Kreisler, as I am leaving Paris early to-morrow morning' Tarr replied.

But the Russian displayed the same persistence with him as he had already observed him to be capable of with the other people.

At last Tarr said 'I don't mind acting temporarily—for a few minutes, now, until you can find somebody else. Will that do? But you must understand that I cannot delay my journey—you must find a substitute at once.'

The Russian explained with business-like gusto and precision, having drawn him towards the door (seemingly to cut off a possible retreat of the enemy), that it was a grave affair. Kreisler's honour was compromised. His friend Otto Kreisler had been provoked in an extraordinary fashion. Stories had been circulated concerning him, affecting seriously the sentiments of a girl he knew regarding him; put about with that object by another gentleman, also acquainted with this particular girl. The Russian luxuriated in his emphasis upon this point. Tarr suggested that they should settle the matter at once, as he had not very much time. He was puzzled. Surely the girl mentioned must be Bertha? If so, had Bertha been telling more fibs? Was the Kreisler mystery after all to her discredit? Perhaps he was now in the presence of *another* rival, existing unknown to him.

In this heroic, very solemnly official atmosphere of ladies' 'honour' and the 'honour' of gentlemen, that the little Russian was rapidly creating, Tarr unwillingly remained for some time. Noisy bursts of protest from other members of the opposing party met the Russian's points. 'It is all nonsense' they shouted; 'there could be no question of honour here!—Kreisler was a quarrelsome German. Kreisler was drunk!'

Tarr liked his own farces: but to be drawn into the service of one of Kreisler's was a humiliation. Kreisler, without taking any notice of him, had turned the tables in that matter.

The discussion was interminable. They were now speaking French: the entire Café appeared to be participating. Several times the principal on the other side attempted to go, evidently very cross at the noisy scene. Then Anastasya's name was mentioned.

'You and Herr Kreisler' the Russian was saying patiently and distinctly 'exchanged blows, I understand, this afternoon, before this lady. This was as a result of my friend Herr Kreisler demanding certain explanations from you which you refused to afford him. These explanations had reference to certain stories you are supposed to have circulated as regards him.'

'Circulated—as regards—that chimpanzee you are conducting about?—what does the ape mean! What does he mean!'

'If you please! By being abusive you cannot escape. You are accused by my friend of having at his expense—.'

'Expense? Does he want money?'

'If you please! Allow me! I am sorry! You cannot buy off Herr Kreisler; but he might be willing for you to pay a substitute if you find it—inconvenient—?'

'I find you, bearded idiot—!'

'We can settle all that afterwards sir. You understand me? I shall be quite ready! But at present it is the affair between you and Herr Kreisler—.'

In brief, it was the hapless Soltyk that Kreisler had eventually run to earth, and had just now publicly smacked, having some hours before smacked him privately.

CHAPTER 2

KREISLER'S afternoon encounter with Anastasya and Soltyk had resembled Tarr's meeting with him and Bertha. Kreisler had seen Anastasya and his new Café friend one day from his window: his reference to possible nose-pulling was accounted for by this. The next day he had felt rather like looking Anastasya up again, his interest revived somewhat. With this object, he had patrolled the neighbourhood. About four o'clock, having just bought some cigarettes at the 'Berne,' he was standing outside considering a walk in the Luxembourg, when Fräulein Vasek appeared. Soltyk was with her. He went over at once. With urbane timidity, as though they had been alone, he offered his hand. She looked at Soltyk, smiling: but she seemed quite pleased to see Kreisler. They began strolling along the Boulevard, Soltyk showing every sign of impatience. She then stopped.

'Mr. Soltyk and I were just going to have the "five o'clock"* somewhere' she said.

Soltyk looked pointedly down the Boulevard, as though that had been an improper piece of information to communicate to Kreisler.

'If you consent to my accompanying you, Fräulein, it would give me the greatest pleasure to remain in your company a little longer.'

She laughed. 'Where were we going, Louis? Didn't you say there was a place near here?'

'There's one over there. But I'm afraid, Fräulein Vasek, I must leave you.—I have—.'

'Oh must you? I'm sorry.'

Soltyk had appeared mortified. He did not go, looking at her doubtfully and then at Kreisler, with an incredulous smile, suggesting that her joke was in bad taste and that she had better bring it to a conclusion. At this point Kreisler had addressed him.

'I said nothing, sir, when a moment ago you failed to return my salute. I understand you were going to have tea with Fräulein Vasek. Now you deprive her suddenly of the pleasure of your company. So there is no further doubt on a certain point.—Will you tell me at once and clearly what objection you have to me?'

'I don't wish to discuss things of that sort before this lady, sir.'

'Will you then name a place where they may be discussed? I will then take my leave?'

'I see no necessity to discuss anything with you.'

'Ah, you see none—I do. And perhaps it is as well that Fräulein Vasek should hear. Will you explain to me, sir, how it is that you have been putting stories about having reference to me, and to my discredit, calculated to prejudice my interests—since this lady no doubt has heard some of your lies, it would be of advantage that you take them back at once, or else explain yourself.'

Before Kreisler had finished, Soltyk said to Anastasya 'I had better go at once, to save you this—.' Then he turned to Kreisler:

'I should have thought you would have had sufficient decency left—.'

'Decency, liar? Decency, *lying swine*? Decency—? What do you mean?' said Kreisler, loudly, in crescendo.

Then he crossed quickly over in front of Anastasya and smacked Soltyk smartly first upon one cheek and then upon the other.

'There is *liar* branded on both your cheeks! And if you should not wish to have *coward* added to your other epithets, you or your friends will find me at the following address before the day is out.' Kreisler produced a card and handed it to Soltyk.

Soltyk stared at him, paralysed for the moment at this outrage, his eyes burning with the sweet intensity Tarr had noticed later that day, taking in the incredible fact. He got the fact at last. He lifted his cane and brought it down on Kreisler's shoulders. Kreisler snatched it from him, broke it in three and flung it in his face, one of the splinters making a little gash in his under-lip.

Anastasya had turned round and begun walking away, leaving them alone. Kreisler also waited no longer, but marched rapidly off in the other direction. Soltyk caught Anastasya up, and apologized for what had occurred, dabbing his lip with a handkerchief.

After this Kreisler felt himself fairly launched upon a most satisfactory little affair. Many an old talent would come in useful. He acted for the rest of the day with a gusto of professional interest. For an hour or two he stayed at home. No one came, however, to call him to account. Leaving word that he would soon be back, he went in search of a man to act for him. He remembered a Russian he had had some talk with at the Atelier, and whom he had once visited. He was celebrated for having had a duel and blinded his opponent.* His instinct now led him to this individual, who has already been seen in action: his qualifications for a second* were quite unique.

Kreisler found him just finishing work. He had soon explained what he required of him. With great gravity the solemn Otto set forth his deep attachment for a 'beautiful girl,' the discreditable behaviour of the Russian, who had sought to prejudice her against him: he gave in fact, a false picture of the situation in which the heart was substituted for the purse, and Anastasya for Vokt. His honour *must* now be satisfied: he would accept *nothing less* than reparation by arms: such was Kreisler, but he was that offended and deeply injured self with a righteous cynicism. He had explained such curiosities of the Kreisler *geist* to Vokt after the following manner: 'I am a hundred different things; I am as many people as the different types of people I have lived amongst: I am a "Boulevardier" (he believed that on occasion he answered fully to that description), I am a "Rapin"—I am also a "Korps student."'

In his account of how things stood he had, besides, led the Russian to understand that there was more in it than met the eye or than it was expedient to say, or in fact than he *could* say (suggesting that he did not care to compromise third parties of sexes that it was the duty of all men of honour to shield and defend). Whatever attitude might be taken up by his proposed adversary, this gentleman, too, knew, he hinted, that they had come to a point in their respective relations towards this 'beautiful girl' at which one of them must disappear. In addition, he, Kreisler, had been grossly insulted in the very presence of the 'beautiful girl' that afternoon: the outrageous Pole had made use of his cane.

The Russian, Bitzenko by name, a solemnly excitable bourgeois of Petrograd, recognized a situation after his own heart: excitement was a food he seldom got in such qualities as was promised here, and pretending to listen to Kreisler a little abstractedly and uncertainly to start with, he was from the first very much his man.

Kreisler and his newly-found henchman had thenceforth gone about their business silently and intently, laying their plans like a pair of gunmen; their proposed victim had been located some quarter of an hour before Tarr's appearance, and stared out of countenance upon the spot by the implacable Otto.

CHAPTER 3

THE passionate effervescence gradually subsided: but the child of this eruption remained: the group of Poles found the legacy of the uproar as cold as its cause had been hot: Bitzenko inspired respect as he scratched his beard, which smelt of tobacco, and wrinkled up imperturbably small grey eyes.

But, the excitement over, the red mark on Soltyk's cheek became merely a fact: his friends found themselves examining it obliquely, as a relic, with curiosity—he had had his face smacked earlier in the day, as well. How much longer was his face going to go on being smacked? Here was the Russian still with them: there was the chance of an affair—a duel—a duel, for a change, in our humdrum life, c'etait une idée.

Who was the 'beautiful girl' the idiot-Russian kept mentioning? Was she that girl he had been telling them about who had a man-servant? Kreisler was a Freiherr?—the Russian had referred to him as 'my friend the Freiherr.'

'Herr Kreisler does not wish to take further measures to insure himself some form of satisfaction' the Russian said monotonously.

'There is always the police for drunken blackguards' Soltyk answered.

'If you please! That is not the way—! I beg your pardon, but it is not usually so difficult to obtain satisfaction from a gentleman.'

'But then I am not a gentleman in the sense that your friend Kreisler is. I am not a Freiherr you see.'

'Perhaps not, but a blow on the face—.'

The little Russian said 'blow on the face' in a soft inviting way, as though it were a tidbit with powers of fascination of its own not to be easily resisted.

'But it is most improper to ask me to stand here wrangling with you' he next said.

'You please yourself.'

'I am merely serving my friend Herr Kreisler. Will you oblige me by indicating a friend of yours with whom I can discuss this matter?'

The waiter who had brought in the card again approached their table. This time he presented Soltyk with a note, written on the Café paper, and folded in four.

Tarr had been watching what was going on with curiosity. He did not believe in a duel: but he wondered what would happen, for he was certain that Kreisler would not let this man alone until he had brought something unpleasant off. What would he have done in Soltyk's place? He would have refused of course—if you had to fight a duel with any man who liked to hit you on the head—! Kreisler, moreover, was not a man with whom a duel need be fought: he was in a weak position to claim such privileges, in spite of the additional blacking on his boots. Tarr himself could have taken refuge in the fact that Englishmen do not duel—but what would have been the next step, this settled, had he been in Soltyk's shoes? Kreisler was waiting at the door of the Café: as soon as the Pole got up and went out, at the door he would once more have his face smacked. His knowledge of Kreisler convinced him that that face would be smacked all over the Quarter, at all hours of the day, for many days to come: Kreisler, unless physically overwhelmed, would smack it in public and in private until further notice. He would probably spit in it, after having smacked it, occasionally. So Kreisler must be henceforth fought by the Pole wherever met. Would this state of things justify the use of a revolver?* That depended on the Pole. Kreisler should be maimed probably; it all should be prepared with great thoroughness; exactly the weight of walking-stick and so forth: the french laws would sanction quite a bad wound.* But Tarr felt that the sympathetic young Pole would soon have Bitzenko on his hands as well. There was every indication that this would shortly be the case. Bitzenko was very alarming.

Kreisler, although evicted from the Café, had been allowed by the waiters to take up his position on a distant portion of the terrace: there, legs crossed and his eye fixed upon the door with a Scottish solemnity,* he squatted with rigid patience. He was an object of considerable admiration to the Café staff: his coolness and persistence appeared to them admirable and typical: his portentousness aroused their wonder and respect. *Celui-là* meant business. He was behaving correctly.

Soltyk opened the note at once. On it was written in german:

'To the cad Soltyk

'If you make any more trouble about appointing seconds, and continue to waste the time of the gentlemen who have consented to act for me, I shall wait for you at the door and try some further means of rousing your courage.'

Sitting next to Soltyk was a small swarthy rat-like person who had taken no part in the discussions or protests but who had watched everything that happened like some observer of another species, dangerously aloof. He now reached out his hand, took up the letter as though it had been a public document, and read it. He then bent towards Soltyk and said:

'What is really the matter with this gentleman?'

Soltyk shrugged his shoulders.

'He's a brute and he is a little crazy into the bargain: he wants to pick a quarrel with me, I don't know why.'

'Doesn't he want to be taken seriously, only? Let his shaggy friend here have a chat with a friend of yours. He may become a nuisance—.'

Soltyk looked sharply at the rat-like figure with dislike.

'What nonsense you're talking Jan! Why are you talking such nonsense?'

'I think Jan's right!' said another.

'I never heard such a stupid remark! If he comes for me at the door, let him! I wish that little man there would go away: he has annoyed us quite enough!'

'Louis, will you give me permission to speak to him on your behalf?'

Soltyk looked the rat-like figure in the eyes with astonishment and enquiry.

'*Why* are you talking like this, Jan?'

'I think it is the best way out, Louis. Shall I act for you?'

Soltyk hesitated.

'If that will give you any satisfaction' he said coldly.

Jan Pochinsky got up without another word and put himself at Bitzenko's disposition. The whole party became tumultuous at this.

'What the devil are you up to Jan? Let them alone!'

'You're not going——?'

'Tell them to go to hell! What on earth are you doing Jan?'

'Jan, come back you silly fool! You must be mad. Louis, tell that fool to sit down! He hasn't your permission to——? Jan! Come here!'

Jan took no notice, except to mutter: 'This is the best thing to do.'

'The best thing? What do you mean? Louis is not going to take that imbecile seriously! You are mad, completely mad!'

Jan shrugged his shoulders, as he reached up on tiptoe for his hat.

'Do you want this to last the whole evening?' he said.

He followed Bitzenko out, and Tarr followed Bitzenko.

CHAPTER 4

THEY went over to a small, gaudy, quiet Débit on the other side of the Boulevard, Kreisler watching them, but still with his eye upon the door near at hand. Tarr was amused now at his position of dummy:* he enjoyed crossing the road under Kreisler's eye, in his service. He would not have missed this for a great deal.

Bitzenko was the prophet of the necessity of this affair, more than Otto Kreisler he was the initial figure: it might have been that, given the outraged Freiherr behind him as solid as a rock, nothing would have saved their proposed victim. But as an agent of destiny he was promptly eclipsed by Jan. When he sat down opposite this almost dwarfish, dusky and impassible, second—who avoided his eyes with a contemptuous expression and waited for him to speak—he was non-plussed and mastered; he felt in his bones, in the extremity of his toes, in the mangy bristles of his peasant-beard, that he would rise from that council-board a beaten man.

His veiled cold and disgusted eyes fishily fastened upon the leg of a chair, Jan asked him to state his case. He stated it, as before, and Pochinsky said:

'Do you consider that an adequate reason for asking my principal to meet this mountebank?'*

Bitzenko leapt to his feet.

'Excuse me! Excuse me!' he rapidly stuttered. 'I cannot allow you to refer to the Freiherr—! I really cannot dream of allowing the Freiherr! Really the Freiherr cannot be referred to—! Excuse me! I must ask you!'

Tarr yawned: the sing-song and complaining french of his russian colleague irritated him.

'Excuse me!' he exclaimed, in conscious parody. 'Do not let us come to blows over the Freiherr whatever we do.'

'By all means! More exactly! But do not let us stand by—we cannot stand by—!'

'Nothing of the sort! I did not expect that.'

Jan, sunk in a frigid lethargy of measureless contempt, sat with his little arm thrown over the back of the chair, his round-shouldered rat-like trunk hanging from this boney hook, the semitic sharpness of his features turned away in a patient oblivion.

Bitzenko resumed his seat with violence.

'It is too much! Excuse me! I am exasperated!'

'What does the Freiherr wish?' asked Jan, his eyes still veiled.

'He desires immediate satisfaction.'

'What order of satisfaction?'

'Satisfaction at the sword-point or with army-pistols.'

'But does the nature of the dispute demand such an extreme issue as that? Our principals might be killed if they used such arms as you mention, might they not? I ask in ignorance.'

Bitzenko gasped.

'That is a possibility that my principal has duly weighed!' he hissed and panted.

Jan was silent: his judicial calm and immobility imposed so much upon the astonished Bitzenko and the perplexed Tarr that they found themselves sitting spellbound until this Sphinx* should give utterance to his thoughts.

'You are prepared to accept no compromise on behalf of your principal?' at length Jan asked indifferently.

'None! I have stated his terms. He does not see his way—as a man of honour—in such a case as this—to compromise—to compromise—in any sense. Those are my instructions.'

There was another momentous silence.

Jan rose without looking at them, pushed his chair aside and said under his breath:

'You will stay here? I will see my principal.'

Bitzenko watched him withdraw with the deepest misgivings. These he immediately expanded in conversation with his colleague.

Jan re-entered the Café des Sports Aquatiques and sat down beside Soltyk.

'Well?'

His friends leant forward and there was a silence.

'Well I'm afraid I was mistaken, Louis: your German means business. I wash my hands of it—I admit I was wrong. The challenge should have been disregarded.'

The gathering gasped and uproar ensued.

'Disregarded? It's absurd absurd absurd! Tell the whole damned crew to go to the devil! How many of them are there?'

'What possessed you Jan to butt in—what business was it of yours! What do you know at all—na! Now—!'

'Yes! You acted on your own initiative. What possessed you—?'

Jan protested coldly and lazily, his arm hooped over the back of his chair.

'Excuse me. I went at Louis' request.'

'You did not!'

'At Louis' request? When?'

'What did they say?'

Everyone shouted at once. The new polish pandemonium attracted the bright attention of the american painting-ladies in the neighbourhood.

'Who is this Bitzenko!' one of the least active of the Poles enquired strengthlessly.

'Don't you know him?' another screamed. 'Lurioff used to know him, but *intimately*, he used to be a friend of Bobby's, a great friend of Bobby's! You know the large studios rue Ulm, near the Invalides, yes behind the Metro—he lives there: he's rich, quite fairly well-off. He is of good family, he is mad.'

Soltyk patted his cheek gently, watching Jan, who kept his eyes upon the ground.

'He once had a duel and blinded a man!'

'Who—that bird—?'

'How—*blinded* him?'

'Yes indeed—blinded him, in both eyes—bang! bang!'

'No! how could he in a duel! In both eyes!'

'But I tell you that is so! Both I assure you! There are duels in which you have a right—.'

'Oh shut up! Do stop talking about duels! I'm sick of the word *duel*! What is a duel? Who ever heard?'

While they wrangled Soltyk continued to pat his cheek without speaking. Now everyone was silent, they lay back exhausted.

'Well?' Soltyk addressed Jan.

'Well!' replied Jan. 'As I said I give it up—I wash my hands of it. Henceforth it's your funeral.'

'How do you mean Jan, *wash your hands of it*, you're not going to leave me in the lurch!'

Jan coloured, but kept his eyes upon the floor.

'You're not surely going to be so mean as to leave me in the lurch—having taken the matter up with such good will: you're not going to throw up the sponge for me Jan at the first difficulty?'

Jan fidgeted in his chair.

'I have acted for the best.'

'Yes' Soltyk insisted 'but you are not going to leave off acting for the best, are you, by any chance? None of these other people here, you know, will act for me! Not one of them would have taken the matter up in the splendid zealous way you did—there's not a potential "second" among them! Look at them! Not one! Whatever shall I do Jan, if you desert me?'

Soltyk continued to pat the red mark upon his cheek, as though to draw attention to it, while he kept his gaze fixed upon the lowered eyelids of Pochinsky. The others watched in complete silence, mostly staring at Jan.

Jan raised his eyes and glanced at the ring of faces. With a slight sneer he then remarked:

'You seem annoyed with me Louis.'

A murmur of protest rose from the others. One exclaimed:

'What did you appoint yourself Louis' "second" for—"second" "second"! What need had he of your services anyway—the whole affair is *pour rire*—why have you acted like this! Tell us, your behaviour after all requires explaining! Now you *wash your hands*—what is that I should like to know?'

'Well you all seem annoyed with me. But there is no need to be—there is no occasion Louis for you to fight, none whatever.'

Again there was a clamour.

'But this is too much! *No need to fight!* What's the man talking about!'

'I think Jan had better have a round with Bitzenko if he's so interested in fighting, as he calls it!'

Soltyk was frowning now: he continued to hold his hand to his cheek.

'How have you left the matter Jan?' he asked.

'I'm out of it!' Jan repeated shortly.

'Yes but how did you leave it, when you left it—for me?'

'*You* are out of it too, unless you wish to be otherwise—there's no use being cross with me Louis, I have acted for the best—what more could I do? I thought you wanted me to go and see what I could do.'

'And what did you say before you came back? Are they still there?'

'All—still there!'

'Will you oblige me by returning Jan and making the terms that you consider appropriate?' Soltyk asked him.

Grumbling in an offended undertone Jan said:

'You must do your own dirty work Louis—I have got no thanks—in fact you seem very angry with me! I've done nothing. Anyone would think that I had—.'

Soltyk laughed:

'Smacked my face? Is that what you mean, yes?'

'No—I seem to have done something to displease you.'

'Well: go Jan and find out the sort of duel it is I am expected to "fight." This is getting most awfully boring. Let us get all this nonsense over for heaven's sake. He will be in here again soon, smacking me, or he may even kick this time!'

The others once more clamoured.

Jan got up and on tiptoe reached his hat.

'I'm off!' he said.

Soltyk seized him by the arm, exclaiming:

'What? But I never heard of such a thing! My Second in flight? What would everybody say to that? No Jan, you must see me through with it now.'

'Don't be absurd Louis' one of the others exclaimed. 'Do let's drop all this nonsense. It's Jan's fault that we're still talking about it. Let him go. He wants to go to bed—it's a pity he didn't go before!'

'A great pity!'

'It's a pity Jan—.'

'Jan! Sit down!' Soltyk pulled him down. 'Jan—arrange all this for me, before you leave us. I rely on you Jan.'

Soltyk's personal friend, Pete Orlinski, rose from his seat and came round and leaning upon his shoulder began pouring out a stream of alarmed protestation. His voice rose and fell in an intense torrent of close-packed sound, close to Soltyk's ear: his face shone and the veins stood out in it. He gathered his arguments up in the tips of his fingers in little nervous bunches and held them up for examination, thrust them under his friend's nose as though asking him to smell them. Then with a spasm of the body, a twanging vibration on some deep chord, a prolonged buzz in the throat, he dashed his gathered fingers towards the floor.

Two more of Soltyk's closer business friends began overwhelming him with protests.

'Have you gone mad Louis! You are not going to pay any attention to this drivel about libels, about "beautiful girls—!"'

'You are surely not so mad as to take this German seriously? Louis! you must be quite mad! Let Jan go, let him go, do let him go!—Jan—*go away!* Please leave at once! You see what a mess you've made, please take yourself off!'

Soltyk still held his self-appointed Second by the sleeve.

Bitzenko entered by the swing door, followed by Tarr.

'Here they come! My dear Jan, *please* go and make all the necessary arrangements for my execution!'

Soltyk grew pale as this sinister figure, so bourgeois, prepossessing and mildly-bearded, with its legend of blindings and blood—its uncanny tenacity as a second—approached: he turned quickly to a good-looking sleek, sallow youth at his elbow and said:

'Khudin, will you act for me—you understand—assist Jan in his preparations for the final scene?'

The angry voices of his friends on the one hand threatened the approaching Bitzenko, on the other hand reproached their friend.

'Louis! Remain where you are! take no notice of this clown!'

'Send for the manager! Waiter! Are these people to be allowed to disturb us! This is a great scandal!'

Soltyk, flung suddenly into a state of shrill excitement, was exclaiming:

'This is too boring—it is past belief, really quite past belief! Will you *settle* with those persons—Jan will you please go over and *settle*—arrange what you please, so that we can be left in *peace*?'

Bitzenko stopped a few yards from the table and signalled to Jan. Jan rose and, in the midst of cries and protests hurled after him by his compatriots, went over to Bitzenko, his face lighted by what was an internal grin, as it were—an exultant tightening in the regions out of sight where all his passions had their existence for himself alone.

Tarr was astonished at the rapid tragic trend of these farcical negotiations.

'How angry that man must be to do that' he thought. But he had not been smacked the evening before; yet he remembered he had been passably angry.

CHAPTER 5

THE new partnership of Kreisler and Bitzenko was one purely of action: but a miraculous solidarity resulted upon the spot and they operated as one man. Their schemes and energies flew direct from mind to mind, without the need for words; Bitzenko with his own hand had brushed the back of Kreisler's coat; on tiptoe doing this he looked the picture of an amiable child: they were together there in Kreisler's room before they started like two little schoolboys dressing up in preparation for some escapade.

When he had entered the Sports Aquatiques, Kreisler had been anxious: his eyes had picked out Soltyk in a delicate flurry, he had been afraid that he might escape him. Soltyk looked so securely bedded in life—he wanted to wrench him out: he was not at all bad-tempered at the moment: he would have extracted him quite 'painlessly' if required: but bleeding and from the roots he must come out! (Br-r-rr. The berserker rage.)

He was quite quiet and well-behaved; above all things, the *well-behaved!* The mood he had happened on for this occasion was a virulent snobbery.

The *duel* theme suggested this. With eagerness he recalled that he was a german gentleman, with a *university education*, who had never worked, *a member of an honourable family!*—he remembered each detail socially to his advantage: he had arbitrarily revived even the title of Freiherr that, it was rumoured in his family, his ancestors had borne. With Bitzenko he had referred to himself as 'the Freiherr Otto Kreisler.'

The snob that emerged was, in this obsession of disused and disappearing life, the wild assertion of vitality: it was the clamour for universal recognition that life and the beloved self were still there: he was almost dead (he had promised his father his body for next month and must be punctual), but people already had begun treading upon him and treating him as a corpse: as to fighting with a man who was practically dead to all intents and purposes, one mass of worms—a worm, in short—that was not to be expected of anybody, not even with the poorest sense of values. So he became a violent snob.

At the opening of the late offensive, Kreisler had fixed his eyes upon Soltyk from his table with alert provocation. He had practised these manners in the *Luitpold** for many a year: he knew the proper way to *fix*. As to the Poles, a gentle flame of social security and ease danced in their eyes and gestures: he was out in the dark, they were in a lighted room! He wished their fathers' affairs would deteriorate and their fortunes fall to pieces, that their watches could be stolen, and their tick attacked by insidious reports: as he watched them he felt more and more of an outcast. He saw himself the little official in a german provincial town that his father's letter foreshadowed: or a clerk in a *Reisebureau*, looking up the times of the trains for Paris or the Tyrol. One or two of them pointed him out: his *fixing* was an operation that could not escape notice: it was a contemptuous laugh of Soltyk's that brought him to his feet.

As he was slapping his enemy he woke up out of his nightmare: he was like a sleeper having the first inkling of his solitude when he is woken by the violent climax of his dream, still surrounded by tenacious influences: but had anyone struck him then, the blow would have had as little effect as a blow aimed at a waking man by a phantom of his sleep. The noise around him was a receding accompaniment.

Next Soltyk's quietness developed hypnotic tendencies: the sweet white of the face made him sick. To overcome this he stepped forward again to strike the dummy a further blow, and then it moved suddenly. As he raised his hand his glasses almost jumped off his nose and at that point he was seized by the waiters. Hurried out on to the pavement he could still see, at the bottom of a huge placid mirror just inside the swing-door, the wriggling backs of the band of Poles. Drawing out his card-case he had handed the waiter a visiting-card. The waiter at first refused it. Then he took it shrugging his shoulders and shuffled off with it. Kreisler saw in the mirror the tearing up of his card. Fury once more, not so much because it was a new slight as that he feared his only hope, Soltyk, might slip through his fingers.

The worry of the hour or so in which Bitzenko was negotiating told on him so much that when at last his emissary announced that an arrangement had been come to, in the sense desired by him, he questioned him incredulously.

Bitzenko accompanied Kreisler to the door of his lodgings, and promising to return within half an hour, disappeared with nervous speed. Tarr, having, as he had stipulated, left the critical phase over, Bitzenko first went in search of a friend to serve as Second. The man upon whom his choice had fallen was already in bed: at once, half asleep, without preparation of any sort, he consented to do what was asked of him.

'Will you be a Second in a duel to-morrow morning at half-past six?'

'Yes.'

'At half-past six?'

'Yes': and after a minute or two, 'is it you?'

'No, a German a friend of mine.'

'All right.'

'You will have to get up at five.'

Bitzenko's next move was to go to his rooms, put a gently tick-ing little clock, with an enormous alarum on the top, under his arm, and so return to Otto Kreisler. He informed his friend of these last arrangements made in his interests: he suggested it would be better if he put him up for the night, to save time in the morning. He attached himself to Kreisler's person: until it were deposited in the large cem-etery near by or else departed from the Gare du Nord in a deal box for burial in Germany, it should not leave him. In the event of victory and he being no longer responsible for it, it would of course disappear as best it could. The possible subsequent conflict with the police was not without charm for Bitzenko: he regarded the police force, its func-tions and existence, as a pretext for adventure. But that was another matter, distinct from this.

The light was blown out. Bitzenko curled himself up upon the floor: he insisted. Kreisler must be fresh in the morning and do him justice. The Russian could hear the bed shaking for some time, he pricked his ears but could not make head or tail of it. Kreisler was trembling violently: a sort of exultation at the thought of his success caused this nervous convulsion.

At about half-past four in the morning Kreisler was dreaming of Vokt and a pact he had made with him in his sleep never to divulge some secret, which there was never any possibility of his doing in any case, as he had completely forgotten what it was. His whole being was shattered by a dreadful explosion. With his eyes suddenly wide open he saw the little clock quivering upon the mantelpiece beneath its large alarum. When it had stopped Kreisler could hardly believe his ears, as though this sound had been going to accompany life, for that day at least, as a destructive and terrifying feature. Then he saw the Russian, already on foot, his white and hairy little body had appar-ently emerged from the scratch bed simultaneously with the deton-ation of his clock, as though it were a mechanism set for the same hour.

They both dressed without a word. Kreisler wrote a short letter to his father, entrusting it to his Second. His last few francs were to be spent on the taxi that would take them to the place of meeting, outside the fortifications.*

They found the other Second sound asleep: he was more or less dressed by Bitzenko. They set out in their taxi to the rendezvous by way of the Bois.*

The chilly and unusual air of the early morning, the empty streets and shuttered houses, destroyed all feeling of reality for Kreisler. Had the duel been a thing to fear, it would have had an opposite effect. His errand did not appear as an inflexible reality either, following upon events that there was no taking back: it was a caprice they were pursuing, as though, for instance, they had woken up in the early morning and decided to go fishing: they were carrying it out with a dogged persistency, with which whims are often served.

He kept his mind away from Soltyk. He seemed a very long way off, it would be fatiguing for the mind to go in search of him.

Nature, with immense fugue,* had pushed Kreisler to a certain course: this feat accomplished, nature had departed, assured that his life would go steadily on in the bed gauged for it by this upheaval. But she had left the Russian with him to see that all was carried out according to her wishes. Kreisler's german nature that craved discipline, a course marked out, had got more even than it asked for: it had been presented with a mimic Fate.

Bitzenko took his pleasure morosely. The calm and assurance of the evening before had given place to a brooding humour: he was only restored to a silent and intense animation on hearing his 'Browning'* speak. This he produced somewhere in the Bois, and insisted upon his principal having a little practice, as they had plenty of time to spare. This was a very imprudent step, it might draw attention to their movements, but Bitzenko overruled their objections. Kreisler proved an excellent shot. Then the Russian himself, with impassible face, emptied a couple of chambers into a tree trunk. He put his 'Browning' back into his pocket hastily, after this, as though startled at his own self-indulgence.

A piece of waste land, on the edge of a wood, well hidden on all sides, had been chosen for the duel. The enemy was not on the ground when they drove up. Kreisler was quite passive; he was in good hands. Until this was all over he had nothing to worry about.

Bitzenko's friend was a tall, powerfully built young russian painter, who, with his great bow legs, would take up some straggling and extravagantly twisted pose of the body, and remain immobile for minutes together, with an air of ridiculous detachment. This combination of a tortured, restless attitude, and at the same time the statuesque tendency, suggested something like a contemplative contortionist.

A mouth of almost anguished attention associated with little calm indifferent eyes, produced similar results in the face.

Fresh compartment—The duel became for him as he stood on the damp grass conventional: it was a duel like another. He was seeking reparation by arms: had he not been libelled and outraged? 'A beautiful woman' was at the bottom of it. Life had no value for him! *Tant pis* for the other man who had been foolhardy enough to cross his path! His coat collar turned up he looked sternly towards the road, his moustaches blowing a little in the wind. He asked Bitzenko for a cigarette. That gentleman did not smoke, but the other Russian produced a khaki cigarette* with a long mouthpiece. He struck a light. As Kreisler lit his cigarette, his hand resting against the other's, a strange feeling shot through him at the contact of this flesh. He moistened his lips and spat out a piece of the mouthpiece he had bitten through.

The hour arranged came round and there was still no sign of the other party. The possibility of a hitch in the proceedings dawned upon Kreisler. Personal animosity for Soltyk revived. He looked towards his companions, alone there on the ground of the encounter: they were an unsatisfactory pair. These Russians! he reproached himself for having chosen Bitzenko in this affair.

Bitzenko, on the other hand, was deep in thought: he was rehearsing his part of Second. The duel in which he had blinded his adversary was a figment of his boyish brain, confided with tears in his voice one evening to a friend. His only genuine claim to be a man of action was that, in a perfect disguise, he had assisted the peasants to set fire to his own manor-house during the revolution of 1906,* for the fun of the thing and in an access of revolutionary sentiment. Later on he had assisted the police with information in the investigation of the affair, also anonymously. All this he kept to himself: but he referred to his past in Russia in a way that conjured up more luridness than the flames of his little château (which did not burn at all well) warranted. As to duelling, he knew nothing at all about that, but hoped soon to do so.

Kreisler felt his hands getting so cold that he thought they might fail him in the duel. But a car was heard beyond the trees, on the Paris road. This masterful sound struck steadily and at once into brutish apathy: it so plainly knew what it wanted. Men in their soft bodies still contained the apathy of the fields: their mind had burst out of them and taken these crawling pulps up on its back.

It was Soltyk's new four-seater bought with the commission derived from a sale of jewels, family heirlooms, belonging to Miss Vasek: with its load of hats it drew up. The four members of the other party came on to the field, the fourth a young polish doctor. They walked quickly. Bitzenko went to meet them—Pochinsky protested energetically that the duel must not proceed.

'Monsieur Bitzenko, this duel must not be proceeded with!'

'On no account!' exclaimed Khudin emphatically. 'It is monstrous!'

'That is a point of view, gentlemen, I cannot accept. On what grounds—?'

'Our principal has proved his respect for Herr Kreisler's claim by accepting this place of meeting.'

Bitzenko stiffened.

'Is there anything in Herr Kreisler that would justify Monsieur Soltyk in considering that he was condescending—?'

'The attitude attributed to our principal is not his attitude' Jan then said, looking at the ground.

'Is the implication that my principal has misrepresented the facts?'

Soltyk's eyes steadily avoided Kreisler's person. He hoped this ridiculous figure might make some move enabling them to abandon the duel. His stomach had been out of order the day before—he wondered if it would surge up, disgrace him: he might in fact be sick at any moment he felt: he saw himself on tiptoe, in an ignominious spasm, the proceedings held up, friends and enemies watching. He kept his eyes off Kreisler as a bad sailor on board ship keeps his eyes off a plate of soup.

Kreisler, from a distance of twenty yards stared through his glasses at the group of people his energy had collected at that early hour of the morning, as though he had been examining the enemy through binoculars. Obediently erect and still, he looked rather amazed at what was occurring. Soltyk, in rear of the others, struggled with his bile: he slipped into his mouth a sedative tablet, oxide of bromium and aniseed.* This made him feel more sick: for some moments he stood still in horror, expecting to vomit. The blood rushed to his head and covered the back of his neck with a warm liquid sheet.

Kreisler's look of surprise deepened. He had observed Soltyk slipping something into his mouth, and was puzzled and annoyed. What was he up to? Poison was the only guess he could make; but what was that for?

Having taken part in many Mensurs he knew that for this very serious duel his emotions were inadequate for the occasion: his nervous system was as dead as that of a corpse. He became offended with his phlegm: this wealth of instinctive resistance to the idea of Death, the indignity of being nothing, was rendered empty by his premature insensitiveness. In a few minutes he might be dead!—but how absurd—that had so little effect that he almost laughed.

Then, with better results, he occupied himself with the notion that that man yonder might in a few minutes be wiped out—he would become a disintegrating mess, more repulsive than vitriol or syphilis* could make him: all that organism he, Kreisler, would be turning into dung, as though by magic. He, Kreisler, is insulted: he is denied equality of existence, his favourite money-lender is corrupted and estranged: he, Kreisler, lifts his hand, presses a little bar of steel and the other is swept away into the earth. Heaven knows where the insulting spirit goes to! Heaven cares! But the physical break-up at least is beautifully complete. He went through it with painstaking realism. But he was too near the event to benefit properly by his fancy: possibilities were weakened by the nearness of Certainty.

People refused to treat him as anything but a sack of potatoes, however. Four or five men had been arguing about him over there for the last five minutes and they had not once looked in his direction. He coughed to draw attention to himself. They all looked round in surprise.

Clearly Bitzenko was defending his duel. Why should Bitzenko go on disposing of him in this fashion? This busybody took everything for granted; he never so much as appealed to him, even once. Had Bitzenko been commissioned to hustle him out of existence?

But Soltyk: there was that fellow again slipping something into his mouth! A cruel and fierce sensation of mixed origin but berserker stamp rose self-consciously in a hot gush around his heart. He *loved* that man! Na ja! it was certainly a sort of passion he had for him! But—mystery of mysteries!—because he loved him he wished to plunge a sword into him, to plunge it in and out and up and down! Oh why had pistols been chosen?

For two pins he would let him off! He would let him off if——yes. He began pretending to himself that the duel might after all not take place. That was the only way he could get anything out of it.

He laughed; then shouted out in German:

'Give me one!'

They all looked round. Soltyk did not turn, but the side of his face became crimson. Kreisler felt a surge of active passion at the sight of the blood in his face.

'Give me one' Kreisler shouted again, putting out the palm of his hand, and laughing in a thick, insulting, hearty manner. He was now a *Knabe* a *Bengel*—he was young and cheeky. His last words had been said with quick cleverness: the heavy coquetting was double-edged.

'What do you mean?' Bitzenko called back.

'I want a jujube.* Ask Herr Soltyk! Tell him not to keep them to himself!'

They all turned towards the other principal to the duel, standing some yards beyond them. Head thrown back and eyes burning, Soltyk gazed at Kreisler. If killing could be embodied in the organ that *sees* a perfect weapon would exist: but Soltyk's battery was too conventional to pierce the layers of putrefying tragedy, Kreisler's bulwark. His cheeks were a dull red, his upper lip was stretched tightly over the gums: the white line of teeth made his face look as though he were laughing. He stamped his foot on the ground with the impetuous grace of a Russian dancer, and started walking hurriedly up and down. He glared at his seconds as well, but although sick with impatience made no protest.

A peal of drawling laughter came from Kreisler.

'Sorry, sorry, my mistake' he shouted. 'Don't disturb yourself. Take things easy!'

Bitzenko came over and asked Kreisler if he still, for his part, was of the same mind, namely, that the duel should proceed. The principal stared impenetrably at the Second.

'If such an arrangement can be come to as should—er—' he began slowly. He was going to play with Bitzenko too, against whom his humour had shifted. A look of deepest dismay appeared in the Russian's face.

'I don't understand. You mean?'

'I mean that if the enemy and you can find a basis for understand-ing—' and Kreisler went on staring at Bitzenko with his look of false surprise.

'You seem very anxious for me to fight, Herr Bitzenko' he then exclaimed furiously.—With a laugh at Bitzenko's miserable face, and with evident pleasure at his own 'temperamental' facial agility, the quick-change artist every inch, he left the Russian, walking towards the other assistants. Addressing Pochinsky, his face radiating affabil-ity, stepping with caution, as though to avoid puddles, he said in a finicky caressing voice:

'I am willing to forgo the duel at once on one condition. Otherwise it must go on!' he barked fiercely. 'If Herr Soltyk will give me a kiss I will forgo the duel!'

He smiled archly and expectantly at Pochinsky.

'I don't know what you mean!' Jan piped with a dark delighted snigger.

'Why a kiss? You know what a kiss is, my dear sir.'

'I shall consider you out of your mind. Men do not kiss men. Men *fight*—but kiss! That is not manly behaviour—.'

'That is my condition.'

Soltyk had come up behind Pochinsky.

'What is your *condition*?' he asked loudly.

Kreisler stepped forward so quickly that he was beside him before Soltyk could move: with one hand coaxingly extended towards his arm he was saying something, too softly for the others to hear.

By his rapid action he had immobilized everybody. Surprise had shot their heads all one way: they stood, watching and listening, screwed into astonishment as though by deft fingers. His soft words, too, must have carried sleep: their insults and their honey clogged up his enemy. A hand had been going up to strike: but at the words it stopped dead. So much new matter for anger had been poured into the ear that it wiped out the earlier impulse: action must again be begun right down from the root. Soltyk stared stupidly at him.

Kreisler thrust his mouth forward amorously, his body in the attitude of the Eighteenth-Century gallant, right toe advanced and pointed, as though Soltyk had been a woman.*

Soltyk became white and red by turns: the will was released in a muffled explosion, it tore within at its obstructions, he writhed upright, a statue's bronze softening, suddenly, with blood. His blood, one heavy mass, hurtled about in him, up and down, like a sturgeon in a narrow tank. All the pilules* he had taken seemed acting sedatively against the wildness of his muscles: the bromium fought the blood. His hands were electrified: will was at last dashed all over him, an arctic douche and the hands become claws flew at Kreisler's throat. His nails made six holes in the flesh and cut into the tendons beneath: his enemy was hurled about to left and right, he was pumped backwards and forwards. Otto's hands grabbed a mass of hair, as a man slipping on a precipice seizes a plant: then they gripped along the coat sleeves, connecting him with the engine he had just overcharged with fuel: his face sallow white, he became puffed and exhausted.

'Acha—acha—' a noise, the beginning of a word, came from his mouth. He sank down on his knees. A notion of endless violence filled him. Tchun—tchun—tchun—tchun—tchun—tchun his blood 'chugged'—he collapsed upon his back and the convulsive arms came with him. The strangling sensation at his neck intensified.

Meanwhile a breath of absurd violence had smitten everywhere. Khudin had shouted:

'That "crapule" is beneath contempt! Pouah! I refuse to act! Whatever induced us—! Pouah!'

Bitzenko had begun a discourse. Khudin turned upon him, shrieking 'Foute-moi donc la paix, imbécile!'

At this Bitzenko had rapped him smartly upon the cheek. Khudin, who spent his mornings sparring with a negro pugilist, gave him a blow between the eyes, which laid him out insensible upon the field of honour. But Bitzenko's russian colleague, interfering when he noticed this, seized Khudin round the waist and after a sharp bout, threw him, falling on top of him.

Jan, his face radiant with unaffected malice, hurried with the physician to separate Soltyk and Kreisler, scuffling and exhorting. The field was filled with cries, smacks, harsh movements and the shrill voice of Jan exclaiming 'Gentlemen! gentlemen!'

This chaos gradually cleared up: Soltyk was pulled off; Khudin and the young Russian were separated by the surgeon with great difficulty. Bitzenko once more was upon his feet. Everybody on all hands was dusting trousers, arranging collars, picking up hats.

Kreisler stood stretching his neck to right and left alternately. His collar was torn open; blood trickled down his chest. He had felt weak and quite unable to help himself against his antagonist. Actual fighting appeared a contingency outside the calculations or functioning of his spirit. Brutal by rote and in the imagination, if action came too quickly, before he could inject it with his dream, his energies became disconnected. This mêlée had been a most disturbing interlude: he was extremely offended by it. His eyes rested steadily and angrily upon Soltyk now. This attempt upon the part of his enemy to escape into physical and secondary things he must be made to pay for! Kreisler staggered a little, with the dignity of the drunken man: his glasses were still in place, they had weathered the storm, tightly riding his face, because of Soltyk's partiality for his neck.

The physician, flushed from his recent work, took Soltyk by the arm.

'Come along Louis: surely you don't want any more of it? Let's get out of this, I refuse to act professionally. This is a brawl not a duel. You agree with me Pochinsky don't you?'

Soltyk was panting, his mouth opening and shutting. He first turned this way, then that: his actions were those of a man avoiding some importunity.

'C'est bien, c'est bien!' he gasped in French. 'Mais oui, je sais bien! Laisse-moi.'*

All his internal disorganization was steadily claiming his attention.

'Mais dépêche-toi donc! Tu n'as plus rien à faire ici.'* Half supporting him, the doctor began urging him along towards the car: Soltyk, stumbling and coughing, allowed himself to be guided. Jan followed slowly, grinning.

Bitzenko, recuperating rapidly, observed what was happening. With a muffled cry for assistance, he started after them.

———

Kreisler saw all this at first with indifference. He had taken his handkerchief out and was dabbing his neck. Then suddenly, with a rather plaintive but resolute gait, he ran after his Second, his eye fixed upon the retreating Poles.

'Hi! A moment! Your Browning! Give me your Browning!' he said hoarsely. His voice had been driven back into the safer depths of his body: it was a new and unconvincing one. Bitzenko did not appear to understand.

Kreisler plucked the revolver out of his pocket with an animal deftness. There was a report. He was firing in the air.

The retreating physician had faced quickly round, dragging Soltyk. Kreisler was covering them with the Automatic.

'Halt!' he shouted 'halt there! Not so fast! I will shoot you like a dog if you will not fight!'

Covering them, he ordered Bitzenko to take one of the revolvers provided for the duel over to Soltyk.

'That will be murder—if you assist in this, sir, you will be participating in a murder! Stop this—.'

The doctor was jabbering at Bitzenko, his arm still through his friend's. Soltyk stood wiping his face with his hand, his eyes upon the ground. His breath came heavily and he kept shifting his feet.

The tall young Russian stood in a twisted attitude, a gargoyle Apollo:* his mask of peasant tragedy had broken into a slight and very simple smile.

'Move and I fire! Move and I fire!' Kreisler kept shouting, moving up towards them, with stealthy grogginess. He kept shaking the revolver and pointing at them with the other hand, to keep them alive to the reality of the menace.

'Don't touch the pistols Louis!' said the doctor, standing with folded arms beside his friend, as Bitzenko came over with his leather dispatch case. 'Don't touch them Louis! They daren't shoot! They dare not. Don't touch!'

Louis appeared apathetic both as to the pistols and the good advice.

'Leave him both!' Kreisler called, his revolver still trained on Soltyk. Bitzenko put them both down, a foot away from Soltyk, and walked hurriedly out of the zone of fire where he found himself beside Jan, who had withdrawn upon the arrival of Kreisler and his Automatic.

'Will you take up one of those pistols or both?' Kreisler asked.

'Kindly point that revolver somewhere else and allow us to go!' the indignant physician called back.

'I'm not speaking to you, pig-face! It's *you* I'm addressing. Take up that pistol!'

He was now five or six yards from them.

'Herr Soltyk is unarmed! The pistols you want him to take have only one charge. Yours has twelve.* In any case it would be murder!'

Kreisler walked up to them. He was very white, much quieter and acting with some effort. He stooped down to take up one of the pistols. The doctor aimed a blow at his head. It caught him just in front of the ear, on the right cheek bone: he staggered sideways; tripped and fell. The moment he felt the blow he pulled the trigger of the Browning, which still pointed towards his principal adversary. Soltyk threw his arms up, Kreisler was struggling upwards to his feet, he fell face forwards on top of him.

Believing this to be a new attack, Otto seized the descending body round the middle, rolling over on top of it. It was quite limp. He then thought the other man had fainted or perhaps ruptured himself. He drew back quickly: two hands grasped him and flung him down on his stomach. This time his glasses went. Scrambling after them, he remembered his Automatic which he had dropped: he shot his hands out to left and right, forgetting his glasses, to recover the revolver. He felt that a blow was a long time in coming.

'He's dead! He's dead!'

The doctor's voice, announcing that in french, he heard at the same time as Bitzenko's panting in his ear:

'What are you looking for? Come quickly!'

'Where is the Browning?' he asked. At that moment his hand struck his glasses: he put them on and got to his feet.

At Bitzenko's words he had a feeling of a new order of things having set in, a sensation he remembered having experienced on two other occasions in his past life. They came in a fresh surprising tone: it was as though they were the first words he had heard that day. Something was ripped open, and everything was fresh loud and new. The words themselves appeared to signify a sudden removal, a journey, novel conditions.

'Come along, I've got the gun. There's no time to lose.' It was all over; he must embrace practical affairs. The Russian's voice was business-like: something had finished for him too. Kreisler saw the others standing in a peaceful group; the doctor was getting up from beside Soltyk.

He rushed over to Kreisler and shook his fist in his face and tried to speak. But his mouth was twisted down at the corners, and he could hardly see. The palms of his hands pressed into each of his eyes, the next moment he was sobbing, walking back to his friends. Jan was looking at Kreisler but it seemed with nothing but idle curiosity.

Bitzenko's bolt was shot: Kreisler had been unsatisfactory. All had ended in a silly accident: this was hardly a real corpse at all. But something was sent to console him. The Police had got wind of the duel. Bitzenko his compatriot and Kreisler were walking down the field, intending to get into the road at the farther end and so reach the nearest station. The taxi had been sent away, Kreisler having no more money, and Bitzenko's feeling in the matter being that, should Kreisler fall, a corpse can always find some sentimental soul to look after it. There was always the Morgue, a most satisfactory place for a body.

Half-way along the field, a car passed them on the other side of the hedge at full tilt. Once more the Russian was in his element. His face cleared: he looked ten years younger—in the occupants of the car he had recognized members of the police force!

Calling 'run!' to Kreisler he took to his heels, followed by his com-patriot—whose neck shot in and out and whose great bow legs could almost be heard twanging as he ran. They reached another hedge, ran along the farther side of it, Bitzenko bent double as though to escape a rain of bullets. Eventually he was seen careering across an open space quite near the river, which lay a couple of hundred yards beyond the lower end of the field. There he lay ambushed for a moment, behind a shrub: then he darted forward again, eventually disappearing along the high road in a cloud of dust. As to his athletic young friend, he made straight for the railway-station, which he reached without inci-dent, and returned immediately to Paris and to bed. Kreisler for his part conformed to Bitzenko's programme of flight: he scrambled through the hedge, crossed the road, and escaped almost unnoticed.

The truth was that the Russian had attracted the attention of the police to such an extent by his striking flight, that without a moment's hesitation they had bolted helter-skelter after him. They contented themselves with a parting shout or two at Kreisler. Duelling was not an offence that roused them very much and capture in such cases was not so material that they would feel very disposed for a cross-country run. But they were so impressed by the Russian's business-like way of disappearing that they imagined this must have been a curiously venal sort of duel: that he was the principal they did not doubt for a moment. So they went after him in full cry, rousing two or three vil-lages in their passage, whose occupants followed at their heels, pour-ing with frantic hullabaloo in the direction of the capital. Bitzenko, however, with admirable resourcefulness, easily outwitted them. He crossed the Seine near Saint Cloud,* and got back to Paris in time to read the afternoon newspaper reports of the duel and flight with a tranquil satisfaction.

CHAPTER 6

FIVE days after this, in the morning, Otto Kreisler mounted the steps of the police station of a small town near the german frontier. He was going to give himself up.

Bitzenko had pictured his principal, in the event of a successful outcome to the duel, seeking rapidly by train the german frontier, disguised in some extraordinary manner. Had the case been suggested to him of a man in this position without sufficient money in his pocket to buy a ticket, he would then have imagined a figure of melodrama hurrying through France, dodging and dogged by the police, defying a thousand perils. Whether Kreisler were still under the spell of the Russian or not, this was the course, more or less, taken by him. He could be trusted not to go near Paris: that city nothing would have persuaded him to re-enter.

The police disturbing the last act of his sanguinary farce was a similar contretemps to Soltyk's fingers in his throat. At the last moment everything had begun to go wrong: for this he had not been prepared because the world had shown no tendency up till then to interfere.

Soltyk had died when his back was turned, so to speak: he got the contrary of comfort out of the thought that he could claim to have done the deed. The police had rushed in and broken things off short, swept everything up and off—the banquet had terminated in a brutal raid. A sensation of shock and dislocation remained in Otto's mind: he had been hurried so much! He had never needed leisure, breathing space, so much: had he been given time—only a little time—he might have put that to rights—this sinister regret could only imply a possible mutilation of the corpse.

A dead man has no feeling, he can be treated as an object: but a living man needs time—does not a living man need so much time to develop his movements, to lord it with his thoughtful body, to unroll his will? *Time* is what be needs clearly. As a tramp, hustled away from a Café by the personnel, protests, at each jerk the waiter gives him, that he is a human being, probably a *free* human being—yes probably *free*; so Kreisler complained to his fate that he was a living man, that he required *time*—that above all it was *time* he needed—to settle his affairs and withdraw from life. He whined and blustered to no effect.

Soltyk's death dismayed him deeply: if you will think of a demented person who has become possessed of the belief that it is essential for the welfare of the world that he should excuperate* into a bird's nest while standing upon one leg on the back of a garden seat, but who is baulked, first of all by the seat giving way, and secondly by the bird's nest catching fire and vanishing because of the use by the bird of certain chemical substances in its construction, combined with the heat of the sun, you will have a parallel for Kreisler's superstitious disappointment.

He was superstitious as well in the usual way about this decease: in the course of his spiritless and brooding tramp he questioned if it were not he that had died, and not Soltyk at all, and if it were not a ghost who was now wandering off nowhere in particular.

One franc and a great many coppers remained to him. As he jumped from field to road and road to field again in his flight, they rose and fell in a little leaden wave in his pocket, breaking dully upon his thigh. This little wave rose and fell many times, till he began to wait for it and its monotonous grace. It was like a sigh: it heaved and clashed down in a foiled way. That evening he spent it on a meal in a small village hotel. The night was dry: he slept in an empty barge. Next day, at four in the afternoon, he arrived at Meaux.* Here he exchanged what he stood up in, hat and boots as well as clothes, for a shabby workman's outfit. He gained seven francs and fifty centimes on the transaction. He caught the early train for Rheims,* travelling 35 kilometres of his journey at a sou a kilometre. A meal near the station, and he took another ticket to Verdun.* Believing himself nearer the frontier than he actually was, he set out on foot: at the next large town, Marcade,* he had too hearty a meal. His money gave out before the frontier was nearly reached. For two days he had eaten hardly anything: he tramped on in a dogged careless spirit.

The *nearness* of his home-frontier began to rise like a wall in front of him. This question had to be answered: Did he want to cross the german frontier? Did he really want, having reached it, to cross it?

His answer to this question had been to mount the steps of the
local police-station.

———

His prussian severity of countenance, now that he was dressed in every
point like a vagabond—without hat and his hair disordered, five days'
beard on his chin—this sternness of the german officer-caste gave
him the appearance of a forbidding ruffian. The 'agent' on duty, who
barred his passage brutally before the door of the inner office, scowling too, classed him as a dangerous vagabond. His voluntary entrance
into the police station he regarded as an act not only highly suspicious
and unaccountable in itself, but of the last insolence.

'Qu'est-ce qu'il te faut?'

'Foir le gommissaire' returned Kreisler.

'Tu ne peux pas le voir. Il n'y est pas.'*

A few more laconic sentences followed. The 'agent' reiterated sulkily that the official he desired to see was not there. But he was eyeing
Kreisler doubtfully and turning something over in his mind.

The day before two Germans had been arrested in the neighbourhood as spies.* They were now under lock and key in this particular
building, until further evidence should be collected. It was extremely
imprudent for a German to loiter on the frontier on entering France, it
was naturally much wiser for him to push on at once—looking neither
to right nor to left—for the interior. This was generally realized by
Germans. But the two men in question were carpenters by profession:
both carried huge foot-rules* in their pockets. Upon this discovery
their captors were in a state of consternation: they shut them up, with
their implements, in the most inaccessible depths of the local clink.
But it was in the doorway of this building that Kreisler now stood.

The 'agent' who had recognized a German by his accent at length
turned and disappeared through the door. He reappeared with two
colleagues. They crowded the doorway and surveyed Kreisler blankly.
One asked in a very knowing voice:

'What's the game Fritz?* What are you doing here? Come about
your pals?'

'I had tuel and killt man;* I have walked for more days—.'

'Yes we know all about that!'

'So you had a duel eh?' asked another: they all laughed with nervous suddenness at the picture of this hobo defending his honour at
twenty paces.

'Well is that all you have to say?'

'I would eat.'

'Yes I daresay! Your two pals inside also have big appetites. But look sharp, come to the point! Have you anything to tell us about your compatriots inside there?'

His throttling by Soltyk had been Kreisler's last milestone: he had changed, he now knew he was beaten, and that there was nothing to do but to die. His body ran to the german frontier as a chicken's does down a yard, headless, from the block.

It was a dull and stupid face he presented to the official. He did not understand him. He muttered that he was hungry. He could hardly stand; leaning his shoulder against the wall, he stood with his eyes upon the ground. The police bristled. He was making himself at home! What a toupet!*

'*Va-t'en!* If you don't want to tell us anything, clear out—look sharp about it. A pretty lot of trouble you cursed Germans are giving us! You'll none of you speak when it comes to the point: you all stand staring like boobies. But that won't pay here. Off you go—double march!'

The two others turned back into the office and slammed the door. The first police officer stood before it again, looking truculently at Kreisler. He said:

'Passez votre chemin! Don't stand gaping there!'

Then, giving him a shake, he hustled him to the top of the steps. A parting shove sent him staggering down into the road.

Kreisler walked on for a little. Eventually, in a quiet square, near the entrance of the town, he fell upon a bench, drew his legs up and went to sleep.

At ten o'clock, the town lethargically retiring, all its legs moving slowly, like a spent insect, an 'agent' came gradually along the square. He stopped opposite the sleeping Kreisler, surveying him with lawful indignation.

'En voilà un qui ne se gêne pas, ma foi!' He swayed energetically up to him.

'Eh! le copain! Tu voudrais coucher à la belle étoile?'

He shook him.

'Oh là! Tu ne peux pas passer la nuit ici! *Houp!* Dépêche-toi. D'bout!'*

Kreisler responded only by a tired movement as though to bury his skull in the bench. A more violent jerk rolled him upon the ground.

Thereupon he awoke and as he lay there he protested in german, with a sort of dull asperity. He scrambled to his knees and then to his feet.

At the sound of the familiar gutturals of the neighbouring Empire the patriot in the policeman came to life. Kreisler stood there, muttering partly in german and partly in french, he was very tired. He spoke with some bitterness of his attempt to get into the police station: he criticized the inhospitable reception he had received. The 'agent' understood several words of german—notably 'Ja' and 'Abort.' The consequence was that however much might be actually intended on any given occasion, by anyone speaking in german, it could never equal in scope intensity and meaning what he thought he distinguished.

He was at once convinced that Kreisler was threatening an invasion*—he scoffed loudly in reply. He understood Kreisler to assert that the town in which they stood would soon belong to Germany and that he would then sleep not upon a bench, but in the best bed their dirty little hole of a village could offer. He approached this contumelious Boche* threateningly. Eventually he distinctly heard himself apostrophized as a 'sneaking *flic.*' At that his hand grasped Kreisler's collar, he threw him in the direction of the police station. He had miscalculated the distance: Kreisler, weak for want of food, fell at his feet. Getting up, he scuffled a short while. Then, it occurring to him that here was an excellent opportunity of getting a dinner and being lodged after all in the Bureau de Police, he suddenly became docile.

Arrived at the police station—with several revolts against the brutal handling he was subjected to—he was met at the door by the same inhospitable man as earlier in the day. This person was enraged beyond measure: he held Kreisler, while his comrade went into the office to report: he held him as a restive horse is held, and jerked him several times against the wall, as if he had been resisting with a desperate fougue.

Two men, one of whom he had formerly seen, came and looked at him. No effort was made to discover if he were really at fault: by this time they were persuaded that he was a ruffian, if not a spy then a murderer, although they were inclined to regard him as a criminal enigma. They felt they could no longer question his right to a night's lodging. He was led to a cell where he was given some bread and water at his urgent request.

On the following morning he was taken up before the Commissaire. When Kreisler was brought in, this gentleman had just finished cross-examining for the fifteenth time the two german carpenters detained as spies. They had not much peace: they were liable to be dragged out of their cells several times in the course of an afternoon, as often as a new theory of their guilt should occur to one of the numerous staff of the police station. They would be confronted with their foot-rules and watched in breathless silence; or be cross-questioned and caught out as to their movements during the month previous to their arrest. The Commissaire was perspiring all over with the intensity of his last effort to detect something. Kreisler was led in and prevented from becoming in any way intelligible during a quarter of an hour by the furious interruptions of the enraged officer. At last he succeeded in conveying that he was quite unacquainted with the two carpenters; moreover, that all he needed was food, that he had decided to give himself up and await the decision of the Paris authorities as regards his duel. If they were not going to take any action, he would return to Paris—at least as soon as he had received a certain letter; and he gave his address. He was sent back to his cell in disgrace.

He slept the greater part of the day. The next he spent nervous and awake. In the afternoon a full confirmation of his story reached the authorities. It was likely the following morning, he was told, that he would be sent to Paris. It meant, then, that he was going to be tried, as a kind of murderer: there would be the adverse witnesses who would maintain that he shot a defenceless man deliberately.

He became extremely disturbed as he sat and reflected upon what was in store for him—Paris, the vociferous courts, the ennuis of a criminal case. All the circumstances of this now distant affair would be resuscitated. Then the Russian—he would have to see him again. Sorrow for himself bowed him down. This prospective journey to Paris was ridiculous—noise, piercing noise, effort, awaited him revengefully. There was no detail he could not forecast. The energy and obstinacy of the rest of the world, the world that would cross-question him and drag him about from spot to spot, at last setting him to pick oakum,* no doubt, these frightened him as something mad. Bitzenko appealed most to this new-born anxiety: Bitzenko was like some much-relished dish a man has one day eaten too much of, and will never be able to see again without wishing to vomit.

*

On the other hand, he became quite used to his cell: his mind was sick and this room had a clinical severity. It had all the severity of a place in which an operation might suitably be performed. He became fond of it. He lay upon his bed: he turned over the shell of many empty and depressing hours he had lived: in all these listless concave shapes he took a particular pleasure. 'Good times' were avoided: days spent with his present stepmother, before his father knew her, gave him a particularly numbing and nondescript feeling.

He sat up, listening to the noises from the neighbouring rooms and corridors. It began to sound to him like one steady preparation for his removal: steps bustled about getting this ready and getting that ready as though for a departure.

The police station had cost him some trouble to enter: but from the start they had been attracted to each other. There is no such thing as a male building perhaps, all buildings are probably female: what are they?—they are the most highly developed 'things.' This small modern edifice was having its romance; Otto Kreisler was its *liebhaberei.*

It was now warning him, it was full of rumours: it echoed sharply the fact of its policemen.

After his evening meal he took up his bed in his arms and placed it upon the opposite side of the cell, beneath the window. He sat there for some time as though resting after this effort. The muttering of two children on a doorstep in the street below came to him on the evening light with dramatic stops and emptiness. It bore with it an image, like an old picture, bituminous* and with a graceful queer formality: this fixed itself before him in the manner of a mirage. He watched it muttering.

Slowly he began to draw off his boots. He took out the laces, and tied them together for greater strength. Then he tore several strips off his shirt and made a short cord of them. He went through these actions with an unconscious deftness, as though it were a routine. He measured the drop from the bar of the ventilator with puckered forehead calculating the necessary length of cord, like a boy preparing the accessories of some game. It was only a game, too: he recognized what these proceedings meant, but shunned the idea that it was serious. In the way that a person disinclined to write a necessary letter may take up his pen, resolving to begin it merely, but writes more and more until it is in fact completed, so Kreisler proceeded with his unattractive task.

Standing upon the bed, he attached the cord to the ventilator. He tested its strength by holding it some inches from the top, and then, his shoulders hunched, swaying his whole weight languidly upon it for a moment. Adjusting the noose, he smoothed his hair back after he had slipped it over his head. He made as though to kick the bed away, playfully, then stood still, staring in front of him. The last moment must be one of realization. His caution had been due to a mistrust of some streaks of him, the most suspect that connected with the nebulous tracts of sex.

A sort of heavy confusion burst up as he withdrew the restraint. It reminded him of Soltyk's hands upon his throat. The same throttling feeling returned: the blood bulged in his head: he felt dizzy—it was the Soltyk struggle over again. But, as with Soltyk, he did not resist: he gently worked the bed outwards from beneath him, giving it a last steady shove. He hung, gradually choking—the last thing he was conscious of his tongue.

The discovery of Kreisler's body caused a profound indignation among the staff of the police station. They remembered the persistence with which this unprincipled vagrant had attempted to get into the building. It was clear to their minds that his sole purpose had been to hang himself upon their premises. From the first he had mystified them. Now their uneasy suspicions were bitterly confirmed. Each man felt that this corpse had personally insulted him and made a fool of him, still worse. They thrust it savagely into the earth, with vexed and disgusted faces.

Herr Kreisler paid without comment what was claimed by the landlord in Paris for his son's rooms; and writing to the authorities at the frontier-town about the burial, paid exactly the sum demanded by this town for disposing of the body, without comment of any sort.

CHAPTER 7

ANASTASYA had personally liked Kreisler. That was why the spectacle of Fräulein Lunken excusing herself, in the process putting Kreisler in a more unsatisfactory light, had annoyed her. But apart from that, Bertha's undignified rigmarole after the Club dance had irritated her: to cut it short she brutally announced that Kreisler's behaviour was due simply to the fact that he fancied himself in love with her, Anastasya. 'He was not worrying about Fräulein Lunken: he was in love with me' the statement amounted to, it had been an irritated exhibition of frankness as immodestly presented as possible, to shock this little bourgeois fool. Bertha! how could Tarr consort with such a *dumm* cow? Her aristocratic woman's sense did not appreciate the taste for the slut, the Miss or the suburban queen. The apache, the coster-girl,* the whore—all that had *character*, oh yes! Her romanticism, in fact, was of the same order as Bertha's but much better class.

————————

Two days after the duel she met Tarr in the street. They agreed to meet at Vallet's for dinner. The table at which she had first come across Otto Kreisler was where they sat.

'You knew Soltyk didn't you?' he asked her.

'Yes. Poor Soltyk!'

She looked at Tarr doubtfully. A certain queer astonishment in her face struck Tarr. She spoke with a businesslike calm about his death.

'I knew him only slightly' she then said. 'You know how he made a living? He sold *objets d'art*. I had several things I wanted to sell, he put the thing through for me, and advised me about some other things I was disposing of in Vienna.'

'He was your agent, or something of the sort.'

'That's it. He was an excellent business-man, I think. I believe he was rather too sharp for me over one transaction.'

'Indeed?'

'I think so. I'm not quite sure yet.'

'You can't do anything about it, I suppose?'

'Not now.'

She knew people referred to her as the 'woman in the case.' Soltyk possessed a rather ridiculous importance, being dead—the fact was bigger than the person. Her sinister prominence she took no interest in, but with Tarr she preferred to make clear the nature of the public misunderstanding.

Kreisler she had come to abominate: to have killed, to have killed someone she knew—it was a hostile act to bring death so near to her! She hoped he might never come back to Paris: she did not wish to meet Kreisler again.

'I don't know what grounds there are for it, but they say Soltyk was not killed in a duel' Tarr continued. 'Kreisler is to be charged with murder or at least manslaughter.'

'Yes I have heard too that Kreisler shot him before he was ready or something——.' She shrugged her shoulders.

'He was shot when he was unarmed, that's the story. There was no duel at all.'

'Oh that is not the version I have heard.'

She did not seem interested in this subject.

'I was Kreisler's Second for half an hour' Tarr said in a minute.

'How do you mean, for half an hour——?' she asked laughing.

'I happened to be there and was asked to help him until somebody else could be found. I did not suspect him, I may say, of meaning to murder your business agent!'

'Of course not. What was the cause of it all, do you know?'

'According to Kreisler, there had been some smacking and caning earlier in the day——.'

'Yes. I as a matter of fact was a somewhat puzzled witness of that. Herr Kreisler met Soltyk and myself. We had just been finishing up the last of the deals of which I spoke.'

'Yes.'

'If you ask me, I think that Soltyk was a little in the wrong.'

'I dare say.'

Tarr's sympathies were all with Kreisler. He had never been attracted by the Poles of Paris: deep square races were favoured by him: and Kreisler was an atavistic creature whom on the whole he preferred. Some of his passion for Bertha flowed over on to her fellow countryman.

What hand had his present companion in the duel, he wondered; her indifference or her patronage of Kreisler seemed to point to something unexplained. Kreisler's ways were still mysterious!

As they were finishing the meal, after turning her head towards the entrance-door Anastasya remarked, with mock concern:

'There is your fiancée. She seems rather upset——.'

Tarr looked towards the door. Bertha's white face was close up against one of the narrow panes, above the lace curtain. There was four foot of window on either side of the door.

Her eyes were round, vacant and dark, the features very white and heavy, the mouth steadily open in painful lines. As he looked the face drew gradually away, and then sank into the medium of the night, in which it had appeared. It withdrew with a glutinous, sweet slowness: the heavy white jowl seemed dragging itself out of some fluid trap where it had been caught like a weighty body.

Tarr knew how the pasty flesh would nestle against the furs, the shoulders swing, the legs move just as much as was necessary for progress, with no movement of the hips. Everything about her in the chilly night would give an impression of warmth and system: the sleek cloth fitting the square shoulders tightly, the underclothes carefully tight as well, the breath from her nostrils the slight steam from a contented machine.

He caught Anastasya's eye and smiled.

'Your fiancée is pretty' she said, affecting to think that that was the correct answer to the smile.

'She's not my fiancée. But she's a pretty girl.'

'I heard you were engaged—.'

'No.'

'It's no good' he thought. But he must spare Bertha in future such discomforting sights.

PART VII

SWAGGER SEX

CHAPTER 1

BERTHA was still being taken in carefully prepared doses of about an hour a day: from say half-past four to a quarter to six. Anyone else would have found this much Bertha insupportable under any conditions: only Tarr had been used to such far greater doses that this was the minimum he considered necessary for a cure.

He came to her daily with the dull regularity of an old gentleman at a german watering-place taking his spring-water at the regulation hour. But the cure* was finishing: there were signs of a new robustness, hateful to her (equivalent to a springy walk and a contented and sunny eye) that heralded departure. His clockwork visits, with their brutal regularity, did her as much harm as they did him good.

The news of Soltyk's death, then Kreisler's, affected the readily melodramatic side of her nature peculiarly. Death had made himself 'de la partie.'* Kreisler had left her alone for a few days: this is what had occupied him. The sensational news made her own case, and her own tragic sensations, more real: they had received, in an indirect way, the authority of Death. Death—real living Death—was somewhere upon the scene: His presence was announced, was felt. He had struck down somebody among them.

In the meantime this disposed of Otto Kreisler for ever. Tarr, as well, appeared to feel that they were left in a tête-à-tête: a sort of chaperon had been lost in Otto. His official post as protector or passive 'obstacle' had been a definite status: if he stayed on now it would have to be as something else. The day of the arrival of the news of Kreisler's end he talked of leaving for England. Bertha's drawn face, longer silences, and above all her sharp darting glances, embarrassed him very much.

He did not go to England at once. In the week or two succeeding his meeting with Anastasya in the restaurant he saw her frequently. In this way a chaperon was found to take Kreisler's place. Bertha was officially presented to her successor. When she learnt that Anastasya

had definitely been chosen, her energy reformed: she braced herself
for a substantial struggle.

CHAPTER 2

On August the tenth Tarr had an appointment with Anastasya at his
studio in Montmartre. They had arranged to dine at a restaurant with
a terrace upon the rue de l'Obelisk. It was their tenth meeting. Tarr
had just come from his daily cure. He hurried back and found her
lounging against the door, reading the newspaper.

'Ah there you are! You're late, Mr. Tarr.'

'Have you been waiting long?'

'No. Fräulein Lunken I suppose—.'

'Yes. I couldn't get away.'

'Poor Bertha!'

'Poor Bertha!'

He let her in. The backwardness of his senses was causing him
some anxiety: his intellect now stepped in, determined to do their
business for them. He put his arm round her waist and planting his
lips firmly upon hers, began kissing. Meanwhile he slipped a hand
sideways beneath her coat, and pressed still tighter an athletic, sinuous hulk against him. The various bulging and retreating contacts
of her body brought monotonous german reminders and the senses
obediently awoke.

It was the first time he had kissed her: she showed no disinclination, but no return. Was Miss Vasek in the unfortunate position of an
unawakened mass? He felt a twinge of anxiety. Had she not perhaps,
though, so rationalized her intimate possessions that there was no
precocious fancy left? Mature animal ardour must be set up perhaps:
he had the sensation of embracing a tiger, who was not unsympa-
thetic but rather surprised. Perhaps he had been too sudden or too
slow—he had not the technique *des fauves, des grands fauves*:* he ran
his hand upwards along her body: all was statuesquely genuine. His
hand took a more pensive course. She took his hand away.

'We haven't come to that yet' she said.

'Haven't we?'

'I didn't think we had.'

Smiling at each other, they separated.

'Let us take your greatcoat off. You'll be hot in here.'

Her coat was all in florid redundancies of heavy cloth, like a Tintoretto mantle.* Underneath she was wearing a very plain dark belted smock and skirt, like a working girl, which exaggerated the breadth and straightness of her shoulders. Not to sentimentalize it, she had open-work stockings on underneath, such as the genuine girl would have worn on her night-out, at two-and-eleven-three the pair.*

'You look very well' Tarr said.

'I put these on for you.'

Tarr had, while he was kissing her, recovered his sensual balance; his senses indeed had flared up in such a way that the reason had been offended and exercised some check at last. Hence a conflict: *they* were not going to have the credit—!

He became shy: he was ashamed of his sudden interest, which had been so long in coming, and hid it instinctively from her. He was committed to the rôle marked out by reason.

'I am very flattered' Tarr said 'by your thoughtfulness.'

'I am on show Tarr.'

He sat smoking, his eyes upon the floor lest his sudden cupidity should be too apparent.

'Do you think we shall always be the audience?'

'Whatever do you mean by that—who are your *we*?'

'I meant the remark about "on show," menfolk of course being the audience.'

'I see what you mean: I should think the spectators' rôle was the one to be preferred but I can quite imagine the audience breaking up and the rôles being reversed. Meantime I'm the puppet.'

Fixing upon him a diabolical smile, set in a precocious frill of double chin and punctuated with prominent dimples she lay back in the chair. A most respectable bulk of hip occupied the space between the two arms of the chair, not enough completely to satisfy a Dago,* but too much to please a dandy of the West. Tarr furtively noted this opulence and compared it with Bertha's. He confessed that it outdid his fiancée's.

'Yes I am even a peep-show for all peeping Toms and Dicks—you know when the Principal Boy turns round, you know the supreme moment of Pantomime?'*

'When she is stern-on?'

'Well I'm like that too when I'm going away and not facing the audience, and tell me how you would like to be a show-girl anyway Tarr? You shake your head—a little girlishly—all the same I can see you're not the show-girl sort, but why should I? I have got these things here' she laid a hand upon the nearest breast to it 'as a stark high-brow I ask you, can you respect such objects upon a person, right on top of a person?'

'I don't mind them. I think they are nice.'

'Not as a high-brow, it's imposs;* they class me, I am one of the Bertha-birds, all the small boobies know what I'm made for when I run to catch a bus. "Look at that milch-cow short of wind—here! wait till I catch you bending!" It's beastly.'

'What's it matter what they say? They are street-arabs* merely.'

'They roam the gutters but they have eyes in their heads.'

'I am all for a breast or two.'

'No, you are laughing at me too—you are being a small boobie.'

'No' Tarr quavered: then he added at once: 'I am hallucinated.'

'That's what it is, you have hit the nail on the head, once I was like you and liked this—I might even learn to love it again' she muttered, casting her eyes into a distant recess.

'The Man dreams but what the Boy believed.'*

'The Man dreams—what is that? What the Child believes to be real with his eyes open, the Man can only believe in—in his sleep and then not quite—I know, there was a time when I was a child of nature who took myself for granted from top to toe, I was mad then.'

'You make me mad now, in a way. Yes' he touched himself with the tips of his fingers: 'I am mad, that's correct: just a touch of passion and off you go again—you are a mad believer once more for the moment!'

'Have you just a touch of passion?'

'Just a touch.' He grinned passionately. 'Something is real.'

She sighed, and licked her lips.

'Aside from that' she said, and lifted up her breast a little way in the palm of her proud hand, 'what would you do under the circumstances Tarr—it's a handicap, there's no blinking the fact.'

'I should do nothing.'

'And there is nothing to do—*rien à faire!* it's all part of the beastly shop-window—I have to stick frills around them even, just as pork-merchants in their shop-fronts decorate the carcasses of their sucking-pigs.'

Tarr laughed as he pictured to himself the lattice-work of the silk receptacle, and as she threatened deliberately to pout, remarked:

'It is part of the reality is lady's underwear—what the child *believes* and the adult only dreams, though they both see it—when visited with a little passion which goes a long way I can believe and become quite genuinely mad, but I am with you if you object to those ravings which would then issue from my mouth being given out as reason, or even as beauty. It's not Beauty. It is Belief, if you like.'

'Of course it's not—we agree in the most marvellous way Tarr. These things, all things that are stamped feminine gender, is not a thing that bears cold print, unless it is to be read by madmen.'

'Of course not.'

'But as you say a little passion goes a long way and I can go anywhere and pass myself off as a most lovely creature. It's a fact.'

'Can you do that?'

'Why yes—I'll pass myself off on you if you're not careful.'

'Je ne demande pas mieux!' Tarr said indifferently, peering over at her as if through a gathering mist.

'I'm still here' she answered. 'What are we going to do about it?'

'It's—it's not the *thing itself*—.'

'Why no. But it is no use, no woman should be intelligent, it's no use.'

But Tarr rejoined, with mock-indignation:

'Nor he-men for the matter of that, it's six one and half a dozen the other—have you ever considered what a man has to carry about with him too?'

'What.'

'It's just the same, I am a man, I trim my moustaches for instance as though this hole here were the better for a black frill of hair—is it?— it's as bad as your sacro-sanct dugs, my kisser's no better!'

'I don't think so: men have never sat down and become lace-makers to embellish their strange hairy beauties like us women. Their little pigs stay at home.'

'I think they are just as bad. They are terrible.'

'Oh no.'

Tarr decided to marry Anastasya after they had finished talking, for the sake of her little pigs, that went to market so beautifully.

'I think Tarr I know your opinion of women with intellects—how right you are, how right you are!'

'Not at all!'

'No, you are, I agree with you all along the line: it must madden you to hear me talking about this in such a matter-of-fact way—have I disgusted you, I expect so? Some things *should* be sacro-sanct!'

She crossed her legs. The cold grape-bloom mauve silk stockings ended in a dark slash each against her two snowy stallion thighs which they bisected, visible, one above the other, in naked expanses of tempting undercut, issuing from a dead-white foam of central lace worthy of the *Can-Can* exhibitionists* of the tourist resorts of *Paris-by-night*.

Tarr grinned with brisk appreciation of the big full-fledged baby's coquetry pointing the swinish moral under the rose and mock-modestly belowstairs, and he blinked and blinked as if partly dazzled, his mohammedan eye* did not refuse the conventional bait; his butcher-sensibility pressed his fancy into professional details, appraising this milky ox soon to be shambled in his slaughter-box, or upon his high divan.

'Sacro-sanct' she repeated heavily, letting fall upon him a slow and sultry eye, not without a Bovril-bathos* in its human depths—like all conversational cattle, it hinted! Expelling its wistfulness, it looked him squarely in the whites, and she said passionately:

'It's usual and we should do as the Romans* do—not that these are Romans!—we should observe a decent emotionality about these coarse mysteries—worship and appetite are one!—who said you could dispense with the veil?—it is impossible, try it!—there should be a blush of animal shame upon the joint of mutton—.'

'You will break my heart!'

She pursued impetuously—

'I don't need you to tell me—there should be no trifling with the objects of sexual appetite—they are sacro-sanct I have agreed, under the fanatical frown of the mosaic code*—we are not pagans—you need not say it, I am already reminded!'

She recrossed the two massive dangling serpents of her legs—up above their thick white necks flashing as she changed them—up under her fore and aft serge apron.

'We intellectuals' she insisted 'talk far too much about things that simply will not bear talking of and looking into—a high-brow girl

such as me must be sexually (oh that's very very american) an abom-
ination: I am convinced that with me a man would become impotent
within a month at the outside, I mean it.'

Sitting crouched like a stage Whittington cat* upon his chair,
with eyes devoutly riveted upon the exhibits of the demonstration as
though he expected a Brocken ghost-mouse* to hop out and were sitting at the cock to pounce when it did, Tarr grinned painfully, without
removing his eyes from the neighbourhood of the supposed exit.

'A man's leg in Ladies' Hose is just as nice as a woman's leg' she
remarked.

Tarr did not let go, unblinking he made haste to answer, motionless:

'Or just as dull, as you would have it; both are—outside the
imagination that is—.'

The intensity of his painful stare deepened and his face flushed.
She uncrossed her legs and brought them to attention, pushing her
skirt down enquiringly.

'*Outside the imagination*—what is that? What do you consider the
imagination is?'

Tarr flung himself back in his chair, took a cigarette from a yellow
packet at his side, and lighted it with anxious fixity, the fixed look
transferred from the mightier cylinders of meat to it, puny nothing
of smoke.

'In the case of the sucking-pig' said Tarr, magisterially, flinging his
flushed face up for air towards the ceiling 'it is the tongue. The thing
seen is merely disgusting to the eye, but it is delightful to the tongue:
therefore the eye passes beneath the spell of the palate, and it is not
an image but a taste—much more abstract, in consequence—that it
sees—if one can say that it sees. The body of the sucking-pig is blotted out.'

Anastasya sniffed.

'I think you forget that it is my breast from which we started this
rambling argument. Also I would take leave to observe that it is not so
easy to blot out a food-unit as you appear to think.'

'You sound like the Duchess in Alice.'*

'Who on earth may that be—the Duchess of What?'

'Of Alice.'

'Oh. I was saying, it is by no means so easy—.'

'I'm with you, I'm with you, you lovely contraption! But nevertheless it is time I were gone!'

'He bursts into song!'

Tarr sprang up in his chair and delivered himself rather breath-lessly as follows:

'Listen to my explanation, I would give all the world from the Baltic to the Rhine—*bis an den Rin*—Geliebte—* darling—pig-girl! to embrace a sucking-pig if it possessed all the other attributes, of body and the rest, of the person I am now addressing, but I meant only that everything we *see*—you understand, this universe of dis-tinct images—must be reinterpreted to tally with all the senses and beyond that with our minds: so that was my meaning, the eye alone sees nothing at all but conventional phantoms.'

Anastasya laughed shrilly and stretched up her arms above her head, looking down at the expansion of her breasts as she extended her torso to its limit.

'So long as we understand each other—that is everything!'

He stood up.

'I am hungry, let us go and discuss these matters over a rump steak' she said rising after him, shivering a little. 'How damp this place is! I am cold.'

He crossed the room to where his hat and coat were lying.

'What does the good Bertha say to your new workshop? Now there's a real woman for you! There's no mistake about *her*!'

'Yes good old Bertha's the right stuff: she's prime!'

'My dear, she must be the world's premier sucking-pig!'

'The *ne plus ultra!*'

'The *Ding an sich!*'* in the driest and most prolonged american she sang and they turned laughing unkindly at a certain homely womanly form towards the burnished door of the new workshop, passing the easel upon which the greek athlete, attacked with religion, disinte-grated before the eyes of a watching harpie.*

As they descended the Boulevard Rochechouart* Tarr stepped with an unmistakable male straddle: no bourgeoise this time! thought he to himself, but the perfect article! It rolled and swept beside him and more and more of its swagger got into his own gait until he was compelled to call a halt: he halted 'the face that launched a thou-sand ships'*—a thousand transports crowded in her carriage and the impetuous rush of her advance—before a Charcuterie.

'Delicatessen!' he hissed significantly in her ear. In a protracted reverie they both directed their gaze upon a Frankfort sausage.

They passed on, Tarr toning himself down as best he could but rehearsing to himself her perfections—No Grail-lady or any phantom of the celtic mind* but perfect meat, horse-sense, accent of Minnesota, music of the Steppes,* german *Weltweisheit*, *Wesengefühl** and what-not—a prodigious mate!

They entered an expensive trippers' restaurant* and devoured the Menu with hungry eyes from top to bottom in an immediate scamper. They ordered oysters: they would be his first, he had never before dared to eat an oyster, because it was alive.

When he told her that it was his first oyster she was exultant.

'You perfect savage—your palate is as conservative as an ox's. Kiss me Tarr—you have never done that either properly.'

The use of his gentile name was a tremendous caress. She presented her salt wet eating lips, he kissed them properly with solemnity, adjusting his glasses afterwards.

'Why have you never eaten oysters?'

'The fact that they were alive has so far deterred me but I now see that I was wrong.'

'You are afraid of everything that is alive!' she assured him with a portentous nod.

'Until I find that it is really not to be feared on that score I believe that is true.'

'You have a marked prejudice in favour of what is dead?'

'But all human food is killed first and is dead—all except oysters' he objected.

'You have a down on life—it's no good!'

'I am an artist.'

'Yes I've heard that before!' she blustered gaily with a german conviviality that made him feel more than ever at home. 'But the artist has to hunt and kill his material so to speak just as primitive man had to do his own trapping butchering and cooking—it will not do to be squeamish if you are to become a great artist, Mister Tarr!'

Tarr looked the great artist every inch as he haughtily replied:

'Nevertheless there stands the fact that life is art's rival in all particulars. They are *de puntos** for ever and ever, you will see, if you observe closely.'

'That I do not see.'

'No because you mix them up in your own practice.'

'The woman, I suppose?'

Tarr gave her a hard dogmatic look and then asserted roundly, and probably finally:

'*As such*, and with such resources, you are the arch-enemy of any picture.'

Anastasya looked pleased, and looked a picture.

'Yes I see how I might be that. But let us have a definition here and there. What is art?—it sounds like Pompous Pilate!'*

'Life with all the humbug of living taken out of it: will that do?'

'Very well: but what is life?'

'Everything that is not yet purified so that it is art.'

'No.'

'Very well: *Death* is the one attribute that is peculiar to life.'

'And to art as well.'

'Ah but it is impossible to *imagine* it in connection with art—that is if you understand art—that is the test for your understanding. Death is the *motif* * *of* all reality: the purest thought is ignorant of that *motif*.'

'I ask you as a favour to define art for me, you have not. A picture is art if I am not mistaken, but a living person is life. We sitting here are life, if we were talking on a stage we should be art.'

'A picture, and also the actors on a stage, are pure life. Art is merely what the picture and the stage-scene represent, and what we now, or any living person as such, only, does *not*: that is why you could say that the true statue can be smashed, and yet not die.'

'Still.'

'This is the essential point to grasp: *Death* is the thing that differentiates art and life. Art is identical with the idea of permanence. Art is a continuity and not an individual spasm: but life is the idea of the person.'

Both their faces lost some of their colour, hers her white, his the strong, almost the 'high,' yellow.* They flung themselves upon each other socratically,* stowing away course after course.

'You say that the actors upon the stage are pure life, yet they represent something that *we* do not. But "all the world's a stage," isn't it?'

'It was an actor that said that.* I say it's all an atelier—"all the world's a workshop" I should say. Consider the content of what we call art. A statue is art. It is a dead thing, a lump of stone or wood. Its lines and proportions are its soul. Anything living, quick and changing is bad art always; naked men and women are the worst art of all, because there are fewer semi-dead things about them. The shell of the tortoise, the plumage of a bird, makes these animals approach nearer to art. Soft, quivering and quick flesh is as far from art as it is possible for an object to be.'

'Art is merely *the dead*, then?'

'No, but deadness is the first condition of art. The armoured hide of the hippopotamus, the shell of the tortoise, feathers and machinery, you may put in one camp; naked pulsing and moving of the soft inside of life—along with elasticity of movement and consciousness—that goes in the opposite camp. Deadness is the first condition for art: the second is absence of soul, in the human and sentimental sense. With the statue its lines and masses are its soul, no restless inflammable ego is imagined for its interior: it has *no inside*: good art must have no inside: that is capital.'

'Then why should human beings be chiefly represented in art?'

'Because it is human beings that commission and buy the art.'

A mixed grill *Montebello* and two *Poulets grain* had disappeared; a *Soufflé Rothschild* was appearing through the hatchway of the lift and a *corbeille* of fruit, comprising figs, peaches, nectarines and oranges, was held in readiness, a prominent still-life, upon a dresser.* Anastasya now stretched herself, clasping her hands in her lap. She smiled at Tarr. She had been driving hard inscrutable Art deeper and deeper into herself: she now drew it out and showed it to Tarr.

'Art is all you say—have it your way: also something else: we will stick a little flag up and come back another day. I wish intensely to hear about life.'

Tarr was staring, suspended, with a defunct smile, cut in half, at the still life. He turned his head slowly, with his mutilated smile, his glasses pitched forward somewhat.

He looked at her for some time in a steady, depressed way: his eye was grateful not to have to be gibing.* Kindness—*bestial kindness*—would be an out-of-work thank God in this neighbourhood. The upper part of her head was massive and intelligent, the middle of her body was massive and exciting, there was no animalism-out-of-place in the shape of a weight of jaw—all the weight was in the head and hips. His steadfast ideas of the flower surrounded by dung were certainly challenged: but he brooded not yet convinced. Irritants were useful—he reached back doubtfully towards his bourgeoise: he was revolted as he recalled that mess, with this clean and solid object beneath his eyes, but he remained pensive. He preferred a cabin to a palace, and thought that a villa was better for him than either. The second bottle of champagne was finished; its legendary sparkle damped his spirits.

'What did you make of Kreisler's proceedings? He was a queer fish!' she asked.

'Most.'

'Do you suppose he and Bertha got on very well?'

'Was Bertha his mistress? I can't say. That is not very interesting is it?'

'Not Bertha, of course, but Kreisler had his points.'

'You're very hard on Bertha.'

She put her tongue out at him as much as a small almond, and wrinkled up her nose.

'What were Kreisler's relations with you by the way?' he enquired.

'My relations with Kreisler consisted in a half-hour's conversation with him in a restaurant, no more: I spoke to him several times after that but only for a few minutes. He was very excited the last time we met. I have a theory that his duel was due to unrequited passion for me. Your Bertha, on the other hand, has a theory that it was due to unrequited passion for her. I merely wondered if you had any information that might confirm her case or mine.'

'No, I know nothing about it. I hold, myself, a quite different theory.'

'What is that? That he was in love with *you*?'

'My theory has not the charming simplicity of your theory or Bertha's. I don't believe that he was in love with anybody, I think that it was however a sex-tumult of sorts—.'

'What is that?'

'This is my theory. I believe that all the fuss he made was an attempt to get out of Art back into Life again. He was like a fish floundering about who had got into the wrong tank. *Back into sex* I think would describe where he wanted to get to: he was doing his best to get back into sex again out of a little puddle of art where he felt he was gradually expiring. He was an art-student without any talent you see, so the poor devil was leading a slovenly meaningless existence like thousands of others in the same case. He was very hard up, also. The sex-instinct of the average sensual man had become perverted into a false channel. Put it the other way round and say his art-instinct had been rooted out of sex, where it was useful, and naturally flourished, and had been exalted into a department by itself, where it bungled. The nearest the general run get to art is *Action*: sex is their form of art: the battle for existence is their picture. The moment they *think* or *dream* they develop an immense weight of cheap stagnating passion. Art, in the hands of the second-rate, is a curse, it is on a par with "freedom"—but we are not allowed to say *second-rate* are we' he grinned 'in the midst of a democracy! particularly such a "cultivated" one as this! But if you are forbidden to say *second-rate*, why then you must leave behind you all good sense—*nothing* can be discussed at all if you can't say *second-rate!*'

The drunkenness of Tarr had passed through the first despondent silence, and as his intelligence grew less firm in battle with the *Roederer** he began to bluster in a sheepish sing-song interlarding his spasms of argument with dumb *prosits*.

'Nobody's claim is individual—*issit!*' he hiccuped at his vis-à-vis, who now did nothing but eat. She shook her head, her mouth full.

'Nobody's!—an important type or original—as a pattern, *that* is the sanction of the first-ranker, am I right? The Many they are the eccentric—what do they matter? am I right or not?—they are "the individuals," yes. Individuals! Well! Prosit Anastasya, let us drink to their confusion! To hell with economy, in any shape or form, to hell with it! Long live Waste! Hoch!'

'I'll drink to that!' she exclaimed raising her glass. 'Here's to Waste. Hoch! Waste!'

'Of course! Curse curse the principle of Humanity, curse that principle! Mute inglorious Miltons* are not mute for God in Heaven— they have the Silence!'

'Ah. The Silence, that's what they must have—Heaven is silent! How did you guess that?'

'Bless Waste—Heaven bless Waste! Hoch Waste!'

'Hoch!'

'Here's to Waste!' Tarr announced loudly to the two waiters in front of the table. 'Waste, *waste*; fling out into the streets: accept fools, compromise yourselves with the poor in spirit, it will all come in handy! Live like the lions in the forests, with fleas on your back. Above all, down with the *Efficient Chimpanzee!*'

Anastasya's eyes were bloodshot, Tarr patted her on the back.

'There are no lions in the forests!' she hiccuped, aiming blows at her chest. 'You're pulling my leg.'

They had finished the fruit and were sitting before coffee filters while the *sommelier* hunted for vodka. Tarr had grown extremely expansive in every way: he began slapping her thighs to emphasize his points, as Diderot was in the habit of doing with the Princesse de Clèves.* After that he began kissing her when he had made a successful remark, to celebrate it. Their third bottle of wine had put art to flight; he lay back in his chair in prolonged bursts of laughter. She, in german fashion, clapped her hand over his mouth. He seized it with his teeth and made pale shell shapes in its brown fat.

In a Café opposite the restaurant, where they next went, they had more vodka. They caressed each other's hands now continually and even allowed themselves more intimate caresses: indifferent to the supercilious and bitter natives they became lost in lengthy kisses, their arms round each other's necks.

In a little cave of intoxicated affection, a conversation took place.

'Have you darling often?'

'What's that you say dear?' she asked with eager sleepy seriousness. The 'dear' reminded his dim spirit of accostings in the night-streets.

'Have you often, I mean are you a grande amoureuse—on the grand scale?'

'Why do you ask? are you curious?'

'Only out of sympathy, only out of sympathy!'

'I mustn't tell you, you'd despise me terribly.'

'I promise not to!'

'I know I shall regret it!'

'Never.'

'I shall, all men are the same.'

'Make an exception with me!'

'Oh I mustn't!'

'Mustn't you?'

'Well I'll tell you!'

'Darling! Don't if it hurts you!'

'Not at all. Well then—I know you'll hate me—well then, only one old Russian—oh yes and a Japanese, but that was a mistake.'

'Have you only, with one old Russian?'

'I knew you'd despise me, I should not have told you!'

'Only one old Russian!'

'There was the Japanese—but he was a mistake.'

'Of what nature? Are you quite sure?'

'Alas yes! He betrayed me upon the links* in New England.'

'The cad!'

'He was a caddie—but he apologized, he was most polite: he assured me it was an accident and I believe it was an accident.'

'But how grim—I should have thought the colour line—.'*

'He explained how it was a complete misunderstanding. His politeness left nothing to be desired, he was a perfect gentleman!'

'Oh I am so glad!'

'You despise me now?'

'No women pals?'*

'Nothing nothing nothing! I have told you except one old Russian!'

She began sobbing upon his shoulder, her face covered with a lace handkerchief. He kissed her through the handkerchief and struck her gently upon the back.

'Never mind' he muttered 'it's all over now. It's *all* over now!'

She put her mouth up to be kissed exclaiming brokenly:

'Say you don't despise me too terribly Tarr! I want *you* so much! I really do want you—so much, so much! *You* will make up for everything!'

A frown had gathered upon his flushed forehead.

'Shall I? Why should I? I'm not going to be made a convenience of!'

'I want you, I really do, enormously, I know you don't believe me! I feel most terribly, oh! back-to-nature-like—*do please* believe me!'

He thrust her rather brutally away on to her chair and himself lurched in the opposite direction, eyeing her askance.

'Why should I? I don't see that! One paltry—*one*—!'

'Tell me what you want!'

'I want a woman. What I want is a woman, you understand, I want a woman badly, that's all!'

'But I am one!'

'I agree, of sorts—very much of sorts!'

She whispered in his ear, hanging upon his neck.

'No no!' he answered: 'all that may be true but—.'

'It is.'

He sat frowning intently at the table.

'Don't be quarrelsome Tarr!'

For a moment she considered him then she pushed her glass away, lay back and remarked with rapid truculence.

'It's all right when you're talking about art but at present you are engaged in the preliminaries to love with a woman.'

'So you say.'

'This is something that can die! Ha! Ha! we're in life my Tarr: we represent *absolutely nothing* thank God!'

'I realize I'm in life, but I don't like being reminded of it in that way. It makes me feel as though I were in a "mauvais lieu."'*

'My confession has been unavailing I observe.'

'To cut a long story short, you disgust me!'

'Give me a kiss you *efficient chimpanzee*.'

Tarr scowled at her but did not alter the half embrace in which they sat.

'You won't give me a kiss? Silly old *in*efficient chimpanzee!'

She sat back in her chair, and head down, looked through her eyelashes at him with arch menace.

'Garçon! garçon!' she called.

'Mademoiselle?' the waiter said, approaching slowly, with dignified scepticism.

'This gentleman, waiter, wants to be a lion with fleas on his back— at least so he says! At the same time he wants a woman if we are to believe him. I don't know if he expects the woman to catch his fleas or not, I haven't asked him: but he's a funny looking bird isn't he?'

The waiter withdrew with hauteur.

'What's the meaning of your latest tack you great he-man of a german art-tart?'

'What am I?'

'I called you german pastry on the large side, with the icing laid on with a shovel.'

'Oh, *tart* is it—?'

'Quite well made, well puffed out, with a great line of talk—.'

'And what, good God, shall we call the cow-faced specimen you spend the greater part of your days with—?'

'She, too, is german pastry, more homely than you though—.'

'Homely's* the word!'

'But not quite so fly-blown and not above all, at least, *pretentious*— yes pre-ten—.'

'I see, and takes you more seriously than other people would be likely to: that's what all your "quatsch" about "woman" means. I guess you know that?'

She had recovered from the effect of the drinks. Sitting up stiffly she examined him as he spoke.

'I know you are a famous whore who becomes rather acid in her cups!—when you showed me your legs this evening I suppose I was meant—.'

'Assez! Assez!!' She struck the table with her fist and flashed her eyes picturesquely over him.

'Let's get to business.' He put his hat on and leant towards her. 'It's getting late. Twenty-five francs, I'm afraid, is all I can manage, you've cleaned me out with the meal.'

'Twenty-five francs for *what*? with you—it would be robbery! Twenty-five francs to be your audience while you drivel about art? Keep your money and buy Bertha an—*efficient chimpanzee*—she will need it poor bitch if she marries you!'

Her mouth uncurled, a thin red line, her eyes glaring and her hands in her overcoat pockets she walked out of the door of the Café.

Tarr ordered another drink.

'It's like a moral tale told on behalf of Bertha' he pondered. That was the temper of Paradise!

Much sobered, he sat in a grim sulk at the thought of the good time he had lost. For half an hour he plotted his revenge and satisfaction together. With a certain buffoonish lightness he went back to his studio with smug, thick secretive pleasure settling down upon his body's exquisite reproaches and burning retaliations.

CHAPTER 3

TARR went slowly up the stairs feeling for his key. He arrived at the door without having found it. The door was ajar: at first this seemed quite natural to him and he continued the search for the key. Then suddenly he dropped that occupation, pushed the door open and entered his studio. The moonlight came heavily through the windows: in a part of the room where it did not strike he became aware of an apparition of solid white. It was solid white flowed round by a dark cloud: it crossed into the moonlight and faced him, its hands placed like a modest statue's: the hair reached below the waist, and flowed to the right from the head. This tall nudity began laughing with a harsh sound like stone laughing.

'Close that door!' it shouted, 'there's a draught. You took a long time to consider my words. I've been waiting chilled to the bone my dear. Forgive me, Tarr, my words belied me, the acidulated demi-mondaine* was a trick. It occupied your mind—you didn't notice me take your key!'

Tarr's vanity was soothed: the key, which could only have been taken in the Café, justified the harsh dialogue.

She stood before him now with her arms up, hands joined behind her head: this impulse to be naked and unashamed had the cultural hygienic touch so familiar to him: the dark ash of the hair was the same colour as Bertha's only it was darker and coarser, Bertha's being fine. Anastasya's white face, therefore, had the appearance almost of a mask.

'Will you engage me as your model sir? Je fais de la réclame pour les Grecs!'*

'You are very ionian—hardly greek.* But I don't require a model thank you, I never use nude models for my pictures.'

'Well I must dress again, I suppose.' She turned towards a chair where her clothes were piled. But Tarr shouted 'I accept, I accept!' a simultaneous revolt of all his tantalized senses shouted its veto upon further acts of that sort. He seized her from behind and heaving her up from the ground, kissing her in the mass, as it were, carried his mighty, luminous burden through the door at the back of the studio leading to his bedroom.

———

'Tarr be my love! we'll be the doviest couple on the *erdball* honey!' Next morning, the sunlight having taken the place of the moonlight, but striking on the opposite side of the house, they lay in muscular masses side by side, smoking and drinking coffee.

'You'll never hear the horrid word *marriage* from me—I want to rescue you from your Bertha habits. We're very well together, aren't we? I'm not doing Bertha a bad turn, either.'

'How do you make that out?'

'Why when that sort of cattle mix themselves with the likes of us, it's at their peril! They suffer for their effrontery.'

Anastasya rolled up against him with the movement of a seal.

'Thank you Tarr for being so nice to me just now. It was perfect.'

Tarr drove the smoke away from his face and wiped his eye.

'You are my efficient chimpanzee then for keeps?'

'No I'm the new animal; we haven't thought up a name for him yet—the thing that will succeed the Superman.'*

CHAPTER 4

TARR crawled towards Bertha that day upon the back of a St. Germain omnibus: as he crawled his mind lazily wandered in the new scene to whose first landmarks he had now grown accustomed. He also turned back into the old with a fresh eye. He really had never meant to leave Bertha at all, he saw: he had not meant to leave her altogether. He had just been playing. A long debt had accumulated, it had been deliberately increased by him because he knew he would not repudiate it.

To-day he must break the news to Bertha that he could no longer regard himself as responsible. The debt was not to be repudiated but he must tell her that he only had himself to pay with, and that his person had been seized and was held by somebody else.

He passed through her iron gateway with a final stealth, although making his shoes sound loudly upon the gravel. It was like entering a vault. The trees looked like weeds, the meaning or taste of everything, of course, had died: the concierge looked like a new one. He had bought a flower for his button-hole: he kept smelling it as he approached the house.

During the last week or more he had got in the habit of writing his letters at Bertha's, to fill up the time. Occasionally he would do a drawing of her (a thing he had never done formerly) to vary the monotony. This time there would be no letter-writing: this visit would be more like the old ones.

'Come in Sorbett' she said, as she opened the door. The formality of the terms upon which they at present met must not be overlooked: prerogatives of past times were proudly rejected. The same depressed atmosphere as the day before, and the days preceding that, penetrated his consciousness. She appeared stale, in some way she was deteriorated and shabby, her worth in the market as in his eyes had dwindled, she was extremely pitiable. Her 'reserve' (a natural result of the new equivocal circumstances) removed her to a distance, as it seemed; it also shut her up inside herself, in an unhealthy dreary and faded atmosphere, she who was naturally so over-expansive. She was shut up with a mass of reserves and secrets, new and old. One was a corpse, as Kreisler was one of her secrets. Mournfully reproachful, she mounted guard over her store of bric-à-brac that had gone out of fashion and was getting musty in a neglected shop: such was her manner, such were her sensations.

Greeted with long mournful glances, he felt she had thought out what she should say; this interview meant a great deal to her. The abject little room seemed to be thrust forward to awaken his memories and ask for pity. An intense atmosphere of teutonic suicide permeated everything: he could not move an eyelid or a muscle without wounding or slighting something: it was like being in a dark kitchen at night, where you know at every step you will put your foot upon a beetle—there was indeed a still closer analogy to this in the disgust he felt for these too naked and familiar things upon which he was treading. He scowled at Beethoven, who scowled back at him like a reflection in a mirror: it was the fate of both of them to haunt this room. The Mona Lisa was there and the breton sabots* and jars. She might have a change of scenery sometimes!—he had the feeling that these tiresome things had been deliberately left in the same place to reproduce a former mood in him. His photograph was prominent on her writing-table: she seemed to say (with a sort of sickly idiocy) 'You see, *he* is faithful to me!'

She preceded him to her sitting-room: as he looked at her back he thought of her as taking a set number of paces, then turning round abruptly, confronting him. From a typical and similar enervation of the will to that which was at the bottom of his troubles, he could hardly stop himself from putting his arm round her waist while they stood for a moment close to each other: he did not wish to do this in response to any renewed desire, but merely because it was the one thing he must not do. To throw himself into the abyss of perplexity he had just escaped from was an almost irresistible temptation: the dykes set up were perpetually threatened by his neurasthenia in this fashion. He kept his hands in his pockets.

When they had reached the room, she turned round, as he had half imagined, and caught hold of his hands.

'Sorbert! Sorbert!'

The words were said separately, each emphatic, each significant. The second was a repetition only of the first. She seemed calling him by his name to conjure back his self again. Her face was a strained and energetic mask.

'What is it Bertha?'

'I don't know!'

She dropped his hands, drooped her head to the right, and turned away.

She sat down. He sat down opposite her, his hat still on his head.

'Anything new?' he asked.

'Anything new? Yes!' She gazed fierily at him, with an insistent meaning.

He concluded this was just the usual, with nothing more behind it than what was always there.

'Well. I have something new as well!'

'Have you Sorbett?'

'To begin with how have my visits struck you lately? How did you explain them?'

'Oh, I did not: why bother about an explanation? Why do you ask?'

'I thought I might as well clear that up.'

'Well?'

'My explanation to myself was this: I did not want to leave you brusquely and I thought a blurred interlude of this sort would do no harm to either of us. Our loves could die in each other's arms so to speak—a comfort to both.'

She stared with incredulous fixity at the floor: her spirit seemed arched over like a swan, and to be gazing down hypnotically.

'That was what I said to myself. The real reason was simply that being very fond of you, I could not make up my mind to give you up. I claim that my visits were not frivolous.'

'Well?'

'I would have married you, if you had considered that advisable.'

'Yes? And—?'

'The rest I find it rather difficult to say.'

'What is difficult?'

'Well, I still like you very much. Yesterday I met a woman, we got on well, I have just left her. I love her too. I can't help that. What must I do?'

Bertha turned a slightly stormier white.

'Who is she?'

'You know her. She is Anastasya Vasek.'

The news struck through something else, and, inside, her ego shrank to an almost wizened being. It seemed glad of the protection the cocoon, the 'something,' afforded her.

'You did not—find out what my news was.'

'I did not. Is there anything particular—?'

'Yes. I am enceinte.'*

———

He thought about this in a clumsy and incredulous way. What a woman, there was no end to her—a Roland for his Oliver:* now she was going to have a baby! With what regularity she countered him. Perhaps Anastasya was getting one too? Bertha's news rose up in opposition to the night he had just spent. Hopes of swagger sex in the future were dashed a little. He was crestfallen at once. He looked up with a gleam of hope.

'Whose child is it?'

'Kreisler's.'

No, no good! There you are! he thought.

Tarr got up and stepped over to her with a bright relieved look in his face.

'Poor Mensch!' he said. 'That's a bad business. But don't go on about it or worry yourself: we can get married and it can always pass as mine: if we do it quickly enough.'

She looked up at him obliquely and sharply, with suspicion grown a habit. When she saw the pleasant, assured expression, she saw that at last things had turned. Sorbert was denying reality! He was ending with miracles—against himself. Her instinct had always told her that generosity would not be lost.

She could have told him at this juncture the actual circumstances under which the child had come. But the idea having occurred to her she had the presence of mind to refrain. She knew that by that her case would be so terribly weakened (whatever the satisfaction to her) that Tarr might immediately take back what he had said.

CHAPTER 5

WHEN he got outside Bertha's house, Bertha waving to him from the window with tears in her eyes, he came in for the counter-attack.

One after the other the protesting masses of good sense rolled up. He picked his way out of the avenue with a reasoning gesticulation of the body; a chicken-like motion of sensible fastidious defence in front of vulgar violence. At the gate he exploded in harsh laughter, looking bravely and raillingly out into the world through his glasses; then he tramped slowly off in his short jacket, his buttocks moving methodically just beneath its rim.

'Ha ha! Ha ha! Kreisleriana'* he shouted without his voice.

The indignant plebs of his glorious organism rioted around his mind.

'Ah-ha! Ah-ha! dirty practical joker, dirty intellect, where are you leading us now?' They were vociferous. 'You have kept us fooling in this neighbourhood so long and now you are pledging us to your fancy fool for ever. Ah-ha! Ah-ha!'

A faction clamoured 'Anastasya!' Certain sense-sections attacked him in vulnerable spots with Anastasya's voluptuous banner unfurled and fragrant. He buffeted his way along, as though spray were dashing in his face, watchful behind his glasses. He met his thoughts with a contemptuous stiff veteran smile: this capricious and dangerous master had an offensive stylistic coolness, similar to Wellington breakfasting at Salamanca while Marmont hurried exultingly into traps:* they were of the same metal, enemies of demagogues and haters of the mob.

Those thoughts that bellowed 'Anastasya!' however, held him up. He answered them.

'Anastasya! Anastasya! You shall have her, what do you take me for? you will still have your Anastasya all right, I am not selling myself or you, a man such as I am does not dispose of himself in such a matter as this. I am going to marry Bertha Lunken: well and what of it, shall I be any the less my own master for that? If I want to sleep with Anastasya I shall do so. "Why marry Bertha Lunken and shoulder all that contagious mess?" Because it is only the points or movements in life that matter, and one of those points is in question; namely, to keep faith with another person: then I show my world by choosing the "premier venu" to be my body-servant and body-companion my contempt for it and for my body, too. Are you satisfied?'

Anastasya he sacrificed with a comparatively light heart. He came back to his earlier conclusions: such successful people as Anastasya and himself were by themselves: it was as impossible to combine or *wed* them as to compound the genius of two great artists. If you mixed together into one whole Gainsborough and Goya* he argued, you would get *nothing.* A subtle lyrical wail would gain nothing from living with a rough and powerful talent, or vice versa: success is always personal. More than ever he was steadily convinced that above a certain level co-operation, group-genius was a slavish pretence and in fact absurd. Mob-talent or popular art was a good thing, it was a big, diffuse, vehement giant; but he was quite sure the only songs of the popular muse that were exciting were composed by great individuals, submerged in an unfavourable time.

He saw this quite clearly: he and Anastasya could not combine otherwise than at present: it was like a mother being given a child to bear the same size already as herself. Anastasya was in every way too big; she was too big physically, she was mentally outsize: in the sex department, she was a Juggernaut.* Did sex not alter the nature of the problem? No. The sexual sphere seemed to him to be an average from which *everything* came, from it everything rose or attempted to rise: there was no mysterious opposition extending up into Heaven, and dividing Heavenly Beings into Gods and Goddesses. God was man: the woman was a lower form of life. Everything started female and most so continued: a jellyish diffuseness spread itself and gaped upon all the beds and bas-fonds of everything: above a certain level sex disappeared, just as in highly-organized sensualism sex vanishes. On the other hand, *everything* beneath that line was female. Jameson, Lowther, Jeffries, Willie Silver, Eddie Watt, Massie, Polden, MacKenzie—he enumerated acquaintances palpably below that absolute line: a lack of energy, permanently mesmeric* state, almost purely emotional, they all displayed it, they were true 'women.' That line had been crossed by Anastasya: he would not be a pervert because he had slept with her, but more than that would be peculiar.*

That evening he met Anastasya as appointed: the moment he saw her he was completely routed: he was humbled and put out of conceit with his judgment. This, he realized later, was the cause of his lack of attachment. He needed an empty vessel to flood with his vitality, and not an equal and foreign vitality to coldly exist side by side with. He had taken into sex the procédés and selfish arrangements of life in general. He had humanized sex too much. He frequently admitted this, but with his defence lost sight of the flagrancy of the permanent fact.

For the first time he now saw in Anastasya an element of protection and safety: she was a touch-wood and harbour from his perplexed interior life. She had a sort of ovation from him.

They went to the same restaurant as the night before. He talked quietly, until they had drunk too much, and Bertha was not mentioned.

'And what about Bertha?' At last she asked:

'Never mind about Bertha.'

'Is she extinct?'

'No. She threatens an entirely new sort of eruption.'

'Oh. In what way new——?'

'It doesn't matter: it won't come our way.'

'Are you going there to-morrow?'

'I suppose I must. But I shall not make many more visits.'

'What's that?'

'I shall give up going I say.' He shifted restlessly in his chair: he had enough Bertha for one day.

After breakfast next morning Anastasya left to go to the painting school. Butcher, whom he had not seen for some days, came in. Tarr agreed to go down into town and have lunch with him; he put on a clean shirt. Talking to Butcher while he was changing, he stood behind his bedroom door: men of ambitious physique, like himself, he had always noticed, were inclined to puff themselves out or let their arms hang in a position favourable to their muscles while changing before another man: to avoid this he seldom exhibited himself unclothed.

After lunch he left Butcher and went to the Mairie of a fashionable Quarter* and made enquiries about civil marriages. After that he went to a lawyer.

He was particularly amiable with Bertha that day, he told her about his going to the Mairie, and he made an appointment with her at the lawyer's for the next day.

Daily, then, he proceeded with his marriage arrangements in the afternoons. He saw Bertha regularly, but without modifying the changed 'correctness 'of his attitude. The evenings he spent with Anastasya.

By the time the french marriage preliminaries had been gone through and Bertha and he could finally be united, his relations with Anastasya had become as close as were those with Bertha formerly. With the exception of the time from three in the afternoon to seven in the evening that he took off every day to see his fiancée, he was with Anastasya.

————————

On September 29th, three weeks after Bertha had told him that she was pregnant, he married her—in the time between three in the afternoon and seven in the evening set aside for her. Anastasya knew nothing about these happenings. Neither Bertha nor she were seeing their german women friends for the moment.

After the marriage at the Mairie Bertha and Tarr walked back to the Luxembourg Gardens and sat down. She had not during the three intervening weeks mentioned Anastasya; it was no time for generosity, she had done too much of that.

They sat for some time without speaking, as though they had quarrelled. She said, then:

'I am afraid Sorbert I have been selfish—.'

'You—selfish—how is that possible? That would be something new.' He had turned to her at once with a hurried fondness genuinely assumed. She looked at him with her wistful, democratic face, full of effort and sentiment.

'You are very unhappy Sorbert—.'

He laughed convincingly.

'No I'm all right.'

'I don't believe you Sorbert.'

'I'm sorry. All right, I'm sad.'

'Are you depressed?'

'I am a little meditative: that is only natural on such a solemn occasion. I was thinking, Bertha, if you want to know what my thoughts were, that we must set up house somewhere and announce our marriage. We must do this for appearance's sake. You will soon be hors de combat—.'*

'Oh I shan't be just yet.'

'In any case, we have gone through this form because—for certain reasons: we must make this move efficacious. What are your ideas as to an establishment? Let us take a flat together somewhere round here: the rue Servandoni* is a capital street: it is narrow, but it is good, it is cheap. There there are apartments. Do you know it?'

'No.' She put her head on one side and puckered up her forehead.
'Near the Luxembourg Museum.'*

He discussed the details of their movements: she had a great many things to pack—there was the chaise-longue, the pictures, the plaster casts of Beethoven and of the Drowned Girl;* he would lend her a hand.

He got up.

'It's rather chilly. Let's get back.'

They walked for some time without speaking. So much unsaid had to be got rid of, without necessarily being said: Bertha had no idea where she was. Their 'establishment', as discussed by Tarr, appeared very unreal and also, what there was of it, disagreeable. What was he going to do with her, she wondered.

'You remember what I said to you some weeks ago?' he asked. 'About Anastasya Vasek. I am afraid there has been no change in that. You do not mind that?'

'No Sorbert. You are perfectly free.'

'I am afraid I shall seem unkind. This is not a nice marriage for you. Perhaps I was wrong to suggest it?'

'How, wrong? I have not been complaining.'

They arrived at the iron gate.

'Well I'd better not come up now. I will turn up to-morrow—at the usual time.'

'Good-bye Sorbert. A demain!'

'A demain!'

CHAPTER 6

ANASTASYA and he were dining that night in Montmartre as usual. His piece of news hovered over their conversation like a bird hesitating as to where to alight.

'I saw Bertha to-day' he said at last.

'You still see her then.'

'Yes, sometimes. For form's sake.'

'I don't understand you.'

'I married her this afternoon.'

'You *what?* Was heisst das—married! Was that for form's sake? What do you mean?'

'What I say, my dear. I married her.'

'You mean you—?' She put an imaginary ring upon her finger.

'Yes. I married her at the Mairie—over there.'

He slung his head to the right.

Anastasya looked blankly into him, as though he contained cheerless stretches where no living thing could grow.

'You mean to say you've done that!'

'Yes I have.'

'Why?'

Tarr stopped a moment.

'Well, the alleged reason was that she is enceinte.'

'But!—whose is the child?'

'Kreisler's, so she says.'

The statement, she saw, was genuine: he was telling her what he had been doing. They both immediately retired into themselves, she to consider the meaning of this new fact; he to wait, his hand near his mouth holding a pipe, until she should have collected herself. But he began speaking first.

'Things are exactly the same as before. I was bound to do that. I had allowed her to consider herself engaged a year ago, and had to keep to that. I have merely gone back a year into the past and fulfilled a pledge, and now return to you. All is in perfect order.'

'All is *not* in perfect order. It is Kreisler's child to begin with you say—.'

'Yes, but it would be very mean to employ that fact to evade an obligation.'

'That is sentimentality.'

'Sentimentality!—Cannot *we*, you and I, afford to give Bertha *that*? Sentimentality—what an absurd word that is with its fierce use in our poor modern hands. What do we mean by it? has life become such an affair of economic calculation that men are too timid to allow themselves any complicated pleasures? Where there is abundance you can afford waste: sentimentality is a cry on a par with "the Simple Life": the ideal of perfect Success is an invention of the same sort of individual as the propagandist of Equal Rights and the Perfectibility of the Species.* Sentimentality is a *privilege*, that I admit, hence its unpopularity, it is a luxury that the crowd does not feel it can possibly afford in these hard times, and it is quite right.'

'That may be true as regards sentimentality in general: but in this case you have been guilty of a popular softness—.'

'No. Listen. I will make it clear to you. You say it was *Kreisler's* child—? Well, that is my security! It is a guarantee that the altruistic origin of the action shall not be forgotten?'

'But that is surely a very mean calculation?'

'Therefore it takes the softness out of the action to which it is allied.'

'No. It takes its raison d'être away altogether. It leaves it merely a stupid and unnecessary proceeding. It cancels the generosity but leaves the fact—your marriage.'

'But the *fact itself* is altered by that!'

'In what way? You are now married to Bertha—.'

'Yes but what does that mean? I married Bertha this afternoon: here I am punctually and as usual at your side this evening—.'

'But the fact of your having married Bertha this afternoon will prevent your making anyone else your wife in the future.'

'You don't want to be my wife.'

'No, but supposing I had a child by *you*—not by Kreisler—it would be impossible to legitimatize him. The thing is of no importance in itself: but you have given Kreisler's child what you should have kept for your own!'

'You would never want a child.'

'How do you know? What's the use of giving your sex over into the hands of a swanky expert, as you describe it, if you continue to act on your own initiative? I throw up my job. Garçon, l'addition!'

But a move to the Café opposite satisfied her as a demonstration. Tarr remained passive. She extorted a promise from him, namely to conduct no more obscure diplomacies in the future.

———

Bertha and Tarr took a four-room flat in the rue Festus, not far from the Place des Vosges,* a long way out, a peripheral home. It was a cheap place. They gave a party to which Fräulein Liepmann and a good many other people came. Tarr maintained the rule of four to seven, roughly, for Bertha, with the utmost punctiliousness. Anastasya and Bertha did not meet.

Bertha's child was born, and it absorbed her energies for upwards of a year. It bore some resemblance to Tarr. Tarr's afternoon visits became less frequent. He lived now publicly with his illicit and more splendid bride.

Two years after the birth of the child, Mrs. Tarr divorced him: she then married an eye-doctor and lived with a brooding severity in his company and that of her only child.

Tarr and Anastasya did not marry. They had no children.

Tarr, however, had three children by a lady of the name of Rose Fawcett, who consoled him eventually for the splendours of his 'perfect woman.' But yet beyond the dim though solid figure of Rose Fawcett, another rises. This one represents the swing back of the pendulum once more to the swagger side. The cheerless and stodgy absurdity of Rose Fawcett required as compensation the painted, fine and enquiring face of Prism Dirkes.*

APPENDIX
PREFACE TO THE 1918 AMERICAN EDITION

LEWIS wrote an epilogue for the initial serial publication of *Tarr* in *The Egoist*. A version of that epilogue appears as a preface to the 1918 American edition. It also appears in amended form, divided into a prologue and epilogue, in the 1918 English Egoist Press edition. Lewis omitted this material from the 1928 revision of the novel, in part because it was originally intended to alert readers to the fact that Lewis created the character of Kreisler before the First World War, and that *Tarr* was therefore to be read during wartime as a prediction rather than a reflection of contemporary relations between England and Germany.

Lewis later regretted what he saw as the preface's nationalism, writing 'the first edition was disfigured, I am sorry to say, by a "patriotic" preface . . . it was a moment of great popular excitement, and I had been infected by it'.[1] But the preface also criticizes aspects of the English national character, and, perhaps more importantly, it explicitly establishes Lewis's claim of authorial distance from his protagonist. It is probably this latter element that led him to omit the preface from the 1928 revision. The preface gives away part of the novel's game before it has even begun, and according to some of his friends' criticisms threatened to lapse into pedantry.[2]

The preface is reproduced below from the 1918 American Knopf edition. A set of variant paragraphs from the prologue of the 1918 English Egoist Press edition follows.

Preface to the 1918 American Knopf Edition

This book was begun eight years ago;* so I have not produced this disagreeable German for the gratification of primitive partisanship

---

[1] *Rude Assignment: An Intellectual Autobiography*, ed. Toby Foshay (Santa Barbara: Black Sparrow Press, 1984), 162.

[2] The poet and artist Sturge Moore (1870–1944) had written to Lewis, 'I rather regret the preface and epilogue: they will distract reflection from the book itself to the doctrine it will be supposed to illustrate . . . they are like a rope anchoring it to Pound's Little World, whereas it might sail the blue quite unattached with advantage' (*The Letters of Wyndham Lewis*, ed. W. K. Rose (Norfolk, Conn.: New Directions, 1963), Sept. 1918, p. 99). In his review of *Tarr* for the *Little Review* Pound noted a similar stricture, writing that in comparison to Kreisler, 'Tarr is less clearly detached from his creator. The author has evidently suspected this, for he has felt the need of disclaiming Tarr in a preface' (*Little Review* (1918); repr. in *Literary Essays of Ezra Pound* (New York: New Directions Books, 1968), 425).

aroused by the war. On the other hand, having had him up my sleeve for so long, I let him out at this moment in the undisguised belief that he is very apposite. I am incidentally glad to get rid of him. He has been on my conscience (my conscience as an artist, it is true) for a long time.

The myriads of Prussian germs, gases, and gangrenes released into the air and for the past year* obsessing everything, revived my quiescent creation. I was moved to vomit Kreisler forth. It is one big germ more. May the flames of Louvain* help to illuminate (and illustrate) my hapless protagonist! His misdemeanours too, which might appear too harshly real at ordinary times, have, just now, too obvious confirmations to be questioned.

Germany's large leaden brain booms away in the centre of Europe. Her brain-waves and titanic orchestrations* have broken round us for too long not to have had their effect. As we never think ourselves, except a stray Irishman or American,* we should long ago have been swamped had it not been for the sea. The habits and vitality of the seaman's life and this vigorous element have protected us intellectually as the blue water has politically.

In Europe Nietzsche's gospel of desperation, the beyond-law-man, etc., has deeply influenced the Paris apache, the Italian Futurist *littérateur*,* the Russian revolutionary. Nietzsche's books are full of seductions and sugar-plums. They have made 'aristocrats' of people who would otherwise have been only mild snobs or meddlesome prigs; as much as, if not more than, other writings, they have made 'expropriators' of what would otherwise merely have been Arsène Lupins:* and they have made an Over-man of every vulgarly energetic grocer in Europe.* The commercial and military success of Prussia has deeply influenced the French, as it is gradually winning the imagination of the English. The fascination of material power is, for the irreligious modern man, almost impossible to resist.

There is much to be said for this eruption of greedy, fleshy, frantic strength in the midst of discouraged delicacies. Germany has its mission and its beauty. But I do not believe it will ever be able to benefit, itself, by its power and passion. The English may a little more: I hope Russia will.

As to the Prophet of War, the tone of Nietzsche's books should have discredited his philosophy. The modern Prussian advocate of the

Aristocratic and Tyrannic took *everybody* into his confidence. Then he would coquet: he gave special prizes. *Everybody* couldn't be a follower of his! No: only the *minority*: that is the minority who read his books, which has steadily grown till it comprises certainly (or would, were it collected together) the ungainliest and strangest aristocratic caste any world could hope to see!

The artists of this country make a plain and pressing appeal to their fellow-citizens. It is as follows: They appeal:

(1) That at the moment of this testing and trying of the forces of the nation, of intellect, of character, they should grant more freedom to the artists and thinkers to develop their visions and ideas. That they should make an effort of sympathy. That the maudlin and the self-defensive Grin* should be dropped.

(2) That the Englishman should become ashamed of his Grin as he is at present ashamed of solemnity. That he should cease to be ashamed of his "feelings": then he would automatically become less proud of his Grin.

(3) That he should remember that seriousness and unsentimentality are quite compatible. Whereas a Grin usually accompanies loose emotionality.

(4) That in facing the facts of existence as he is at present compelled to do, he should allow artists to economize time in not having to circumvent and get round those facts, but to use them simply and directly.

(5) That he should restrain his vanity, and not always imagine that his leg is being pulled. A symbolism is of the nature of all human effort. There is no necessity to be literal to be in earnest. Humour, even, may be a symbol. The recognizing of a few simple facts of that sort would help much.

In these onslaughts on Humour I am not suggesting that anybody should laugh less over his beer or wine or forgo the consolation of the ridiculous. There are circumstances when it is a blessing. But the *worship of the ridiculous* is the thing that should be forgone. The worship (or craze, we call it) of Charlie Chaplin* is a mad substitution of a chaotic tickling for all the other more organically important ticklings of life.

Nor do I mean here that you or I, if we are above suspicion in the matter of those other fundamentals, should not allow ourselves the little scurvy totem of Charlie on the mantelpiece. It is not a grinning face we object to but a face that is mean when it is serious and that takes to its grin as a duck takes to water. We must stop grinning. You will say that I do not practise what I preach. I do: for if you look closely at my grin you will perceive that it is a very logical and deliberate grimace.

In this book you are introduced to a gentleman named Tarr. I associate myself with all he says on the subject of humour. In fact, I put him up to it. He is one of my showmen; though, naturally, he has a private and independent life of his own, for which I should be very sorry to be held responsible.

From the Prologue of the 1918 Egoist Press Edition

Kreisler in this book is a German and nothing else. Tarr is the individual in the book, and is at the same time one of the showmen of the author. His private life, however, I am in no way responsible for. The long drawn-out struggle in which we find this young man engaged is illuminated from start to finish by the hero of it. His theory, put in another way, is that an artist requires more energy than civilization provides, or that the civilized mode of life implies; more *naïveté*, freshness, and unconsciousness. So Nature agrees to force his sensibility and intelligence, on the one hand, to the utmost pitch, leaving him, on the other, an uncultivated and ungregarious tract where he can run wild and renew his forces and remain unspoilt.

Tarr, in his analysis of the anomalies of taste, gives the key to a crowd of other variants and twists to which most of the misunderstandings and stupidities in the deciphering of men are due. He exaggerates his own departure from perfect sense and taste into an unnecessary image of Shame and Disgust, before which he publicly castigates himself. He is a primitive figure, coupled with a modern type of flabby sophistication: that is Bertha Lunken. The Munich German Madonna stands nude, too, in the market-place, with a pained distortion of the face.*

Tarr's message, as a character in a book, is this. Under the camouflage of a monotonous intrigue he points a permanent opposition, of life outstripped, and art become lonely. He incidentally is intended to bring some comfort of analysis amongst less sifted and more ominous perplexities of our time. His message, as he discourses, laughs, and

Preface to the 1918 American Edition   289

picks his way through the heavily obstructed land of this story, is the message of a figure of health. His introspection is not melancholy; for the strange and, as with his pedagogic wand he points out, hideously unsatisfactory figures that are given ingress to his innermost apartments become assimilated at once to a life in which he has the profoundest confidence. He exalts Life into a Comedy, when otherwise it is, to his mind, a tawdry zone of half-art, or a silly Tragedy. Art is the only thing worth the tragic impulse, for him; and, as he says, it is his drama. Should art, that is some finely-adjusted creative will, suddenly become the drama of the youth infatuated with his maiden, what different dispositions would have to be made; what contradictory tremors would invade his amorous frame; what portions of that frame would still smoulder amorously? These questions Tarr disposes of to his satisfaction.

So much by way of warning before the curtain rises. Even if the necessary tragic thrill of misgiving is caused thereby (or are we going to be 'shocked' in the right way once again, not in Shaw's 'bloody' schoolgirl way?),* it may extenuate the at times seemingly needless nucleus of blood and tears.

P. WYNDHAM LEWIS

1915

EXPLANATORY NOTES

Tarr is a highly allusive Modernist novel, and appreciation of Lewis's achievement depends in part on familiarity with the referents of the novel's erudition and the details of its cultural world. These notes provide information about Paris and the life of the artist before the First World War; about the histories and practices of British and European painting, literature, and philosophy; and about the popular and intellectual life of Europe during the period in which *Tarr* takes place.

As an 'international novel' *Tarr* contains a good many non-English words and phrases. Translations of those words and phrases that require no further explanation will be found in the Glossary of Foreign Words and Phrases. Words and phrases requiring more detailed context or commentary are glossed below.

On occasion Lewis's German spelling is idiosyncratic, and at other times (as the substance of his opening quotation from Montaigne suggests) the French and German in his characters' speech reflect dialectical usages, foreign accents, and characters' errors of grammar. In these annotations I have tried to note and distinguish between these different kinds of non-standard language.

3 *period of illness and restless convalescence*: bouts of confinement to bed during 1915, caused by septicaemia. See Paul O'Keeffe, *Some Sort of Genius: A Life of Wyndham Lewis* (London: Jonathan Cape, 2000), 164–5.

6 *Epigraphs*: passages from the *Essais* of Renaissance French author Michel de Montaigne (1533–92), the first from 'Sur des vers de Virgile' ('On some verses of Virgil'), Book III, Chapter v:

> I would have done it better elsewhere, but the work would have been less my own; and its principal end and perfection is to be precisely my own. I would indeed correct an accidental error, and I am full of them, since I run on carelessly. But the imperfections that are ordinary and constant in me it would be treachery to remove.
>
> When I have been told, or have told myself: 'You are too thick in figures of speech. Here is a word of Gascon vintage. Here is a dangerous phrase'. (I do not avoid any of those that are used in the streets of France; those who would combat usage with grammar make fools of themselves.) 'This is ignorant reasoning. This is paradoxical reasoning. This one is too mad. You are often playful: people will think you are speaking in earnest when you are making believe.' 'Yes,' I say, 'but I correct the faults of inadvertence, not those of habit. Isn't this the way I speak everywhere? Don't I represent myself to the life? Enough, then.' (*The Complete Works of Montaigne*, trans. Donald M. Frame (Stanford: Stanford University Press, 1957), 667)

The second from the essay *De l'expérience* ('On Experience'), Book III, Chapter XIII:

> The more simply we trust to Nature, the more wisely we trust to her. Oh, what a sweet and soft pillow is ignorance and incuriosity, to rest a well-made head! (*Complete Works*, trans. Frame, 822)

7 *Baedeker*: a series of small burgundy-coloured travel guides published by Verlag Karl Baedeker in Germany, and in English from 1878 to 1918, so popular before the First World War that the name became generic to mean a guidebook of any kind. References in these notes to *Baedeker* are to the 1907 *Paris and Environs with Routes from London to Paris*.

western Venuses: attractive (and most probably American female tourists, whose voices are louder and more nasal than those of the Parisians, and who are reduced to near-silence ('hushed to soft growl') by their awe at, or their socially expected deference to, the art of Paris. The adjective 'Western' may distinguish these living beauties from the Venus de Milo, the best-known statue in Paris.

Thébaïde: a hermitage or place of contemplation—in this sense the title of a drawing in Lewis's portfolio *Timon of Athens* (1912)—but also suggesting the early play *La Thébaïde* (*The Story of Thebes*, 1664) by French author Jean Racine (1639–99), which recounts the hatred and war between Oedipus' sons. Together the allusions suggest that Paris is both an Edenic retreat and the site of potentially fratricidal tragedy.

Vitelotte Quarter: Lewis's fictional name for Montparnasse, a neighbourhood of Paris on the Left Bank of the Seine in the 14th arrondissement. The *vitelotte* is a variety of purple French potato, brightly coloured but essentially prosaic, a sardonic name for a painter's quarter.

Hollywood . . . buttocks: Westerns were a popular staple of the early silent cinema in Europe as well as the United States. 'Gun', short for 'gonoph', is nineteenth-century urban slang for a thief. Thus, the effects of the cowboy's swaggering walk are superimposed on attempted pickpocketing. The 1907 *Baedeker* warns visitors to 'be on their guard against the huge army of pickpockets and other rogues, who are quick to recognize the stranger and skilful in taking advantage of his ignorance' (p. xxv).

Henri Murger's Vie de Bohème: French novelist, 1822–61. His *Scènes de la vie de bohème* (*Scenes of Bohemian Life*) appeared in episodes from 1847 to 1849 and was published in book form in 1851. It provided a romanticized vision of the life of the Parisian artist, and became the source of the libretto for the opera *La Boheme* by Italian composer Giacomo Puccini (1858–1924).

linseed oil: a common base in oil paint, derived from flax seeds.

Boulevard du Paradis . . . Boulevard Kreutzberg: invented names suggesting the intersection of a French Garden of Eden ('Paradis') with a Germanic site of Crucifixion (from Ger. 'Mountain of the Cross'). A fictionalization of the intersection of the Boulevard Raspail and Boulevard Montparnasse, where Lewis lived for a time in the Hôtel de la Haute Loire.

Campagnia: a region of southern Italy, now spelled 'Campania'.

Tussaud's of the Flood: 'Madame Tussauds' is a renowned wax museum on Marylebone Road in London created by Marie Tussaud (1761–1850); 'the Flood' refers to the story of Noah in the Old Testament (Genesis 6–9), in which near-universal destruction follows upon man's failure to live according to God's laws.

8 *Cambridge*: Hobson is in many ways a lampoon of painter and art critic Roger Fry (1866–1934), who was educated at Cambridge and was a member of a prominent Quaker family. Fry was a powerful taste-maker in London, who lauded French post-Impressionism at the expense of the newer schools of experimental art, such as Cubism, and of English painters in general. Fry was an early supporter of Lewis's painting, but they broke in 1913 over Lewis's belief that Fry stole a commission from Lewis and the Vorticists. Lewis lambasts Fry in his aesthetic writing of the 1910s and 1920s: in the Vorticist journal *Blast* he labels Fry 'THE BRITANNIC AESTHETE', the 'GOOD WORKMAN', and 'ART-PIMP' (*Blast* 1, pp. 15–16).

travesty of a Quaker's Meeting: a spiritual gathering of The Religious Society of Friends, founded in England in the seventeenth century, and known for its dedication to pacifism. Participants at such a meeting may sit in silence for substantial periods of time until a member chooses to speak.

fetish: an inanimate object worshipped for its presumed magical powers, or as being animated by a spirit; used here to refer to that spirit itself.

9 *daimon*: from the Greek for 'divinity', an indwelling spirit or genius.

A B C waitresses: servers at branches of the Aerated Bread Company, a popular chain of bakeries and tea rooms in London. In *Blast* 2 Lewis blesses 'All A.B.C. Tea-shops (without exception)' (p. 93).

Bloomsbury: a fashionable residential area of central London in the borough of Camden, associated with the 'Bloomsbury Group' of writers and artists, including novelists Virginia Woolf (1882–1941) and E. M. Forster (1879–1970), biographer and essayist Lytton Strachey (1880–1932), economist John Maynard Keynes (1883–1946), and the painters and art critics Roger Fry, Duncan Grant (1885–1978), and Clive Bell (1881–1964). Lewis loathed Bloomsbury in part because of his personal battles with Fry and Bell, but also because he believed that the Bloomsbury artists endorsed an aesthetic that was merely decorative, feminine, and crypto-Victorian.

10 *Walt Whitman . . . Buffalo Bill . . . Thomas Carlyle*: three notable nineteenth-century men who wore long hair: Walt Whitman (1819–92), American poet and author of *Leaves of Grass*; William Frederick 'Buffalo Bill' Cody (1846–1917), American bison hunter and showman; and Thomas Carlyle (1795–1881), Scottish essayist and historian, author of *Sartor Resartus* and *The French Revolution*.

10 *"Roi . . . daigne"*: Fr., 'I am not the King, I do not condescend to be the prince', a variant of 'Roi ne puis, prince ne daigne, Rohan je suis' ('King I cannot be; prince I do not deign to be; I am a Rohan'), the immodest motto of the aristocratic Rohan family of Brittany.

Hobson's choice: proverbial for having no real choice. Derived from the business practices of Thomas Hobson (*c.*1544–1630), a carrier and renter of horses in Cambridge, England, who offered his customers only the next horse in line or no horse at all.

Panthéon: a neoclassical building in the Latin Quarter originally built as a church dedicated to St Geneviève, but primarily known as the burial place of many of France's greatest men.

Rue Lhomond: a street in Paris in the 5th arrondissement, not far from the Panthéon.

Rowlandson . . . the epoch: Thomas Rowlandson (1756–1827), English satiric artist and illustrator. Rowlandson's career lasted well beyond the major period of eighteenth-century satire into the Georgian period. Lewis endorsed Rowlandson as a model for contemporary English satire in his journal *The Tyro* (1921).

11 *'Carrion-Crow'*: an allusion to the lines 'Old Adam, the carrion crow, | The old crow of Cairo; | He sat in the shower, and let it flow | Under his tail and over his crest', from a song in Act V, Scene iv, of the play *Death's Jest-Book* by English poet and dramatist Thomas Lovell Beddoes (1803–49) (*The Works of Thomas Lovell Beddoes* (Oxford: Oxford University Press, 1925), 184).

12 *cantab*: short for 'Cantabrigian', a student of Cambridge University. The adjective 'Cairo' continues the allusion to Beddoes's *Death's Jest-Book*.

philogermanic: adj., 'loving German culture'.

13 *panurgic*: 'skilled in all kinds of work', also, 'meddling', from the Gr. *pano-yrgiko*, 'knavish'. Also echoes the name of the character Panurge, a crafty libertine and coward in *La Vie de Gargantua et de Pantagruel* by François Rabelais (*c.*1494–1553), whose name derives from the same root.

Flaubert . . . Bouvard et Pécuchet: an unfinished novel by French novelist Gustave Flaubert (1842–80), published posthumously in 1881, a satire about two hapless Parisian copy-clerks and their quest for erudition. Flaubert's *Le Dictionnaire des idées reçues* (*The Dictionary of Received Ideas*), a kind of pendant to the novel, was published in France in 1911–13. This collection of platitudes, based on notes that Flaubert gathered in the 1870s, holds the mirror up to the middle-class French 'squalor and idiocy' of which Tarr speaks.

14 *Rembrandt . . . old Jews*: Rembrandt van Rijn (1606–69), Dutch painter and etcher, frequently used his elderly neighbours in the Jewish district of Amsterdam as models for his paintings of Old Testament themes.

Falstaff: Sir John Falstaff, one of William Shakespeare's greatest comic characters, a fat and boastful knight who appears in *Henry IV, Part I*,

Henry IV, Part II, and *The Merry Wives of Windsor*, where he is associated with images of grease throughout: he is called in this last play 'this whale (with so many tuns of oil in his belly)'(II. i. 64–5) and 'this greasy knight' (II. i. 107–8).

Socrates . . . shrew: Xanthippe, the wife of the Greek philosopher Socrates (469–399 BC), the proverbial model of a shrewish wife. In Xenophon's *Symposium* Antisthenes describes her as 'beyond dispute, the most insupportable woman that is, has been, or ever will be' (*The Complete Works of Xenophon*, trans. Ashley, Spelman, et al. (Edinburgh: William P. Nimmo & Co., 1881), 605).

picture post cards: by the first decades of the twentieth century, collecting picture postcards had become a worldwide hobby of unprecedented proportions, but Tarr particularly alludes to the beautiful, and likely vapid, women who modelled for the erotic Parisian photographs that became known throughout the English speaking world as 'French postcards'.

Tadema: Sir Lawrence Alma-Tadema (1836–1912), Dutch-born late-Victorian English painter. Admired in his time for his superb draftsmanship and depictions of classical antiquity, by the early twentieth century progressive artists viewed him as hopelessly academic and out-of-date.

Raphael: Raffaello Sanzio (1483–1520), Italian Renaissance painter and architect, known for his technical perfection and ennobling treatment of the human form.

cubism: avant-garde art movement that revolutionized modern painting and sculpture, pioneered in Paris between 1907 and 1914 by Pablo Picasso (1881–1973) and Georges Braque (1882–1963).

15 *eugenist*: one who advocates the improvement of human hereditary traits through planned social and scientific intervention. Eugenics had many prominent supporters among writers and thinkers in the early twentieth century, but lost its scientific reputation in the 1930s when eugenic rhetoric entered into the racial policies of Nazi Germany.

Napoleon . . . captivity: Napoleon Bonaparte (1769–1821), French military and political leader. Imprisoned and exiled by the British to the island of St Helena in 1815, Napoleon lived there as recluse until his death.

voice-culture practitioner: a follower of the vocal training methods of François Delsarte (1811–71) who believed that it offered aesthetic and social benefits for the singer, orator, and average speaker alike, and whose ideas were popularized in the late nineteenth century by such books as *Society Gymnastics and Voice Culture, Adapted from the Delsarte System* (1890, Genevieve Stebbins). Tarr's use of the term as an insult suggests that 'voice culture' was the sort of effete late-Victorian trend typically embraced by Hobson's coterie.

pierrotesque: in the manner of Pierrot, a melancholy, silent, white-faced clown often portrayed as moonstruck, the French version of a stock character of the Italian *Commedia dell'arte*.

16 *chimera*: an unreal creature or imaginary amalgam. From a beast of Greek mythology that was composed of parts of several different animals.

17 *Turner... washerwoman at Gravesend*: J. M. W. Turner (1775–1851), English Romantic landscape painter, watercolourist and printmaker, who lived for more than fifteen years at the end of his life with Sophia Caroline Booth. Booth was described as 'good looking' and 'illiterate' (A. J. Finberg, *The Life of J. M. W. Turner, R.A.* (Oxford: Clarendon Press, 1961), 438), and had run a boarding house in Margate before becoming Turner's housekeeper in Chelsea. She exemplifies a woman of low class and intelligence who provides romantic and sexual satisfaction to a man of genius, although Tarr misidentifies both Booth's profession and the seaside town where she and Turner first met.

gallant: a fashionable young man.

18 *ego*: Latin for 'I'. Less an allusion to Freud than to the idea of the ego propagated in *Der Einzige und sein Eigentum* (*The Ego and Its Own*), a work of pre-Nietzschean philosophy by Max Stirner (real name Johann Kaspar Schmidt (1806–56)). Stirner's idea of a self that transcends the limitations of religion and politics also inspired the name of Dora Marsden's journal *The Egoist*, and Lewis alludes prominently to Stirner and *The Ego and Its Own* in his play *Enemy of the Stars*.

old fruit-tin: familiar British address of the period, comparable to 'old bean'. Perhaps also playing upon another period usage of 'fruit' to mean 'easy mark' or 'one who is easily deceived'.

Dr. Jekyll... Mr. Hyde: the main character(s) in *Strange Case of Dr Jekyll and Mr Hyde* (1886), a short novel by Scottish author Robert Louis Stevenson (1850–94). Subsequently a catchphrase for a person who manifests two irreconcilable sets of behaviours and personalities in different situations.

collages: Fr., 'gluing, sticking', but also a work of visual art, strongly associated with Cubism, where an aesthetic whole is created from an assemblage of different forms and materials. According to the *Oxford English Dictionary* the word 'collage' first appears in English in Lewis's 1919 aesthetic treatise *The Caliph's Design*.

Oh Sex! oh Montreal!: a lampoon of the refrain 'O God! O Montreal!' from 'A Psalm of Montreal', a satirical poem by Samuel Butler (1835–1902). The poem pokes fun at the Victorian prudery of the Montreal Museum of Natural History, which has stored away two plaster casts of classical statuary. As the custodian explains to the visiting Butler, 'The Discobolus is put here because he is vulgar, | He has neither vest nor pants with which to cover his limbs.' The poet responds, as Tarr might ask Hobson about Bloomsbury, 'Preferrest thou the gospel of Montreal to the gospel of Hellas?' (*The Shrewsbury Edition of the Works of Samuel Butler*, vol. xx (London and New York, 1926), 393).

19 *bear-garden*: an arena designed for the baiting of bears, a popular spectacle in England in the sixteenth and seventeenth centuries. Figurative for a place where riotous behaviour is common and permitted.

our emancipated Bohemia: since the late 1840s a byword for a community of freethinking artists who live apart from middle-class convention, by association with the actual Bohemia, a region of Central Europe now part of the Czech Republic, thought to be the place of origin of the Roma people, who are popularly known as 'gypsies'.

20 *invert-spinsters*: 'inversion' was a period term for homosexuality, first used by the British sexologist Havelock Ellis (1859–1939), author of *Sexual Inversion* (1897). Given the propensity towards both bisexuality and homosexuality in the Bloomsbury group, these 'invert-spinsters' may be understood to be either unmarried lesbians or effeminate males.

vegetable ideas: perhaps in any of its obsolete senses of 'organic', 'capable of growth', or 'of the soul', as in the 'vegetable love' mentioned in 'To His Coy Mistress' by poet Andrew Marvell (1621–78). However, Tarr likely means 'vegetable' in one of its modern senses, as featureless, monotonous, and dull, the mode in which Lewis curses 'VEGETABLE HUMANITY' in *Blast* (1, p. 15).

roses and Victorian lilies: common subjects of Victorian painting and verse; the lily was a standard emblem of Victorian femininity, as in *Sesame and Lilies* (1865) by art critic John Ruskin (1819–1900). The allusion insults both Hobson's masculinity and his credentials as a Modernist.

Yellow Press: unscrupulously sensationalist newspapers, which often featured scurrilous personal attacks on public figures. The name derived from an issue of the *New York World* in 1885 that featured a colour cartoon of a child in a yellow garment ('The Yellow Kid'), as an eye-catching experiment to increase sales.

21 *Chelsea artist*: an area of south-west London, home to the Chelsea School of Art, which was founded in 1895. Chelsea was known as London's bohemian quarter from mid-Victorian times until roughly the First World War, and was associated with painters, writers, and political radicals.

Wilde: Oscar Wilde (1854–1900), Irish playwright, novelist, and society wit. The 'Wilde decade' was the 1890s, a time associated with decadence, the art movement Aestheticism, and during which Wilde was imprisoned for 'gross indecency' with another man. Wilde attended Magdalen College (Oxford) from 1874 to 1878.

Liberalism: a political philosophy that emphasized individual rights and property ownership, and limited central government, emerging from the Enlightenment and associated in the mid-nineteenth century with the party and governments of Prime Minister William Ewart Gladstone (1809–98). By the mid-1880s so-called 'classical' liberalism found itself under threat by the emergence of socialism, and the 'death of liberalism' became a subject for debate for some decades. See, for instance, the book *The Strange Death of Liberal England* (New York: H. Smith & R. Haas, 1935) by George Dangerfield (1904–86).

suburb of Carlyle and Whistler: i.e. Chelsea, home to Thomas Carlyle and painter James McNeill Whistler (1834–1903).

21 *barley-water*: a bland British soft drink, usually flavoured with lemon, popular in the 1890s.

lost generations described in Chekov: a frequent subject of the plays of Russian playwright Anton Pavlovich Chekhov (1860–1904), particularly his last play *The Cherry Orchard* (1904). They were the fading landed aristocracy and 'superfluous men' of the mid- to late nineteenth century in Russia, who were soon to be swept away by the powerful forces of a rising middle class and by the political upheavals of the Russian Revolution.

communism: a socioeconomic and political doctrine based on the theories of German philosopher Karl Marx (1818–83), who desired the establishment of a classless society in which property and the means of production are owned communally. Tarr finds Hobson an 'advanced-copy' of Communism because Hobson has subordinated himself in thought and fashion to the ideas of a larger group, and because from the vantage point of 1928 he represents the kind of privileged 'parlour socialist' that Lewis criticized in 1927 in *Time and Western Man* (ed. Paul Edwards (Santa Barbara: Black Sparrow Press, 1993), 124–6).

take water with it: 'moderate your ideas and rhetoric', from the use of water to dilute strong whisky.

22 *Baudelaire's fable*: a description of the first part of the 1864 prose poem 'Assommons les Pauvres!' ('Let's Beat Up the Poor!') by Charles Baudelaire (1821–67), number 49 of the collection of short prose poems published posthumously as *Le Spleen de Paris* in 1869. The parallel with Tarr and Hobson breaks down at the parable's end, however, where the poet identifies the beggar as his equal, shares his purse with him, and urges him to treat other beggars in a similar manner according to the '*théorie que j'ai eu la* douleur *d'essayer sur votre dos*' ('theory I have had the *sorrow* of testing out on your back'; *Œuvres Complètes, Petit poëmes en prose* (Paris: Louis Conard, 1926), 172). The beggar agrees with the poet's advice—an unlikely response from Hobson.

misnamed wideawake: usually 'wide-awake', a soft, low-crowned felt men's hat resembling those worn by American Quakers. It is 'misnamed' because Tarr considers Hobson to be spiritually and aesthetically 'asleep'.

23 *gangster cut*: a men's fashion inspired by Parisian fascination with American popular culture and crime stories.

cocaine: an addictive drug originally used as an anaesthetic in Germany in the 1880s, but adopted recreationally by bohemian circles in Hollywood and Europe before the First World War. When applied to the gums the drug can produce this 'frozen' expression.

in excelsis: Lat., 'to the highest extent', from 'Gloria in excelsis Deo' (Lat., 'Glory to God in the highest'), the Gloria of the Catholic and Anglican mass, known also as the Greater Doxology.

Charenton: a south-eastern suburb of Paris, or the nearby Charenton asylum, later the Esquirol hospital, where the Marquis de Sade (1740–1814) was famously confined from 1803 to 1814.

Romanys: the Roma people, gypsies.

24 *Pernot*: slight misspelling of Pernod Fils, the most popular brand of absinthe, a green anise-flavoured liquor with supposed narcotic properties derived from the substance thujone. One of the most popular alcoholic beverages in Paris, it was banned in France and most of Europe in 1915.

the Lunken: a rendering into English of an Italian mode of referring to a woman to a third party as 'la' followed by the subject's first name or surname. (See also 'the Fuchs', p. 156.)

25 *Balzac . . . character*: Honoré de Balzac (1799–1850), nineteenth-century French novelist. He was subject to a neglectful childhood, and his novels often feature young men trying to make their way in the world after difficult beginnings. In his novel *Cousin Pons* he wrote 'La misère . . . donna cette grande, cette forte éducation qu'elle dispense à coups d'étrivières aux grands hommes, tous malheureux dans leur enface' ('Indigence . . . put them through that hard and stringent course of education which she dispenses in the form of whippings to great men, all of whom have had an unhappy childhood') (French edn (Paris: Éditions Garnier Frères, 1962), 64; trans. Herbert J. Hunt (Harmondsworth: Penguin Books, 1968), 79).

26 *Boulevard Sebastopol*: a thoroughfare running north–south in central Paris that divides the 1st and 2nd from the 3rd and 4th arrondissements.

aryan: pertaining to the ancient Indo-European Aryan people, in particular a racialist notion of the French diplomat, writer, and ethnologist Joseph-Arthur, Comte de Gobineau (1816–82), whose *Essai sur l'inégalité des races humaines* (*Essay on the Inequality of the Human Race*) (1853–5) identified the Germanic with the Aryan peoples as the peak of racial civilization. At the time of *Tarr* the term was not yet identified with the Nazi racial policies of the 1930s, or specifically with anti-Semitism.

27 *Gioconda*: an alternative name for the *Mona Lisa*, a painting of a woman wearing an enigmatic expression by Leonardo da Vinci (1452–1519). One of the world's most recognizable paintings and, as part of the Louvre, one of Paris's most popular tourist attractions.

28 *platonic*: in the sense of 'ideal', taken from Plato's theory of forms, rather than the common contemporary usage, derived from *The Symposium*, to describe an intimate but non-sexual friendship between a man and a woman.

30 *Ancient Britons . . . coracles*: the indigenous Celtic inhabitants of pre-Roman Britain. A 'coracle' is a small, lightweight boat used by the early Britons, and still used in parts of Wales.

31 *bum*: American slang for a disreputable or dissolute man; also a fool, sometimes intended teasingly. The *Oxford English Dictionary* lists a quotation from the *Observer* for 2 April 1933: ' "Bum", a term of affectionate obloquy which young American friends have applied to me . . . means not merely a fool, but a droning fool.'

31 *Passy*: a considerably upscale area of Paris in the 16th arrondissement, west of the Louvre and the Champs-Élysées on the Right Bank, a suggestion of the success of Butcher's automobile business.

Samaritaine: a large department store, located in the 1st arrondissement.

32 *'Monsieur Lounes . . . sortir'*: Fr., 'Mr Lowndes? I think so. I didn't see him leave.' 'Lounes' represents 'Lowndes' phonetically as pronounced by the French porter.

34 *Boswell*: James Boswell (1740–95), Scottish lawyer, diarist, and author of *The Life of Samuel Johnson* (1791), a biography of his friend and man of letters Samuel Johnson (1709–84), and thereafter a byword for a constant companion, observer, and recorder.

36 *sombrero*: a broad-brimmed Spanish hat, rather than the more commonly pictured Mexican variety, usually made of felt or some other soft material, used to protect the head from sun.

impressionist's . . . represented: the invention of portable easels and oil paints in tubes allowed the Impressionists to move out of the studio, thus their emphasis on painting directly before the subject. For early twentieth-century avant-gardists Impressionism—with its emphasis on the subjectivity of vision and blurring of the object's contours—represented a faded and already institutionalized radicalism.

37 *Floridas of remote invasions*: an echo of *Blast* that suggests that Paris is 'invaded' by an American mildness from across the ocean: 'A 1000 MILE LONG, 2 KILOMETER Deep BODY OF WATER even, is pushed against us from the Floridas, TO MAKE US MILD' (*Blast* 1, p. 11).

38 *balzacian . . . comic*: in the 1842 'Avant-Propos' to his enormous fictional project *La Comédie humaine* Balzac wrote that he wished to emulate in fiction naturalists such as Georges Cuvier (1769–1832) and Étienne Geoffroy Saint-Hillaire (1772–1844) by attempting to understand 'Espèces Sociales comme il y a des Espèces Zoologiques' ('Social Species as though they were Zoological Species') (*Œuvres complètes, Études de Mœurs: Scènes de la vie privée, 1* (Paris: Édition Louis Conard, 1953), p. xxvi).

Petit Suisse: an unripened soft cheese from the Normandy region, literally Fr. 'little Swiss', served in individually sized cylinders and either seasoned with herbs or sweetened and eaten as dessert.

Luxembourg Gardens: The Jardin du Luxembourg, the largest public park in Paris, located in the 6th arrondissement.

39 *Venus of Milo*: a Hellenic statue from the late second century BC, discovered in 1820 on the Aegean isle of Melos. A popular tourist destination at the Louvre and one of the most recognizable pieces of art in the world.

westphalian: adj., from Westphalia, a historical region and former duchy of west-central Germany east of the River Rhine.

air-baths: exposing one's naked body to the air, thought by theorists and practitioners to offer benefits for physical and mental health.

sanguine of an Italian master: a drawing done with blood-red chalk or crayon, sometimes used for preliminary studies for oil paintings. Used extensively by artists of the Italian Renaissance, including Leonardo da Vinci, who made sanguines as sketches for *The Last Supper*.

Dryad-like on one foot: like a tree nymph of Greek mythology, portrayed in the Pre-Raphaelite painting *The Dryad*, painted in 1884–5 by Evelyn De Morgan (1855–1919) as standing with one foot on the ground and one foot in the hollow of the tree.

40 *bourgeois-bohemian*: Lewis's coinage for a way of life that claims to be radical but that recapitulates the middle-class mores against which it claims to rebel.

Islands of the Dead: *Die Toteninsel*, a nightmarish painting by the Swiss painter Arnold Böcklin (1827–1901). It exists in five different versions, all of which portray an isolated rocky island with 'gigantic cypresses' in the centre, and a small boat moving towards it in which stand a white-clad oarsman—perhaps Charon, the boatman of the dead from Greek mythology—and what appears to be a coffin.

brass jars . . . Normandy: souvenirs from the northern region of France known for its copper and coppersmithery; brass is an alloy of copper and zinc.

sinking feeling: i.e. Bertha's domestic decorations are a distressing manifestation of her middle-class taste.

41 *Klinger*: a work by Max Klinger (1857–1920), German Symbolist painter and sculptor.

43 *bouffonic*: Lewis's coinage, presumably 'comic, ridiculous', from Fr. *bouffe* (in the sense of *l'opéra bouffe*, 'comic opera'), or Eng. 'buffoon'.

'Berthe' . . . 'Oui': Fr., 'Bertha, you're a good girl!' 'You think so?' 'Yes.' In this context *brave* is a weak compliment, even slightly pejorative.

Schatzes: Ger., 'sweethearts', lit. 'treasures'. The proper German plural is *Schätze*; Tarr pluralizes *Schatz* as though it were an English noun.

44 *coup de foudre*: Fr., 'love at first sight'. The context of smashed icons suggests, however, that Lewis is calling upon the phrase's literal meaning, 'a stroke of lightning'.

eikon: alternative spelling of 'icon', an image or likeness, particularly associated with religious images of the Eastern Orthodox Church.

'Vous . . . Geschmack': Fr. and then Ger., lit. 'You are to my taste', i.e. 'You're my type'. Bertha's use of the formal *vous* to a male lover is not unusual for French speaker-address of the period, despite her use of the informal *Du* in German.

caravanserai: an Eastern roadside inn, a large quadrangular building with a spacious court in the middle, where travellers by caravan could rest from the day's journey.

Pasha . . . incog.: a Turkish officer of high rank; abbreviated adv. meaning 'incognito', 'with one's real name and identity disguised'. The theme of the disguised ruler circulating among his people is a staple of both Eastern and Western folk tales and plays.

44 *villégiature*: Fr., 'holiday, vacation', in parallel with 'caravanserai' here short for *lieu de villégiature*, 'holiday spot'.

Khalife: alternative spelling for French *calife*, a caliph or the chief civil and religious ruler of a Muslim country. A caliph figures prominently in the titular parable of Lewis's essay on art and architecture *The Caliph's Design* (1919).

45 *Hymen*: the god of marriage in Greek and Roman mythology, represented in art as a boy crowned with flowers and carrying a burning bridal torch.

46 *'Oh dis Sorbert . . . Dis!'*: Fr., 'Oh, tell me Sorbert! Tell me! Do you love me? Do you love me? Tell me!' Bertha's shift to the informal *tu* marks her sudden desperation.

'Oh . . . m'aimes!': Fr., 'Oh, tell me. Do you love me? Tell me that you love me!'

Schopenhauer: German philosopher Arthur Schopenhauer (1788–1860), best known for his work *Die Welt als Wille und Vorstelung* (1818, *The World as Will and Representation*). Schopenhauer was notoriously hostile to women, and in his essay 'Über die Weiber' (1851, 'On Women'), he writes: 'Women are qualified to be the nurses and governesses of our earliest childhood by the very fact that they are themselves childish, trifling, and short-sighted, in a word, are all their lives grown-up children; a kind of intermediate stage between the child and the man, who is a human being in the real sense' (*Parerga and Paralipomena: Short Philosophic Essays*, vol. ii, trans. E. F. J. Payne (Oxford: Clarendon Press, 1974), 614–15).

astral baby: in the late-nineteenth-century hermetic practice of theosophy the 'astral plane' was considered to be the next step above the terrestrial or sensible world. The 'astral body' was a sort of psychic body or aura made up of emotions, as the physical body was composed of matter.

49 *Ganymed*: a 1774 poem by German writer Johann Wolfgang von Goethe (1749–1832). Dealing with the mythic seduction of the boy Ganymede by Zeus, who is disguised as Spring, the poem was also familiar as the basis of art song settings by Austrian composers Franz Schubert (1797–1828) and Hugo Wolf (1860–1903). Tarr reads the first stanza beginning with the second line:

> All round me, you glow upon me,
> Oh spring, oh my lover!
> With the rapture of a thousand loves
> It thrusts at my heart,
> This sacred sense
> Of your eternal ardour,
> Oh infinite beauty!

(trans. David Luke, *Goethe: Selected Poetry* (London: Penguin Books, 2005), pp. 7, 9)

50 *Armageddon*: the place of the last decisive battle at the Day of Judgement in the Book of Revelation in the New Testament, thus, allusively, any final cataclysm.

54 *more metropolitan speech*: in a more urbane and sophisticated manner.

56 *earliest Science . . . holes*: Plutonism, an early school of geology in the eighteenth century associated with Scottish scientist James Hutton (1726–97), theorized that sedimentary rocks were forced to the surface by earthquakes and volcanoes, which were created by pressure originating from a subterranean molten core.

amazon: member of a tribe of warrior women in Greek mythology.

58 *Geschmack*: Ger., literally 'taste', in this context, 'fondness'.

59 *redskin impassibility*: a stereotype about the Native American peoples taken from nineteenth-century fiction and ethnography. See, for instance, a passage from *The Deerslayer* (1841), the popular American novel by James Fenimore Cooper (1789–1851): 'It is well known that the American Indians, more particularly those of superior characters and stations, singularly maintain their self-possession and stoicism . . . Chingachgook had imbibed enough of this impassibility to suppress any very undignified manifestation of surprise' (New York: D. Appleton & Company, 1901), 333.

game of grabs and dashes: obscure: perhaps a version of 'grab', a children's card game listed in the *New English Dictionary* (1900), in which two or more cards of equal value are placed on the table and the player who is quickest to recognize and grab them adds them to his own hand. Or perhaps a game such as 'capture the flag', where both players try to seize a prize held by the opposition, and dash away before the opponent can tag him or her 'out.'

60 *a cat may look at a king*: English proverb. Despite his far greater status a king has no power over the behaviour of a cat—thus, 'I can do what I want despite what you may wish.'

61 *Breton*: the historic Celtic language and culture of the inhabitants of Brittany, a region of northern France adjacent to Normandy.

62 *antediluvian*: adj., extraordinarily old; literally, from before the time of Noah's Flood.

64 *'FRAC'*: in Fr., It., and Sp., a formal jacket for evening wear, comparable to Ger. *frack*, and the English 'frock coat'.

Kreisler: Otto Kreisler's first name derives from Otto von Bismarck (1815–98), the Prussian statesman and the architect of a unified Germany who was known as 'The Iron Chancellor'. His surname comes from the literary character Johannes Kreisler, a tormented and increasingly eccentric composer who appears in the work of German Romantic author and composer E. T. A. Hoffmann (1776–1822), most notably in the essay *Des Kapellmeisters Johannes Kreislers musikalische Leiden* (*The Conductor Johannes Kreisler's Musical Sufferings*, 1814), later included as the opening section of *Kreisleriana* (1814–15), and the novel *Lebensansichten des Katers Murr nebst Fragmentarischer Biographie des Kapellmeisters Johannes Kreisler in Zufälligen Makulaturblättern* (known in English by the abbreviated title *The Life and Opinions of the Tomcat Murr*) (1819, 1821). Hoffmann writes of his Kreisler, 'His friends maintained that in his formulation nature had tried a new recipe but that the experiment had gone wrong . . . that balance which is essential to the artist, if he is to survive in this world . . . had been destroyed' (*E. T. A. Hoffmann's Musical Writings*, ed. David Charlton, trans. Martyn Clarke (Cambridge: Cambridge University Press, 1989), 79).

64 *ratiocination*: the process of reasoning.

Mont-de-Piété: a public pawnshop, literally Fr. 'mount of piety', authorized and controlled by the French government, that lent money at reasonable rates, particularly to the poor.

necropolis: from Gk., 'city of the dead', an ancient burial ground, especially one with elaborate tombs.

65 *Gillette blade*: a men's safety razor, patented in 1904, manufactured by the Gillette Safety Razor Company of Boston, Massachusetts.

bismarckian Prussian: a product of military Prussia, a historic state of northern Germany, who has been trained in the tradition of Bismarck. Prussians prided themselves on their organization, discipline, and obedience to authority; others, particularly outside Germany, associated Prussians with regimentation, repression, and arrogance.

german student . . . duels: the *Mensur*, or student duel fought with swords, as practised by German fraternities through the late nineteenth and early twentieth centuries; a scar from such a match was seen as a badge of honour. Such duels were so common among German students that nineteenth-century university administrators sold confiscated student weapons to local garrisons of the military.

droop: in the early nineteenth century the Prussian guard wore large moustaches, which became essential to Bismarck-era military fashion—and which gave birth to a European industry of combs, brushes, and waxes with which to groom them.

66 *Pas de Calais*: a *département* (administrative division) of northern France.

pop: chiefly British slang, 'to pawn'.

'*Je ne sais pas vous savez!*': Fr., 'I don't know, you know!' The suppression of an expected comma in dialogue is a feature of Lewis's style of the late 1920s, particularly when transcribing inane speech, as frequently in *The Apes of God* (1930).

67 *serried*: adj., pressed close together, like a rank of soldiers.

68 *Get your father off on your fiancée*: an echo of the novel *The Brothers Karamazov* (1880) by the Russian author Fyodor Dostoyevsky (1821–81), in which Dmitri, the oldest of the brothers, vies with his father Fyodor for

the favours of the young woman Grushenka. This violent rivalry leads to Dmitri's conviction for his father's murder.

69 *Gare de Lyon*: one of Paris's six large railway stations, which offers mainly train service to the south.

Goths . . . second century: the Gothic Wars actually took place from AD 376 to 382, and Rome was sacked by King Alaric I and the Visigoths in AD 410. It is ironic that Kreisler blames a Germanic people for the degeneration of civilized Rome.

'Un Viagre!': Kreisler is asking in a heavy German accent for *un fiacre*, a hackney-coach or cab, so named because in seventeenth-century Paris the first carriages for hire were stationed at the Hôtel de St Fiacre.

70 *Big Boulevards*: 'Les Grands Boulevards' refers to eight large streets— Madeleine, Capucines, Italians, Montmartre, Poissonière, Bonne Nouvelle, St-Denis, and St-Martin—that stretch across Paris from the Madeleine to the Place de la Bastille.

'Paris by Night': a phrase associated with the seamy side of Parisian tourism, with implications ranging from the innocent admiring of city lights to indulging in sex for hire. As early as 1871 a London publication titled *Paris by Night* offered as part of its subtitle 'A Description of the Casinos, Ball-Rooms, Cafés Chantants, and "Fast" Resorts of the Pleasure Seekers, Grisettes, and "Demi-Monde" of Paris', and noted that the Paris of the time had upwards of thirty-five thousand prostitutes (cover reproduced in David Price, *Cancan!* (London: Cygnus Arts, 1998), 12).

71 *that side of the town*: the Right Bank and Montmartre, as opposed to the Left Bank, home to artists and students.

kokotten: Ger., 'cocottes', women of loose morals, prostitutes. In *Blast* 1 Lewis blasts France's 'Naively seductive Houri salon-picture Cocottes' (1, p. 13).

Berck-sur-Mer: a commune of northern France, in the *département* of Pas-de-Calais.

73 *Sagraletto*: obscure: perhaps a dialectical form of It. *sacrilegio*, 'sacrilege', or a phonetic rendering of *dissacra letto* ('bed desecrator') with the first syllable elided. *Sporco Tedesco*, It., 'filthy German'.

75 *Gauguins . . . South Sea Islands*: Paul Gauguin (1848–1903), one of the leading French post-Impressionist painters. In 1891 Gauguin moved to Tahiti, and lived there for two years, returning to the South Seas in 1894 and dying on the Marquesas Islands. His painting came to reflect the colours and forms of the Pacific Islands, and his canvases of the period contain many striking images of Polynesian women.

Fauve: the Fauves (from Fr. 'wild beasts') were a loose association of twentieth-century painters who exhibited together in Paris from 1905 to 1908, including Henri Matisse (1869–1954) and André Derain (1880–1954). Their work was characterized by the use of vivid colours, and effects derived from applying paint to the canvas directly from tubes.

75 *cocotte*: see note to p. 71.

76 *'Also . . . gewesen?'*: Ger., 'So where is he then, our properly authentic Teuton? I guess he hasn't been here.'

78 *'tick'*: debt.

79 *The dot*: generally Fr., the dowry, a sum of money given to the groom as part of a marriage agreement, usually by the bride's family. The 'obscurity' of the dowry—its size or origin—implies some additional and unspecified irregularity in the affair.

80 *Magog of Carnival*: Gog and Magog were traditional figures of Carnival, Old Testament giants, in some traditions associated with the ancient Aryan peoples, whose names appear in the Book of Revelation to designate nations who shall war after the Millennium: 'And when the thousand years are expired, Satan shall be loosed out of his prison. And shall go out to deceive the nations which are in the four quarters of the earth, Gog and Magog, to gather them together to battle: the number of whom *is* as the sand of the sea' (Revelation 20: 7–8, King James translation).

'Sacré Otto vas!': Fr., properly 'Sacré Otto va!', 'Oh, you Otto!'

the Academy: the Académie des Beaux-Arts (Academy of Fine Arts), created in 1803 as one of the five academies of the Institut de France.

81 *'J'ai . . . temps!'*: ungrammatical French: 'I've lost the time! . . . I've lost my time!'.

'Qu'est-ce . . . quel genre!': Fr., 'How did he put it? He lost his time? Indeed! . . . That's a first! What a character!'

82 *côtes de pré salé*: chops from a lamb that was raised on the salt marshes of Brittany and Normandy. Considered by some connoisseurs to be the finest such meat in the world, and thus of higher quality than one might expect from a 'tranquil little creamery'.

military morning suit: the Prussian military equivalent of the morning coat, a men's jacket with tails. A degree less formal than the full 'frac', the morning suit was considered to be appropriate wear for daytime formal events. Kreisler is exceedingly overdressed for his surroundings.

Charivari . . . The Brush: a confused cacophony, from the French folk custom of banging cans and creating other noisy distractions under the window of newly married couples, referring here to the mismatched and clashing attire of the student artists.

83 *storm and shock*: lit. trans. of Ger, *Sturm und Drang*. See note to p. 200.

84 *dervish performance*: a dervish is a follower of an order of Sufism, a mystical order of Islam. The Mevlevi order of dervishes are known as the 'whirling dervishes' because of the spinning ritual dance they perform as part of their religious practice.

burnous: a cloak or mantle with a hood, similar to an article of clothing worn in North Africa by Arabs and Berbers.

86 *de profundis*: Lat., 'out of the depths', the first words of Psalm 130, 'De profundis clamavi', 'Out of the depths I cried'. By association, any cry from the depths of misery or degradation.

'smokkin': Fr. and Eng. by adoption, a 'smoking' or 'frac', 'formal evening jacket'. The spelling is a phonetic approximation of Kreisler's attempt at French.

87 *Korps-student*: a student belonging to a German duelling society.

'das Weib': Ger., 'Woman', carrying from the later nineteenth century on an increasingly generic and largely pejorative connotation.

88 *stormy petrel*: proverbially, one who brings discord or trouble; from the sea-bird the 'storm' or 'stormy petrel', associated in sailors' folklore with storms at sea.

91 *blood and iron*: a phrase associated with Bismarck, who gave a speech to the Prussian lower house of Parliament or *Lantag* on 30 September 1862 in which he claimed 'Germany does not look to Prussia's liberalism, but to her power. . . . Not by speeches and majorities will the great questions of the day be decided . . . but by iron and blood.' History misremembers the concluding terms in reversed order. (Cited in Louis L. Snyder, *The Blood and Iron Chancellor* (Princeton: D. Van Nostrand and Company, Inc., 1967), 127; trans. from *Die politische Reden des Fürsten Bismarck*, ed. Horst Kohl (Stuttgart, 1892–1904), ii. 29–30.)

92 *Bonnington Club*: possibly named in imitation of the Bonnington Hotel in Bloomsbury, which opened in 1911, or, with slight misspelling, in honour of English Romantic painter Richard Parkes Bonington (1802–28), who attended the École des Beaux-Arts in Paris. Both possibilities suggest the incursion of an alien British aesthetic sensibility into the heart of Paris.

93 *'Eh bien! . . . comme toi—!'*: Fr., 'Well! If everybody thought as you do—!'

'Où est . . . Tu ne le vois pus?': Fr., 'Where's Mr Vokt? . . . What? He has no money? That's not true. Don't you see him anymore?' The appearance of *pus* instead of *plus* represents a dialectical elision: the word appears as *'p'us'* in the 1918 Egoist edition.

94 *Rue de la Gaieté*: a street in Montparnasse, in the 14th arrondissement.

Petit Parisien: a prominent French newspaper of a conservative bent published between 1876 and 1944 and, despite its name, having at one time the largest newspaper circulation in the world.

Midi: the southern regions of France.

Arras: the capital of the Pas-de-Calais *département* in northern France.

95 *Mensch*: Ger., 'man', in the sense of 'human', i.e. 'What does it mean to be a Man?' The question echoes the claim of German philosopher Immanuel Kant (1724–1804) that the question 'Was ist der Mensch?' ('What is man?') is the most important of the four fundamental questions of philosophy, and the ultimate referent of the other three, which are 'What can I know? What ought I to do? What may I hope?' (Kant, *Lectures on*

     Logic, trans. and ed. J. Michael Young (Cambridge: Cambridge University Press, 1992), 538).

99 *Observatoire*: the national astronomical observatory of France, located in the 14th arrondissement, south of the Latin Quarter.

100 *'tick' account*: a running tab at a bar or restaurant.

     Atelier: an artist's workshop or studio.

     horse-meat chariot: horse meat has long been an accepted food in France, particularly among the poor. In 1866 the French government legalized the eating of horse meat and created special horse butchers' shops called *boucheries chevalines*.

102 *Massier*: a student at an atelier who is elected by his peers to act as secretary and treasurer for the studio, also responsible for posing the models.

     as living statues do in ballets: the statue who comes to life was a popular feature of ballet and melodrama from the time of *Pygmalion* (1762) by Swiss philosopher and composer Jean-Jacques Rousseau (1712–78). The animation of inanimate figures was also a recurrent feature of late nineteenth-century and early twentieth-century ballets, such as *Coppélia* (1870) by Léo Delibes (1836–91); *The Nutcracker* (1892) by Pyotr Ilyich Tchaikovsky (1840–93), which is based on a story by E. T. A. Hoffmann; *Petrushka* (1911) by Igor Stravinsky (1882–1971); and *From Dust Till Dawn* (1917) and *The Truth about the Russian Dancers* (1920) by Arnold Bax (1883–1953).

104 *gyrating . . . Fêtes*: a carousel, a French invention of the seventeenth century, found in many Parisian parks. The 'Fêtes' in question may be either the *fête foraines*, seasonal carnivals that date from the Middle Ages and reached the height of their popularity at the end of the nineteenth century, or specifically the Place de Fêtes, part of the Paris neighbourhood of Belleville in the nineteenth arrondissement which marks a spot where such regional fairs were held.

     Bosche: alternative English spelling of French *Bosch*, derogatory slang term for a German, used originally by French soldiers.

105 *swine-dog*: Eng. translation of Ger. *Schweinehund*, a strong insult.

108 *cinematograph and Reisebuch*: a movie theatre and a travel guide, such as a *Baedeker*.

     vortex: a whirling movement of matter, water, or gas around a central axis; metaphorically a situation that sucks one in and from which one cannot escape. The key symbol of Vorticism, the avant-garde art movement that Lewis created before the First World War.

110 *Maenads*: in Greek myth the frenzied female followers of Dionysus, the god of wine and ecstatic experience; capable of peaceful coexistence with nature when left alone, but when spied upon capable of tearing apart cattle—and Pentheus, the king of Thebes—with their bare hands.

'*Wer . . .*' '*. . . Fräulein*': Ger., 'Who is it?' 'Mr. Kreisler, dear lady!' Kreisler's German construction is unusual—*Der Herr* would typically be used to refer to a third party, not oneself.

111 *Fontenay des Roses*: properly Fontenay-aux-Roses, a commune in the south-western suburbs of Paris.

112 *the 'Concert' of Giorgione*: the 'Pastoral Concert' (*Fiesta campestre*, *c*.1510), one of a handful of known paintings by Giorgio Barbarelli da Castelfranco (*c*.1477–1510), painter of the Italian Renaissance. An inspiration for the painting *Le Déjeuner sur l'herbe* (1863) by Édouard Manet (1832–83), it is now considered to be in part or in whole the work of Giorgione's student Titian (1485–1576).

antimacassar: a covering placed over the back of furniture to prevent it from being stained by macassar, a popular type of hair oil. Associated with the stodginess of traditional Victorian and Edwardian decor.

113 *Jura*: a popular tourist destination, a system of mountain ranges that covers both sides of the Franco-Swiss border, extending from the Rhône to the Rhine rivers.

114 *Peter the Great*: Peter I (1672–1725), tsar of Russia from 1682 to 1725.

raree show: a street show or spectacle.

Great Russian and Little Russian: terms used in the nineteenth century to differentiate between the 'Great Russian' language and culture as opposed to the 'Little Russian' language and culture of the territory of Ukraine.

115 *Quattrocento*: the fifteenth century as a period of art and architecture in Italy. Literally It., 'four hundred', used as shorthand for 'the 1400s'.

118 *Paul Verlaine . . . old age*: French Symbolist poet (1844–96) whose scandalous life included a homosexual relationship with the younger poet Arthur Rimbaud (1854–91), whom he wounded with a revolver during a jealous rage in 1873. In his later life Verlaine degenerated into drug addiction, alcoholism, and poverty. His 'old age' could have been no older than a debauched 51.

119 '*Reformkleide*': properly *reformkleid*, Ger., literally 'reform dress', an unstructured dress than did not require a corset to be worn underneath. Favoured by many *Jugendstil* artists and their wives—many of the subjects painted by Gustav Klimt (1862–1918) are portrayed in *reformkleider*—but derided as ugly by others, particularly depending upon the physique of the wearer. See, for instance, a description from a novel of the period: 'the awful reformkleid was in vogue, and fat German women were displaying themselves in lumps and creases and billows and sections that rolled like the untrammelled waves of the sea' (Gertrude Franklin Horne Atherton, *The White Morning* (New York: Stokes, 1918), 186).

122 '*Homme sensuel! . . . Homme égoïste!*' Fr., 'Sensualist! . . . Selfish!'

122 *siberian exile*: Siberia is a large northern territory of Russia known for its formidably harsh winters, and was used from the early seventeenth century as a penal colony and place of internal exile.

124 *bona-fides*: guarantees of good faith.

126 *megrim*: a headache, also specifically a migraine headache.

128 *Rue de Rennes*: a street in the 6th arrondissement.

'pious mountains': a literal rendering into English of *monts-de-piété*, the government pawnshops.

'Smokkin' . . . *complets*: inaccurate Fr., 'a full ensemble of men's formal wear'.

stoop to Folly: allusion to the poem 'Song (When Lovely Woman Stoops to Folly)' which first appeared in the novel *The Vicar of Wakefield* by Oliver Goldsmith (*c*.1730–74):

> When lovely woman stoops to folly,
> And finds too late that men betray,
> What charm can soothe her melancholy,
> What art can wash her guilt away?
>
> The only art her guilt to cover,
> To hide her shame from every eye,
> To give repentance to her lover,
> And wring his bosom—is to die.

(*Collected Works of Oliver Goldsmith*, iv (Oxford: Clarendon Press, 1966), 379).

flapper: although generally associated with the slender, stylish, and unconventional young women of the 1920s, the *Oxford English Dictionary* lists the use of 'flapper' as early as 1903, to refer to 'a young woman, esp. with an implication of flightiness or lack of decorum'.

'Get thee to a nunnery!': Hamlet to Ophelia in Shakespeare's *Hamlet*: 'Get thee to a nunn'ry, why woulds't thou be a breeder of sinners?' (III. i. 120). 'Nunnery' is usually taken to mean a brothel; Ophelia addresses Hamlet as 'my lord' five lines before.

129 *simoom*: a strong desert wind that occurs in Arabia and the Sahara.

130 *conservatory*: a greenhouse, particularly for delicate plants.

131 *'for it'*: 'done for'.

Love's horns: an allusion to a song from Act 2, Scene 1 of the play *The Bride's Tragedy* (1822) by Thomas Lovell Beddoes. The song portrays Love as a hunter, and begins 'A ho! A ho! | Love's horn doth blow, | And he will out a-hawking go' (*The Works of Thomas Lovell Beddoes* (Oxford: Oxford University Press, 1925), 184).

décor Versaillesque and polonais: interior decoration associated with Versailles, an opulent French palace expanded by Louis XIV in the seventeenth century; the 'polonais' decor in question may be polonaise carpets,

Persian products of the late sixteenth and early seventeenth centuries that were bought by aristocratic collectors from Poland and were among the first such carpets displayed in Europe. It may also refer more generally to the elements of Baroque and Rococo design shared by Versailles with some seventeenth-century Polish art and architecture, which can be seen particularly in the city of Kraków.

132 *en pleine abstraction*: Fr., literally 'in the state of abstraction', with the apparent meaning 'having lost touch with reality'. A play on words that mixes the practice of the Impressionist artists of painting *en plein air*—'in the open air'—with the incompatible practices of abstract painting.

133 *faun*: in Roman mythology, a rural deity associated with lust, portrayed as half-human, half-goat.

satyric: adj., 'like a satyr', the Greek equivalent of the faun.

weibliche Seele: Ger., 'feminine soul', a crudely essentializing term associated with late-nineteenth-century pre-Freudian German sexologists such as Karl Heinrich Ulrichs (1825–95) and Richard von Krafft-Ebing (1840–1902), author of *Psychopathia Sexualis* (1886).

135 *Comme toute la Pologne!*: 'Ivre comme toute la Pologne' ('drunk as all of Poland'), French proverb for being very drunk indeed.

Mephistopheles: a name for the devil, particularly the demon of the Faust legend, whose best-known manifestation appears in the play *Faust* (1808–32) by Johann Wolfgang von Goethe.

136 *'Merry Widow' waltz*: a popular tune from the 1905 operetta *The Merry Widow* (Ger., *Die lustige Witwe*) by Austro-Hungarian composer Franz Lehár (1870–1948).

Bauern Ball: properly *Bauernball*, a peasant's ball (literally Ger. 'Farmer's dance'), a rustic dance typical of the Tyrol, or a German social event held in imitation of such an event, where attendees wear costumes representing the varied rural areas of the German-speaking countries.

137 *berserker warrior*: an ancient Norse warrior known for frenzied and savage fighting: the origin of the modern English work 'berserk'.

140 *'Lass' mich doch, gemeine alte Sau!'*: Ger., 'Leave me alone, you swinish old hag' (lit. 'common old sow').

Gadarene Swine: the New Testament Gospels of Matthew, Luke, and Mark narrate how Jesus exorcized a group of demons from a possessed man in Gadara, casting them into a herd of pigs: 'And he said unto them, Go. And when they were come out, they went into the herd of swine: and, behold, the whole herd of swine ran violently down a steep place into the sea, and perished in the waters' (Matthew 8: 32, King James translation).

141 *A FEST . . . LAUGHTER*: an anti-Romantic echo of the final line of 'Ode: Intimations Of Immortality from Recollections of Early Childhood' (1803–6) by English poet William Wordsworth (1770–1850): 'To me the meanest flower that blows can give | Thoughts that do often lie too deep for tears.' See also p. 164.

141 *fifty-centime piece*: a coin worth half a franc. Very little money in a city where mailing a postcard cost 10 centimes. By comparison, the 1907 *Baedeker* suggests that tourists to Paris budget between 15 and 40 francs per day.

142 *ox-eye*: having large protuberant eyes, like those of an ox; used as an adjective ('ox-eyed') in Greek literature, particularly Homer, to describe the goddess Hera.

Gare St. Lazare: one of Paris's six large train stations, providing service to Normandy.

143 *red-headed . . . Iscariot*: in Christian iconography Judas, the betrayer of Jesus, is often portrayed as a redhead. In France red hair is known as *poil de Judas*.

Sorbett . . . final consonants: because the German Bertha has not learned to pronounce 'Sorbet' in the French manner as 'Sorbay', Tarr spells his pet name with a doubled final 't' to match his orthography to her mispronunciation.

144 *Dieppe*: a port on the English Channel, offering regular ferry service to Newhaven in England.

'Verdammte . . . Donnerwetter!': three German expletives meaning roughly 'Bloody hell', 'The Devil!' (lit. 'Lucifer match!'), and 'Damn!'

oaths of Goethe: aside from the occasional vulgarism in the early play *Götz von Berlichingen* (1773) and the *Walpurgisnacht* scene of *Faust*, Goethe was not particularly associated with crude language. Lewis likely refers in general to the somewhat fusty nature of Bertha's expletives.

'Na . . . Ruhe denn!': Ger., 'Well then, leave me in peace!'

145 *femme*: Fr., in this context 'womanly'.

Salon d'Automne: a prestigious recommendation for Clara's work. The Salon d'Automne (literally Fr. 'autumn salon') was held annually in Paris in the autumn as an exhibition devoted to young artists. It was established in 1903 as an alternative to the conservative official Salon, and early such salons featured paintings by Paul Gauguin (1903 and 1906), Henri Matisse and the Fauvist painters (1905), and Paul Cézanne (1907).

English Review: a literary and cultural journal founded in 1908 and edited by Ford Madox Hueffer (1873–1939, later known as Ford Madox Ford). Lewis published some of his earliest fiction in the *English Review*: 'The "Pole"' in 2/6 (May 1909), 'Some Innkeepers and Bestre' in 2/7 (June 1909), and 'Les Saltimbanques' in 3/9 (August 1909). The passage quoted by Tarr is Lewis's invention.

147 *'Mademoiselle est triste? . . . salaud?'*: Fr., 'Are you sad, miss?' . . . 'Mr. Sorbet has upset you again, hasn't he?' 'Yes, ma'am, he's a bastard,' 'Oh, don't say that, miss: what do you mean, he's a bastard?' Bertha's French contains elementary errors—'il est un salaud' should be 'c'est un salaud'. The use of polite titles is explained by the 1907 *Baedeker* guide: 'It is

also customary to address persons even of humble station as '*Monsieur*', '*Madame*', or '*Mademoiselle*' (p. xxv).

149 *"souillures de ce brute"*: Fr., 'the defilements of that brute'.

152 *reform-clothes*: see note to p. 119.

153 *potty*: British English, 'mad'.

157 *fillip*: a smart tap or blow; something that rouses or excites.

159 '*contretemps*': disagreements, disputes, or mishaps; from a term in fencing, adopted from the French, 'a badly timed thrust'.

160 *quatsch*: nonsense, rubbish.

162 *Modern Girl*: term for an unconventional young girl, mainly used in the 1920s, often as an alternative to 'flapper'. The popular press of the day generally described the 'Modern Girl' as younger, more frivolous, and more overtly sexual than the so-called 'New Woman'. Anastasya's anachronistic status as 'Modern Girl' before the War reflects her social and sexual precocity.

neck: nerve, effrontery.

163 *Eldorado*: a fictitious country or city abounding in gold, believed by the Spanish and by Sir Walter Raleigh to exist upon the Amazon.

Gulf Stream: a warm and fast-moving current of the Atlantic Ocean that originates in the Gulf of Mexico.

164 '*Oh Schwein! . . . du hasslicher Mensch du!*': Ger., 'You pig! Pig! I hate you—I hate you! Pig! Ugh! You revolt me!' (lit. 'You ugliest of men, you!').

a Salon picture: a conventional and unimaginative painting, of the sort typically shown at the official French art exhibition of Paris, held since the early eighteenth century by the Académie des Beaux-Arts (see also note to p. 75).

Susanna-like breast: Susanna is a beautiful young wife in the Apocrypha who attracts two elders; they spy on her in the bath and accuse her of immorality when she refuses to sleep with them. The partially nude Susanna, usually portrayed under the lustful eyes of the elders, was a popular subject for paintings from the time of the Renaissance.

172 *answer . . . outrage*: i.e. if Bertha were home in Germany, a male family member or male admirer would challenge Kreisler to a duel. Although duelling had fallen out of practice in England by the mid-nineteenth century, in Germany and France it was common until the First World War.

173 *Place Clichy*: a square in the 8th arrondissement, north of the Seine and not far from Montmartre. It lies across town from Bertha and Montparnasse.

174 *bibliothèque*: a cabinet originally for the display of books, but used to display any kinds of *objets d'art*.

Place Pigalle: a neighbourhood in Montmartre, known as a centre of decadence. The 1907 *Baedeker* warns ladies that some cafés 'on the N. side of the Boulevard Montmartre should . . . be avoided, as the society there is far from select' (p. 22).

175 *handsome Wellington beak*: a large hooked nose like that of Arthur Wellesley, First Duke of Wellington (1769–1852). His nose was so prominent that geographical features from Scotland to India still bear the name 'Wellington's Nose' and 'The Duke's Nose'.

minor Tennysons: later and lesser poets who imitated the very Victorian dress and poetry of Alfred, Lord Tennyson (1809–92), Poet Laureate of England from 1850 until his death.

176 *hellenizing world . . . greek culture*: the Hellenistic Period (*c.*323–31 BC) was the last great phase of Greek art, following the death of Alexander the Great and the incorporation of the Persian empire into the Greek world. Tarr's painting suggests a struggle between late classicism and the Asian aesthetics it threatened to supplant—which in turn reflects the increasing influence of non-Western forms on artists of the period such as Picasso and the Vorticist sculptors Jacob Epstein (1880–1959) and Henri Gaudier-Brzeska (1891–1915).

two colours . . . curves: an apparent description of Lewis's *The Dancers* (1912).

poxed: syphilitic.

relief ships or pleasure boats: fanciful terms for prostitutes.

177 *'fire-ship'*: mainly eighteenth-century English slang: one suffering from venereal disease, especially a prostitute. From the wartime practice of loading a vessel with combustibles and explosives, and sending it adrift to destroy other ships.

Rive Gauche: Fr., the 'Left Bank' of the Seine, home to Montparnasse and Bertha.

180 *souvenirs*: in the sense of 'remembrances' rather than 'sentimental tokens'.

181 *oreiller... aimer*: Fr., 'Pillow of cool flesh where one cannot love', a description of the somewhat heavy women typically portrayed in paintings by Flemish painter Peter Paul Reubens (1577–1640) taken from Baudelaire's poem 'Les Phares' ('The Beacons'), number 6 of 'Spleen et idéal' in *Les Fleurs du mal* (*Œuvres Complete, Les Fleurs du mal, Les Épaves* (Paris: Louis Conard, 1930), 20).

182 *mercenary troops*: German soldiers for hire played a part in many European and New World wars, from the *Landsknechte* of the fifteenth and sixteenth centuries to the so-called 'Hessians' who fought for England during the American Revolution.

183 *parvenu*: an upstart; someone lacking the accomplishments or polish for their claimed social position.

184 *'Sorbet . . . jeune'*: Fr., 'Sorbet, you are *so young*.'

189 *Young Werther... Sorrows*: in Goethe's novel *Die Leiden des jungen Werther* (*The Sorrows of Young Werther*, 1774) the young hero is characterized by a 'blauen Frack mit gelber Veste' (Ger., 'blue coat and yellow vest') which he is wearing when he is found dying at the end of the novel, a suicide by pistol. The immense popularity of the book during the Romantic period led to what became known as *Wertherfieber* (Ger., 'Werther fever'): young men adopted Werther's colour scheme in fashion, and there was a sharp upturn in youthful suicides.

191 *'Peep-oh!'*: alternative spelling of 'Peep-bo', the child's game of peekaboo.

192 *Romany Rye*: a man who is not a Gypsy but associates with the Gypsies, 'rye' in the nineteenth-century slang sense of 'man, gentleman'. *The Romany Rye* (1857) is the title of an autobiographical book by George Borrow in which he details his semi-fictional experiences with the gypsies of England.

Land's End ... John o' Groats: popular usage to mean 'the whole of Great Britain'. Land's End marks the extreme south-westward point of Great Britain, in western Cornwall; John o' Groats marks the traditionally acknowledged, if not geographically accurate, extreme northern point of Scotland in north-eastern Caithness.

193 *The Tiller girls*: troupes of English dancing girls founded in 1901 by John Tiller (*c.*1851–1925). The original women's precision dance groups, they were trained in England and appeared in music halls and variety shows, including as resident dancers at Paris's Folies-Bergère. They were the direct inspiration for the Rockettes of New York.

bouf!: an interjection of surprise and dismay.

Fasching: a German carnival, a pre-Lenten celebration typified by revelry and humour.

194 *'Deutsches Volk—the folk that deceives!'*: in *Jenseits von Gut und Böse* (*Beyond Good and Evil*) the German philosopher Nietzsche proposes a fanciful etymology for the word *deutsch*: 'man soll seinem Namen Ehre machen—man heißt nicht umsonst das "tiusche" Volk, das Täusche-Volk ...' (*Friedrich Nietzsche: Werke in Zwei Bänden*, vol. ii. (Munich: Carl Hanser Verlag, 1973), sect. 244, p. 133; 'it's not for nothing that the Germans [*die Deutsche*] are called the *"tiusche"* people, the *"Täusche"* (deceptive) people ...' (trans. Judith Norman (Cambridge: Cambridge University Press, 2002), 137).

Wagner: the German composer Richard Wagner (1813–83), a notorious anti-Semite and author of the tract *Das Judenthum in der Musik* (*Jewishness in Music*, 1850), was nonetheless rumoured to have Jewish blood, perhaps because of Nietzsche's claim in *Der Fall Wagner* (*The Case of Wagner*, 1888) that Wagner had a Jewish father.

'See the Continental Press': the anti-British animus of the newspapers of Continental Europe was so apparent that Tarr cites this phrase as a cliché.

Such bias had been clear at least since the mid-nineteenth century: the *Quarterly Review* of 1848 called to task 'those whole classes of the continental press which are the most rancorously hostile to England' (83/165, p. 297). Even at the cusp of the twentieth century the British journal the *Nineteenth Century* would note 'The Continental Press is still intensely hostile' (no. 273 (Dec. 1899), 1029).

194 *malin*: Fr., 'cunning, sneaky'. Kreisler uses the masculine adjective where he should use the feminine, *maligne*.

   whip . . . too: a notorious quotation from *Also sprach Zarathustra* (*Thus Spake Zarathustra*, 1883–5), from the end of the section titled 'Von altern und jungen Weiblein' ('Of little women old and young'), 'Du gehst zu Frauen? Vergiß die Peitsche nicht!' (Friedrich Nietzsche: *Werke in Zwei Bänden*, Carl Hanser Verlag, vol. i (Munich: 589); 'You go to women? Do not forget the whip!', trans. Adrian del Caro (Cambridge: Cambridge University Press, 2006), 50).

196 *bubonic plague*: although apparently comically incongruous, the reference is surprisingly topical. There was a resurgence of plague beginning in 1894, and although the disease was largely confined to Asia, an International Sanitary Conference was held in Paris in 1903 to deal with the potential threat. This meeting and others led to the creation of the Office international d'hygiène publique (International Office of Public Health) in Paris in 1907, the forerunner of the current World Health Organization.

197 *revenant*: one who returns to a particular place, or one who returns from the dead.

   playing . . . gooseberry: to be an unwelcome third party at a lovers' meeting.

198 *rapprochement*: an establishing of harmonious relations.

   atmosphere . . . police-court romance: i.e. of a scene between criminals, or between an accused criminal and an interrogating officer, in a popular crime novel (Fr., *roman policier*).

   casanovaesque stage-coach journey: Giacomo Casanova (1725–98), Italian womanizer and author, whose name became emblematic for the suave seducer. His posthumously published *Histoire de ma vie* (*Story of My Life*, first published in French, 1826–38) is one of the earliest records of extensive travel through Europe via stagecoach. An English translation by Arthur Machen appeared in 1894.

200 *revolutionary storm and stress*: during the 1848 February Revolution, which overthrew the government of Louis Philippe and led to the creation of the short-lived Second Republic in France (1848–52), a government commission on the problems of labour was established in the Luxembourg Palace. 'Storm and stress' is a common English translation of the German phrase *Sturm und Drang* (*Drang* more literally 'urge', or 'drive'), taken from the title of a 1776 play by German author Friedrich von Klinger (1752–1831). The phrase is associated with a pre-Romantic late eighteenth-century

German movement in literature and music in which formal innovation went hand in hand with intensified subjectivity, emotionalism, and rebellion against moral and social conventions. The phrase is frequently used in English, often ahistorically, to refer to Romantic turmoil of any kind.

Lycée Henri Trois: a double misremembrance on Lewis's part, in name and location: the Lycée Henri IV, one of France's most esteemed private schools, lies several blocks away from the Luxembourg Gardens, on Clovis Street in the Latin Quarter. Its grounds are not contiguous with the Gardens.

201 *his Park*: compare to Stephen Dedalus, the protagonist of *A Portrait of the Artist as a Young Man* by Irish novelist James Joyce (1882–1941), who feels similarly possessive of a Dublin park, describing his thoughts while 'Crossing Stephen's, that is, my green' (Harmondsworth: Penguin Books, 1992, p. 271).

'Elle . . . parchemins': Fr., 'She says the word, Anastase, born for eternal parchments.' A quotation from 'Prose pour Des Esseintes' (1885) by the French Symbolist poet Stéphane Mallarmé (1842–98). Called up by Anastasya's name, the phrase is obscure in the original, and in this context is less thematically significant than it is an example of Tarr's erudition.

202 *after a fashion true*: an allusion to the repeated refrain 'I have been faithful to thee, Cynara! In my fashion' from 'Non Sum Qualis Eram Bonae Sub Regno Cynarae' by English poet Ernest Dowson (1867–1900).

Suarès . . . Ibsen: the insight of André Suarès, French writer and critic (1868–1948), into the work of Norwegian playwright Henrick Ibsen (1828–1906). Suarès wrote two essays dealing with Ibsen for the *Revue des deux mondes* in 1903, and the book *Trois hommes, Pascal, Ibsen, Dostoïevski*, in which appears the sentence that Tarr paraphrases: 'Par tout le Nord, il règne une rhétorique d'esprit, qui répond à la rhétorique de mots en faveur au Midi' (Paris: Éditions de la Nouvelle Revue française, 1913, p. 96).

petits-maîtres: lit. Fr., 'small masters', in English a largely derogatory term for minor practitioners of the fine arts; also, by extension, dandies or fops.

203 *garden city . . . London:* Letchworth Garden City, known more commonly as Letchworth, is a town in Hertfordshire, England, that was founded in 1903 as the first manifestation of the urban-utopian ideas of Ebenezer Howard (1850–1928). The garden city was intended to offer the benefits of urban living without the crowding and squalor of the Victorian city, and was much mocked by the Press as a misguided liberal social experiment, although it was embraced both by area Quakers and the Arts and Crafts movement.

The Fabian Society was founded in 1884 and devoted to gradualist, non-Marxist collectivist thinking about social policy, taking its name from the Roman general Quintus Fabius Maximus Verrucosus (*c.*280–203 BC), who was known as *Cunctator* (Lat., 'The delayer') for his cautious tactics in war. The organization was founded in part by economist and reformer Sidney Webb (1859–1947), his wife Beatrice Webb (1858–1943), and Irish playwright George Bernard Shaw (1856–1950), and became the pre-eminent politico-economic intellectual movement of the Edwardian era.

Although Letchworth attracted a number of Fabian residents and had an active Fabian society, the Fabians were in fact against the founding of Letchworth, arguing that resources would be better spent to alleviate conditions in extant cities rather than in building new ones. Tarr uses 'Fabian' as a generic description for English socialist ideas.

203 *reform-dressed*: see note to p. 119.

204 *Jean-Jacques . . . natural man*: Jean-Jacques Rousseau, who particularly in the *Second Discourse* (1755, also known as *Discourse on the Origin and the Foundation of Inequality Among Men*) described the necessary losses entailed by civilization as opposed to the savage state of man. In *Blast* 1 Lewis blasts Victorian 'ROUSSEAUISMS' and 'bowing the knee to wild Mother Nature' (18–19).

205 *Bouillon*: literally Fr., 'broth', here referring to the first popular chain of restaurants, founded in 1855 by the butcher Pierre-Louis Duval (1811–70), who had the idea of offering a single menu item of meat and meat broth at a reasonable price to the food market workers of Les Halles. In the first years of the 1900s restaurateurs opened somewhat more upscale *bouillons* that featured fuller brasserie menus and frequently art deco interiors. It may be this new kind of *bouillon*, blending inexpensive food with a working-class heritage and advanced aesthetic sensibility, that attracts Tarr and Anastasya.

207 *cox of a boat*: short for 'coxswain', a boat's helmsman. Typically, as here, the steersman of a racing shell who sits facing the other rowers, motivates them with loud verbal directions, and coordinates their oar strokes.

209 *like the Cynic's dishonourable condition*: a member of a school of ancient Greek philosophy marked by contempt for worldly pleasure, founded by Antisthenes (445–365 BC), a student of Socrates, and usually assumed to take its name from the Greek word *kunikós*, 'dog-like'. The best-known of the Cynics, Diogenes of Sinope (*c.*404–323 BC), reportedly lived in a tub and committed publicly shameful acts to protest against the artificiality of society's comforts and taboos. His rude behaviour and disbelief in man's honesty made him a byword for misanthropy and harsh self-treatment—to the point where contemporary medicine refers to pathological physical self-neglect, particularly among the elderly, as 'Diogenes syndrome'.

210 *Quixote . . . giants*: in the two-volume comic novel *Don Quixote* (1605, 1615) by Spanish author Miguel de Cervantes Saavedra (1547–1616) a country gentleman, Alonzo Quijana, becomes obsessed with chivalric

romances and comes to believe that he is a knight, setting off on a series of picaresque adventures with his neighbour, Sancho Panza. In vol. i, chapter 8, he tilts at a group of thirty or forty windmills, believing them to be giants. Throughout the novel Quixote misidentifies the common people of his contemporary Spain as the lords and ladies of medieval romance.

211 *HOLOCAUSTS*: sacrificial burnt offerings, complete sacrifices. In the 1920s not yet associated with the mass killings of Jews by the Nazis in the late 1930s and 1940s.

comedian: a comic actor, but likely with an echo of Fr. *comédien*, any kind of actor, including a performer in tragedy.

Café des Sports Aquatiques: Fr., 'The Aquatic Sports Café'.

213 *Schoolgirl Complexions*: from the advertising slogan 'Keep that Schoolgirl Complexion', popularized by Palmolive soap in 1923. In his later writings such as *The Doom of Youth* (London: Chatto and Windus, 1932), 8), Lewis associates the phrase with society's increasingly politicized obsession with youth.

'Moonlight Sonata': the popular nickname for the Piano Sonata No. 14 in C sharp minor *'Quasi una fantasia'*, Op. 27 No. 2, by German composer Ludwig van Beethoven (1770–1827). Such an orchestral arrangement of classical music for cabaret performance was typical of the times, but also serves as another example of the debasement of particularly German Romantic art into middlebrow decoration.

214 *braves*: Native American warriors. On the stereotype of their impassivity, see the note to p. 59.

card upon a plate: a French duel required the formal exchange of calling cards. According to formal etiquette, a gentleman visiting another gentleman at a restaurant or hotel under ordinary circumstances would send in his calling card, often on a servant's silver tray, and wait in the reception area for his acquaintance to come and greet him. Refusal to greet the sender of the card meant rejection of the visitor's society, and ripping it up would have been a grave public insult.

218 *'five o'clock'*: a small late afternoon meal, in imitation of the British tea. The *Pall Mall Gazette* noted in the late nineteenth century that 'the little lunch, the five o'clock, imported from abroad, is now completely acclimatized at Paris' (quoted by the *New York Times*, 18 December 1885).

219 *blinded his opponent*: an absurdity, but possibly a distortion through gossip or imagination of the Russian having participated in a so-called 'blind duel', where only one of the two pistols is loaded.

second: a trusted representative for the participant in a duel, who carries and receives the challenge, arranges the time and place—usually at dawn—makes sure the weapons are equal and properly loaded, and ascertains that the duel is conducted fairly.

222 *justify the use of a revolver*: a matter requiring some nice distinctions in duelling etiquette, for the offence could be neither too slight nor too substantial. Two artists almost duelled in Paris in 1914 when the New York sculptor Edgar Macadams struck a blow at Waldemar George, Polish-French art critic and future contributor to the second issue of Lewis's journal *The Tyro* (1922), knocking him unconscious. George's seconds considered the blow to be too hard to fall under the rules of duelling rather than the purview of the law courts. George explained 'had Mr. Macadams slapped me or called me names swords or pistols would have been in order, but he gave me a knockout blow, which is a form of attack that they classify as a "coup d'apache", too violent for gentlemen to settle among themselves' (*New York Times*, 14 May 1914; for *apache*, see note to p. 252).

the french laws would sanction quite a bad wound: laws dealing with duelling in France were far more liberal than in Germany, because French duels seldom resulted in bloodshed or death—a subject of much derision by Germans, who took the culture of honour, and the bloodiness of its result, far more seriously than their French counterparts. A Frenchman noted in 1890 'when the duel takes place under conditions of irreproachable fairness, even though it should have a fatal issue, adversaries and witnesses escape most of the time unharmed from the tribunal' (quoted by Kevin McAleer, *Dueling: The Cult of Honor in Fin-de-siècle Germany* (Princeton: Princeton University Press, 1994), 184).

scottish solemnity: a national stereotype, associated, among other cultural attributes, with the extreme severity of Scottish Calvinist worship from the time of the eighteenth century.

223 *dummy*: one who acts as a tool for another.

224 *mountebank*: originally a charlatan or seller of dubious goods, or an itinerant street entertainer; more generally, one who makes false claims for personal gain.

225 *Sphinx*: an enigmatic or inscrutable person, from the monster of Greek mythology, having the head of a woman and the body of a winged lion, that terrorized the city of Thebes until Oedipus successfully answered the riddle it posed to all passers-by.

230 *Luitpold*: a famous café in Munich, once the city's most spectacular, named for Prince Luitpold of Bavaria (1821–1912). Lewis spent some time at this café with young German officers during a trip to Germany in 1906 (letter to his mother, *The Letters of Wyndham Lewis*, ed. W. K. Rose (Norfolk, Conn.: New Directions, 1963), Mar. 1906, p. 28).

232 *fortifications*: a fortification wall was built encircling Paris from 1841 to 1845, with a set of polygonal forts added as reinforcement during the late 1870s. Kreisler's taxi will pass the original wall, which was demolished only after the First World War, and probably the Fort Mont-Valérien, which overlooks the Bois de Boulogne (see note below). The modern Paris

ring road or *périphérique* was built in the 1970s in the space left by the demolished fortifications.

Bois: the Bois de Boulogne, a large park located along the western edge of the 16th arrondissement of Paris. The Bois and surrounds were a common setting for Parisian duels.

233 *fugue*: literally 'flight', a term from psychiatry, a reaction to shock that results in a patient's hysterical disassociation from normal identity.

'Browning': a semi-automatic pistol designed by American firearms designer John Moses Browning (1855–1926) and manufactured in Belgium; the Browning no. 2, manufactured in 1903, became a favourite police weapon, and was adopted by several European armies. The Browning became particularly notorious in 1914, when the south Slav nationalist Gavrilo Princip (1894–1918) used a model 1910 pistol to assassinate the Archduke Ferdinand, starting the First World War.

234 *khaki cigarette*: strong Russian cigarettes called *papirosi*, made with dull-brown coloured unfiltered papers that are stuffed with cheap tobacco, usually attached to a tubular cardboard holder. In his 1947 novel *Comrade Forest* Michael Leigh describes them as 'one-third tobacco, two-thirds mouthpiece' (New York and London: Whittlesey House, McGraw-Hill Book Co., 1947), 143).

revolution of 1906: peasant rioting, including the sacking and burning of manor houses, occurred in Russia in the summer of 1905 as part of the Revolution of 1905. After subsiding in late 1905, such rioting resumed on a large scale in 1906.

235 *oxide of bromium and aniseed*: a pill to calm the nerves and settle the stomach. Bromium had been used as a sedative since 1857, usually in the form of potassium bromide, although the 1910 *Practitioner's Medical Dictionary* by George Milbry Gould lists 'Bromid, Basic', 'a compound of a bromid with the oxid of the same base' used to 'allay nervous excitement' (Philadelphia: Blakiston's Son & Co., p. 215). Aniseed was used to treat gas and indigestion; because of its pleasant scent and taste, it was also used to mask the taste of other medicines.

236 *vitriol or syphilis*: two agents capable of inflicting extreme physical harm—concentrated sulphuric acid, and a venereal disease that in its late stages can cause a number of deformations, including the collapse of the cartilage of the nose.

237 *jujube*: a fruit-flavoured lozenge.

238 *body . . . woman*: many images of such beaus, from eighteenth-century paintings to Dresden figurines, feature a similar posture; see, for instance, the central figure of the French dancing master in the print 'The Levee' from *The Rake's Progress* by William Hogarth (1697–1764). However, the posture suggests the aggressiveness of German fencing as much as it does dancing.

239 *pilules*: small pills.

240 *'C'est bien . . . Laisse-moi'*: Fr., 'Fine, fine. Yes, I know. Let me alone.'

'Mais dépêche-toi... faire ici': Fr., 'Hurry up. There's nothing more for you to do here.'

241 *gargoyle Apollo*: a blend of a spout that projects from some Gothic buildings, such as Notre-Dame Cathedral in Paris, made in the shape of a grotesque animal or human figure, and the Greek god of light and the sun, who is often portrayed in art as a handsome young man.

one charge . . . twelve: as a rule duelling pistols were single-shot flintlock guns that required reloading between firings. The semi-automatic Browning could fire multiple rounds from a cartridge without reloading. The physician exaggerates, however: Brownings of the period could fire seven or eight rounds without reloading, whereas Brownings that could shoot a dozen rounds without reloading were not manufactured until 1935. Some duels were in fact, however, fought with Brownings before the First World War: see, for instance, the fictional duel between Settembrini and Naphta in *Der Zauberberg* (*The Magic Mountain*, 1924) by German novelist Thomas Mann (1875–1955).

244 *Saint Cloud*: a commune in the western suburbs of Paris, about 10 kilometres from the city centre.

245 *excuperate*: a word unattested elsewhere in the English language. Presumably, a coinage meaning 'expectorate', from Spanish *escupir* 'to spit'.

Meaux: a commune of Seine-et-Marne, in the metropolitan area of Paris, roughly 40 kilometres east-north-east from the city centre.

Rheims: English spelling of Reims, a city of the Champagne-Ardenne region of northern France, roughly 145 kilometres east-north-east of Paris.

Verdun: Verdun-sur-Meuse, a city and commune in north-east France, in the Lorraine region close to the German border.

Marcade: an apparently fictional town, possibly named after Eustache Marcadé (1390–1440), author of *La Passion d'Arras*, a massive French mystery play about the life and death of Jesus.

246 *'Qu'est-ce qu'il . . . Il n'y est pas'*: Fr., 'What do you want?' 'To see the superintendent.' 'You can't see him. He isn't in.' 'Foir le gommissaire' represents phonetically Kreisler's German-accented attempt to say 'Voir le commissaire.'

spies: France's hysterical fear of German spies, active from the 1870s through the Dreyfus affair of 1894—when a French officer was falsely accused of spying for Germany—reached a new peak in the late 1900s, stoked by both the yellow press and scaremongers in the French military. The *New York Times* reported on 12 September 1909 that 'French officials have seen a German spy in every shadow', and that there were then six spies caught in the act of collecting information from the Germans being held in a prison in Rheims ('German Spy Scare Now Rife in France').

huge foot-rules: most likely 2-foot carpenter's rules, standard tools of the trade. Strips of wood or metal with a straight edge used to assist workmen in making straight work while plastering or keeping surfaces in plane. Such devices folded into four 6-inch lengths for convenience in carrying.

Fritz: nickname for the German name 'Friedrich', used particularly by English soldiers during the First World War as a derogatory term for a German soldier, or by extension any male German.

tuel and killt man: 'I had a duel and killed a man'. Kreisler's heavily accented German French is represented as heavily accented German English.

247 *What a toupet!*: colloquial Fr., 'What nerve!', from the idiom *avoir du toupet*, 'to have the audacity'.

'En voilà . . . D'bout!': 'My word, here's someone who makes himself at home . . . Hey, buddy! You'd like to sleep in the open air? . . . Look here. You can't spend the night here. Upsy-daisy! Hurry up. Get up.'

248 *threatening an invasion*: a common fear among the French in the early twentieth century, intensified by French intelligence, who invented German invasion schemes in the late 1900s and attributed them to British intelligence in an attempt to solidify the alliance between France and England. Fear was also stoked by the popularity of a genre of fiction, the anti-German 'invasion novel', that emerged in England and France in the 1870s as a response to the Franco-Prussian War. A prominent example, *The Invasion of 1910* (1906), by the Anglo-French author William Le Queux (1864–1927), was a best-seller of the period.

contumelious Boche: insolent or disgraceful German.

249 *pick oakum*: to pull to pieces old tarry ropes, which were then used to make new ropes or to cover the planks of wooden ships to make them watertight, work that was very hard on the hands. A common occupation in Victorian and early twentieth-century prisons and workhouses.

250 *bituminous*: containing bitumen, a kind of pigment made from asphalt and oil, associated with the darkening and cracking of surfaces over time found in some paintings of the eighteenth to the mid-nineteenth centuries. It was also used in the world's earliest surviving photograph, taken in 1826 by the French inventor Joseph Nicéphore Niépce (1765–1833). The 'old picture' in question may be a time-damaged painting or an early photograph.

252 *apache, the coster-girl*: period slang for a member of a Paris street gang, by analogy with the Native American tribe; a female costermonger, one who sells food in the street from a barrel, a term sometimes used as a general term of abuse.

255 *the cure*: at German spa towns such as Bad Nauheim and Baden-Baden leisured Europeans who suffered from real or imagined health problems

'took the cure', which often involved drinking from the spa's mineral springs at prescribed intervals.

255 *had made himself 'de la partie'*: Fr., 'had joined in'.

256 *des fauves, des grands fauves*: Fr., 'of the wild cats, of the big wild cats', such as the tiger, but also with an inevitable echo of the bold aesthetic rather than sexual techniques of the Fauvist painters.

257 *Tintoretto mantle*: a loose, sleeveless cloak, often represented in exquisite detail in the paintings of Tintoretto (real name Jacopo Robusti, 1518–94), late-Renaissance Venetian painter.

open-work stockings . . . two-and-eleven-three the pair: lace or 'fishnet' stocking, then as now associated with overt sexuality. 'Two-and-eleven-three' (two shillings, eleven pence, and three farthings) was a common figure of the period used to mean 'inexpensive', if not 'cheap', and suggests that the stockings are of artificial silk, all of which adds to Anastasya's erotic credibility as a working-class 'genuine girl'.

Dago: an offensive term for a Spaniard or Italian, variant of the name 'Diego', at times used to disparage any foreigner.

Pantomime: a form of traditional popular British stage entertainment that tells a fairy-tale-like story, typically performed during the holiday season. The 'Principal Boy', or hero, is traditionally played by an attractive young woman costumed in a short, tight skirt, with fishnet stockings, and knee-high leather boots. At a time when female apparel typically reached down to the ankles, the dress of the Principal Boy had considerable erotic appeal for male viewers—particularly when she stood 'stern-on', with her back to the audience, allowing full masculine appreciation of her legs and posterior.

258 *imposs*: a colloquial abbreviation of the early 1920s for 'impossible' (Eric Partridge, *A Dictionary of Slang and Unconventional English*, 7th edn. (New York: The Macmillan Company, 1970)). An anachronism, given the pre-War setting of *Tarr*, perhaps to demonstrate that Anastasya is well ahead of her time even in her use of slang.

street-arabs: period term for homeless children and vagabonds who lived on the streets, generally used as an insult.

'The Man dreams but what the Boy believed': from 'The Cock and the Fox: Or, The Tale of the Nun's Priest, from Chaucer', in *Fables Ancient and Modern* by English poet John Dryden (1631–1700) (*The Major Works*, ed. Keith Walker (Oxford: Oxford World Classics, 2003), l. 336, p. 715).

260 *Can-Can exhibitionists*: a lively and risqué stage dance usually performed by a line of four women, known for its high kicks that exposed both petticoat and leg. Associated with such tourist night spots as the Moulin Rouge.

mohammedan eye: a lustful eye, from a persistent deprecatory stereotype in English culture about Moslems and 'The Turk', derived in part from the sexualized Houri of the Islamic paradise, and typified by such nineteenth-century erotica as *The Lustful Turk or Lascivious Scenes from a Harum* (1893).

Bovril-bathos: 'Bovril' is the trade name for a concentrated beef extract invented in 1889, usually diluted with hot water to make beef tea—thus, 'highly concentrated' bathos. Also, less commonly, a slang term for a brothel. Both meanings are likely implied here.

Romans: in the early years of the twentieth century, avant-gardists and intellectuals admired the pagan worship of sexuality while Christians condemned it, some attributing a number of pagan practices to the Romans in particular. For the latter see Sidney Calhoun Tapp, who wrote 'When our Lord came, the Christ found all the world bowed down to sex worship, and pagan priests consecrating sex-lust for money. The Roman empire and the Roman world were filled with it' (*The Truth about the Bible* (Kansas City, Mo.: Sidney C. Tapp International Biblical Society, 1916), 29).

mosaic code: usually capitalized: the ancient laws of the Hebrews, named after the prophet Moses, consisting of the injunctions found in the first five books of the Old Testament. The majority deal with sin and forms of uncleanliness in the mode that Ezra Pound termed 'the Mosaic negative' ('A Few Don'ts by an Imagiste', 1912).

261 *stage Whittington cat*: a popular animal character in a pantomime based loosely on the folk tales that accrued around Richard Whittington (*c.*1354–1423), medieval merchant and later Lord Mayor of London. In most versions the intrepid Dick Whittington gains fame and fortune through the rat-catching prowess of his cat, who is played by a costumed actor.

Brocken ghost-mouse: during the phantasmagoric *Walpurgisnacht* scene of Goethe's *Faust*, the protagonist breaks away from dancing with a young female witch when a red mouse hops out of her mouth. Commentators— and one of Havelock Ellis's case informants in *Studies in the Psychology of Sex* (1897–1910, vol. ii, History XIII)—interpret this moment as an emblem of extreme male fear of overt female sexuality.

The Brocken, a mountain peak in the Harz mountains in Germany and the scene's setting, receives its ghostly reputation from an optical illusion in which the light could project a climber's image forward onto a wall of mist, creating an enormous glowing spectre. This phenomenon was much commented upon in Romantic literature, particularly in *Die Harzreise* (1826) by Heinrich Heine (1797–1856).

the Duchess in Alice: a character in *Alice's Adventures in Wonderland* (1865), a fantasy by English author Lewis Carroll (real name Charles Lutwidge Dodgson, 1832–98) who speaks at times in confounding paradoxes, and treats Alice with alternating condescension and affection. She has a baby who turns into a pig under Alice's eyes, and shows little interest in the transformation—rather the reverse of Anastasya, who playfully objects to Tarr's reduction of her body to the abstract status of 'sucking-pig'.

262 *bis an den Rin—Geliebte*: all of Prussia: Ger., 'To the Rhine, beloved', although Tarr mistakes Germany's name for its own longest river, in German the *Rhein*, in French the *Rhin*, for which *Rin* may be a Germanic phonetic approximation.

Ding an sich: literally Ger., 'the thing in itself', a term used by Kant in *Kritik der reinen Vernunft* (*The Critique of Pure Reason*, 1781) to refer to the reality of the object independent of sensory experience.

harpie: usually 'harpy', a filthy, ravenous creature described in Greek and Roman mythology as having a woman's face and body and a bird's wings and claws. Used by association to mean a nagging or shrewish woman.

Boulevard Rochechouart: a road situated at the foot of Montmartre hill and to its south, in the 9th arrondissement.

'the face that launched a thousand ships': a reference to Helen of Troy in the play *The Tragical History of Doctor Faustus* (1st pub. 1604) by Renaissance English poet Christopher Marlowe (1564–93): 'Was this the face that launch'd a thousand ships | And burnt the topless towers of Ilium?' (*A-Text*, v. i. 90–1).

263 *Grail-lady or any phantom of the celtic mind*: the Lady of the Lake in Arthurian legend, a magical and misty figure who gives the sword Excalibur to King Arthur, or perhaps the enchantress Morgan le Fay. Celtic folklore is in general replete with female phantoms and fairies, many of which are described, for instance, in tales collected by the Irish poet William Butler Yeats (1865–1939) in *Fairy and Folk Tales of the Irish Peasantry* (1888).

accent of Minnesota . . . Steppes: Anastaya's multinational background, which combines her upbringing in the American Midwest with her Russian heritage.

Weltweisheit, Wesengefühl: Ger., 'worldly wisdom', and 'feeling for being' (properly *Wesensgefühl*). The term *Weltweisheit* was used regularly in late eighteenth-century German thought to denote the full scope of philosophy; the term *Wesensgefühl* appears in the work of late German metaphysicians such as Eduard von Hartmann (1842–1906) and Ludwig Klages (1872–1956).

expensive tripper's restaurant: a restaurant for wealthy tourists, by inversion of the common nineteenth-century phrase 'cheap-tripper', or budget traveller.

de puntos: a term from the sixteenth-century school of Spanish fencing, meaning thrusting at one another with rapiers or daggers (lit. Sp., 'at points'). See, for instance, Mercutio in Shakespeare's *Romeo and Juliet*, who warns of Tybalt's backhanded thrust, his *punto reverso* (II. iv. 26).

264 *Pompous Pilate*: a play on the name of Pontius Pilate, Roman procurator of Judaea (*c.*26–*c.*36), best remembered for presiding at the trial of Jesus and authorizing his crucifixion. Medieval English mystery plays often portrayed Pilate as a braggart who spoke in comically pompous rhetoric.

motif: Fr., and Eng. by adoption: a recurrent element in a design or work of art, particularly a significant theme or image.

'high,' yellow: an American racialist term, often used offensively, to refer to the light skin of mixed-race people who share some African ancestry.

socratically: in the spirit of philosophic inquiry represented by Socrates, presumably with an allusion to the eating and drinking of Plato's *Symposium*.

"all the world's a stage" . . .' 'It was an actor who said that': a quotation from *As You Like It* by William Shakespeare, spoken by the character Jaques (II. vii. 139). Shakespeare was a working actor who acted in supporting parts in many of his own plays.

265 *A mixed grill . . . dresser*: an opening dish of several grilled meats, named after the Quai de Montebello in the 5th arrondissement, which runs alongside Notre-Dame Cathedral; a main course of two free-range chickens; a desert soufflé made with strawberries, pineapple, and maraschino liqueur; and a closing basket of fruit. The most elegant meal of the novel, juxtaposed with no little irony against the austere abstraction of the conversation.

gibing: mocking, sarcastic.

267 *Roederer*: champagne produced by the house of Louis Roederer (1809–70) in 1833. In 1909 Roederer became the official supplier of champagne to the Imperial Court of Russia.

Mute inglorious Miltons: 'Some mute inglorious Milton here may rest | Some Cromwell guiltless of his country's blood', a line from 'Elegy written in a Country Churchyard' by English poet Thomas Gray (1716–71), a meditation upon the many whose talents remained unfulfilled and have died unrecognized by the world (*The Works of Thomas Gray in Prose and Verse* (London: Macmillan & Co. Ltd, 1884), 76).

268 *Diderot . . . Princesse de Clèves*: Denis Diderot (1713–84), French philosopher and writer. *La Princess de Clèves* (1678) was a novel by Madame de La Fayette (1634–93), but the princess of the anecdote in question was Catherine II of Russia, who is reported to have written to Marie Thérèse Rodet Geoffrin, 'Your Diderot is a very extraordinary man. I cannot get out of my conversations with him without having my thighs bruised black and blue. I have been obliged to put a table between him and me to shelter myself and my limbs from his gesticulation' (quoted in Arthur M. Wilson, *Diderot* (Oxford: Oxford University Press, 1972), 632).

269 *the links*: a golf course.

colour line: the imaginary line segregating the races. In 1903 African-American scholar and activist William Edward Burghardt (W. E. B.) Du Bois (1886–1963) wrote in *The Souls of Black Folk* 'the problem of the Twentieth Century is the problem of the color-line' (Chicago: A. C. McClurg & Co., p. vii).

269 *'No women pals?'*: i.e. 'No lesbian lovers?'

270 *"mauvais lieu"*: Fr., 'a brothel', literally 'a bad place'.

Homely: Tarr uses the word to mean 'inclined to domesticity', Anastasya uses it to mean 'physically unattractive'.

272 *acidulated demi-mondaine*: a woman of doubtful reputation whose outlook on life has soured.

Je fais de la réclame pour les Grecs!: Fr., 'I'm an advertisement for the Greeks', using a now-outdated French term for 'advertisement'.

ionian . . . hardly greek: Ionian sculpture, product of the Eastern region of ancient Greece. Known for giving the human body softer contours than in other Greek sculpture, although generally considered provincial and idiosyncratic when compared to the art of Athens.

273 *the Superman*: the *Übermensch* or superior man postulated by Nietzsche in *Also sprach Zarathustra*, a term first translated into English as 'Overman' in 1895 but given its more common English form by George Bernard Shaw in his 1906 play *Man and Superman*. Anastasya's phrase 'efficient chimpanzee' refers to the popularization (and partial distortion) of the theory of human evolution in *The Descent of Man* by English naturalist Charles Darwin (1809–82) but is also implicit in Nietzsche's prologue: 'What is the ape to a human? A laughing stock or a painful embarrassment. And that is precisely what the human shall be to the overman' (*Thus Spoke Zarathustra* (Cambridge: Cambridge University Press, 2006), 6).

274 *sabots*: Fr., wooden clogs traditionally worn by Breton peasants.

276 *enceinte*: Fr., 'pregnant'.

a Roland for his Oliver: two friends, the former dramatically heroic and the latter commonsensical, battle-comrades in the army of Charlemagne in the medieval French *chanson de geste* 'Le Chanson de Roland' ('The Song of Roland', *c.*1100). Roland ignores Oliver's advice that he summon reinforcements by blowing his horn in battle; later, when the battle is almost lost, Roland blows his horn and dies. Tarr implies that Bertha's pregnancy is another example of a self-defeating gesture performed too dramatically and too late.

277 *Kreisleriana*: the name both of the book by E. T. A. Hoffmann (see note to p. 64) and a major work for piano in eight movements that was inspired by Hoffmann, Op. 16 (1838) by German Romantic composer Robert Schumann (1810–56). In *Kreisleriana* Hoffmann writes of his protagonist 'In a disturbing way, his greatest suffering was frequently expressed in ludicrous terms' (*Musical Writings*, 124).

Wellington . . . traps: the Duke of Wellington supposedly predicted his defeat of Marshal Auguste Marmont's French forces at the battle of Salamanca on 22 July 1812, when he glanced at the troops through spyglasses from an observation post near where he was eating breakfast.

278 *Gainsborough and Goya*: English portrait and landscape painter Thomas Gainsborough (1727–88), and Spanish painter and printmaker Francisco

José de Goya y Lucientes (1746–1828). Great artists of very different sensibilities, impossible to blend. Gainsborough produced aristocratic canvases typified by formal perfection and evanescent colours, while Goya inclined, particularly in his late work, to proto-expressionist explorations of nightmare.

Juggernaut: an unstoppable force that crushes everything in its path, from Hindi *Jagannāth*, literally, 'lord of the world', a title of Vishnu.

mesmeric: hypnotic, from the idea of animal magnetism developed by Franz Anton Mesmer (1734–1815).

peculiar: i.e. because of the 'manliness' of her overt sexuality and superior intellect if Tarr allied himself with Anastasya he would feel like an intellectual 'pederast'. For the German intellectual lineage of Tarr's misogyny and distrust of accomplished women, see, for instance, Schopenhauer, who wrote 'Only the male intellect, clouded by the sexual impulse, could call the undersized, narrow-shouldered, broad-hipped, and short-legged sex the fair sex; for in this impulse is to be found its whole beauty . . . the most eminent minds of the whole sex have never been able to produce a single, really great, genuine, and original achievement in the fine arts, or to bring anywhere into the world a work of permanent value' ('On Women', *Parerga and Paralipomena*, 619–20) or Nietzsche, who writes in *Zarathustra*, 41, 'Women are not yet capable of friendship: women are still cats, and birds. Or, at best, cows.'

279 *the Mairie of a fashionable Quarter*: each arrondissement of Paris has its own *mairie* or town hall, where civil marriage ceremonies were performed. Tarr's choice of a 'fashionable Quarter' suggests his comic partial fall into the bourgeois niceties against which he has railed throughout the novel.

280 *hors de combat*: Fr., 'disabled', literally 'out of combat', referring here to the indisposition of late pregnancy.

rue Servandoni: a street in the 6th arrondissement, near the Luxembourg Gardens.

281 *Luxembourg Museum*: the Musée du Luxembourg, situated near the Palais du Luxembourg.

the Drowned Girl: the peaceful, smiling death mask of 'L'inconnue de la Seine' ('the unknown girl of the Seine'), an anonymous girl who drowned in Paris in the late nineteenth century. Reproductions of the mask were popular for decades among artists and impressionable young women, the subject of a kind of early twentieth-century Romantic cult of suicide. As A. Alvarez notes, 'During the 1920s and early 1930s, all over the Continent, nearly every student of sensibility had a plaster cast of her death-mask' (*The Savage God: A Study of Suicide* (New York: Random House, 1972), 133).

282 *Equal Rights and the Perfectibility of the Species*: in the *Second Discourse* Rousseau describes 'perfectibility' as a quality that separates man from the animals, but also paradoxically 'the source of all of man's miseries . . . the faculty which, by dint of time, draws him out of that

original condition in which he would spend tranquil and innocent days' (Jean-Jacques Rousseau, *The Discourses and other Early Political Writings*, trans. Victor Gourevitch (Cambridge: Cambridge University Press, 1997), 141).

283 *Place des Vosges*: the oldest square in Paris, in the Marais district, part of the 3rd and 4th arrondissements. Although across the Seine, not in fact remarkably far from Montparnasse—closer, indeed, than Montmartre—but in a neighbourhood not associated with artists, and not previously represented in the novel.

284 *Rose Fawcett... Prism Dirkes*: names that suggests Tarr's continued oscillation between women who are respectively like Bertha and like Anastasya. The first combines Bertha's flowery Romanticism ('Rose') with her emotional fluidity ('Faucet'); the second suggests both Anastasya's angular beauty ('Prism') and her dangerous incisiveness (a 'Dirk' is a kind of dagger).

APPENDIX

285 *eight years ago*: probably 1908, although the mathematics would suggest 1907. Lewis signed and dated the Epilogue to the serialized *Tarr* 'P. Wyndham Lewis 1915', an attribution retained in the English 1918 Egoist Press edition.

286 *Prussian germs... past year*: in early 1915 the German army attacked using shells filled with xylyl bromide, and in April 1915 they attacked with poisonous chlorine gas during the second battle of Ypres. Nearly 6000 Allied soldiers died from such attacks before the adoption of gas masks later in 1915.

flames of Louvain: in August 1914 German troops burned and looted most of the Belgian town of Louvain, killing hundreds of civilians and destroying its fifteenth-century university and library. This devastation became an international cause célèbre and a symbol for the brutality of the German war effort.

brain-waves and titanic orchestrations: the influential histories of German philosophy and of titanic Romantic musical composition, from Beethoven to Wagner.

stray Irishman or American: Irish novelist James Joyce and American poet Ezra Pound.

Italian Futurist littérateur: Filippo Tommaso Emilio Marinetti (1876–1944), Italian poet, self-promoter, and founder of the Futurist movement; *littérateur*: Fr., pejorative, 'literary hack'.

Arsène Lupins: versions of the wildly popular fictional gentleman thief, a literary character created in 1905 by French author Maurice Leblanc (1864–1941). The character of Lupin featured in twenty volumes by Leblanc, as well as subsequent sequels by other hands.

Over-man . . . Europe: vulgarized versions of Nietzsche's ideas pervaded intellectual Europe in the years surrounding the First World War. The first serial instalment of *Tarr*, for instance, was followed in the same column by an essay on Nietzsche and German aggression ('Second-Rate Supermen', Honor M. Pulley, *The Egoist* (3/4, 1 April 1916), 63).

287 *maudlin and self-defensive Grin*: an echo of *Blast* 1: 'BLAST HUMOUR Quack ENGLISH drug for stupidity and sleepiness' (p. 17).

Charlie Chaplin: Charles Spencer Chaplin (1889–1977), English comedian and filmmaker, in 1915 an international phenomenon, the most widely recognized and highly paid entertainer in the world. Despite his respect for Chaplin, Lewis came to view the universal popularity of Chaplin's Tramp as a sign of modern culture's increasingly debased childishness, particularly in *Time and Western Man* (1927).

288 *German Madonna . . . face*: the painting *Madonna with the Carnation* (1478–80), also known as the *Munich Madonna*, an early work of Leonardo da Vinci that hangs in the Alte Pinakothek in Munich, Germany. Deterioration and subsequent improper restoration has caused surface distortions to the painting, which is especially noticeable on the Madonna's face.

289 *Shaw's 'bloody' schoolgirl way*: several of the plays of George Bernard Shaw, such as *Mrs Warren's Profession* (1893), were considered scandalous in the early twentieth century. To Lewis their treatment of 'adult' subjects was merely quaintly 'shocking' in a way easily assimilated by middle-class taste. In *Blasting & Bombardiering*, Lewis later wrote, 'I am rather what Mr. Shaw would have been if he had been an artist . . . and if he had been more richly endowed with imagination, emotion, intellect and a few other things. (He said he was a finer fellow than Shakespeare. I merely prefer myself to Mr. Shaw)' (2nd rev. ed.; Berkeley and Los Angeles: University of California Press, 1967, p. 3).

GLOSSARY OF
FOREIGN WORDS AND PHRASES

A demain (Fr.) see you tomorrow

à fond (Fr.) thoroughly

à propos (Fr.) relevance, timeliness

Aber (Ger.) Just a minute, hold on

Abort (Ger.) latrine

Assez (Fr.) enough

ah, ça (Fr.) an exclamation of insistence

ambitieux (Fr.) one who is ambitious

Amoureuse (Fr.) lover, femme fatale

Angriff (Ger.) attack, onslaught

au courant (Fr., and Eng. by adoption) up to date, acquainted with what's going on

Auf wiedersehen (Ger.) goodbye

Ausgelassenheit (Ger.) exuberance, boisterousness

bas-fonds (Fr.) the lower depths

Bureau de Tabac (Fr.) a tobacconist's counter, typically found inside a café

béguin (Fr., colloquial) infatuation

Bengel (Ger.) rascal

blagueur (Fr.) joker

Boulevardier (Fr.) man about town

calinerie (Fr.) coaxing, cajoling

Celui-là (Fr.) that one

C'est peu! (Fr.) That's not much!

cet oiseau-la (Fr.) that character

c'etait une idée (Fr.) There was an idea

champs de manœuvres (Fr.) parade grounds

crime passionel (Fr.) a murder committed in the heat of passion, usually sparked by discovery of a lover's unfaithfulness, often dealt with leniently by the French courts

cochon (Fr.) swine

commerçante (Fr.) shopkeeper

Comment (Fr.) What?

coup (Fr.) blow, sudden move

crapule (Fr.) good-for-nothing

de rigueur (Fr., and Eng. by adoption) obligatory, particularly in matters of etiquette and fashion

Débit (Fr.), short for *débit de boissons*, bar

déchéance (Fr.) degeneration, decline

Dis (Fr.) Say

dumm (Ger.) stupid, dense

enceinte (Fr.) pregnant

en maître (Fr.) like the master, in charge

entresol (Fr.) mezzanine, an intermediate floor between the main floors of a building

erdball (Ger.) globe

esprit de corps (Fr.) group morale, often military

Et alors? (Fr.) So what?

femme de ménage (Fr.) cleaning lady

fiançailles (Fr.) engagement

flic (Fr. slang) cop

fougue (Fr.) ardour, spirit

Foute-moi donc la paix, imbécile! (Fr.) Get lost, idiot!

Freiherr (Ger.) baron

Gang (Ger.) hallway

garçon (Fr.) waiter

Garçon, l'addition (Fr.) Waiter, cheque please

Geist (Ger.) spirit, mind

Geschmack (Ger.) taste

gigot (Fr.) leg of mutton or lamb

gnädiges Fräulein (Ger.) gracious lady

grande amoureuse (Fr.) a great lover (female)

grands messieurs du Berne (Fr.) great men of the Berne

Heraus! (Ger.) Get out!

Herrgott (Ger., interjection) (by) Christ

Himmel (Ger., interjection) Heavens

Hoch (Ger.) Raise your glass (to)

Ich danke sehr (Ger.) Much obliged

Ich hasse dich (Ger.) I hate you

Il n'y a rien pour vous (Fr.) There's nothing for you

intime (Fr.) intimate; also used in English as a self-conscious gallicism

Ja (Ger.) yes

Je ne demande pas mieux! (Fr.) That sounds good to me

Knabe (Ger.) youngster

lasse (Fr.) weary

liebhaberei (Ger.) hobby

loge (Fr.) a caretaker's lodge, either a dedicated living space within an apartment or rooming house or a separate dwelling adjacent to it

Mathematiker (Ger.) mathematician

méchant (Fr.) malicious

même jeu (Fr.) the same story

mœurs (Fr.) manners and customs

Mokka (Ger.) mocha, coffee

mon Dieu! (Fr.) My God!

Monsieur est distrait aujourd'hui (Fr.) The gentleman is absent-minded today

Na (Ger., interjection) Well!

Na ja! (Ger., interjection) more typically *naja*, 'Well now!', implying a degree of ironic detachment

ne plus ultra (Lat.) to the most extreme possible degree

noch einmal (Ger.) once again

nom d'amour (Fr.) pet name

Oh là là (Fr.) variant of 'Ooh là là', an expression of pleased surprise, often used by a man to comment upon the appearance of an attractive woman

parti (Fr.) a suitable romantic or marital match

passe-partout (Fr.) a skeleton or master key

Passez votre chemin! (Fr.) Move along!

perbacco (It., interjection) from 'By Bacchus', used to emphasize a positive comment

Pfui (Ger.) interjection of disgust, comparable to English 'ugh'

pièce de résistance (Fr.) originally 'the most substantial dish of a meal', now more generally 'the prize item in a collection'

plat du jour (Fr.) the daily special

pommes a l'huile (Fr.) a potato salad, made at times with onion and mustard, and dressed with oil and vinegar

poseuse (Fr., and Eng. by adoption) a female poseur, one adopting an affected or pretentious persona

pour rire (Fr.) laughable

premier venu (Fr.) the first person who comes along

procédés (Fr.) processes, behaviours

Prosit (Ger.) a toast; 'Cheers!'

Quel type! (Fr.) What a character!

quoi? (Fr.) What?

raison d'être (Fr.) reason for existence

Rapin (Fr.) an apprentice painter

Reisebureau (Ger.) travel or tourist agency

Salaud (Fr.) bastard

sans gêne (Fr.) lack of embarrassment or restraint

sekt (Ger.) sparkling wine

Schatz (Ger.) sweetheart, lit. 'treasure'

Schauspielerin (Ger.) actress

Schicksal (Ger.) fate

Schurke! (Ger.) Scoundrel!

Schwein (Ger.) pig

Schweinerai (Ger.) disgusting mess, lit. 'piggishness'

Schön (Ger.) Very well

Sois pas bête! (Fr.) Don't be stupid!

sommelier (Fr., and Eng. by adoption) wine steward

sotto voce (It.) in hushed tones

sympathisch (Ger.) likeable, congenial

Table d'hôte (Fr.) lit. 'the host's table', a common table for boarders at a boarding house

tableau vivant (Fr.) lit. 'a living picture'—a motionless person or group of people theatrically posed and costumed to represent a well-known work of art

Tant pis (Fr.) Too bad

terrasse (Fr.) the outside eating area of a café

tête à tête (Fr.) at close quarters, lit. 'face to face'

Tor (Ger.) fool

Tout de suite (Fr.) right away

types (Fr.) guys, blokes

Va-t'en! (Fr.) Go away!

vieille barbe (Fr.) grey beard, old bore

vis-à-vis (Fr.) person facing opposite

Was heisst das (Ger.) What does that mean?

Was wünschen Sie (Ger.) What can I do for you?

Wunderbar (Ger.) wonderful

Zigeuner (Ger.) gypsies

Zut (Fr., interjection) damn

American Literature

British and Irish Literature

Children's Literature

Classics and Ancient Literature

Colonial Literature

Eastern Literature

European Literature

Gothic Literature

History

Medieval Literature

Oxford English Drama

Poetry

Philosophy

Politics

Religion

The Oxford Shakespeare

A complete list of Oxford World's Classics, including Authors in Context, Oxford English Drama, and the Oxford Shakespeare, is available in the UK from the Marketing Services Department, Oxford University Press, Great Clarendon Street, Oxford OX2 6DP, or visit the website at www.oup.com/uk/worldsclassics.

In the USA, visit www.oup.com/us/owc for a complete title list.

Oxford World's Classics are available from all good bookshops. In case of difficulty, customers in the UK should contact Oxford University Press Bookshop, 116 High Street, Oxford OX1 4BR.

JOHN BUCHAN	**Greenmantle**
	Huntingtower
	The Thirty-Nine Steps
JOSEPH CONRAD	**Chance**
	Heart of Darkness and Other Tales
	Lord Jim
	Nostromo
	An Outcast of the Islands
	The Secret Agent
	Typhoon and Other Tales
	Under Western Eyes
ARTHUR CONAN DOYLE	**The Adventures of Sherlock Holmes**
	The Case-Book of Sherlock Holmes
	The Hound of the Baskervilles
	The Lost World
	The Memoirs of Sherlock Holmes
	A Study in Scarlet
FORD MADOX FORD	**The Good Soldier**
JOHN GALSWORTHY	**The Forsyte Saga**
JAMES JOYCE	**A Portrait of the Artist as a Young Man**
	Dubliners
	Occasional, Critical, and Political Writing
	Ulysses
RUDYARD KIPLING	**Captains Courageous**
	The Complete Stalky & Co
	The Jungle Books
	Just So Stories
	Kim
	The Man Who Would Be King
	Plain Tales from the Hills
	War Stories and Poems

	Late Victorian Gothic Tales
JANE AUSTEN	Emma
	Mansfield Park
	Persuasion
	Pride and Prejudice
	Selected Letters
	Sense and Sensibility
MRS BEETON	Book of Household Management
MARY ELIZABETH BRADDON	Lady Audley's Secret
ANNE BRONTË	The Tenant of Wildfell Hall
CHARLOTTE BRONTË	Jane Eyre
	Shirley
	Villette
EMILY BRONTË	Wuthering Heights
ROBERT BROWNING	The Major Works
JOHN CLARE	The Major Works
SAMUEL TAYLOR COLERIDGE	The Major Works
WILKIE COLLINS	The Moonstone
	No Name
	The Woman in White
CHARLES DARWIN	The Origin of Species
THOMAS DE QUINCEY	The Confessions of an English Opium-Eater
	On Murder
CHARLES DICKENS	The Adventures of Oliver Twist
	Barnaby Rudge
	Bleak House
	David Copperfield
	Great Expectations
	Nicholas Nickleby
	The Old Curiosity Shop
	Our Mutual Friend
	The Pickwick Papers